P. J. Grondin

A Lifetime of

Deception

PD House Holdings, LLC

PD House Holdings, LLC
4704 Venice Road, Suite 201
Sandusky, Ohio 44870

Library of Congress Control Number: 2008902413

ISBN10: 0-9815333-2-9
ISBN13: 978-0-9815333-2-2
Published by PD House Holdings, LLC
www.pjgrondin.com
Sandusky, Ohio

Dedication

This book is dedicated to our brave servicemen and servicewomen. Their job is always dangerous regardless of circumstances. The job becomes more difficult when personal problems at home distract them from their mission. It is criminal when their own countrymen take advantage of these heroes while deployed and unable to defend themselves. God Bless all of our fighting men and women in the Navy, Marine Corps, Army, Air Force, Coast Guard, and the National Guard. Without you, freedom is just a dream.

Acknowledgements

Thanks go to my brother, Patrick and my wife, Debbie for their critique of the manuscript, both technical and creative. Their input and feedback were a tremendous help in keeping the story real-to-life.

Prologue
1971

Abbie Glover was on her back with her legs high in the air and her feet in stirrups. She was used to being in this position but this time she was in pain. Sweat poured from her face and neck as the nurses monitored her vital signs and those of her unborn baby. Her gown was soaked, clinging to her shoulders, breasts, and back. The air in the room was cool but Abbie was immune to the chill as her body tensed with each pain. Her contractions were very close now and the Obstetrician was coaching her through her next moves.

She didn't trust the doctor or the nurses. They were all here at the request of the United States Air Force, she was sure of it. They were supposedly staff of Penrose-St. Francis Medical Center but she knew better. She knew the Air Force set up the delivery team. She hated the military. She hated anyone associated with the military. She hated that her baby was going to be born with military doctors and nurses attending. But there was no turning back now. She was here on her back and her baby was going to be born any time now.

"Okay, when you have this next pain, push as hard as you can. I can see the top of the baby's head now." The doctor's instructions went in one ear and out the other. Abbie wasn't thinking about pushing. She was thinking about the bastards that had put her in this position; fifteen years old and pregnant. Her own mother disowned her when she found out Abbie was pregnant. Her father was long gone. He'd bugged out on Abbie's mom fifteen years before, as soon as he found out that she was pregnant. He didn't want to be strapped with a kid. He had a future and he didn't need that sort of baggage holding him back. So she raised Abbie alone as best as she could but she was far too young for that responsibility. Throughout her youth, Abbie was passed from relative to relative until none of them wanted her any longer. She was always in trouble and never did what she was told.

She wound up in foster care in Colorado Springs, Colorado near the Air Force Academy. That's where she learned how to turn on the charm and make a living as the party girl. She made some good cash servicing the young cadets at the academy. She managed to keep from getting pregnant until now. But here she was, legs in the air, pains coming faster than she could handle them. She started to scream as the next contraction hit. "Holy shit! Oh God, this hurts!"

"Push harder, Abbie. You need to push as hard as you can." The doctor was trying his best to be supportive but Abbie was having none of it.

"I'm pushing, you fucking moron! God I hate you Air Force pricks!" She groaned loud then squealed as the contraction started to subside. A nurse took a cloth and wiped sweat from her face and neck. Abbie jerked her head towards the attending nurse and shouted, "Get that away from me you bitch!" The nurse rolled her eyes when she turned her back to Abbie. She got another dry cloth from the stack on the table by one wall of the delivery room and prepared to wipe her face down again when the next contraction started. Abbie let out another scream, this one more intense than the last.

Patiently, the doctor continued to coach in a calm voice, "Abbie, you need to push as hard as you can one more time."

She swore at the doctor again. Less patient people would have walked out of the delivery room and let her deliver her own baby, but they were professional medical staff. They'd heard much of this before. Foul language like this was usually hurled at the father of the newborn during delivery. But there was no father to target today, so the staff took the brunt of the abuse.

Only the man in the far side of the birthing room was actually military. He was there to observe the delivery. His orders were to report back to the Superintendent of the Air Force Academy, Lieutenant General Wilson Chester, as soon as the child was born. Specifically, he was to listen to everything the mother said during and after the birth. The delivery room staff was a bit uncomfortable with the guest but they had no choice. The military, or someone within the military, was paying the bill.

The baby's head was beginning to make its way out of the birth canal and the doctor told Abbie to relax as best she could until the next contraction. "This may be the push that does it so save your strength and try to really push this next time."

Abbie angrily shouted, "Look you motherfucker, there ain't no resting and I'm pushing as hard as I can. If you think you can push this kid out, have at it. AHHH!" The next contraction started. "Ahh! God this hurts. God I hate you bastards! I'll kill every one of you Air Force pricks for this!"

The staff was so stunned at this outburst that they didn't hear the doctor say, "Here it comes." The doctor had to yell to his staff to get moving and take the baby so he could get the umbilical cord clamped and cut. A nurse wiped the baby girl clean. She took the baby's weight and recorded the APGAR score. Seven. Not too bad for the baby of such a young girl.

The doctor said, "Record date and time of birth, February 2, 1971, 1632 hours. Oh, that's 4:32 PM for her civilian records."

Abbie turned her head away from the child when the nurse presented her with her new baby girl. She said, "She doesn't stand a chance with me. Take her away. I don't want to see her."

The nurse protested, "You'll change your mind when you've had some rest. This has been very traumatic."

"What the fuck do you know about me? I said take her away. I want to give her to someone who can love her. I can't. Now get her out of here and get me out of here."

The nurse gave her a sad look and turned with the newborn and headed towards the nursery. Before she left the delivery room she turned and asked Abbie, "Do you have a name for your baby girl?"

Abbie spat, "Bastard."

The entire staff stopped what they were doing for a moment and stared at Abbie. Then one by one, they returned to their tasks. This would be a delivery they would never forget. The nurses decided to call the baby Rebecca because they had just been talking about books they'd recently read. One of the books was *Rebecca of Sunnybrook Farm*. They all agreed that it was a beautiful name and this baby was a beautiful baby. If Abbie came to her senses she could choose whatever name she wanted but for now she was Baby Rebecca.

* * *

Major Harold Trent reported to General Chester that the birth went well and the baby, a girl, was in fine condition and care. He also reported that the woman who gave birth to the infant did not want the child. He was certain that the child would be given up for adoption.

The General's response was, "You make certain that takes place. If that baby can be sent out of state so much the better. When the mother is healthy enough to be discharged, you be there and give her this package. Make sure she goes to the opposite side of the country from that baby. This woman is to have no contact with the baby or the adoptive parents. Is that understood, Major?"

"Yes sir," was his answer, but he did not understand. He figured that the General had his reasons and did not question his orders but he left the office with many unanswered questions.

* * *

On May 15, 1971 at a smoke-filled Colorado Springs pub, four young graduates, now United States Air Force Lieutenants smoked cigars and hoisted a round of shots to their success. They'd completed the tough requirements of the Air Force Academy. They'd also dodged a bullet.

"Hey Milt, we made it." He took a puff on his cigar then held his second shot of Jack Daniels high in the air. His three companions raised their shot glasses as well.

"Hell yea. Salute!" The four drank their shots and put the glasses down hard on the table.

"We need to drink a round to your old man. He saved our asses."

The other three frowned at their fellow graduate. Milton Chester in a quiet, but firm tone said, "Shut the fuck up, man. What if someone overhears you talking about that shit? Our asses could be right back in the sling." The others nodded in agreement. Milton continued, "We have to vow to each other that we'll never talk about this to anyone. Ever! Understood?" He looked hard at each man. They each nodded agreement. "Good." He paused then said, "Fill 'em up."

His old man may have saved their asses but it wasn't before he'd cold-cocked his son for nearly ruining both their careers. Milton put down the shot glass and rubbed his jaw at the memory.

But their little problem was gone. One half left the state heading east, the other heading west. It was time to forget about that little lapse in judgment and move on. There were Air Force careers to be made. The four had their orders. Their bright futures awaited them.

For Abbie, the future looked bleak. She'd been given enough money to get out of town and a little extra to keep her mouth shut.

For baby Rebecca, the future was unknown.

Chapter 1
1987

Randy Divert and Earl Glavin shared a two bedroom apartment with their girlfriends in Summerville, South Carolina. Randy wasn't too keen about the arrangement. He wasn't close friends with Earl. They'd gone through the Navy's Nuclear Power School together in Orlando, Florida and had been transferred to West Milton, New York for the final stages of their training before being permanently assigned to a submarine. In West Milton they'd shared a house with three other sailors who were in the Navy at the training facility in upstate New York. Even then, Randy wasn't pleased to be sharing housing with other sailors, friends or not. There always seemed to be a conflict. Someone was always slack in their duties, most of which were simple chores. But when the trash was overflowing, or the dishes were stacking up, the excuses started flying. They were all busy with studying, working long hours on rotating shifts; all of which were part of the training routine at the Navy's nuclear reactor training facility. But the chores still had to be done, like it or not. When Randy left New York for duty aboard his first real submarine, the last thing on his mind was to share an off base apartment with anyone, much less Earl Glavin.

Randy was a third class Machinist Mate aboard the USS Stonewall Jackson. He was short at 5 feet 7 inches, with sandy brown hair and gray eyes. His slim face didn't seem to be a good fit for his muscular body. He walked with purpose wherever he went. He always turned with quick, abrupt movements which irritated his division officers. They thought he was being insubordinate, trying to be cute by his receiving an order and quickly running off to carry it out. But they soon learned that it was just his nature to not procrastinate. Randy wanted to get the job done with as little fanfare and interruption as possible. He got his orders and did the job. Everyone liked Randy. They especially liked Randy's ingenuity. He had a knack for making special tools to make jobs easier. When the standard tool didn't work exactly right, he would make a slight modification to the tool and the job would take less than half the time it normally did. His fellow Machinist Mates told him that he should patent his tools but Randy said he just did it to make his life easier. He didn't want any rewards for something so simple. It was what he was told that the Navy was all about. It was what his training told him that he should do.

The Navy was in his blood. His father had been a Machinist Mate as had his uncle. When they'd heard that Randy had joined the Navy to follow in their footsteps, they sat Randy down and told him story after story about their off crew escapades.   Many of the stories were hilarious and many were frightening.   One story was about one of their buddies who'd been shacked up with a chick and two of her friends.   When he came back from a 3 month patrol, all of his belongings were gone from his apartment. His bank account had been cleaned out and his car was gone.   He was wiped out.   His dad and uncle told him to never let a woman get that close. They'd said, "Always protect yourself and your stuff.   Somebody's always trying to take your stuff when you're out to sea."   Great advice, Randy thought.

Less than a week after Randy reported to the USS Stonewall Jackson at the Naval Weapons Station in Goose Creek, South Carolina, Earl Glavin showed up and started to hang out with Randy, even when he wasn't invited.   Randy didn't think too much of it.   Earl was a pretty decent guy though he didn't have much of a personality.   He was taller than Randy at 5'11" but weighed much less at only 164 pounds.   He had a light complexion and dark brown eyes.   His eyes were shaped such that he looked almost oriental.   His dark hair was curly but he kept it close cropped. His accent was western Pennsylvania or eastern Ohio.   Everything was 'yuns want to go to the mall' or 'yuns want to get a beer?'   Almost from the moment he met up with Randy at the off crew office, he started to talk about splitting an apartment with him.   Randy wasn't too keen on the idea.

Shelly Mercer was the reason for Randy's reluctance.   Shelly was Randy's girlfriend.   She already had plans for her and Randy to share an apartment together when she moved out of her parent's home in Grand Rapids, Michigan.   She was trying real hard to get her hooks into Randy. She wanted a husband real bad and Randy was her target.

But Earl was being very persistent.   Finally, Randy gave in and the deal was made.   He and Earl would split a place for six months until Shelly moved down.   They'd move out and find a place of their own and Earl would have to find someone else to share the expenses.   That was the plan.

Then the plan changed.

Earl met Colleen Clarkson at a nightclub in North Charleston and immediately fell in love with her.   Colleen was a pretty girl at 5'3", 108 pounds, shoulder length strawberry-blond hair and a slender body.   She was real pleasing to the eyes.   She said that she was 19 but she looked younger. She had nicely shaped breasts, shapely hips, and pouty lips that she used to her advantage.   She had a southern belle accent that just blew Earl away. She'd talk sweet to him; tell him what a gentleman he was and how she 'just loved how he treated her.'   Whenever Earl would say something that she didn't like, she would put on a sad little face, lips turned down slightly, and plead with him to change his mind.   It worked every time.   Earl was hooked and Colleen was reeling him in.

Randy sensed problems right off the bat and tried to tell Earl to slow down. She was always making decisions for Earl even on relatively important matters, like where to spend his money, what to buy for the apartment, what kind of car he should buy. She even recommended that they start a joint checking account. The words of Randy's dad and uncle rang in his ears. *"Always protect yourself and your stuff. Somebody's always trying to take your stuff when you're out to sea."* Randy tried to talk with Earl about the errors of his ways, but he might as well have been talking to a wall. Earl was in love with Colleen and the hook was set . . . deep. They'd only known each other for three weeks but love conquers all, especially a young sailor who'd previously never been out of Beaver County, Pennsylvania. So after a day or so of pleading about a joint checking account, Earl caved and they were off to the bank. Randy didn't even have time to pull him aside and warn him of the danger of such a move.

Randy didn't know Colleen at all when she moved in with them. All he knew was that she had a job as a waitress at Ruby Tuesdays in the Northwoods Mall. She contributed to the rent and the bills and that's what counted as far as Randy was concerned. That made paying the bills easy. Randy was able to save more money. He was going to need all the money he could save to pay for a different apartment, furniture and all the things that a new, young couple needs to get off to a good start in a relationship. He was pleased that he could sock away a good part of his paycheck to help with that goal. It had only been seven weeks in the shared apartment with Earl and Colleen and Randy had saved almost a thousand dollars. He was feeling pretty good.

About this time, Randy's girlfriend, Shelly Mercer, decided that she needed to move in with her man. She couldn't wait another five months. She'd been having problems at home, arguing with her mom so she decided that she was old enough to make her own decisions. She hopped on a bus, headed for South Carolina and moved in with Randy, Earl, and Colleen.

Shelly was a pretty, 18 year old girl. She was shorter than Randy, at 5'2". She had a body that turned heads. She weighed only 112 pounds and a good part of that was on her chest. She also had beautiful blue eyes and platinum blond hair. She was the kind of girl that people used for blond jokes. She was a bit air headed and didn't catch on to things too quickly. When she moved in with her fiancé and his friends she had only a suitcase of clothes and her cosmetics bag, which was almost as large as her suitcase. She didn't wear too much makeup, she just wanted to be sure she had makeup for any occasion.

Shelly and Colleen hit it off right away, which seemed odd to Randy since they were from completely different backgrounds. They had two things in common; they were hot looking and they'd snagged themselves a couple of sailors. That made them both very happy indeed.

Things were going well for the two couples initially. The four of them got along well and didn't annoy each other like many co-habitat situations. Everyone was pulling their weight and doing the things that were necessary to get along. They went out on the town together a few nights each week and generally had a good time. Since Shelly's arrival, Randy was saving less money due to all of the party nights, but he wasn't too concerned since he and Earl were going to be back on the submarine in a few weeks. He'd already coached Shelly about how to budget their money and how much to save out of each paycheck. He had her go over the plan with him several times each day to make sure that she understood what she had to do and how important it was that she follow his instructions as closely as possible.

Randy also told Shelly to be careful with Colleen. She was not to let Colleen know any of the details of their finances. They were all getting along well, but he still had a nagging feeling that Colleen was hiding something. He couldn't put his finger on it but it was always there, lingering just out of reach. She was just a bit too nice; almost phony. Many of his shipmates left their girlfriends in charge of the household when they left for sea. As the day came closer to turn the keys over to Shelly and Colleen, Randy's anxiety level jumped for no apparent reason. He wished he'd never agreed to share the apartment with Earl. His father's advice kept repeating itself in his brain; *Always protect yourself and your stuff.*

Then came the day that most ballistic missile submarine sailors dread; reporting day. Randy, Earl, and the rest of the blue crew reported to the USS Stonewall Jackson at 0530 hours (5:30 am to civilians) on a Tuesday to start turnover with their gold crew counterparts. They spent two more days loading their equipment, manuals, food, spare parts, cleaning supplies and other necessary items to keep a submarine at sea and self sufficient for at least 90 days. Then they spent the next two weeks preparing the submarine for sea. Finally, the crew started up the ship's reactor, main turbines and main engine, lit off and tested all the radar, sonar, communications equipment and weapons systems and headed for the open sea. They would not be heard from for at least 72 days. The only communications from home for the crew of the ship came in the form of a 'family gram'. This little trickle of information from home was limited to 40 words and could contain information only of a general nature. If the message was too specific, containing such things as dates of family picnics that they would be expected to attend upon their return, the family gram would not be sent. The fear was that too much information could pinpoint the date and time of the ships return to port and help the enemy learn the schedules of the United States Nuclear Submarine fleet. So the messages were limited. Most family grams were watered down to 'I love you and miss you' and 'I can't wait until you get home.' Most sailors looked forward to receiving their messages. Randy received all eight of his family grams, each spaced about 1 week apart as he'd instructed Shelly. Each was pretty bland with very little detail, only the bare minimum of information, ending with 'I love you and miss you. I can't wait until you get home. I have lots to tell you.'

Earl, on the other hand, received his first six as scheduled, then didn't receive his last two. He wasn't worried, he'd told Randy. She probably put too much detail in her family gram so the Fleet Communications Center probably wouldn't send them through. Randy agreed with Earl, mostly to try not to worry him about it. The patrol was nearing its end and they had plenty on their minds without the worry of whatever was happening at home. There was nothing they could do about it anyway. They were locked in a big steel tube. They could be twelve miles from the coast of South Carolina or they could be thousands of miles from the nearest land. Only a handful of radiomen and the senior officers of the ship knew for certain. Besides, it would be over soon enough.

* * *

The USS Stonewall Jackson pulled into the Naval Weapons Station, Goose Creek, South Carolina, pier Charlie on Saturday. The weather was hot and muggy, but the sailors on board were just glad to see land. The crowd of wives and children on the pier was as excited as ever as the giant submarine was tied to the pier. When Randy and Earl were finally allowed to leave the ship, they scanned the crowd for Shelly and Colleen. They could see the joy on the faces of their shipmate's wives and children as they looked at the crowd. Many joyous hugs and kisses were almost too passionate in front of children, but who could fault a young couple who hadn't seen each other in nearly three months. For the sailor's part, they hadn't seen a live woman throughout the cruise. The two continued to look around the crowd, then down the pier to see if the ladies had just arrived late and couldn't find a spot to park at the end of the pier. But Colleen and Shelly were nowhere to be seen. Randy asked several of their shipmate's wives if they'd seen the two. Nobody could remember if they'd been seen on the pier or in the parking lot. The two sailors picked up their sea bags and headed to the pay phone near the parking lot. Earl called the apartment phone number but there was no answer, only a continuous ring. He was starting to become annoyed. Earl told Colleen how important it was to him that she be there to meet him. He stepped out of the booth to tell Randy but Randy was already headed to the parking lot.

Earl shouted, "Randy, where are you going? There's no answer at the apartment."

"I heard you. Well, I saw that nobody answered. Maybe they're still in the parking lot. Let's go look. They could have gotten held up in traffic or something." From the look on Randy's face Earl could tell that he didn't believe it. He knew that Randy was upset. His pace was quick like it always was as he headed towards the sea of cars to look for his green

Mercury Sable, but it was not in the parking lot. When the two were tired of looking, they spotted Petty Officer Dan Shannon heading for his car. Dan was a Missile Technician on the Jackson. He was alone as he headed to his car. They flagged him down and asked if he could drive them to their apartment in Summerville. It was about a twenty minute drive from the weapons station and in the wrong direction from where Dan wanted to go, but he wasn't in a hurry because he had no family living in the area. He was single and his only thought was to find his first beer.

"Sure guys. Hop in. How about we stop for a beer on the way?" All three were in their working blue dungaree uniforms so they really couldn't stop in a public bar. They would stand out in the bar as if they were in prison dungarees. They weren't supposed to wear their working uniforms off of the base except directly to or from their homes, but a quick run into a store was generally tolerated, especially for sailors coming back from a long deployment.

"How about we go through the Convenient Market Drive-thru and grab a six-pack," Randy suggested. "We can toss 'em back on the way to the apartment." They all agreed.

When they arrived at the apartment complex, Randy saw that his car was not in the lot. The curtains to their apartment were closed. He was starting to get real worried. His facial expression told the story and both Earl and Dan read the message. Something wasn't right.

"I've got a real bad feeling about this, guys." Randy said.

"Me too." Earl looked as though he'd lost his best friend in the world. "Maybe they just forgot. Maybe Shelly's gone shopping and Colleen's just asleep."

"Well, we're about to find out."

The three went up to the door of the ground floor apartment, Earl and Randy carrying their seabags. Dan went along for moral support. Randy tried his key and the door opened in front of them. They walked into the apartment. Their faces turned to shock. The apartment was completely empty. No furniture, no Colleen, no Shelly. Earl and Randy dropped their seabags in the living room just inside the door.

Randy quickly moved through the empty living room into the kitchen and in rapid succession, opening and closing every cabinet door and all of the drawers. There was nothing in the kitchen cupboards or drawers. The dishes, silverware, pots and pans, small appliances, everything was gone. Randy turned abruptly and headed for the bedrooms. The bedrooms were bare as well. All of the closets were empty. The only thing on the carpet was dust balls and lint and the indentations where furniture used to sit. Randy moved back out into the hall and looked at Earl and Dan, still standing at the door. Randy glared at Earl. All he could think of was that Colleen had ripped them off for everything that they owned. His dad's and uncle's advice raced through his mind as he tried to calm himself enough to think of what he should do next. His first thought was to punch Earl but then he figured that wouldn't accomplish much except hurt his hand. He again began to survey the rooms. There were only two things left in the apartment; the curtains on the windows and a telephone. The phone hung from the kitchen wall. He grabbed the receiver and started dialing.

"Hey, man, who're you calling?" Earl asked.

Randy just stared back at Earl. He was still angry. He couldn't help thinking that Colleen had something to do with this. His mind was racing as the phone rang in his ear. After the third ring, a sweet, young female voice answered, "Hello?"

"Shelly, what the hell are you doing in Michigan?"

"Randy, please don't yell at me. Colleen told me that my mom called and needed me at home. Colleen said that Daddy was sick and Mom couldn't handle everything without me up here."

"Well, is your dad alright?"

"That's the stupid part. Mom said she never called the apartment. When I got up here, Daddy was fine. I've been trying to call Colleen for a week and there's been no answer at the apartment. Have you been there yet?"

"I'm calling from the apartment now. It's empty. Everything is gone." Randy could hardly contain his anger. He wanted to blast her but he didn't have the heart. He was silent for a moment while he thought about what he should say to his very blond, air-headed fiancé. He spoke his next question in measured words. "Shelly, how did you get home?"

"I took a bus."

"Didn't you call your mom before you got on the bus?"

"Well . . . no. Colleen had the ticket purchased already. She gave it to me and she gave me a ride to the station. She said that I wouldn't be able to reach Mom because she was at the hospital with Daddy. She acted like it was an emergency, like she was really concerned that something bad was wrong with Daddy." Shelly's voice started to crack as she lost her composure. Randy could tell that she was starting to cry. "I'm so sorry, I know I screwed up."

"Look Shelly, there's nothing we can do about it now. Did Colleen say anything that would tell you where she might go? Did she say anything about family or where she'd like to visit, or any boyfriends?" He stopped short and looked over at Earl. The pained look on Earl's face made Randy wince slightly.

"No. She didn't say anything." Then Shelly remembered that Colleen had talked about moving to Florida. She mentioned the Florida Keys several times. But she wasn't sure of herself so she just let it go. Instead she started to cry as her emotions washed over her. Her sobs were so loud that Earl and Dan could hear them half way across the apartment. Randy tried to calm her but without success. Finally, Randy told Shelly that he would call back and hung up.

* * *

Colleen Clarkson, the run-away girlfriend of Earl Glavin, was laid out on Higgs Beach in Key West, Florida in her new bikini. She had suntan oil with a #4 sun protection factor because she already had a great tan. Colleen wasn't her real name. The reason she looked young for 19 was that she was really 16. Her fake Florida driver's license would get her into any bar in the south with no questions asked. She'd get plenty of smiles though. Her face appeared 16, but her body said a whole lot more. As she lay on the beach she spent a few minutes assessing her financial situation. She figured that she had enough money to last for another 7 weeks, then she'd have to get a job or find another sucker. *But there are loads of suckers everywhere I go.* She wasn't worried. Seven more weeks in the Keys would take her well into summer. There was plenty of time to plan her next move. She closed her eyes and soaked up more rays. Just as she was finally getting situated on her blanket, a shadow came over part of her body. She opened her eyes to see a tall, slender man standing over her. He was about 6'5", dark hair and somewhat pale skin for the Florida Keys. She figured that he probably didn't tan real well. He couldn't have been in the Keys long with that pale white skin.

"Hi. My name's Bobby. Can I buy you a drink?"

Colleen gave this stranger a broad smile. She looked him over for a moment then said, "Sure."

Chapter 2
1997

Major Francis 'Frank' Hartnett reviewed the order from the office of the Judge Advocate General dated February 19, 1997. He was to assemble a team of military investigative personnel. Their task was to stop a rash of fraudulent acts being committed against deployed members of the armed forces. *Well, this should be as easy as stopping the floodwaters of the Mississippi River. I wonder what desk-jock-genius thought this up?* With his right forefinger, he pushed his reading glasses back on the bridge of his nose. With a sweep of his hand, he brushed the bristles of his close cropped salt and pepper hair. His facial lines showed the stress of prior battles as the wrinkles in his forehead tightened. He was a veteran of several conflicts that took him to several battlefields during his career. He'd faced battlefield conditions that were, at times, unbearable. Now he sat hunched over his large, mahogany desk and read the new battle facing his fellow soldiers and sailors. This battle would take place on the domestic front. It was against an enemy that was far worse than the soldiers from countries that didn't believe in the ideals of the United States. At least you could see those enemies coming, usually by jets or ships. More recently, the terrorists were more difficult to detect but intelligence reports provided enough information about those religious fanatics who were out to destroy our way of life.

Those enemies were not to blame for the horrible acts being perpetrated against our brave men and women. This new enemy wasn't made up of armies with the most modern assault weapons purchased from arms dealers. This new enemy came from within the borders of the United States of America; they were U.S. citizens. They were the lowest of the low life scum that enjoyed the freedoms that so many of our courageous men and women fought and died for over the years. They preyed on the very fighting men and women that continue to guarantee our freedom, and their freedom, from tyranny and from attack by foreign enemies. Major Hartnett received orders to figure out a way to stop this enemy from attacking our young soldiers, sailors, and airmen where they least expected it; from their fellow countrymen.

As Frank Hartnett reviewed the case files on his desk, he couldn't help but wonder how a citizen of the United States of America could take advantage of these brave young men and women. What kind of a mind purposely targets military personnel? Being a 'lifer', Major Hartnett couldn't imagine that these people existed. As he read the file of Randall Divert and Earl Glavin, he had to wonder if this perpetrator had ever been caught. He picked up the next file and read the first three pages. It had a familiar theme. He reread the previous file and compared the details. He finished reading through the case file, leaned back in his high back, overstuffed office chair, removed his reading glasses and rubbed the bridge of his nose. He rubbed his eyes with the palms of his hands.

He'd finished reading several files. All of them were spread out across his desk. The majority of the cases involved young couples who were thrust into military life at a young age. Many of the personnel involved were 18 or 19 years old, just fresh out of high school or jail. Some of these young men and women had just made some bad decisions and were caught by local police. In years gone by, they were given the option of going to jail or going into the military. Many opted for the military and the majority of those grew up quickly. Military training in boot camp was an in-your-face kind of experience. No more mommy and daddy to protect you. You learned very quickly to be self sufficient. You also learned how to work closely with others on your team, even those that you didn't necessarily like. You learned how to become a team player.

Major Hartnett took a deep breath and opened the next case file and read on. Once again, this case had a similar theme as the last that he'd read. This one was about a submariner deployed on a ballistic missile sub out of King's Bay, Georgia. The new bride took off with everything. Similar build, age, eyes, and accent. *Hell, it could be the same girl.* He read on but he didn't need to read another word. The young woman had the same physical characteristics and the same pattern of behavior. There was little doubt that this was the same person. There was definitely enough evidence indicating that at least a percentage of these crimes were performed by a young woman, probably in her twenties who was able to persuade these poor young men to let her into their lives. There wasn't a lot that they could do to defend themselves since they were overseas or out to sea on a ship, far away from the scene of the crime.

But Frank Hartnett was formulating a plan. He had to get a gut check from his long time buddy, Major Augustine Griggs. He picked up the phone and dialed the number for Griggs' office.

A young female voice answered, "Major Griggs' office."

"Good afternoon, Sergeant. Is the Major in?"

"Yes sir. I'll pass you right through."

The wait was only seconds as the administrative sergeant informed Major Griggs that his long time buddy was on the line. In a deep, gruff voice, Gus Griggs said, "Frank, what can I do for you?"

Frank's voice was serious and he skipped any pleasantries. "Gus, I need your help. When can you drop by my office?"

"You sound like this is serious. I'm free in about half an hour.

Can you tell me what's up?"

Frank thought about it for a second then replied, "I'd rather we talk in person but to give you a flavor, I've been tasked with some police work. You'll want to be sure to bring your reading glasses."

Gus raised one eyebrow thinking what this could possibly be. He replied, "I'll be there as soon as I'm free."

"Thanks Gus."

* * *

When Gus Griggs finished reading the case files, he sat back in the chair across from Frank Hartnett's desk and drew in a deep breath. He took off his glasses and looked at his friend. "We've got one hell of a problem here. What exactly are your orders?"

"I'm supposed to assemble a team to track down this woman, assuming it is the same woman, and stop her from taking advantage of our boys." He paused. "This isn't going to be easy. It's not like we can send out a squad and nail her with a sniper bullet. At least with the Royal Guard in Iraq you knew where to look for them. But this woman could be anywhere."

Gus nodded his head in agreement. He looked around the office at all the war memorabilia. Over the years Frank Hartnett had assembled an impressive collection of weapons and swords that were once used against U.S. Forces in various conflicts. They were now being used to decorate the walls and tables in his office. He had artifacts that dated back to World War I. He'd purchased a collection from the widow of a retired Marine Corps Colonel. That acquisition pushed the value of his collection to about $75,000. He wanted to collect more from Iraq but he'd been warned that our government now frowned on taking battlefield spoils. *Political bullshit. If you fight and win, you deserve some rewards.* But rather than face charges of disobeying a lawful order, he decided to get his latest round of goods through legitimate purchases. Even so, his collection always drew stares from anyone who entered his office.

Gus' attention returned to Frank. "You know, this really sounds like FBI work. Since the lady obviously crossed state lines to commit these crimes, the feds will say it's their cases. How will you handle that?"

"I don't know. But for now, it's ours. I need to assemble a team. You need to tell me if the team is good."

"I can do that. In the mean time, how about let's grab a beer. We can chat while we drink."

"Relax. We can toss a few bourbons back while we talk." Frank reached into a cabinet behind his desk and pulled out two tumblers and a bottle of whiskey. He poured a double shot in each and handed one to Gus. They raised their glasses towards each other and said in unison, "Semper Fi!"

Chapter 3

"It's the damnedest thing I've ever seen. Denny Wilson found him laying here in the bedroom with the gun in his hand," Detective Reid Hansen said in his slight Nordic accent. "We got a call from a lady next door, a Mrs. Julie Dornside. She lives in the house to the east. Said she heard a loud noise from the house but said that the lady that lived here moved out several weeks ago. The story was that her husband was killed in Europe." Detective Hansen looked around the small bedroom, being careful not to step in any evidence. The 'evidence' consisted of blood, brain matter and bone fragments. He continued, "Said she didn't know her real well. It must have been the shot that she heard. You can see that it was suicide, but why did this guy kill himself in this empty house? We haven't had a chance to question any of the neighbors yet. He's probably stationed at the Air Force base. He's got the military haircut. The guy looks pretty squared away."

Detective William Banks' face was tight, jaw clenched so that the cleft in his chin was exaggerated. He looked around the bedroom. It was small, about nine feet by eight feet, painted institutional green, like the halls in a hospital or military barracks. The floor was asphalt tile, cream color with light colored streaks running through each tile. A section of tiles near the bedroom were stained grey, nearly white, apparently from a puddle of hot water that had sat until it evaporated, ruining the wax finish. In the hall next to the bedroom was a closet with a slatted door that looked like it housed the furnace or maybe the hot water heater. Across the hall from the closet was the single bathroom. Further down the hall were the other two bedrooms, each nearly the same size as the one in which they stood. The tiles at the perimeter of the room were cracked from where carpet strips had been nailed through them into the concrete slab. Besides the smell given off by the pool of blood and brain matter from the victim's head, the room had the faint, but distinctive, musty smell of dogs. It was a good thing that the carpeting had been removed or the whole house would wreak from the smell. He could almost see three or four dogs lounging around the house, eating scraps of food thrown to them by well meaning owners. Since the call came into the department within an hour of the loud noise that the neighbors had heard, and the police were on the scene within 10 minutes after the call, there was no decomposition of the body. In this temperature, the body could have laid for days without any noticeable decomposition. It was like a meat locker in the house. He asked Reid, "How long have you been out of the Marines; thirty years?"

"Twenty-seven. Why do you ask?"

"I thought only active duty military said *squared away*." Banks stood with his arms at his side and directed his gaze to the body on the floor before him. The pool of blood had stopped expanding and was starting to dry at the outer edges of the flow to the right of the victims head. Significant brain matter and skull fragments were scattered across the room where the exit wound had given way to the explosion inside the young man's head. He was apparently on his knees when the shot was fired and he fell at an angle to the 'V' shaped debris field of human tissue. "Anybody check his ID?"

"Nope. Body hasn't been moved at all yet. We're just getting to that. The crime lab guy just took about a million pictures. He's waiting for us to turn the body over so they can take a million more of him turned right side up." Detective Hansen stood at the victim's feet, hovering over everyone in the room. At 6'5" and 235 pounds of muscle, he looked like he could still be a marine. His blond, but graying hair wasn't cut military close but it was neatly trimmed. He didn't wear a hat. He was dressed in a heavy, thigh-length, black leather, winter coat that was unzipped exposing the shoulder harness that he wore for his Glock 9mm semi-automatic. His heavy gloves were shoved in his coat pockets. From his blue jean pants, he pulled a set of latex gloves and put them on with a snap. He appeared more relaxed than Banks. His casual demeanor around dead bodies used to annoy Banks. At automobile accidents where victims were bloody beyond recognition, Hansen was almost jovial. He would be the one to help pull the bodies from wreckage and assist the coroner or paramedics with getting bodies on gurneys. Banks was going to confront Hansen on this until he found out that Hansen had seen a lot of death in Vietnam. He was in Quang Tri during the Tet offensive and nearly his whole company was killed. He was shot in the left leg and left torso. He only survived because the bullet hit and broke a rib but was deflected away from any major organs. Hansen didn't react to death the way normal people do. Banks still thought that he was too comfortable with it. Death should evoke emotions. Hansen's expressions didn't change in the presence of death, regardless of how grizzly the scene.

The air in the house was nearly as cold as the air outside, another reason why the dog smell that hung in the room was held to a minimum. The temperature had barely reached 30 degrees and the wind chill was brutal. This was typical for North Dakota in early spring. It was Saturday, March 24. Federal taxes were due to be mailed in less than a month. That thought gave William Banks more of a chill than the weather conditions. He still hadn't started his taxes. His plan had been to finish them this weekend and be ready to mail them Monday morning on the way to the police station. His weekend plans had just changed.

Detective William Randolph Banks was dressed in a light-blue, button up shirt and black pants, a black and blue striped tie, and a dark, knee length overcoat, untied and unbuttoned. He wore a navy blue ambassador hat with ear flaps. The hat covered his close cropped blond hair completely. He kept his hair short since leaving the Army 20 years ago. It was habit more than necessity. The Grand Forks Police Department had standards for haircuts but Banks never had to worry about that. His hair would still meet military specs. His shoes were also shined to a high gloss and he always looked like he starched his clothes. No matter how long he worked each day, he looked as neat and pressed at the end of the day as he did at the start.

While pulling on his own latex gloves, Detective Banks looked around the room, but there wasn't much to see. Two walls were blank, nothing on them but paint. A third wall had the only window to the room which faced north. It looked out to the front lawn and the nearly identical houses across the street. The fourth wall had a double closet with bi-fold doors and the door to the room. The room, like the rest of the house, was empty. He looked down at the young man lying sprawled out before him in an unnatural position, his right arm under his body, his left out to his side above is head. He wore a thin coat, a light tee shirt, blue jeans and sneakers; not exactly the right gear for North Dakota this time of year. His skin was tanned, another indication that he hadn't been in town long. The only way to get a tan this dark in North Dakota this time of year was at a tanning booth. This tan looked natural, with white skin behind the left ear, not like the dark, more even tans from an artificial baking.

The gun was a Beretta 92F 9mm, the sidearm issued to military police and combat units. Banks knelt down, cautiously pulled the Beretta from his hand, flipped on the safety with a fingertip and placed it in an evidence bag. He rolled the body on its left side so that he could get into the victim's right rear jeans pocket. He pulled out a black, tri-fold wallet and looked at its contents; $239 cash, a Visa Card, a picture of an older couple, probably his mom and dad, and one military ID, enlisted. Staff Sergeant Kevin R. Reardon, US Air Force. He'd been in since January, 1992.

Banks looked up at Hansen, still standing above the body. "You were right, Air Force, active duty. He was probably stationed at Grand Forks. Is there anything at all in the house?"

"We just started looking, but you can see for yourself, it's pretty well cleaned out. I mean, even the cupboards are bare. Mother Hubbard would've been proud. There's just you, Denny Wilson, and Sven Larson to work the house. Charlie Sams and I will start with the neighbors."

Banks looked around the room again. It was definitely empty, except for the contents of Kevin Reardon's head all over the one side of the room. "Okay. Anything else before we get started?"

"Nope. Just real creepy. Maybe we'll find out he was depressed or something and we can finish this by dinner time. I'm starved. "

Banks gave Hansen a sideways look with a raised eyebrow. "I'm worried about you. You should get some help with your emotional outbursts." Banks looked back down at the body of Kevin Reardon and shook his head. "You know, people are supposed to be getting happier now. Hell winter's over. It's all the way up into the teens at night." They both chuckled.

Hansen and his Senior Patrol Officer headed out the front door of the one story ranch in the western section of Grand Forks. Reid didn't like the look, smell, or feel of the scene. He knew people got depressed in the cold north but the empty house was an odd twist. The look that was etched on Reardon's face was one of despair. The traces along his cheeks appeared to be the path of dried tears. Folks who were depressed for long periods had wrinkles etched into their faces. Their eyes were sunken and baggy. Reardon's face looked young and tight. Except for the missing half of his head, he looked healthy. He was a lean, muscular young man, not like a body builder, but more like a runner. He apparently worked out and dressed neatly. Depression didn't appear to be a factor, though they should find out more from the neighbors. "Charlie, let's head for the neighbors. You head east, I'll head west. Hit the first 5 houses and then cross the street and head back this way. We'll meet and compare notes."

"Ok. Is there anything in particular that we should be asking besides if they knew these folks or heard anything unusual?"

"Yea. Ask everyone if they knew anything about him supposedly being killed overseas and how long ago that was." He thought for a moment. "Ask them if they had dogs. That place stinks in there."

* * *

The neighbors on the quiet block on 7th Avenue North were surprised to hear that a young man fitting Kevin Reardon's description had committed suicide back in the house. He was already supposed to be dead. The story goes that he was on a training mission in Europe where they were making practice in-air refueling runs. Reardon was a Flight Engineer for a refueling tanker. He had been in Europe for about three and a half weeks. He was supposedly killed when a fueling truck ran over him while he was inspecting the tanker. Apparently someone was lying.

The neighbors to the west of the Reardon home, a Mrs. McFarland, said that Mrs. Reardon packed up and was headed to Pensacola, Florida. She said Mrs. Reardon told her that her parents lived down there. In fact, her brother came up to help her pack. She said she was a military brat. Her dad was supposedly in the Air Force. That seemed odd to her husband, Master Sergeant Daniel McFarland, because she seemed a bit spoiled for a military kid and she didn't know the Air Force lingo at all. But not all military kids fit the standard mold.

Mrs. McFarland said one other strange thing was that Mrs. Reardon was selling several of Kevin's power tools before she supposedly learned of her husband's death. Her explanation was that Kevin wanted to sell the tools because he no longer had the time to do any hobby woodworking. She sold several expensive power tools for real cheap. Her husband remarked that he thought Mrs. Reardon was getting ready to leave her husband. He'd seen it many times before where a young military bride gets tired of the separation from a spouse who's been deployed for long periods of time. It puts a real strain on any marriage particularly a new marriage when the bride is young and not used to being away from her husband.

Hansen was just about to pull out of the drive when a woman came up to the car making a circular motion with her hand, the universal signal to roll down the car window. When Detective Hansen did so, the woman introduced herself as Mrs. Lillie Weickoff. Mrs. Weickoff was a short, plump woman in her early thirties. She had a round face and a pair of chins. She was wearing jeans, a heavy jacket and a scarf. She had dark hair and too much blue eye shadow over her dark gray eyes. She said that she was wondering what had happened. When detective Hansen wouldn't offer any information, Mrs. Weickoff said, "Look, I know that there's a dead body in there and folks are saying that it's Kevin Reardon, but I don't think that's right. I met Kevin. He was the nicest man. He'd do anything for you. It's so sad that he was lost over there. His wife was a bit different though, not nearly as nice as Kevin. Her brother was a weird character, too. He didn't look like her too much. They packed up and left just a week ago, March 16th. I remember because we, my husband and I, were going to go to lunch and then head out to Wal-Mart. We needed to get a present for my mother-in-law. So I remember that they packed up and left in a U-Haul. They spent most of the day loading. My husband asked if they needed help and they said no, that they wanted to do it themselves and make sure that nothing got dropped or broken. So we just watched them pack up from our house over there." She pointed to one of the houses across the street.

"Mrs. . . . ?"

"Weickoff. Lillie Weickoff. You can call me Lil, everyone else does."

"Yes, Lil. Tell me about Mrs. Reardon."

"Her name is Belinda. She's short, a little over 5 feet tall and thin except she's built pretty well, if you know what I mean. She turns guy's heads, that's for sure. And she has light colored hair, almost blond, but more sandy colored. Her face is thin and her eyes are a bit sunken. They always looked like she wasn't getting enough sleep, you know, dark circles underneath."

Reid asked Lil, "Did she have any tattoos or piercings, besides ear piercings, I mean? Like an eyebrow or nose?"

Lil folded her arms across her chest and looked thoughtful for a moment, as if studying a picture in the air next to Reid. She slowly shook her head and said, "I don't believe that she did, at least none that I can remember. She seemed like the type that might but I really don't recall seeing any tattoos or any stuff like that. One thing she did have was a birth mark under her left ear. I remember that because it looked like West Virginia. It was about the size of a quarter. It was really unique. I remarked about it one day and I think she was upset. It may have made her feel a bit uncomfortable. You know how some folks are, like a zit that you can't hide."

"What about her hands and fingers. Did she wear any nail polish, bite her nails, have any scars on her hands? Were her hands rough or smooth? Did she wear any rings, like a wedding band or diamond?"

Again, Lil took the thinkers pose. This time, she was quick to answer, though. "Her hands were pretty smooth and she wore a solitaire, about 1/3 carrot."

"Did she work?"

"No, she couldn't have. She never left the house long enough to have a job."

"Do you remember any remarkable characteristics about Mrs. Reardon's brother? Any scars or other distinguishing features?"

"Well, he had jet black hair. It looked dyed black. He was about 6'5" tall or more and about 150 to 160 pounds. He was real skinny."

Detective Hansen asked Mrs. Weickoff, "Can you remember his eye color? Did he have any tattoos or piercings?"

"Sure. He had very dark eyes, so brown that they were almost black. He didn't have any tattoos or other weird markings. His skin was real pale and he didn't have any freckles at all. Same with Belinda. No freckles except her birth mark. But her skin wasn't pale. Odd, huh?" She was going to keep talking but Detective Hansen interrupted.

"What kind of clothes was he wearing? Did he have proper clothes for this climate?"

"Yes, he did. He had a black leather jacket and black leather gloves. Every time I saw him, he wore black. He looked like one of them . . . what do you call it when they have pale skin and wear all black? It's an old word."

Hansen asked, "You mean Gothic?"

"That's it. He didn't wear any spiked collars or wristbands or anything like that, but if you put some of that stuff on him, he'd have fit right in with them."

"Did you ever have a chance to talk with him close up?"

"Absolutely. I talked to him face-to-face a couple of times. He wasn't very talkative, almost introverted I'd say, but he did speak. Of course it may have been that they were mourning with Kevin's death and all. It probably wasn't a real good time to get to know him."

"Lil, would you mind if I show you Kevin's ID? We're trying to figure out what's happened here and it would be helpful if you could positively identify Kevin." Hansen exited the car, went to the house to retrieve the ID card and returned moments later. Mrs. Weickoff was talking with another neighbor. She spoke to Detective Hansen as he approached, "Detective, this is Janice McFarland. She's met the Reardons before and can verify my description."

"I sure can," Mrs. McFarland stated with certainty. "He is, or was, just as Lil described him, if she said 5'10, 160 pounds, brown hair, cut military style."

"That's what she said. Is this Kevin Reardon?" He held the ID card in front of both their faces and held it there for only a second when both ladies nodded their heads in unison.

"That's Kevin." Lil's stated.   Mrs. McFarland nodded in agreement.

"Thanks, ladies. You've been most helpful."

"But who is the dead guy in the Reardon's house?"

"You will probably hear about it on the news but the dead guy in the house is Kevin Reardon."

"Well who was killed in Europe then?"

"That's the question of the day. I hope we can find out quickly. You mentioned that Mrs. Reardon said they were headed to Florida?"

"Yes. Pensacola."

Hansen nodded, got back in the car and backed out of the drive, narrowly avoiding a police car and a rescue truck. He headed north on 20th street then west on US Route 2 towards the Grand Forks Air Force Base.

Chapter 4

Robert Garrett was pissed off. He'd been sitting in the driver's seat of a beat up, red Toyota Corolla at the rest area at mile marker 123 along Interstate 26 near Columbia, South Carolina. He was trying to get a few hours sleep before heading on to King's Bay, Georgia. He'd gone over the events of the past few months to try and figure out what went wrong. The best they could net from nearly two months of work was a meager $3,800.00. On top of that, they'd had to endure the harshest months of the North Dakota winter. *This is unsat. I can't believe that loser showed up early. His stint was supposed to be for another month and a half. No more work north of the Mason Dixon line. It's too fucking cold.* He had to put all of the pieces in place in his mind and figure out why the plan fell apart. It was important to learn from past mistakes to make sure that you didn't repeat them. That was one of life's lessons he'd learned the hard way.

He looked to his left, then his right. No other cars were parked near the picnic area of the rest stop. They were alone for the time being. All he could see were the concrete tables under the shelters, a few covered trash cans, grass and pine trees. The rest area was pleasant looking. The mid-morning sun beat down on many areas of the parking lot but Bobby had selected a spot that was under the shade of a stand of tall pine trees. The air was cool at 56 degrees but there was little breeze, so the sun on the parking area blacktop warmed the car and made it feel comfortable. As Bobby sat thinking, a car drove by, heading back out onto the interstate. Bobby watched out his mirrors as the car passed. The car sped up and was gone in just a few seconds. *A little paranoid, don't you think? You can't be too careful, though.* Bobby laughed to himself, thinking that he might be going crazy, having an ongoing dialogue in his head.

Robert 'Bobby' Garrett was 29 years old. He was tall at 6'5" and had dark black hair. His eyes were so brown that they looked like black dots. His skin was pale which gave him somewhat of a gothic appearance. He was born in Beckley, West Virginia, went to the local public schools, and generally did well with his studies. Then, when he was starting his junior year, his dad announced that he was leaving his mother for a much younger woman. He was in love with her and he just didn't love his mother anymore. Bobby was so enraged that he beat his father nearly to death. His father never fully recovered. The brain damage wasn't severe but his right arm hung at his side, useless for all practical purposes. His speech was so slurred that he sounded dead-drunk when he spoke, which was rarely. For protecting his mother's honor, Bobby spent a year in juvenile detention and was released on his eighteenth birthday. He was approached by a Navy recruiter who told him that he could assist him with finishing high school, starting a career, and seeing the world. Bobby was pretty good with writing and was meticulously organized so the recruiter recommended that he look into becoming a Yeoman. The Navy Yeoman is the ship's administrator. They handle the paperwork for personnel from training records, leave and absence requests, to advancement forms. The job required attention to detail. Bobby was sold. He joined the United States Navy within a week of his release from juvenile hall and headed to Northern Illinois for boot camp at Great Lakes Naval Training Center.

He did well in his career for several years. He was promoted regularly, as early as was possible for an enlisted man. He had a number of positive comments and letters in his personnel file. All things considered, he was on his way to a great career. He'd decided that he liked the Navy, liked the pay, liked to travel and liked the other men on his ship, a fast frigate out of Charleston, South Carolina. He'd achieved the rank of Second Class Petty Officer. Life was great.

Then his temper got the best of him again.

He and several of his shipmates were at a local Charleston, South Carolina bar, having drinks and pretty much minding their own business when several locals started to harass them. Bobby's friends noticed that he was getting annoyed by their comments. They could see his face turning red and his body tense. Apparently the locals could see that, too so they directed their verbal barbs exclusively at Bobby. They made fun of his pale complexion, his thin face, and his dark eyes. Then they started with the Navy jokes. Before they could get the third joke started, Bobby was out of his seat throwing punches. He rarely lost his temper, but when he did he was wild. It was as if he bottled up all the energy from any annoyance over the years and the pressure kept building until he couldn't hold it in any longer. He laid two of the locals out before the other two caught him with a couple of lucky punches. Bobby's shipmates had joined in by then. Within a few seconds, the bar bouncers had the three sailors and the four locals up and out the door. The fighting started again out in the parking lot, but it didn't last long. The Charleston Police had several cars on the scene within minutes of the seven being thrown out of the bar.

Bobby was charged with assault. After a night in jail and missing his duty muster on board ship the next day, he was sent to Captain's Mast, the Navy's form of misdemeanor punishment. He was fined half a month's pay for two months and confined to the ship for three months. He was also reduced in rate, which meant that he lost a stripe which bumped him down to Petty Officer Third Class. The captain suspended that punishment with the condition that he had to stay out of trouble for at least another six months. If he kept his nose clean, he kept his stripe. If not, he lost it and the pay that goes along with a demotion.

Bobby kept his end of the bargain and stayed out of trouble. During his confinement to the ship, he used his time to study paperwork used by the military for different situations. Since he was a Yeoman, he had access to the mountain of forms used by any branch of the military for any situation. There were the typical forms that appeared in every sailors personnel file; copies of the DD4-Enlistment/reenlistment Document Armed Forces of the United States, to DD93-Record of Emergency data, to DD1624-Leave and Earnings Statements. He used these daily in his normal job duties. Then there were obscure, little used forms for things that would never occur to the average civilian. It was amazing that the military could create a form for nearly every occasion. But they were very proficient at creating useless paperwork. They were quite poor at disposing of those forms once they became obsolete. Why would anyone need a form DD1205-Soil Moisture-Content determination? But the Department of Defense had a form just for that.

Then there were the personnel forms that were rarely used, for example DD1075-Convoy list of remains of deceased personnel, and DD1077-Deceased Personnel, Collection Point register of. And form DD565-Statement of recognition of Deceased. Bobby was intrigued by these forms and their use. As he studied the forms he wondered if he'd ever have to process any of these. They were rarely used in peacetime. Even while he was confined to the ship for those three months, he was thinking that there had to be a way to make money from the massive forms maze the military had created. How could anyone keep track of the path that these forms had to follow from start to finish? His mind raced while he plotted and schemed and made up different scenarios in his mind on how he could capitalize on his knowledge of military paperwork. He came up with several ideas, but he needed help with his schemes.

Bobby coasted through the remainder of his Navy enlistment. He'd been discharged from the Navy for a few years but never landed a job that he felt was worthy of his talents. He had a number of women move in and out of his life, the last being an older woman with a pretty bizarre view of life. She was interesting and sexy even for a middle aged lady. She had some strange ideas on how to make a living. She'd scam sailors in bars and do a little flesh peddling. She took care of his sexual needs, too. Her tastes were just south of kinky; a bit too much for Bobby. It was okay for a while but she started to get too far out for him. She had her seven year old son living with them as well. That was what pushed him over the edge.

Then he met Rebecca Lippert in Key West, Florida. She had all the skills, talent, and intelligence that he needed in a business partner. And she was the second most evil person he'd ever met.

Becky Lippert was asleep in the passenger seat of the beat up Toyota Corolla. Her long sandy-blond hair hung over her face and she breathed deeply, nearly snoring. She was wearing a loose, low cut sweater, blue jeans, and sandals. She had on large dream catcher earrings. She wore heavy eye shadow and dark, rusty red lipstick. When Bobby started the engine she began to stir. He turned to her as she sat up and rubbed her eyes.

"Where are we? Last thing I remember we were in the mountains and it was just getting light."

Bobby stared at her cleavage as she stretched, her arms above her head, back arched, a groan coming from her throat. Bobby thought she looked sexy even when she was waking from a restless sleep. He gathered his thoughts again and said, "We can't ever screw up like this again."

She was still half asleep and she really didn't understand Bobby's comments. "What baby? I didn't hear a word you said. I'm so tired."

With a little more force in his voice he said, "Wake up, Becky. This is important. We have to keep better track of these guys. I mean we were almost sitting in the driveway packing the van when this guy showed up."

That was a bit of an exaggeration. They actually were gone for almost a week before Kevin Reardon showed up at the house. But Bobby was trying to make a point that he didn't plan on going to prison and she better start keeping closer track of her "husbands."

She shook her head, trying to shake the cobwebs loose. She looked around at the rest area then turned to Bobby. "How am I supposed to do that? They don't tell us wives anything until the last minute." She put a sarcastic emphasis on 'wives'. She paused to look at the trees. Two robins were hopping along the ground in search of a wormy treat. She was relaxed. She really wasn't in the mood for any of Bobby's orders. She let him think that he was in charge and it worked for the most part. Once in a while he got a little pushy. Then she would turn on her wicked charm and he was right back in line. She let him think that he got his way, but she was in control and she knew it.

Bobby went on with his speech, "You better make friends with someone from the command then. Make yourself available to one of the officers who handle that information. You know how to do it. Just don't be too obvious. You can keep his mind off of work. I've seen you in action. Just turn on you're little helpless wifey-pooh act. You know the one . . . You're new at this having just been married and all. Your new hubby is deployed and you just don't know what to do. You'll have them eating out of your hand in no time."

"Oh, yea. I can do that alright. But it won't be my *hand* that their eating from. How would you like a little taste right now?" She smiled a sleepy little smile that told Bobby what she was thinking about.

"We don't have time for any of that right now. We have to get to King's Bay for a week or so, then back to Jacksonville. There should be a paycheck there soon. Remember your poor, deceased husband, Mrs.

Sharp?"

Her sleepy smile curled into a wicked smile as she thought about the Serviceman's Group Life Insurance Policy check that was waiting for them. He was amazed at how sexy she could be. She looked so young for being in her mid twenties, but she had the moves that made men go wild. And she did it with a subtlety that, before you knew what was happening, you were in her arms with your heart in her one hand, your testicles in the other and she was putting the squeeze on you. Oh yea, she was evil, but so hot. Bobby leaned over to kiss her. Before he reached her lips she lifted her sweater and directed him to her breasts while she pulled the lever on her seat. Before he knew what was happening, she had his balls in her hand and she was squeezing.

"Let me show you what I can do to keep your mind off your troubles."

And she did.

* * *

The show in the rest area didn't go on without an audience. The view through the binoculars was as clear as watching a TV show. The middle-aged woman watching Bobby and Becky was steaming mad. She thought, *You will pay for this little escapade, Bobby Garrett. It might take a while, but you will definitely pay, you bastard. You were planning on taking my cut. That ain't right.*

Chapter 5

Wilson Brush sat with his friend and shipmate, Doug Farrell at Tommy's Place near the southern entrance to the Kings Bay Navy Submarine Support Base north of St. Mary's, Georgia. It was 9:45 on a Friday night and the bar was just starting to get busy. They'd been back from sea for about ten weeks. In a few weeks they'd have to report back for duty in preparation for taking the USS Nevada back from the Blue Crew. The time during off crews always passed faster than the time aboard ship. As members of a "two-crew" ballistic missile submarine, they enjoyed their time off while the other crew had the strenuous task of being out to sea, meandering around, just waiting to unleash massive destruction upon the enemies of freedom. That destruction was in the form of nuclear warheads delivered by Trident D-5 missiles. Each missile is capable of pinpoint delivery of multiple independent reentry vehicles, which means that it can deliver many bombs to different locations. One missile can destroy numerous large cities. Each Trident submarine had the capacity to carry 24 missiles. So a handful of Trident subs can take out a major portion of the northern hemisphere. Of course, no one likes to think about all that destruction when you're riding around in a big black tube capable of delivering a significant portion of that annihilation, so you have to stay busy. And while you were aboard ship, you were busy.

The routine was always the same. When the sub enters port for turnover, the off-going crew docks the ship and gathers all of their personal and crew belongings. They get their things off the ship while the oncoming crew finds their bunks, and load their personal belongings in the tiny compartments that are allocated for that purpose. Then turnover begins. The off-going crew hands over all of the maintenance information regarding failed equipment, depleted spare parts, and other data to the on-coming crew. After about two days of turnover, the off-going crew departs the ship and the on-coming crew begins the grueling task of making the ship ready to set to sea. Duty sections are set up in port and starboard, which only means that you have no life except what the Navy tells you. When you had duty, you were on the ship for 24 hours out of 24 hours of the duty day. The next day, you are on the off duty day which means you only have to work about 12 of the 24 hours in that day. On the third day, you are back on duty again. And that goes on forever, so it seems.

Wilson and Doug were talking about their first four weeks of off crew which consisted of reporting to the base twice a week to muster with the crew. After muster, you were dismissed. This is done primarily to ensure that you were in the area and available to report if needed. That first four weeks after turning the submarine over to the other crew was heavenly. It was intended to allow sailors of the ballistic missile force time to relax and get rested for the next deployment. The captain of the USS Nevada determined that the muster days were Tuesday and Thursday at 8:00 am. So after each Thursday muster, Wilson and Doug usually headed for Daytona Beach, Florida for a long weekend. They loved the heat, sun and bars at Daytona. And the scenery wasn't bad either. There were always plenty of young ladies to look at, many tanned and trim. And that was the topic of their conversation at Tommy's. They had planned to head for Florida for the weekend but Doug was employed part-time by the Chief of the Boat, or the COB. The COB had quite a few rental properties and occasionally had some tenant issues that needed to be handled outside of the normal, strictly legal, means. Doug was 21 years old; a big guy, 6'6" and about 250 pounds. He looked like a bouncer and had that cocky attitude that a bouncer needs to ensure control of the rowdies at bars. The COB knew that his presence was a big help in convincing tenants that they should either pay up or move out. So Doug would accompany the COB on visits with his problem tenants. In most cases, when the tenant got a look at Doug, the problem disappeared.

Doug was a handsome young man and always seemed to attract the women, young and not so young, even though he treated them with indifference. They'd work hard trying to talk to him and he'd pay just enough attention to them to keep their interest. That was one reason why Wilson liked hanging out with him. There were always plenty of good looking women hanging around.

Wilson, at 22, was a pretty decent looking guy himself. He was 6'1" tall and slender. He kept a neat appearance and dressed well. He looked sharp even in casual clothes. This evening he had on a pair of new looking jeans and a golf shirt that looked as if it had just come off the rack. His light, sandy-brown hair was close cropped and neatly trimmed, well within Navy Specs, but not a buzz-cut. He had soft blue eyes that caught people's attention. When Wilson and Doug came into a bar, most people noticed them, especially the women.

Tommy's was typical of bars in most Navy towns, catering to off-duty sailors looking for some down time to relax. With two dart boards, two worn, quarter operated pool tables, a handful of video games, 10 bar stools and a dozen and a half tables and booths, the bar could comfortably accommodate over 80 people. The lights were dim, partly because there weren't enough and partly because the lens covers had a yellow, cigarette-smoke-covered film. The bar always had a smoky haze filling the air. Behind the bar was a mirror that ran the entire length of the wall. The shelves in front of the mirror were stocked with all the popular brands of commercially-available booze. They had a great choice of beer, both domestic and imported.

Tommy's kept the crowds pretty well under control. It was known for keeping its patrons in line and they had no problem throwing out the trouble-makers. It was located on Point Peter Place just off of USS Kamehameha Avenue which ran into the southeastern entrance to the base. Sailors and their girlfriends or wives, groups of wives whose husbands were out to sea, and groups of sailors were the typical crowds that filled Tommy's on a regular evening. This Friday night looked no different, until a very young looking lady walked in alone. Wilson elbowed Doug and nodded in her direction. Doug's eyes turned that way. Doug liked what he saw but acted as if it was no big deal. This young lady, a girl by all appearances, was new to Tommy's. She was slender with attractive facial features, at least from 35 feet away. She walked slowly with an attitude that said, 'I know you're looking at me.' Doug looked around the room and her attitude was right on target. She was getting attention from most of the testosterone in the room. There was at least one guy who got a stiff elbow from his girlfriend. Another lady grabbed her husband's jaw and pulled it towards her face as if to say *you look at me and not that tramp.* Wilson stared at her as she walked up to the bar and asked the bartender a question. The bartender smiled at her, but shook his head. She said something back and turned towards the crowd. She briefly scanned the room then made her way to a booth near a window that looked out over the parking lot. A minute later, the bartender walked over and set a mixed drink in front of her. She smiled, nodded thanks to the bartender as he moved away, then she returned her gaze to the window.

"I wonder if she's meeting someone." Wilson asked Doug.

"Yes she is. She's waiting for you, my friend."

With that, Wilson Brush picked up his beer, walked over to her table, introduced himself and asked if she was waiting for someone in particular. She replied that she was planning to meet a friend but that her friend had said she may not be able to make it. Wilson asked if she wouldn't mind some company while she waited, and she said with an easy smile, "That would be great."

"My name's Wilson."

"Tanya. Tanya Walters." She held out her hand and Wilson took it. Her hands were soft and small. Her nails were perfectly painted in a rust polish that stood out against her tan skin. She had matching lipstick on, also applied perfectly. Her face was slender, matching her body. Her eyes were blue and were perfectly proportioned. She was short, about 5'3", and her straight blond hair hung about six inches past her shoulders, parted slightly to the right of center.

She wore a flower print blouse with the top two buttons open and showed just enough cleavage to let Wilson see the top portion of two seriously luscious breasts. She had as close to a perfect body as he'd ever seen, at least as much as he could see.

"So, tell me about yourself, Tanya Walters. Do you live nearby? Are you married, single, seeing anyone?"

"Whoa. Slow down Wilson. I just got here. First, a question for you. What's your last name?"

"Oh. Sorry. Brush. Wilson Brush. I live here in Marysville but I'm originally from East Liverpool, Ohio."

"East Liverpool. I know where that is. I've been through that town on the way to West Virginia from Cleveland. The place looks pretty run down along the river."

"It's pretty run down most places in town. That's one reason I joined the Navy. I had to get out of there. My folks still live north of town near Calcutta. Things are a little better there. My dad's about to retire. He's a foreman at a glass factory there. That place used to be the largest producer of specialty glass in the world. Practically everybody in town worked for one of the glass factories. Then foreign competition ate our lunch and one by one, the factories started closing or moving south or overseas. Hey I'm rambling on about myself. Now it's your turn for a while."

"Well, I'm originally from West Virginia, near Parkerstown. I was raised by my Aunt and Uncle. My parents were killed in a fire at the factory where they both worked. I was real young so I never really knew them."

Wilson's face turned grim. "I can't imagine how that must feel, not knowing your parents."

"It wasn't all that bad, really. My Auntie Jenn and Uncle Walt are the only parents that I've ever known so it wasn't like I lost them after having known them for years. Once in a while I do think about what it would have been like growing up with my real mom and dad. But there's no sense dwelling on it. You can't change the past." She smiled and seemed to not let the gravity of the conversation ruin her mood.

Wilson watched her smile for a moment before remarking, "I guess I understand that. I haven't ever experienced anything like losing a parent so I really don't know how I'd feel. So are your aunt and uncle still in West Virginia?"

"No, they moved to Arizona, near Phoenix. I haven't seen them in a couple of years. I talk to them on occasion but they're getting on in years now. They are actually my great aunt and uncle. Uncle Walt can hardly hear now. Aunt Jenn has to use a cane to walk. She may have to get a walker soon. But they're in their seventies so that's pretty much expected. They worked hard all their lives. My Uncle Walt tells me that they 'have pains in places that 'us yunguns don't even know exist.' He's still got his sense of humor anyway." She smiled, her eyes gazing out the window to the parking lot while she thought about the lie she'd just told. Her 'Uncle Walt and Aunt Jenn' didn't exist.

"He sounds great."

As they were talking, a tall slender man with dark hair and dark eyes entered the bar and took a bar stool near the hall to the restrooms. He looked around at the other patrons, but paused briefly when he saw Tanya. He turned to the bartender and ordered a Bud Light draft. He pulled out a cigarette, lit it and blew smoke into the air towards the hall. Doug noticed the guy sitting there alone. He looked out of place in this bar that was typically occupied by short-haired squids. He had hair that definitely wasn't military spec. It was parted in the middle and covered his ears, almost to his shoulders. He slouched over at the bar. He had pale looking skin and wore black clothes which made his skin appear all the more pale. Doug glanced back at Wilson and Tanya. They were deep in conversation, looking each other directly in the eyes, smiling once in a while, looking serious then laughing. Wilson seemed to be enjoying himself so Doug looked around the room again. A number of the guys were still glancing over at Tanya who clearly was the hottest looking lady in the bar. He noticed a table with two young ladies. They were glancing his way quite a bit but he played his usual indifference card and looked away. He decided to visit the head before ordering another drink. As he got up he bumped into the tall, pale guy who had been at the bar. He was heading for one of the pool tables with his beer in hand. Almost losing his balance, Doug reached his hand over and grabbed the guy by the arm to keep them both from tumbling to the floor.

"Whoa, fella. Are you okay?"

"I'm fine but you should watch where the hell you're going. You almost knocked me on my ass." His voice was raised so that it could be heard above the Brian Purcer and the Hot Licks song playing on the juke box. That drew some attention because Brian Purcer played loud rock and roll. If you were louder than the juke box, you were loud. Wilson and Tanya also looked in the direction of the two. Wilson tensed in case he had to go to the aid of his friend, which he quickly realized was pretty silly. Doug could handle most anyone in a one-on-one fight. As Tanya looked at the pale guy, he glanced her way and made brief eye contact. There was familiarity in the glance. She got a chill from his gaze and quickly turned away towards the parking lot. Wilson didn't notice the exchange and continued to look at the two men, now standing square to each other, sizing the other up. Wilson edged towards the end of the booth to prepare himself for action. Just then, Tanya put her hand on his and broke his attention away from the boiling feud of words in the middle of the bar.

Doug said, "Lighten up dude. I didn't see you. Last time I looked, you were at the bar."

"Well try opening your eyes instead of eyeballing the chicks."

"Look pal, just move on. Nobody's hurt and let's keep it that way."

"No, you look. Just watch where the fuck you're going next time." Doug was getting irritated by this guy's attitude. He quickly looked him up and down and figured he could take this guy in seconds. It wasn't worth his trouble. He looked closer to make sure he didn't have a gun or knife in his pocket but didn't see any bulges that would give a weapon away. He looked the guy directly into his dark brown eyes and said, "Maybe you should watch your mouth around these ladies. You should have seen me get up. You could've stopped instead of ramming into me."

The tall guy stared back and said, "If you're looking for an apology, you're looking in the wrong place. If you're looking to take this outside, well, that's your decision. I'm game."

Conversation in the bar had stopped. Everybody was watching the two of them. Maybe there would be some live entertainment tonight after all.

Then the pale guy said, "Just forget it, asshole. You fuckin' squids are all alike. Think you own the bar or something, just because a few of you hang out here. I'll leave it alone for now. Just watch what the fuck you're doing the next time."

With that, the altercation de-escalated. The skinny, pale guy withdrew and left the bar without paying for his drink and Doug watch him leave. Doug waited for a few seconds then went to the head as he'd originally planned. He was only gone for a few minutes, but when he returned, Wilson and Tanya were nowhere to be seen. *Way to go, Wilson.*

Doug ordered another beer. As he waited for his beer to arrive, a smiling young lady approached him and with a strong southern accent said, "Hi. My name's Cindy. I liked the way you handled that weirdo-freak. So, you're Doug, right?"

"That's right. How did you know?"

"Well, all those folks yelling, 'way to go, Doug' had something to do with it."

Doug smiled and looked down at his beer. "What are you drinking? I'll get you another one."

Cindy replied, "I'm not that thirsty. But I would like to talk for a while if you don't mind."

"We can talk as long as you like, Cindy."

Things were looking up.

Chapter 6

Pat McKinney and his 5 year old son, Sean sat in the anchored 22 foot Bayliner Capri fishing boat within 200 yards of shore on Lake Dora near Tavares, Florida. As they looked out over the lake, the sun reflection on the water provided an array of colors, from dark green where trees were reflected, to light blue where the reflection mirrored the clear sky. They both had life jackets on securely and each had a bottle of water opened at their side. The cooler that had once held a twelve pack of cold water now contained only two bottles. Pat would have preferred a six pack of beer but he knew that he couldn't drink a six pack and drive home with his son in the car with him. He knew his wife, Diane, would have his hide for a stunt like that. Besides, he wanted to set a good example for his young son. The ice that had kept the water cold was now a memory, though the water in the cooler was still far below air temperature. The container of earthworms was getting low as well. They'd managed to feed quite a few fish with limited success at pulling many into the boat. They hadn't come close to landing a trophy bass. It was about 10:00 AM and the sun was just starting to beat down on the two anglers. They'd been on the lake since 7:00 that morning. They were both dressed in shorts, tee shirts and sandals and were coated in sunscreen with a 30 SPF rating, but the oppressive heat was starting to get to Pat. The fish had been biting earlier but things had slowed considerably. Pat caught a couple decent sized large mouth bass. Sean had caught just one little bluegill and was getting restless. He was constantly reeling in his line and casting it back out. Pat tried to get his son to be more patient but at just shy of six years old, Sean couldn't sit still.

Pat was recently discharged from the United States Navy and had quite a bit of free time to spend with his family. He'd recently had a significant amount of stress removed from his life, none of which had anything to do with the Navy. As he sat in the boat next to his son he reflected on the last eight years of his life. He subconsciously rubbed the scar on the left side of his chin with his right, middle finger; a habit that he couldn't seem to break. Pat and his two brothers, Joe and Mike, had been in the nursery business growing indoor foliage plants and selling them wholesale to department stores and florists throughout the southeast. It was a thriving and expanding business.

Nine years earlier, the brothers were building a greenhouse to expand the business. It was a typical hot, humid summer day in Florida and Pat was getting tired. While attempting to hammer a nail into a rafter board on a greenhouse, Pat lost his grip on the hammer. It mis-struck the16 penny nail causing it to ricochet into his jaw. The nail stuck about an inch into the skin along his jaw bone. There was no permanent damage, but over the years the scar turned white. Pat had a habit of rubbing the scar with the middle finger of his right hand whenever he was concentrating on an idea or when his thoughts wandered, like they were now.

Seven years ago, Pat's youngest brother Mike married Julie Mallernee. Everyone was very happy for Mike and Julie. Pat could still see her young, pretty face, always smiling. She was a perfect sister-in-law. She was slim, attractive, and always upbeat. She was the type of person who walked into a room and immediately brightened the mood. Everyone enjoyed her company. Mike and Julie returned from their honeymoon and were getting settled in their new house when she was brutally raped and murdered. The perpetrators of the crime were supposedly close friends of the McKinneys. Even worse, nearly the entire crime was captured on a home video tape recorder. Through some deception and theft of evidence by a Sheriff's deputy who was on the payroll of a notorious drug kingpin, the four accused rapists and murderers were set free. Aside from the video tape, no other evidence was recovered from the scene. It was a major blunder by the sheriff's department and the four never stood trial. To top it off, they laughed in the McKinney's faces and all but bragged about committing the crime. Pat and Joe swore to take revenge on the perpetrators but Mike was too distraught to take part in the plan. Pat and Joe joined the service; Pat the US Navy, Joe the US Marines. They got out of central Florida and away from their new adversaries and worked every day at planning their revenge. Pat and Joe's youngest brother, Mike moved to Nevada and never returned.

Finally the time came for their plan to be executed. But just as they kicked off the plan, it seemed to take on a life of its own. Their enemies started showing up dead without the brothers' lifting a finger. Each victim was murdered in the exact way that the brothers had planned. They were questioned about the murders but had alibis that were air tight because, for the most part, they were true.

While Pat and Joe were busy trying to figure out why their plan was being executed by someone else, Mike was overcome by despair and committed suicide. Years of depression, alcohol and drug abuse pushed him over the edge. The death of his young wife of only two weeks was too much for him to bear. After more than seven years of self-blame for not protecting her, he purposely overdosed on whiskey and Percodan and died. Mike's death stunned Pat and Joe and caused them even more anxiety as the remaining perpetrators came after Pat and his family. Pat sat in the hot Florida sun on the rented boat going over the events in his mind when he was jolted back to reality.

"Dad!"

Sean's excited voice caused Pat's body to jerk as he looked over at his son. Sean's fishing pole was bent over in an exaggerated arc. Sean was hanging on for dear life as the 5 year old struggled to maintain control of the rod.

"You're alright, son, just don't let go. Hang on to the rod tight with your right hand and put your left hand on the reel and start to reel him in." Pat moved closer to his son in case he needed to help with the catch which looked to be a real big fish.

"I can't, Dad. I'll drop the pole!"

"No you won't. Just make sure you hold on tight with your right hand. Do you have a good grip?"

Sean nodded. He was almost too scared to say anything as he fought with the fish at the end of the line.

"Okay. Now let go with your left hand but make sure you keep your grip with your right hand. You can do it." Pat was being very deliberate with his words, trying to reassure his son.

Sean tried to let go but he quickly grabbed the rod again. He didn't feel confident that he could keep his grip on the rod with just one hand. "I can't, Dad. It's too hard!"

Again in measured words, Pat asked his son, "Do you want me to help you reel the fish in?"

"No!" Sean's reply was quick and angry. He didn't have the confidence to do it himself but he wasn't going to let Pat help no matter what. He wasn't going to have his dad telling everyone that he had to help him reel in his fish. "I'll do it," Sean shouted. "Just let me do it by myself!"

"Okay. You're on your own."

Pat sat back and watched Sean try to work out how he would hang on to the rod and get his other hand on the reel to haul in what was obviously a pretty big fish. The rod continued to bow as the line moved back and forth in the lake water. Sean carefully put the handle of the rod between his legs and leaned the rod against the wall of the boat for more leverage. He slowly moved his left hand to the reel and began reeling the line in. He worked slowly at first but then gained more confidence as he worked the handle of the reel. The fish was working his way around to the back of the boat but Sean held the rod tightly in place. After seven full minutes the huge large-mouthed bass was within sight. Pat was pretty excited as Sean continued to haul in the fish. When the fish was close enough, Pat reached the net over the side and scooped up the trophy bass. He set the net on the floor of the boat, pulled the great fish out of the net and removed the hook.

Pat shouted, "You did it! Wow, that's a monster fish. Great job, son. This is one of the biggest bass I've ever seen."

Sean laughed and pumped his fist in the air then shouted, "Yes! I told you I could do it!"

Pat put out a hand for a 'high-five' and Sean smacked his dad's hand.

Still excited for his son, Pat said, "He's gonna taste great."

"You mean we have to eat him?"

"Well, yes. What did you think we were going to do with it?"

"Yuck. Fish taste terrible. You can eat it."

"Well, maybe we can have him stuffed and make a trophy for your room. Would you rather do that?"

"Yea. That'd be cool."

"Alright then, it's settled."

Pat just smiled to himself as he thought about what Diane's reaction would be. He tried to think back to when he was five years old. Did he like fish back then? Absolutely not. As they were baiting up Sean's hook for another cast, Pat's cell phone rang. He looked at the number. "Your mom's calling. She has me on the electronic leash."

"What's an electronic leash?" Sean's puzzled look accompanied his question.

"You'll understand soon enough."

Pat pressed 'talk' and in a pretty excited voice, he said, "Hi Babe. You should see the bass your son hooked. It's enough fish for a meal for all of us but I think we're going to have it stuffed and mounted on the wall in Sean's room. You should have seen him reeling it in. He's quite a fisherman."

Pat continued rambling on about Sean's catch when Diane interrupted, "How soon can you get home?"

The edge in Diane's voice made Pat tense. Then he asked, "What's going on?"

"Your mom called. It's your dad. He's in the hospital. She thinks he's had a heart attack. The doctors can't be certain but you need to bring Sean home so you can head down to Ft. Myers."

Pat's head started to swim. He knew that his dad wasn't in the greatest of health, but a heart attack? He started to think about his mom and how she must be in a panic. She wasn't real good during a crisis. He was certain that she was on the verge of a nervous breakdown by now.

Pat thought for a moment. No need to panic. If he was already at the hospital the doctors must have him stabilized by now or it was already too late. *Remain calm.* "We'll get home as quick as we can. I have to get the boat turned in. It should take less than an hour to get home from here. Did the doctors say how bad it is?"

Diane didn't answer for a couple of seconds. The delay caused Pat's heart to ache. "You need to hurry, Pat. But please be careful."

"I will, Sweetheart. Is Mom okay? How did she sound?"

"Scared. Do you want me to call Joe?"

"No. I'll do that."

"Okay. I'll see you in a bit. Drive careful Sweetheart."

Immediately after disconnecting with Diane, Pat hit the speed dial for his brother Joe. He wished that he knew more details but they would know soon enough.

* * *

Diane McKinney, Pat's wife of six and a half years packed his suit case while she waited for her two fishermen to arrive home. She wished he could fly so he didn't have to drive while thinking about his dad's condition. She thought about getting a plane ticket for Pat to Ft. Myers but it probably would take just as long to fly as it would to drive. The closest airport with commercial flights was Tampa International, over 100 miles away. By the time Pat drove to the Tampa International Airport, parked, got through security, waited for the flight and boarded, he could drive the rest of the way to Fort Myers.

Diane could tell by the sound of her mother-in-law's voice that Pat's mom was under a lot of stress. The normally steady, composed voice was shaking and choked up over the phone. '*I feel so helpless. I want to go in and see him and tell him he's going to be alright . . ..*' She'd stopped in mid sentence. Diane asked her if there was anyone with her and she'd said that friends of theirs were there. They offered to stay as long as she needed them. Diane assured her that Pat would be there as soon as he could. She also let her know that Pat would call Joe and make sure he knew where to go.

An hour after she first called Pat, she heard two car doors shut. She opened the front door, smelled the fishy scent on her son's hands and clothes and told him to get ready to take a bath. "You can tell me about your big day fishing afterwards." She smiled as best she could under the circumstances and put her hand on his back to help move him along into the house. When Sean was inside Diane turned to Pat. "Mom said that Dad is pretty bad. They're not sure about his chances. Is Joe on his way down?"

"Yes. He was leaving right away after I talked to him. I called him right after I hung up with you. He should be down there in about 3 hours or so. It'll take me about 4 hours to get down there. What all do I need to get ready?"

"You should be all set. I packed your suitcase. I left your shaving kit out so you could get a shower before you leave." She pinched her nose indicating that Pat smelled like fish then continued, "I packed for about 4 days worth. Please drive careful. You've already been driving for about an hour and the sun is really beating down. Make sure you have the air conditioning on high. You don't want to be dozing off. You and Sean were up early this morning."

"I know, Babe. If I get tired, I'll pull over and walk around the car or something. I really should eat something."

"I packed you a sandwich, pop, and chips. They're next to your suitcase."

"I don't know what I'd do without you Babe. Where is Anna?"

Their young daughter was taking a nap and was fast asleep in her room. Little Anna McKinney had a long morning of playing with her dolls. She was just too tired to stay awake and Diane knew that she would be a terror if she didn't get her nap.

"Give her a big kiss for me."

"You know I will." Diane moved closer to Pat, put her arms around him and put a soft kiss on his lips. Pat pulled her tight and kissed her harder with passion. When he stopped, he hugged her tight.

"I'll call you when I get to the hospital and let you know how Dad's doing. You never know with this stuff. Heart care's come a long way in the last few years. Just say a little prayer that it'll be alright.

"I'll be saying a lot of prayers, for your dad and you. You drive careful."

"You know, you've already told me that about six times."

"And I'll tell you six more so it sinks into that thick head of yours, you big dope." She smiled, but it was a sad smile that told Pat of the worry and loneliness that she already felt even before he walked out the door. Pat saw the first tears in her eyes. He wiped the tears away with his thumbs and pulled her close again. He kissed her and hugged her gently. He held her for a long time then turned, picked up his mini-cooler and suitcase and walked out the door.

* * *

Lisa Goddard was working on her tan early this year. She was getting ready for a trip to Key West and wanted to have a good base tan before the trip. It was just after 10:00 AM and the sun was already hot on her tan, oily body. She was a slender 110 pounds without a visible ounce of fat on her well proportioned body. When she walked down to the apartment pool, she drew lots of attention from the young men that lived in the complex in Pine Hills. Even in her Publix Supermarket uniform, she turned heads. But when she stretched out by the pool, as she was now, you could almost smell the testosterone cooking in the vicinity. She was every guy's dream girl. Lisa worked out several nights each week to keep herself in shape and it was definitely working. But now she was simply laid out by the pool, her eyes closed, thinking about her good fortune. She was young, healthy, happy, employed, and in love.

Her boyfriend, Joe McKinney, wanted to take her on vacation before she started school in the fall. They were planning to spend 2 weeks away from Orlando and take a leisurely drive down along the east coast of the Sunshine State until they reached Key West at the end of US 1. On the way back north, Joe was planning a bit of a surprise. He told her that they were driving along the west coast of the state so that they could see the Gulf Coast beaches and see the difference between the Atlantic Ocean and the

Gulf of Mexico. His real motive was to introduce her to his parents in Fort Myers.

Lisa sensed that someone was standing nearby, blocking the sun from reaching her skin. The shadow of Joe McKinney's broad shoulders was cast over most of Lisa body. He was looking her over from head to toe, his eyes stopping at her breasts, her firm stomach, then her bikini bottoms. He lingered there for a moment too long.

"See anything you like?"

Busted. "I like everything I see. Do you need any oil rubbed on that skin? You may have missed a spot."

"Umm. That sounds interesting. But I'm pretty well oiled up. Maybe you can wash it off in the shower later."

That brought a smile to Joe's face. "Is that an invitation?"

"Oh Yea," she replied in a sensuous voice.

Oh boy, Joe thought to himself. Then he remembered the reason he came down to the pool. He wished he didn't have to tell her about his father but there was no way around it. The expression on his face turned serious and he took a deep breath. "Hey, listen. I'm going to have to take a rain check on that shower."

Lisa propped herself up on her elbows. She took a moment to look at Joe's face. His eyes were gray with a hint of blue. He had a cleft in the middle of his slightly square chin. He was 5' 11" and solid muscle. He was trim, not bulky like a weight lifter. He kept his hair short and neat, a habit that he couldn't break since his discharge from the United States Marine Corps. It wouldn't meet strict Marine Corp regulations but it wouldn't take much trimming to get within 'spec'. Lisa looked Joe square in the eyes and said, "Don't tell me you're leaving me for another woman already?" She smiled and winked.

Joe's look told her that this was serious. "I have to drive down to Fort Myers. My dad's had a heart attack. He's at the hospital now."

Lisa sat up quickly and gave Joe a serious look. "Oh my God, Joe, I'm so sorry. How bad is it?"

"The doctors don't really know. He just went in about a half hour ago." He sat down on the lounge chair next to Lisa and stared down at the ground. Lisa moved closer to him and put her arms around his shoulders and leaned her head against his right shoulder. Neither of them said anything for several moments.

"When are you leaving?"

"I need to get on the road pretty much right away. It'll take me about 3 hours to get down there if I stay at just above the speed limit. I have to confess something before I go. The trip to Key West was a ploy to get you to Fort Myers to meet my parents."

Lisa smiled with her face still against his shoulder. Finally, she looked up into his eyes and said, "I was hoping that's what you had in mind.

Do I really need to pass their inspection?"

Joe smiled back. "It doesn't matter what they say. You already passed my inspection. But they will love you." He paused for a second then said, "Listen, I don't know how long I'll be down there. Depending on what happens with Dad, it may be just a few days . . . "

Lisa put her right hand up to his lips to stop him. "You do what you need to do. Take as long as you need. I'll be here when you get back. Then we'll go on our vacation. Just take care of your family. That's important."

"I know, but you're important to me, too. I can't tell you how much." He leaned in closer and kissed her passionately. After they broke for air, Joe stood and walked back towards his apartment to pack for the drive to Fort Myers. Lisa followed him with her gaze. She would certainly miss him but she knew he would be back as soon as he could. She was hoping to hear the big question, but that would have to wait. *If he doesn't ask me soon, I may ask him first.* She shouted out to Joe as he walked away, "Joe. I love you."

He looked back her way and blew her a kiss. Then he turned the corner of the apartment building near the pool and he was gone.

Chapter 7

"What do you think, Gus? This sounds like we've got a real problem here."

Major Frank Hartnett sat in a cushioned chair in the office of his long time friend and colleague, Major Augustine 'Gus' Griggs. His and Gus' military careers had crossed numerous times, both on the battlefield and in administrative positions. Both were seasoned battlefield veterans and both boasted a chest full of ribbons for military achievements and participation in battlefield engagements throughout the world.

Gus Griggs' large desk was neat and orderly with a series of file folders on the left side, a clean space in the middle and another series of file folders to his right. The folders were color coded to indicate the relative importance of its contents. The stacks were grouped by folder color. The folders on the right had yellow folders on top and green on the bottom. The folders on the left were all red. The red folders were 'top priority' with the yellow being second and green being lowest. Nothing crossed Griggs' desk without being in a folder with little sticky plastic arrows directing him where to sign a particular form. The red pile on the left side of his desk already had his signature. They were on the way out. Between meetings, one member of his clerical staff would deliver a new stack of files. They would place the new folders on the bottom of the appropriate stack to make sure that older issues were dealt with first. He had a reputation to be brutal on anyone who fouled up his system. To his credit, the people that worked for him liked him once they learned how he wanted his office run. The odd thing about this is he was once a real disorganized administrator until he had a young female clerk set up the current system. He took over as the head of the local Naval Criminal Investigative Service division at Camp Lejeune. The NCIS handles criminal investigations for the Marine Corps as well as the Navy. He liked it so well that he kept the system exactly as she set it up. She received an early promotion based on his recommendation and he lost her services to a more senior officer.

The current discussion with Major Hartnett was about the third priority on the list; the criminal abuse that his soldiers and sailors were taking, not at the hands of a foreign enemy, but at the hands of some low-life American citizens. These were some of the same citizens that they were sworn to protect 'from all enemies, foreign and domestic.' So, the military had to protect its citizens and it also had to protect its own members from a small fraction of those citizens who were determined to take advantage of young men and women in uniform. At the very time that these young men and women were deployed, protecting the interests of our country, unscrupulous predators were taking advantage of them, stealing their belongings and money.

"I agree, Frank. It looks like its open season on our boys . . . and girls of course. But it looks like young submariners are the biggest target. It happened some during the Iraq invasion, too, but it looks like sailors are easy pickings for these bastards."

Each man held several pages of a report from one of the red folders on Griggs' desk. By a factor of almost 2 to 1, Submarine sailors were singled out for theft of their belongings; both physical and financial. Many times it was a case of a young couple who'd just been married. The husband and wife, both newly graduated from high school, deeply in love, thrust into military life by a bad economy or a serious twinge of patriotism. Then the realization of long periods of separation set in due to the husband's deployment to sea or overseas. The young bride stays home in an unfamiliar house, an unfamiliar city or base, without the assistance of Mom or Dad. The young girl simply can't take the pressure of being a new military wife or can't take the home-sickness that invades her mind. She simply packs up and heads for home. Other times, the bride meets a new man who fills up this new void in her life created by her husband's deployment. She doesn't plan to be unfaithful, but the need for love is too great to hold back. She feels guilty after a one night stand or a short affair and flees for the shelter of home before the return of her unknowing husband. These cases, though heartbreaking, are understandable. Some just can't handle military life, especially those very young women who haven't experienced life outside the protection of a parent's home.

Then there is the real threat; the bottom feeders. These are the predators that prey on unsuspecting military personnel and take them for their life savings leaving these young men and women broken and bitter. How could someone take advantage of these poor kids when they have no way of defending themselves? They thought that the enemy was overseas while the real enemy was at home, like a virus, striking from within.

"If you look at the three summary cases on top, they all have similar MOs. I mean the perpetrators use the same tactics. We're talking some serious bucks here. The houses were cleaned out, the bank accounts cleaned out, and the men were declared KIA. So a life insurance claim was filed for and distributed. That's a big chunk of change; sometimes as much as $250,000. It all depends on what they elect for coverage. Somebody knows our process pretty damn well. We've got a handwriting specialist looking at the forms and it looks like the same person filling out the forms. We'll know more in a few days. It'll take him time to process ink samples and paper fabric comparisons but it looks like the same person or persons may be behind these three."

Gus Griggs asked, "So, you think we're looking for ex-military?

Do we know anything about this person, maybe a profile of this guy?"

Frank Hartnett was processing those questions. He was leafing through the papers to find a psych profile. He handed over the five page report to Gus Griggs and remarked, "We believe that there are multiple persons involved, at least two. One is believed to be male, the other female. It appears that the female makes contact with the enlisted man, gets him to 'fall in love', then convinces him to marry her. This usually takes place just before a deployment of some type. About a month or two into the deployment, a letter appears that states that the individual was killed in action. Then paperwork is processed to Serviceman's Group Life Insurance to pay the Death Benefit. It all looks official with signatures and stamps, the whole nine yards. No one becomes aware of the fact that the serviceman is still alive until it's too late."

Gus Griggs rubbed his square chin for a moment. He was deep in thought about how this worked. Then he turned is attention back to the reports in front of him on the desk. He read in silence for a few minutes and thought again. Finally he asked, "Who do we have for the lead investigator?"

"Captain Nancy Brown, USMC. She's been looking into these cases and provided most of the detail in these reports. We plan to keep her on the job for the duration. She's a great field investigator as well as an excellent judge of people. She has a degree in criminal justice, military justice and a minor in forensics."

"Does she have any combat experience?"

"Nope," Hartnett replied. "She's never been in field."

"I want someone on this that has some field experience and I mean battlefield experience. She doesn't know how it feels to put your life on the line. She wouldn't know how a sailor or soldier felt after putting it all out there for your country only to find that someone that you're fighting for has stabbed you in the back. I have someone in mind to assist her. Do you think that she'd mind an equal partner on the case?"

"Gus, I think she could handle this alone. She's tough as nails. But you tell me who you have in mind and I'll make sure she knows what our decision is. She'll accept that. Who do you have in mind?"

Griggs' lips formed a sly smile. "Joe McKinney. He's on reserves but he'll be happy to be back on active duty."

* * *

"The Marine Corps is calling you back to active duty? This sucks. You can't go back to active duty now! Hell Dad's still in intensive care and Mom's a wreck! How can they do this to you?"

"It's real simple, Pat. I'm a Marine reservist. If they need me, they call me and I say, "Yes sir, yes sir, three bags full." Then I pack away my civilian clothes, unpack my Marine uniforms and head for the airport. I have three days to report to Camp Lejeune. I'll be reporting directly to

Major Gus Griggs and a friend of his, Major Frank Hartnett. It's some investigation, not even a deployment to the field. I was hoping that it was some sniper training. It isn't training but I don't know the details. I won't know that until I get briefed."

"Have you told Lisa yet," Pat asked his younger brother? Lisa Goddard was Joe's girlfriend of only three months.

"Nope. I just read the recall letter a few minutes ago. I picked my mail as I left the apartment but didn't get a chance to look at it until now. I wanted you to be the first to know because somebody's got to take care of Mom while Dad's in recovery. Can you handle it?"

Pat looked at Joe and said, "Look, you're a jarhead. You have to go. I can handle this. Diane will take care of things at home and I know she'll help with Mom and Dad. You do what you have to do. Go get all your arrangements made and let me know the details. You've got another call to make, you know. Lisa's gonna freak out when you tell her."

"I'm not calling about this. I'll drive back and tell her face to face."

"Good plan. That way she can cut off your nuts and hand them to you in person."

They both smiled sadly at Pat's comment. Joe shook Pat's hand and headed back into their Father's room. His next tough conversation was with his Mother. This would only add to her worries. But it couldn't be avoided. Joe owed it to her to tell her face to face.

Chapter 8

Pat and Joe McKinney stood with their mother, Emma McKinney in the pale, white hallway outside of the hospital's heart surgery operating room. Pat and Joe helped pass the time, pacing the halls by exchanging small talk about the weather, about Pat and Sean's fishing expedition, and about anything they could think of to keep their mother's mind off of her husband's heart surgery. The smell of the hospital was sterile, but not clean. On occasion, the air changed to a more human smell, like a primitive rest room with no running water. But those odors didn't last long as the powerful ventilation system of the hospital wing quickly removed the offensive air and replaced them with the highly treated and filtered air, loaded with disinfectant chemicals. The staff on the floor always appeared to be in motion, taking clipboards from one room to another along with pills or a syringe loaded with some type of medication or another. There was not much conversation going on in the wing considering the grave nature of the business performed here. Afternoon visiting hours were long over and there was virtually no one in street-clothes roaming the halls. Everyone on the floor had either a white, green, or multi-color smock. Several patients were walking down the badly lighted hall, encouraged by a physical therapist.

Even conversations at the nursing station were spoken in hushed tones so that the details of the exchanges were kept private. The mood was that of a library, where any words spoken above a near-whisper drew glances from anyone in close proximity. So quiet was the noise level in the hall that one could hear the sound of a flushing toilet in rooms far down the corridor or the wheels squealing as an IV post was being moved along side a patient out for a slow, but necessary therapeutic walk.

The series of doors to hospital rooms were separated by a seating area for guests off to one side of the corridor about midway between the double door entrance to the operating rooms and the opposite end of the hallway to the elevator vestibule. The sitting area had a number of vinyl covered chairs and end tables with plastic flower arrangements. A large window allowed an unflattering view of the parking garage some 100 yards away. Between the window and the parking garage was the stone and rubberized roof of another section of the hospital. Ventilation stacks protruded from the roof. Several air conditioning units were scattered about. A sliver of the Gulf of Mexico and the southern-most tip of Sanibel Island were barely visible beyond the corner of the parking garage. The small thread of water had an orange glow from the setting sun that was no longer visible behind the parking garage.

"Mrs. McKinney? I'm Doctor Panjani Doshi, your husband's heart doctor. Let us sit for a moment. I will explain what is happening with your husband."

Emma Louise Kelly McKinney's face was ashen with fear when Dr. Doshi approached her. Pat and Joe were by her side. The look on the doctor's face gave no indication of the status of her husband's condition. Her mind raced as he approached. She feared that the news was bad. She depended on her husband, Daniel Ryan McKinney for everything. He was the best husband a wife could ever desire.

He'd been her rock during their early lives together when both of their fathers had been working class laborers in the Ford Auto Assembly Plant in Lorain, Ohio. They learned how to get by on very little money when they were just starting their family. They lived in a rented, wood frame, two-bedroom house. The paint on the side of the house was peeling and the landlord said he had no money to paint it. Dan McKinney went to the landlord and offered to paint the house if he supplied the paint. Their landlord, in turn said that if Dan bought the paint, he'd take the cost of the paint off their next month's rent. So he set about painting the little frame house on the weekends.

When little Patrick was born, Emma had a bad case of post partum depression. Even though Pat was a good baby, she was always depressed with little desire to get out of bed, much less run a household. But her young husband encouraged her each day to get up and remain as active as possible. He used to do little things to cheer her up, like bring her flowers when he came home after work. He picked them in the city park, which was really illegal, but he knew he had to work to keep his wife out of her dark moods. She thought back on a particular Friday when he came home after work and announced that they were going out to dinner and a movie. He'd lined up a baby sitter and they headed out the door. She worried about her newborn the whole night but Dan kept reassuring her that everything was fine at home. When they finally arrived home after an evening filled with worry and anxiety, they found that little Patrick was asleep and the babysitter was watching TV. Dan turned to his wife and said, "You see? Everything is just as I told you. Little Patrick is fine, the house is fine. You're fine. And I want to thank you for a fine evening out on the town."

Dan took the babysitter home and when he arrived back at the house, his wife was sobbing, her eyes red and swollen. Dan went to her and held her and asked what was wrong. Through sobs, Pat's mom said, "Nothing. Absolutely nothing. That's why I'm so scared. I can't stop crying about nothing." Dan held her tight for what seemed like an eternity. The next day they went to a specialist on post partum depression. With a mild daily dose of the antidepressant Elavil, her depression went away for good.

So Dan and Emma McKinney had their happy household, held

together by a little yellow pill. Dan didn't like that his wife was taking anti-depressants but he thought that he understood it was necessary. He'd talked with a close friend whose wife was going through the baby blues, too. They would compare stories and each realized that this really was a condition that was best medicated rather than ignored.

Emma would have to take her Elavil for several months after each of her three sons were born but she always managed to get over her blues. After 90 days, she would stop taking the pills, cold turkey. There were days when she was tempted to get back into the medicating routine, but, with her husband's help, she would stay clean. After her third child, Michael, she never took the pills again. Now she thought that she might need some chemical assistance to get through this most recent crisis.

Dr. Doshi, Emma McKinney, Pat and Joe moved to a waiting area off the main hallway. The brothers took seats on either side of their mother who sat on a small, dark green couch. The doctor sat on a table directly across from Emma, took her hands in his and looked her directly in the eyes. "Mrs. McKinney, I just left your husband and he is resting right now. We completed the surgery on your husband's heart and he appears to have made it through with sailing colors." In his pronounced Indian accent, Dr. Doshi misused the expression 'flying colors.' Pat and Joe had to think about what he meant for a moment. "But he must now rest, so you should go home to rest yourself. I can tell you that he had three major blockages in his arteries that were choking off the blood flow to his heart. We performed a triple bypass to restore the blood flow. We will have him out of recovery by late tomorrow but he will have to take it slow for a while. We will make sure that he gets out of bed for exercise. We have found over the years that the sooner the patient gets up and moving, the recovery period is made smaller." Dr. Doshi's accent was getting harder to understand. "We will set him up for a regiment of exercises that will get progressively more difficult but we'll explain all that tomorrow." He paused before continuing. "Is there anything I can answer for you?"

Emma shook here head. Pat and Joe shook their heads as well.

"Will you need anything to help you sleep tonight?" She looked back at him, not understanding the question. "Do you need a sleeping aid, such as a pill to help you get to sleep? You will need to get rested because your husband has a long recovery ahead of him." She shook her head, indicating that she didn't want any pills.

The relief on Emma McKinney's face was visible. She seemed to nearly collapse on Joe's shoulder with the news. Then she tensed again as she looked from Joe to Pat. "I should stay here tonight in case your father wakes. He'll need me to be here."

Pat turned to his mother and said, "Mom, you should let me drive you home. It's not that far and we can be back here in the morning. Dad's out of it and won't be awake for hours. You need to rest. This is just the beginning of a long process."

"Your son is correct," Dr. Doshi said in a heavily accented but calm, soothing voice. "Your husband will be out for at least 12 hours due to the medication. You will not do him or you any good to be staying here. Go Home. Get your rest. You'll see him tomorrow about mid-morning. We will call you if anything happens or he wakes early, but I can assure you, he will not be awake for some time now."

Emma turned to her sons to see if the expression on their faces would give her assurances that they agreed with the doctor. When they both nodded to her, she again relaxed and said, "Alright. If you both think that I should, I'll go. But we'll come back in the morning. I need to be here when he wakes up. He needs me."

And you need him, Pat and Joe both thought to themselves. Pat knew that his mother would have a very difficult time if their father passed away. Emma needed her husband to fully recover from the heart attack. He was just 59 years old; too young to have heart problems. She could be strong for a while, but without his support, she would have a difficult time maintaining her sensibilities. Pat was afraid that she would become depressed. Maybe he feared that her depression would return. Pat's dad had described her severe depression after he, Joe and Mike were each born. Pat found the stories hard to believe, knowing the bright and happy persona his mom always appeared to have. But Pat had read about post partum depression and how it drove otherwise happy, normal mothers to do unbelievably evil things to their own children. He knew that their mother had never been that bad, but maybe it was because their father had always been there to help her through the hard times. Their dad made it through the worst of it, but that didn't mean that he was out of the woods yet. Even after he recovered, would he actually ever be fully recovered to the point where he could do all the things that he did before? He was once self assured and confident; strong as an ox even though he was a scholar by trade.

Joe, without knowing what Pat was thinking, had similar thoughts going through is mind. He was worried for his dad's health and his mom's well being. It was going to be a long road to recovery. Joe's thoughts turned to his own personal dilemma; telling Lisa that he was an active duty Marine again. That wasn't going to be much fun. But he had a plan. His plan was to pop the question. He had a long drive back to Orlando first to work up the guts to ask her to marry him. He figured that they'd wait until Joe's dad recovered sufficiently to attend the wedding. He also had to consider how her folks from Ohio would be able to make the wedding. Those were details that could be easily resolved. But the change in his civilian status threw in a few new twists. He didn't know how long this new assignment would last. He didn't know where he was being sent to serve his country. He was only told that it wasn't a foreign combat deployment. That narrowed down the possibilities to about a million.

Pat and Joe were both wondering how much their younger brother's tragic death just months before played into their dad's heart problems. Mike was the youngest sibling. He was the most favored son. Dan and Emma Ryan spoiled him far more than Pat and Joe. When Mike committed suicide using alcohol and Percodan, their father kept his emotions hidden. The brothers wondered if this added stress could have been the trigger that caused his heart attack. They couldn't dwell on that for there was no way to know the answer. They could only deal with the current reality.

Pat tapped Joe on the shoulder and motioned him towards the window. The sun had nearly set and the water on the Gulf was a dark green now. They stood near the window as Pat turned to face Joe. "I'll tell Mom tomorrow about your heading to active duty. She doesn't need to hear that now." Joe nodded in agreement. Pat continued, "Have you figured out what you're going to tell Lisa?"

"Not exactly but I have a three and a half hour drive ahead of me. I'll figure it out. Maybe I'll take her shopping, buy her about $1000 worth of girly crap then slip the news to her as she's having a shopping orgasm."

"Great plan. Ruin her moment of ecstasy. Like I said, she'll rip your nuts out and hand them to you."

Joe grimaced at the thought. "Really, I have a plan. I'll call and tell you how it goes. But like I said, I have a long drive and plans can change. Let's get Mom home and then I'll get on the road."

"You have a long drive ahead of you and it's getting late. I'll take care of Mom. Go on and head out. You rested enough to drive tonight?"

"Yep. Rested and ready. Take care of Mom. I'll call tomorrow to check on Dad."

The brothers shook hands then gave each other an awkward man-hug. Pat said, "I really miss Mike and I know part of what Mom is feeling is left over pain from when Mike . . ." Pat's voice trailed off. Joe noticed his eyes tearing up.

"I know, man. I miss him, too." With that, Joe walked back over to his Mother, gave her a long hug and some words of encouragement. Then he headed down the corridor to the elevators. He needed to call Lisa to let her know he was on his way back to Pine Hills. This was the short call before the long, face-to-face encounter.

* * *

The drive back to Orlando was agonizing. Joe practiced telling Lisa that he had to go back on active duty. He was a Marine after all, and he couldn't turn away when duty called. As he traveled up I-75 near Tampa, evening traffic was heavier than he expected. The average speed was just short of 90 miles per hour. Joe had a difficult time thinking about what he would say to Lisa since he had to concentrate on his driving. He made the I-4 interchange in good time and was glad to start heading northeast away from the Tampa-St. Petersburg area. He knew that he had some rough traffic ahead as he approached the Walt Disney World interchanges. His mind raced with all the emotions running through him. He couldn't keep his mind off of Lisa. What should he say to her? He told Pat that he had a plan but the truth was he didn't have a clue what to say. Should he wait until morning or pop the big question tonight? Should he tell her about his dad first or hold that until after she was already mad about his recall back to the Marines? He could use the sympathy card and start out with his dad's condition. That would be pretty low, though. Then he decided. He would be straight with her and tell her about the Marines first. Then anything after that would be good news, wouldn't it? Well then, that was settled; Marines first, Dad's condition second, then pop the question. He thought for a moment. *It should be about 11:30 by the time I hit Pine Hills. I could be disemboweled by 11:40.* He shook his head and tried to keep his concentration on the traffic.

Then Joe thought about his dad. He knew that Dr. Doshi had said the operation was a success but what did that mean for his dad's future. Would he come out of this a new man or would the entire ordeal take its toll and ultimately leave him weak and unable to enjoy life. He wasn't an old man by any standards but he wasn't a spring chicken either. No one in the family saw the heart attack coming. He didn't have any bad vices. He'd been a moderate drinker in his younger years and didn't do drugs at all. His diet was pretty bland; meat and potatoes for the most part. He and Pat would have to ask the doctor if there was anything else, maybe a hereditary issue that they didn't know about. They would need to know that for their children's sake. *Well, for Pat's children's sake anyway. By the time Lisa's done with me, I'll be lucky to be able to have kids.*

Once again, he wondered how much, if anything, his brother, Mike's death had to do with his dad's condition. He knew that Mike was closer to both their mom and dad than he or Pat. Mike seemed to be their favorite from the moment he was born. He was the youngest and therefore the least disciplined. Pat and Joe had broken in their dad on the behavior side. By the time Mike came along, their parents were tired of yelling "Stop that." So Mike sailed through his youth with "A Most Favored Son" status. Mike's suicide was devastating to Pat and Joe. It must have really ripped their parent's hearts out. Their dad was a trooper through the ordeal with Mike. He seemed so much in charge of his emotions and manner. Maybe that's what took the biggest toll, trying to contain all that emotion so that he shouldered the burden for the entire family. Now it was their mom's turn to be strong. This was going rough for their mother because she had her husband to lean on for strength. Now the strong had become the weak and the weak had to step up and take over. Joe knew that he and Pat would help out as much as possible but the drive to Fort Myers from both

Dunnellon and Pine Hills was over three hours long. Helping from that distance was going to be challenging at best. Since he was heading to the Marines for active duty Pat would have to shoulder the load for the time being. Joe thought about how hard this would be on Diane, having to take care of the kids, the house and yard, and all the day to day things that Pat helped with now. Joe was amazed at how many people were affected by their dad's heart attack. The consequences were far reaching.

His thoughts shifted to his assignment. He really had no clear picture of what he might be asked to do for the US Marine Corps. It all seemed pretty hush-hush; confidential was the word Major Griggs had used. Not top secret but Joe knew that he shouldn't talk much to anyone about the fact that he was heading back to active duty. But if Major Griggs asked for him, it must be important and something that they wanted to keep away from the average grunt Marine. At least it wasn't a battlefield deployment, he was assured of that. He would still have answered the call, as if he had a choice, but he would have done so with a bit more reluctance.

Chapter 9

Lisa Goddard sat next to Joe at his dining room table, her long sandy blond hair pulled behind her ears, her brown eyes staring at Joe in disbelief. She couldn't believe what she was hearing. She was dressed in a long tee shirt that she wore to bed each night and nothing on underneath. Joe was in a pair of his Marine boxer shorts and a desert patterned brown and tan tee shirt. They'd just finished a breakfast of French toast and coffee. Lisa had cleared the dirty dishes from the table but the smell of the meal and fresh coffee still hung in the air. Joe decided on his way home from Ft. Myers that he'd first tell Lisa about his recall to active duty and then ask her to marry him. It wasn't going exactly as planned. He wasn't sure if he was ever going to make it to the part where he pops the big question and they live happily ever after. Joe McKinney, normally in control and self assured, was tripping over his own words. When he arrived at her apartment the night before, they didn't take the time to talk. They'd kissed, stripped off each other's clothes and made love for what seemed like hours. Then they fell asleep. This morning, they hadn't gotten past his recall so she had no idea about his dad's current condition or his prospects for a full recovery. They also hadn't talked about her going back to college and working towards her degree in Criminal Justice. He'd planned to offer to pay for her college and that she didn't have to pay him back. He thought that she would take offense to that because she was pretty independent. But he believed that after he asked her the big question that she couldn't refuse because his money would be hers as well. She told him before that she didn't know where she would get the money to pay for college. Joe had wanted to wait for the right time to make his offer but the right time hadn't come. The way things were developing, it didn't look promising during the course of this conversation. They'd been dating seriously for over 4 months now and Joe thought he felt pretty comfortable letting her in on a few of his life's secrets. He really wanted to marry this woman so he tried to get the conversation back on track.

"Lisa, you knew I was in the Marines when we started dating. I also told you that I am a reservist and that there is always a chance that I would get recalled. I know I told you the chances were small but there's always that chance. This may not be the last time either."

She paused for a moment to process this. When she spoke, her manner was more sad than angry. "I know. I just didn't think that it would be this soon. I'm afraid that I'll never see you again." She looked up into his eyes, hers pleading with him to stay with her and not leave. "What if you're sent to Iraq, or Afghanistan? How will I get in touch with you? How will I know that you're safe?"

He looked back in to those pleading eyes and said, "You're not getting rid of me that easy. I don't know exactly what my assignment is, but I do know that it isn't in Iraq or any other foreign country. I'm going to Camp Lejeune in North Carolina. I have to report to my old boss, Major Griggs. Apparently he has something that he feels only I can do or he wouldn't be recalling me."

"Do you know how long you'll be gone?"

That was a tough question to answer because he had no idea. "I wish I could tell you but I honestly don't know. All I know is when I have to be there. Tomorrow afternoon, I have to be at camp headquarters and report directly to Major Griggs. From there, I'll get my orders. When I know more, I will call you."

This seemed to satisfy Lisa a bit and her mood lightened. Then her face turned serious. "I'm sorry. We started talking about your recall and I haven't asked about your dad at all. How is he?"

"He's doing alright, all things considered. He had a serious heart attack brought on by blockages in three arteries. He went through the surgery just fine. His Surgeon was an Indian guy named Dr. Doshi. He seems very competent. Anyway, Dad will be in therapy for several weeks and he can't do a lot of things that he's used to doing. Someone's going to have to keep a close eye on him while he gets his strength back. Mom is going to have her hands full. He'll try to sneak around and be the macho man. He's always pushed it to the limit.

Lisa thought about the time she and Joe had first met. Joe was lifting weights alone in the apartment complex weight room. When she walked in, she thought that he was having a heart attack because he had the barbells loaded and he was straining. Now she knew where he got his stubborn side.

"I seem to remember another guy who likes to push things, Mr. 'I like to work out alone.' The day we met . . . "

Joe smiled and cut her off. "Alright already. Guilty as charged. At least you know I get it honestly." He decided to ask her about school again and what she planned to do. "Have you figured out when you're going back to college and where you'd like to go?"

Lisa went into the kitchen and poured her and Joe each a cup of coffee, then returned to the table and sat. "Yes and no. I'd like to go to University of Central Florida but it costs a ton of money. I really can't afford to pay the tuition and books and still eat. I'd have to get scholarships. With me being out of school for so long, I don't even know if I'm eligible for any. I'm sure there are some but they're few and far between. I might just have to save for several years before I go back."

Joe took a deep breath before he started. "I have an idea. Listen to me all the way through before you say anything." He had her interest and she leaned forward a bit. "Let me pay for your college." She started to protest but he held up a hand and stopped her before she could say a word. "I thought you were going to listen first." He lowered his hand and went on. "Lisa, I can pay for your college and books and all you have to do is go to school and get your degree. I can afford to do this for you with absolutely no strings attached."

Lisa looked back at Joe with a confused look in her eyes. Then she asked, "How can a guy your age, an ex-Marine, afford to pay for my school? I know that your mom and dad are still alive so you didn't inherit a fortune. Where did you get all this money? Do you rob banks for a living?"

"Yes." He paused looking at Lisa's face for her reaction. When he didn't get one he said, "Okay, I'm kidding. I've already told you some of my past. You know that Pat, Mike and I owned an orange grove and a nursery. They made pretty good money. Remember, we sold them a few months ago."

"Yes, but as I recall you didn't make a killing on the sale."

"True. But what I didn't tell you is where we made our real money."

Joe took a deep breath and proceeded to tell her about their illegal marijuana business. He knew this was going to be difficult because of Lisa's brother Gary Goddard. Gary also sold drugs, though he didn't limit his choice of drugs to marijuana. He sold anything he could to make a buck. But Gary wasn't careful. He was caught red handed. His financial woes became his parent's problems. They posted his bail and paid for his attorney. In the end, he was convicted and spent time in prison. That punishment wasn't nearly as brutal as the financial debacle he caused his parents.

So when Joe told her the source of the majority of his wealth she wasn't happy. The conversation took a turn back to where it was when he told her about his recall to the Marines. He was in hot water again. He was explaining that they didn't intend to get into the business but circumstances kept the business growing. Before they knew it, they were in very deep.

Joe tried to explain. "Honey, we got out of it for two big reasons; we were being robbed at every turn and . . . "

"And it serves you right. Don't you realize how dangerous drugs are? They nearly killed my brother and they bankrupt my parents. Gary's drug use and dealings cost my folks a fortune. They've never recovered from that." Her face was turning red with anger and her voice was raised to the point where Joe was afraid that the neighbors might hear their conversation. She'd told Joe previously about how her brother had nearly died from a drug overdose and how it had affected the entire family and many of his close friends who saw it coming.

"I know. You told me about it and I agree. It must have been devastating."

"It still is. Mom and Dad talk about it all the time. They can't retire because of it. My folks spent tens of thousands of dollars covering my brother's legal bills. He's such a loser. He still asks them for money. They just can't afford to have that anchor around their necks anymore. I called him last week and told him to never ask Mom and Dad for money ever again. He tells me it's none of my business. Do you see what it's done to my family? And there are millions more like mine, I'm sure." Lisa looked at Joe and saw that she was tugging at something in his heart. She knew about Joe's sister-in-law's murder and his brother's suicide. She could see it in his eyes.

Joe said, "Yes, I know. That's why we stopped. I've told you about Mike and Jenny and our so-called friends. We learned the hard way what harm it causes. But this would be different. This could do some good. Don't you see? This could help you get the degree that you need to help fight this problem? It's kind of like money that drug enforcement agencies confiscate and use against dealers, except this money is already there. You don't have to work for it. You don't have to pay it back. It's yours for the taking. It's the least I can do for you. It isn't doing anyone any good just sitting in stocks and bonds. Please, let me do this for you."

Lisa turned her head away from Joe. He was finally making inroads and getting the conversation back on track. After a few moments of looking at the pictures on the wall in the dining area, Lisa looked back at Joe and said, "I'll think about it. But, if I do this, I will pay you back with interest."

"I'm already interested."

"You know what I mean." Lisa still had her head turned slightly away from Joe, but looked at him with a sideways glance, and gave him a sly smile. "I don't know why I can't stay mad at you."

"Because you love me?" Now Joe had a sly smile on his face. "Which brings me to my next topic." Joe paused for a moment to gather his courage for the big question. He was starting to get nervous again so he took a deep breath and looked Lisa square in the eyes. "Lisa, . . ."

The phone rang. Joe paused again, still looking at Lisa then exhaled. "I'd better get that."

Joe paused a third time, then on the third ring, went to the kitchen and grabbed the phone. To Lisa's surprise, she heard Joe say, "Yes Ma'am, she's right here." Joe handed the phone to Lisa, mouthed the words 'It's your mother,' and watched the expression on her face. He knew from the sound of Lisa's mother's voice that this was not a social call. Her voice was raspy and filled with tension, not unlike his own mother's voice just yesterday at the hospital in Ft. Myers, Florida. He watched Lisa as the color drained from her face. He heard the strained responses to what her mother had to say. Then she slowly turned to him with a frightened look and handed him he receiver. Joe put the receiver to his ear and heard only a dial tone, then hung the phone back on the cradle.

Lisa's voice was a monotone filled with fear. "Daddy's had a stroke. It sounds bad. Mom's a mess. I have to get up there."

Up there was Oak Harbor, Ohio. Joe grabbed Lisa and held her close. When he released her he told her to pack for the trip and make sure that she had enough clothing for at least a week. He said he'd check for flights out of Orlando International Airport to Toledo Express Airport and get a ticket for her. They'd initially taken her dad to Magruder Hospital in Port Clinton, but he was being transported to St. Vincent's Medical Center in Toledo. Joe asked Lisa if she would be able to drive on her own or if she'd need money for taxi service.

About 30 minutes passed since her mom's call and she was starting to get a grip on the situation. She assured Joe that she would be alright. She had no idea how long she would be gone. Joe told her not to worry about anything but her mom and her dad's health.

"Everything else can wait. Take care of your family. Did your mom get in touch with your brother?"

Anger flashed across her face briefly. "That bastard told her he was too busy to get home but he'd be by sometime in the next few days. Can you believe that? He's too busy." Lisa shook her head, the anger creeping up inside her. Joe thought to himself that maybe he should put plan number two together to take care of this problem. Then he shook his head like an Etch-o-Sketch as if to erase those thoughts.

Later in the evening, at Orlando International Airport, Lisa's jet was being boarded. The group with her seat number had just been called when she turned to Joe and asked, "I almost forgot, you were going to ask me something before my mom called." Joe thought about asking Lisa to marry him in some dramatic fashion, like a movie love story, but he thought better of it. He leaned to her, kissed her hard on the lips and pulled away. "I forgot what it was about. When I remember I'll call you. Get on board. Your mom's alone and needs you." He thought *I'll hold the question until we both get home.* Lisa looked back at Joe with eyes that contained three parts fear and one part loneliness. The fear was for her dad's health, her mom's future, and a nagging feeling that she might not ever see Joe McKinney again. He was going away on some unknown mission for the US Marine Corps and not knowing was tugging at her heart, which only made the one part loneliness all the more painful. Lisa threw her arms around Joe and kissed him hard again. Joe kissed her back. They held that way for two full minutes which passed all too quickly. Then Lisa turned and headed down the boarding ramp on her way to Ohio.

* * *

Pat McKinney arrived home two days after his father's surgery. Diane and the children were waiting at the open door to their Dunnellon, Florida home as he pulled his suitcase from the trunk of the Ford Taurus. Diane gave him a tight embrace. When they released, Pat leaned down and picked up his 3 year old daughter, Anna, and gave her a hug. Sean walked up to Pat and looked up with a worried expression and asked Pat, "Is Grandpa's heart going to be alright?" Pat handed Anna to Diane and knelt down in front of his son. He looked Sean right in the eyes and said, "Your grandpa is going to be fine. He's going to be a little weak for a while, but then he'll get stronger and stronger every day. And you know what? When he does, your Grandpa, you and I are going to go fishing out on the lake again. Would you like that?"

Pat could see the tension leave Sean's face and he jumped into Pat's arms.

"I think that would be fine," Sean said in a matter-of-fact tone.

Pat gave him a big hug, and was surprised to see how heavy his son was. He squeezed him one more time and set him back down again. He seemed so mature for his age. And he was a serious boy. Everything seemed to be important to Sean. Pat worried that his son would have an ulcer before he was 10.

"Let's get inside so your dad can get into the air conditioning." They all turned and headed for the door. Diane placed a hand on Pat's arm to slow him down.

"How is he really?" Diane asked when the kids were out of ear-shot.

"Not great, but he is getting up and around. He's real slow. It's going to be a while before he can lift anything or do any kind of real work. I expect that he'll try to rush it." Diane's expression was one of agreement. "I told Mom that if he tried to do anything that was against the doctor's orders to call me or Joe and we'd talk with him. We told her to threaten him with getting a 350 pound live in nurse if he didn't follow his recovery plan to a 'T'. We'll see how long it takes before he's ignoring the plan; probably within a day."

When they got inside, the kids headed for the living room so Anna could play with her doll house and Sean headed for his room and closed the door. Diane and Pat moved into the kitchen and talked a while longer about the hospital and the Ft. Myers area in general, how difficult it was to get from one side of town to the other. Pat grabbed a beer from the refrigerator and asked Diane if she wanted anything to drink. She said no that maybe she would get a glass of wine later. Pat raised an eyebrow at that. They sat at the kitchen counter next to each other. Pat commented that it was going to be a difficult recovery period for his dad. And it was going to be tough for his Mother, too. Dan McKinney would not be an easy patient to handle. Pat took a long pull on his beer.

"You know, it's a really long drive to go down there several times a week. Have you given any thought to having your folks move in with us for a while? We have plenty of room. We're not working so we have time. Joe could help, too."

Pat grimaced. "I didn't have time to tell you but Joe's been recalled to active duty."

Diane's exasperated look showed her total disbelief. "That's terrible! When did he find out?"

"Yesterday, right before he drove to the hospital. He has to head out day after tomorrow, I think, to Camp Lejeune. He isn't going to do any battlefield stuff, at least that's what they told him, but he really doesn't know what his assignment will be, so he won't be around for at least the next few weeks. He was really bummed out, but you know Joe, gung-ho Marine; Duty, God and Country. I actually admire him for his dedication to the Corp but it's really going to impact his personal life. I should wait until it happens, but he's going to ask Lisa to marry him. He plans to pop the question right before he leaves for North Carolina. I'm not sure what I'd say first; 'Hey Babe, let's get married' or 'Oh, by the way, I'm leaving you for a few days, or a few weeks or months. I'm not sure.' That'll go over real big."

Pat was shaking his head, glad that he didn't have to go through that with Diane. He was a Navy Veteran but didn't have to serve any reserve time. His EAOS, End of Active Obligated Service was also his end of any military service requirement. Pat had no desire to continue with any ties to the military. His stint had served its purpose. It got him out of central Florida for six years and gave him the training and discipline to work on a plan of revenge against his former enemies. At the same time that Pat was in the Navy, Joe did a six year stint in the Marines. He became proficient in battlefield tactics and learned the fine art of command and control in battle. Joe's level of discipline was far above Pat's. Joe worked out every day and was in great physical shape. In addition to his physical shape, Joe was mentally alert and noticed even the slightest detail that was out of place. He was a trained marksman and before he left the Marines, was a 'Sniper' instructor. That was nearly unheard of in the Marine Corps. Most of the instructors were seasoned veterans with battlefield experience. But Joe had proven himself in competition and in the combat theater that he was among the best in the Marine Corps.

When the two returned to Florida to carry out their plan, they didn't have to lift a finger. The plan seemed to execute on its own. In the end, all of their enemies were killed, most quite brutally. They finally learned the secret to why the plan was completed without their taking action. On the day that they learned what had really happened, they returned to their property in Apopka, Florida. The building that they used as their base of operations for their former business was a steel vault, built by an orange grove owner in the early 1960s during the Cuban Missile Crisis. The former owner's widow sold the McKinney brothers, Pat, Joe, and Mike, the property, which included an orange grove, a foliage plant nursery, and the bomb shelter; known to the McKinney brothers as the Vault. From this formidable structure, the brothers had a thriving marijuana business. Prior to the purchase of the grove and nursery, their marijuana business was simply to support a growing habit to get free pot. It grew into a serious enterprise, taking in hundreds of thousands of dollars in a few months time. That's when the trouble started.

Their customers and friends started to become jealous of the brothers success. They plotted against the brothers and stole nearly $100,000 in money and pot. Then they raped and murder of Mike's wife. Pat and Joe were enraged. Mike was beyond devastation.

That's when they started to formulate their plan of revenge. Pat and Joe were ready to go but Mike was so distraught that he moved away to Las Vegas to a private apartment community. He drank his life away and finally committed a drug and alcohol induced suicide, never recovering from the loss of his bride at the hands of people he thought were his close friends.

It was now four months since the vault was torn down, the day that Pat and Joe learned how the plan was executed. Pat and Joe never spoke of the plan after that day. It was the final chapter in a former life that was best left forgotten. They learned a very hard lesson about illegal activities and the devastation that can result. Never in their wildest dreams could they imagine that selling weed would cause such heartache and pain, both mental and physical. Neither spent a single day in jail but they both received a life sentence. They lost a brother and best friend and his wife. They lost seven years of their lives chasing the sweet taste of revenge. In the end, they were denied those fruits. They were satisfied with the level of justice delivered on their behalf, but nothing could make up for the suffering that they'd caused. It only took one look into their mother's eyes to see all the way to her heart, and the anguish that tore into the fiber of her being. Sure, they made lots of money, but they would give it all back to undo what they had done. It was simply too late for that and they both had to live each day with the knowledge that their pot dealing was the root of the evil that hung like a dark cloud over them.

"Is anyone home," Diane sang.

Pat gave a jerk like he'd been tugged by the arm. He'd been rubbing the small scar on his chin where he'd been struck by an errant nail. He shook his head slightly and said, "Whoa. I got lost in my head there for a second."

"No kidding. I thought you were going to cry for a second there. I'd like that glass of wine now, please." She paused while Pat got up and pulled a bottle of White Zinfandel from the refrigerator. Then she continued, "Your dad's going to be okay, Honey." She walked around the counter into the main area of the kitchen, took her glass of wine from her husband, gave him a little kiss and said, "Listen to me. You said yourself, it'll take time but, physically he's going to get better. Mentally, it's going to take some work because he's so independent. I think that's where Joe gets his personality. I'm a little worried about you though. Are you going to be okay?"

Pat put his arms around his wife and said, "I'll be fine. How could I be anything else with you by my side?" They both smiled, looking into each others eyes. Then they kissed passionately, foretelling a night to remember.

Chapter 10

Brian Purcer and the Hot Licks, the hottest new heavy rock band to be signed by Deep South Sounds, a division of Atlantic Records, had been on tour for three weeks. They were scheduled to play in every major arena around the southeast. So far, every show had been a sell-out and the crowds were loud and enthusiastic. Their songs were heating up the airwaves, especially their biggest hit, *I Know You Better Than You Think*. That song hit number one on the rock charts the first week after their CD was released and remained at the summit ever since. Brian's wildest dream had become a reality. But what made this dream even better than he'd imagined was the lady sitting beside him. They were back stage at the Lakeland Civic Center after another sold out show in front of a wild, energetic crowd. The band was in wind down mode, sipping beer and cooling off in the air conditioned room, trying to slow down the adrenaline rush that they'd been caught in for the last three hours. They were physically drained and needed some isolation from the crowd. The last of the chosen few that were allowed backstage passes were escorted out of the room so only the band members and the selected groupies remained.

Ginny Parks sat next to Brian leaning into his shoulder, sipping a glass of champagne. She was still in awe of the spectacle that surrounded the band and their shows. The crowds were there to see her man, Brian. Really they were there to see the band, but without Brian, there was no band. He was the attraction; him and his wailing Stratocaster, that seemed to talk as Brian stroked, plucked, and picked those magic strings. The guitar and those strings, without an artist, might as well be a piece of furniture. But when Brian picked up that guitar and began to play, the instrument came to life, telling a story, or screaming at the crowd to get up and get loud. Brian was the artist. He was the life blood of the group of guys known as Brian Purcer and the Hot Licks. The remaining band members were excellent with their own instruments and would be great in any rock band. But when they played with Brian, their skills were taken to a new level, a higher plain. The result was the hottest new band in nearly a decade coming out of the south. Many of the old bands were still touring but most were relegated to playing at county fairs and local speedways. There was little in the way of fresh, new sound coming from the south. The Hot Licks were far from a rebirth of southern rock. Their sound was a new direction; more raw than southern rock but not as deafeningly loud as heavy metal. It was a cross between new wave, heavy metal, and southern rock that had a real class of its own. It was a sound that was destined to be copied by many young garage bands, looking for a way to make it big.

Brian took a pull on his long neck bottle and made a smacking sound and a loud sigh. His ears were still ringing a bit from the volume of the show that had ended some thirty minutes ago. Every member of the band had a wide smile plastered on their faces as they swam in the intoxication of another outstanding, high energy show. They were on top of the world and loving every minute of it. Rick Wessler, the band's drummer, asked Brian about his plans for the next few days. The bands manager, Arnold Jet, answered before Brian had a chance.

"You guys have a few days off and I don't think you need to do any rehearsing so I'd recommend that you use it to rest up and get your bodies and minds recharged. We have to get everyone back together on Tuesday morning. We're heading for Jacksonville Coliseum for a show on Wednesday, to Savannah Civic Center for a Friday show, then to Colonial Center in Columbia, South Carolina on Saturday. This is going to be a rough stretch coming up. It's going real well, but it is going to start to get to you, trust me. Enjoy your break, but for Pete's sake, get some rest."

"That's going to be rough for Brian," Rick joked and smiled Brian's way. He was alluding to the fact that he and Ginny were hot and heavy these days. It seemed that every time he and Ginny Parks had an extra couple of hours, they were headed to a hotel room. That wasn't necessarily true but it sure seemed to be a trend noticed by the other band members.

"Hey, I'm getting plenty of rest. As a matter of fact, Ginny and I are leaving in a few minutes to get even more rest." Brian smiled at Ginny as she blushed. She wasn't sure how to take some of Brian's comments. Rick's comments were innocent enough now, but as the band's schedule started to get more intense, the other band members might not like having Ginny along. She didn't want to be a burden on Brian. She sure didn't want to be compared to Yoko Ono. No matter. That particular problem would be solved within the next week when Ginny had to get back to school and concentrate on her studies. She had summer classes that would keep her very busy for the next eight weeks. She knew that was going to be difficult with Brian out on tour, being exposed to all these little teen hussies, throwing themselves at her man. Yes, studying would be difficult at best. But tonight, they were headed to the Gaylord Palms in Orlando to celebrate their three month anniversary. They'd stayed at the Palms on their first overnight together. Brian had signed his contract with the record company that day and he'd wanted to share that occasion with her. He'd bought her a fabulous bracelet that she wore this evening. She didn't care now if Brian ever bought her another bracelet, ring, necklace, blouse, or anything. She was in love with this man. Keeping Brian to herself wasn't going to be easy. He was a rising star. His stock was rocketing in the world of rock and roll. This lifestyle had destroyed many a great person and reduced them to nothing more than blithering idiots, or worse, put them in a grave. But Ginny knew that Brian could handle the stress and strain. He had a level head and he had friends that could help him in both his financial concerns and his personal issues. He was blessed in many ways.

Brian turned towards Ginny and said, "Let me know when you're ready, Babe. I just have to finish this beer and we can head out. The car's waiting in the back lot and I have the keys."

"Take your time. There's no rush. Let me freshen up and I'll be right back." Ginny headed for the rest room.

Arnold got Brian's attention and said that he had a note for him from a friend. It was from Pat McKinney. He smiled as he ripped the envelope and pulled out the two page letter.

Hey Brian, I've been watching the entertainment news. Sounds like you're having a blast. According to the people in the know, you're the hottest band from the south since Lynard Skynard. That says a lot. I can't turn on the radio without hearing that damn song, 'I Know You Better Than You Think'. What a great tune. I find myself tapping the steering wheel or my desk whenever I hear it. Diane yelled at me the other day for singing it in the shower.

Pat went on to tell Brian about his dad's heart attack and that he was in recovery. He also wrote about Joe being recalled into the Marine Corps and how he was going to ask Lisa to marry him when her dad took ill with his stroke. A stretch of bad luck, Pat called it. But he did say that when Joe, Lisa, Diane and Pat were together that they'd catch one of Brian's upcoming concerts.

Pat ended with; *Thanks for being there for me when we were under the gun. Your friendship and trust mean a lot to me. The talk at the vault helped me get it back together and understand what I really have in my family, especially Diane. She and the kids are my world.*

Good luck with the tour. Keep your head on straight and make a fortune. I talked with Jerry, my money guy. He's ready to help you in any way he can. Just let him know when you're going to break from the tour.

Brian was just finishing the letter when Ginny returned, looking fresh and beautiful. She asked who the letter was from and Brian told her. "Pat's dad had a heart attack and Lisa's dad had a stroke last week. Bad luck strikes in threes. I hope that's just a myth."

"I didn't know you were superstitious, Mr. Purcer," Ginny smiled as she leaned over to kiss her man. This brought a round of hoots, kissing noises and taunts from the rest of the band and their friends. Brian got up, his face showing the red blush as he took Ginny's arm and headed for the door. He turned his head towards the band as he got to the door, smiled a devilish smile and flipped the room a bird. When they got into the rented

Cadillac CTS, Brian's face took on a more serious, worried look. Ginny noticed and asked, "What is it, Brian?"

"I'm worried about Pat and Diane, Joe and Lisa. I'm worried about whether the band can hack the touring and constant pressure. I'm worried about my folks. If I ever meet your folks, I'll be worried about them. Hell, I'm worried about everything. I'm at the most exciting time of my life and I'm worried. What's wrong with me?"

"This is all new, that's all. There's a whole lot happening right now. I have a suggestion; why don't we spend the night at the Palms like we planned tonight and then call Pat and Diane. If they're home and don't have plans, we can spend the day with them. They'd love to see you and you can relax. Take a load off that mind of yours. It's in overdrive."

Ginny watched Brian as his eyes brightened in the reflection of the parking lot lights. "You know, you're amazing. That's a great idea." Brian reached into his pocket and pulled out a hair tie and pulled his long, frizzy hair into a pony tail. He rubbed his eyes, started the car then leaned over and kissed Ginny. To their surprise, they heard loud hoots, hollers and kissing noises coming from the door to the backstage at the Lakeland Civic Center. Brian looked and saw Rick Wessler and the other band members standing outside the door, looking their way. Brian honked the horn, gunned the engine and took off for the Gaylord Palms.

Chapter 11

Detective William Banks was staring at the file folder in the middle of his desk. The rest of his case files had been pushed to one side of his large desk. His phone was nearly buried in the pile of manila folders with mostly old cases that he'd pulled out several days ago because he was getting bored. No homicides had occurred in Grand Forks for nearly a year. Even now, this wasn't a homicide, but it was a violent death and the homicide detectives were the best trained men to handle the investigation. He and his partner, Reid Hansen, had been trying to determine where to go with the investigation into Sergeant Kevin Reardon's death. They spoke with the military brass on the Air Force base at Grand Forks but they were getting nowhere. The military command would not divulge any information about why the young man had been declared Killed in Action in Europe or how he showed up dead in Grand Forks. He drummed his pen on the folder while he rubbed his forehead with his left hand. He laid down his pen, reached for his coffee cup and raised it, but stopped half way to his mouth and put it back down, noticing that it was empty. He looked around the office of the Grand Forks Police Department. The office was quiet and nearly empty. Bill looked up at the clock on the wall above the file cabinets at the far end of the office. It was 5:30 in the afternoon and most of the patrol officers were out on the street. Only he and Reid were at their desks.

"So, Reid, what do you make of all this? We find a dead flyboy and the brass at the base wouldn't even acknowledge that he was in the Air Force until we told them about his military ID. What kind of bullshit is that? The least they could have done was tell us what he was doing in Europe. Hell, the neighbors knew that much. It's not like it's a matter of national security. We're sure as hell not trying to muscle in on their territory. He was found off base." Bill looked back down at the file and began to flip through several pages of information and forms that were filled out to document the investigation so far. He reached for his coffee cup again then shook his head and set it back on the desk. He got up and headed for the coffee pot but noticed that it was empty, too. He returned to his desk. "Shit. No frickin' coffee," he said in his slightly Nordic accent. He looked at Reid who was reading through his notes, frowning.

Reid looked up from his notebook and ran his hand over the top of his close-cropped, blond hair. He leaned back in his office chair and stared at the ceiling for a moment. "Nothing. There's nothing here that makes any sense at all. Why would a guy blow his brains out if he were reported dead in Europe? We don't have enough of the pieces of this puzzle. This guy wasn't screwed up in the head. He was a member of a team that did some pretty precise maneuvers. They don't send up dumb-asses in half billion dollar aircraft to fuel billion dollar jets. No matter what part you play on one of those mid air refueling teams, you have to know your stuff. This guy had to know what he was doing. Why won't the brass from the base work with us?"

Bill listened to Reid's questions. He heard the frustration in his voice and saw the animation in his face. He also agreed with his assessment that they didn't have even the most minimal information that they needed to even start to formulate a theory, much less put together a timeline of events. They had only a few pieces of a very complex puzzle, or so it seemed. "Let's call it a night, Reid. All this will be here in the morning. Maybe by then, the folks at Grand Forks will have a change of heart and decide to cooperate with us."

"Right . . . and pigs will fly."

"Stranger things have happened, buddy. Besides, we're out of coffee and I can't drink anymore anyway. All I'll do is keep myself awake. I can't think straight as it is."

Reid rubbed the stubble on his face with both hands then swept them over the top of his head, stopping at his neck as he stared at the notebook on his desk. "Let's do one more thing before we call it a night. Let's take another look at the timeline. At least we'll have that updated. We need to fill in the blanks and there's a bunch of them."

Bill hesitated for just a moment then said, "Alright, I'm game. Where do we start?"

Reid stood and walked to the white board behind his desk, picked up a black dry erase marker and tried to write a slanted line for today's date. The marker was dry. He recapped it and threw it in the trash can by his desk and picked up the red marker. It was also dry. This marker he threw against the wall and picked up the orange marker. He took a deep breath and drew a long, orange, slanted line on the board, then turned to Bill who was wearing a broad grin. "No problem. We're making progress now."

"What's our starting point?" Bill was serious again.

Reid held the bottom of the dry erase marker to his squared chin. "Let's start with the date Sergeant Reardon joined the Air Force. Do we know any other pertinent dates before that?"

"Not yet. If we find any, we can add them. Right now, we can add the date of his death. Also, add the date that he was reported to have been KIA. We'll have to use the date that the neighbors gave us."

Reid wrote down the couple of dates that they had, then looked at the board. "Still real thin, not much to go on. How about the date that Mrs. Reardon moved out?"

Bill flipped through his notebook and found the entry where the chatty neighbor, Lillie Weickoff, said that Belinda Reardon moved out and headed for the panhandle of Florida. March 16. "That's about a three day drive from Grand Forks if a person drove ten hours or so per day. That means that they, Belinda and her brother, would have arrived about March 19th or 20th. They've been there for over two months if they did what they told their old neighbors."

"Do we know anyone in Pensacola?" Bill asked Reid, hoping that they had a connection in law enforcement there?

"Nope. If I did, do you think that I'd be living up here? Hell, I'd have made captain in Pensacola by now. Anyway, they're probably not there."

The timeline, from left to right looked like a very sparse arrow feather; a straight line with lines starting at the main line and extending up to the right at a 45 degree angle. On the slanted lines, dates were written with additional information about the event that occurred on that date. So far they had the month that Kevin Reardon joined the Air Force, January, 1992. Next, February 2, 1997, Reardon is sent to Europe followed by his reportedly being Killed in Action on about February 23. Reid also wrote down the approximate date that Belinda Reardon moved out with the help of her brother; March 16. Finally, Saturday, March 24. The date that Reardon's body was found in the house on 7th Avenue North.

"It sure is thin on detail," Reid said as he looked at the board. "Can you think of anything else? We can fill in the details from our interview notes under the last entry. It's been two months since we found the body. We've been back to the neighbors twice. Should we start back in the neighborhood again and see if any of the neighbors remember anything else?"

Bill looked over the board and shook his head. He had his hand on his coffee cup again but removed it before he lifted it, remembering that it was empty. "We're grasping at straws. But if straws are all you have, I guess we should start grabbing."

"It's getting near 6:00. I'm starving. Would you like to get a bite then come back for a few hours and see if we can think of anything else?" Reid was really hoping that Bill would say to forget it and start fresh in the morning. It appeared that he was about to do just that. Then Bill's phone rang.

"Detective Banks, Grand Forks Police." Bill's eyes were staring down at the folder open on his desk as he listened to the caller. He slowly looked up at his partner as the words started to sink in. He got a kind of half grin on his face as his eyes met Reid's. Reid heard him say, "Yes, Major. Absolutely. Where did you say that you're stationed? And how did you hear about Staff Sergeant Reardon?" At the mention of Reardon's name, Reid listened more closely. "Yes sir, Major. I'll be frank. We haven't had much cooperation from the brass at the base up here. We welcome any assistance that we can get from the military. Obviously we'll have to set some ground rules but we're anxious to share anything that we have so far in exchange for continued involvement in the case. You do know that the body was found in town, so technically, it is our jurisdiction." There was a pause for several seconds while the voice at the other end of the receiver was filling Bill Banks in on what they had in mind. As he listened he scribbled down several notes on a pad. Reid was trying to crane his neck around to try and decipher Bill's handwriting but to no avail. "We really need to have you folks involved if we're going to figure out what happened to Kevin Reardon. It's what we all want, I believe." There was another pause before Bill answered. "Yes. That's right. I look forward to meeting with your team. When will they be here?" The final pause was just a few seconds while the caller told Bill the details of the arrival of their military team in Grand Forks. "Excellent, Major. We're looking forward to meeting with them." Bill finished by giving the Major directions to the Grand Forks Police Department from the Air Force base. When he placed the receiver on the cradle, he had a half grin on his face, with his lip cocked up on one side. All he said was "That was interesting."

Reid said, "Well are you going to swallow that mouse and tell me or are you just going to sit there with that shit eatin' grin?"

"That was Major Frank Hartnett, US Marine Corps. He's stationed at Camp Lejeune, North Carolina. He has a file on one dead Staff Sergeant Kevin Reardon. He is investigating numerous cases in which our military personnel are being 'taken advantage of', per the Major's description. He is offering to assist us in our investigation, if you can believe it." As Bill finished his remarks, he put his left elbow on his desk and rubbed the stubble on his chin. He narrowed his eyes as he thought about the possible reasons for the military's decision to get involved in their investigation.

Hansen appeared to read his mind. "Why would a Major from North Carolina want to get involved in a case like this? Did he say?"

"He mentioned that he had files on a number of cases where citizens of our great country took our military men, or women, for a ride; left them penniless and homeless. He said there were a handful of cases that are very similar to Reardon's."

Reid's left eyebrow went up, indicating he was now interested. He looked back up at their timeline and wondered if this new involvement might fill in some of the rather large holes that were staring back at the detectives. "So when does the cavalry arrive?"

"Sooner than you might expect; tomorrow evening."

* * *

Major Frank Hartnett and Major Gus Griggs were exchanging glances during the short call to Grand Forks Police Department. They really weren't sure just what to expect when they spoke with the local civilian authorities. The military and police, regardless of the level of government involved, didn't have a reputation for cooperation. So when the detective from North Dakota appeared to be pleased at the offer of assistance that also pleased Frank Hartnett.

"Well, at least we're in the door. This Detective Banks seemed downright happy that we called. I'll bet they're getting nada, zip, nothing from our flyboy buddies at Grand Forks. I can see them now, declining to assist as if they have everything under control. They'd probably be thrilled if they could just call it a suicide and be done with it. Who cares if he was declared dead in Europe? They probably figure that it was just a paperwork snafu." Major Hartnett grunted and shook his head in disgust. The military was supposed to take care of its own. It just wasn't right in his mind. He looked over at the U.S. Marine Corps plaque on the wall in his office and hoped that his comrades never abandoned his fellow Marines like that. Of course, he knew better. The Corps would always go back after their dead, regardless of the circumstance, whether in battle, a barroom brawl, or odd circumstances like these. The brotherhood would remain strong.

Gus Griggs broke the silence. "When does Sergeant McKinney get here?"

"He'll be here tomorrow at 0900 hours. Captain Brown will also be here. We'll brief them both then, give them their orders and they'll be on a flight to Grand Forks by 1100 hours. They should be at the Grand Forks Air Force Base by dinner. Is McKinney going to have a problem working with Captain Brown?" Hartnett looked directly at his friend and peer to see how he would react to the question.

Without a hint of doubt Gus Griggs answered, "McKinney will have no problem working with the Captain, I'm absolutely certain of that. He is one of the best Marines I've ever seen in action. I believe that your Captain is going to learn a few things about investigative techniques and working in the field."

"Don't sell Brown short. She may be a looker but she's very sharp, mentally, I mean. I look forward to the competition between them. I already told Captain Brown that she would have to hustle to keep up with McKinney. I could see the hair on the back of her neck stand up." Griggs smiled as Hartnett described how he challenged the young female Captain. "I bet that they make a good team."

"What kind of experience does she have? Has she ever run a broad investigation like this before? I mean, she's the lead for the several cases with similarities, right?"

Hartnett lifted the eight folders on the left side of his desk. "She has every one of these. They all appear to have the same M.O. A couple of them go back a pretty long while. Then there's a gap of about 7 or 8 years and they start up again. There are only slight differences. This Reardon case though, it's the only one where someone ends up dead."

"Well Frank, I'm going to head for home. I'll meet you back here at about 0830 hours and we can get the show on the road. I think that you'll be impressed with Sergeant McKinney. I know I am."

"I look forward to meeting the sergeant. See you in the morning, Gus."

With that, Gus Griggs headed out into the early evening at Camp Lejeune. He was thinking about young Sergeant Kevin Reardon and the report on his death. *Sergeant Reardon, whoever did this to you will pay if I have anything to do with it. Sergeant McKinney and I will see to it.*

Captain Nancy Brown stood at ease in Major Frank Hartnett's office promptly at 0900 hours. She was in her US Marine Corps service dress uniform with service insignias. One of them was a marksman insignia. She held her cover in her hand behind her back. She wore no makeup but still looked remarkably polished and very beautiful. She'd been in the office less than 30 seconds as the clock approached the time for their brief. Just as the clock started to chime, Sergeant Joe McKinney walked sharply into the room and stood next to Captain Brown. He didn't say a word until after Major Griggs simply said, "McKinney?" It was the manner in which he said it that prompted a response to the implied question, *How are you?*

"Major Griggs, sir. Good to see you again, sir," Joe replied in crisp tones. He was back into it. Back into the Corps and he felt like he never left. He was ready for action regardless of his orders. He took an oath to defend the constitution of the United States against all enemies, foreign and domestic and he was eager to uphold that oath.

Major Griggs replied calmly, "At ease, son. You look well, fit. You're taking good care of yourself. Have you been doing any shooting in the civilian world?"

Joe relaxed some as he assumed the At Ease stance. "Not enough, sir. I'll need some time at the range, no doubt."

"Sergeant McKinney, I'd like for you to meet Captain Nancy Brown, US Marine Corps JAG office, Camp Lejeune. You will be working with her on this assignment." This caused Joe's right eye brow to rise ever so slightly. The Judge Advocate General's office was the legal office of the military. If they were involved, he definitely wasn't going into battle, not directly anyway. But there are many battlefields in the world. Not all of them are fighting a uniformed enemy. Joe turned to face the Captain and extended his hand which she grasped and shook. Her grip was strong and firm but not overly aggressive. Her hands were soft, but Joe could tell she worked with her hands at something. She definitely had rough points on her fingers and hands. As they shook, Joe said without a smile or hint of emotion, "Captain."

She returned with a just as bland, "Sergeant."

He quickly and covertly looked her over from face to toe. She was very attractive and fit and looked exceptionally sharp in her service dress uniform. *At least this mission has some benefits.* He completed his once over and returned to face the major. He had to keep his mind on the task at hand which he really didn't know yet. He also had to keep in his mind that he had a steady girlfriend who was now up in Ohio with her very ill father and grieving, worried mother.

Major Hartnett entered the room from a side door as the brief introductions were completed. He walked directly up to a spot in front of Captain Brown and Sergeant McKinney and extended his hand first to the Captain, then to Joe and introduced himself. "Please be seated," and he motioned the two to the chairs in front of his desk. Gus Griggs took a chair at the side of Frank Hartnett's desk, facing the two invited guests. Major Hartnett stared at his desk for a moment as if to collect his thoughts, then looked up at his team members. His eyes shifted between the two for a moment.

Major Hartnett began, "You're here because we have a problem that is seriously undermining the ability of our young men and women to protect our country and its citizens. We believe that you can help us put a serious dent in this problem and set up a systematic method to deal with this problem in the future. The problem is that we have civilians taking advantage of the men and women in various branches of the military;" he raised the volume of his voice as he said, "our military!" His face actually started to turn red as his anger was starting to show. "Major Griggs will go into detail with you on what your specific assignment is, but I want you to know just how serious this problem has become. A few months ago an Army Private was declared Killed in Action in Afghanistan. His mother was called and informed of this. She made funeral arrangements for him. His town was planning a celebration for his heroic efforts. Then the young man was dropped off at home, alive and well. His mother nearly had a heart attack seeing him alive. Some of the town's folks thought that his mother staged the whole thing for publicity. It was becoming a real circus. Fortunately, we were able to talk to this soldier's mother and the local media and let them know that there was a mix up in paperwork and all is well. But in the mean time, this soldier's unit is without his services while he's at home, straightening the mess out." Joe is sitting there thinking *what's the problem that I've been called up to solve here? Do I have to chase down some paper pusher and teach them how to fill out their forms correctly?* Then Major Hartnett got to the nasty part. "This young man's wife of three weeks cleaned his clock, so to speak. She emptied his bank account, sold his belongings, which included a real expensive gun collection and coin collection. She sold all of their furniture and she was able to collect on his SGLI. This young man is out putting his life in harms way, getting shot at in a foreign country and his real enemy is at home and he can't do a damn thing about it." Again his face was beat red with anger. "This is happening with more frequency than we'd like to admit, but we have admitted it. That's where you two come in. You're going to help solve this problem. You may be asking yourselves how, but Major Griggs will explain that to you. Are you both up to the task?"

In unison, Captain Nancy Brown and Sergeant Joe McKinney answered with a sharp, "Yes Sir." And they both meant it.

And they both thought to themselves *How in the hell are we going to stop this?*

* * *

Petty Officer Wilson Brush was laid out on a beach towel under the bright Daytona Beach sun, lathered up with high SPF sun protection lotion. His fair skin would have been burned to the texture of bacon in less than an hour without the added protection. He didn't have the opportunity to get a tan in East Liverpool, Ohio before he joined the Navy. Now that he spent a lot of time beneath the ocean on a submarine, he was lucky to see the sun more than 200 days per year. Being a member of a ballistic missile submarine gave him more opportunity than his fast attack submarine counterparts. On good years, they were lucky to see the sun for 100 days. Not because they were under the water so much as they were always on the ship. When you were on the ship, whether at sea or in port, you never saw the sun. At least the missile subs had a second crew to take the ship and free up some time for R and R; rest and relaxation. Wilson Brush was on the tail end of his nearly three months R and R period. He and the rest of his crew had to take back the ship in less than 4 weeks. But while he was off he planned to make the most of this off crew. He was about to make a life changing move. That is, if he could get the cooperation of one fine young lady. Over the last 2 weeks he'd fallen in love and he believed that Tanya Walters felt the same way. He turned his head sideways to see his girlfriend lying beside him. He watched as she soaked up the sun, her tan skin glistening with suntan lotion of a much lower SPF than his own. She already had a base tan and was merely getting darker with each passing minute. Wilson admired her near perfect body, from her ample breasts, to her tight tummy, and her muscular legs. She must have sensed that he was looking at her because she turned her head slightly in his direction and smiled.

"So, how's the scenery?" she asked in a playful tone.

He smiled back at her and replied, "Everything I see is beautiful." He paused and propped himself up on his left elbow and looked her over once again, this time from a higher angle. From this vantage point he could see tiny droplets of sweat on her breasts and above her lip. A few beads had connected to form a running drip down her tight tummy. Her hair was matted along her forehead where her sweat had mingled with several strands. He thought that she could easily be a model. She was perfect. "I just wish we had more time before I have to report back to the boat. It's coming up fast. I'm afraid that you'll be gone when I get back. Three months is a long time to be gone."

"Don't worry about that. I'll be here. We've had a really great time this last couple of weeks. It isn't going to end just because you have to do your job." She smiled up at Wilson with a sexy little smile. "We're going to have lots of great times, trust me."

This also brought a smile to Wilson's face. He leaned over and kissed her lightly on he lips. He started to back away, but she put her hand behind his head and drew him to her and returned his kiss hard. They embraced for several minutes, kissing deeply and hugging close with passion.

Tanya broke their embrace and looked longingly at Wilson, cupping his head in her hands. "When do you have to head back to the base and check in?"

"Not for three days." Wilson said.

"Let's get a room for a few nights. We can stay here and enjoy the beach and sun . . . and each other."

Wilson didn't miss a beat. "Let's go. We can get a room right now." Within 2 minutes, they were up, in the car, heading for the ramp off the beach. Within 20 minutes they were in a room at the Sea Crest Hotel, on the bed making love in a heat of passion. Another 30 minutes and they were resting in each other's arms.

Wilson looked Tanya in the eyes and said, "I'm afraid that I'm falling in love with you." She tightened her hold on the young sailor, rested her head on his shoulder and thought to herself, *Yes, I've got him.* She backed away, looked in his eyes and in a shy voice said, "I think I'm feeling the same way, too," and hugged him tight again.

Then he asked her the $100,000 question. "Tanya, I know we've only known each other a short while, but," a pause that seemed to Tanya like ten minutes, "will you marry me?"

Without hesitation and with a big smile that wasn't faked, Tanya Walters, also known as Rebecca Lippert and Laurie Sharp, said an emphatic "Yes! I'd marry you right now if there were a preacher here! Of course, this might be a little embarrassing. But yes, yes, yes!" And she kissed him over and over again. They made love a second time. When they were through, Wilson closed his eyes and thought he was in heaven. Through a love induced brain fog, Wilson asked if a wedding in three weeks would suit her and she readily agreed. Tanya closed her eyes, drifted off to sleep, feeling like $100,000. And with a little luck, she'd have it in her hands in less than 9 weeks.

Chapter 12

The flight to Grand Forks International Airport west of Grand Forks, North Dakota was uneventful. Sergeant Joe McKinney, active duty for three hours, and Captain Nancy Brown talked for nearly an hour. The discussion surrounded details of the various case files and how to proceed with identifying and tracking down the first set of perpetrators. There were six cases where the details of the crime were very nearly identical. A young military man would meet a pretty young lady, fall in love, get married and have his new bride move in with him. Within the first week, all of the legal adjustments to the young man's checking and savings account were changed to a joint account, last will and testaments were revised, and car titles or property deeds were changed to reflect joint ownership. The young man was always within two to three weeks of being deployed overseas to a battlefield assignment or, for the Navy men, heading out to sea for at least a twelve week deployment. In each case, the young bride was apparently from the mid-west, possibly eastern Ohio or western Pennsylvania. She had blue eyes, and was short but well built. The hair color was varied but that was as easy to change as a pair of underwear. Each folder placed her weight at about 105 to 115 pounds. Most of the estimates were at the lower end of that range. In every case, a young man with dark hair and a light, almost pale complexion assisted the young woman in moving after the husband was rumored to have been killed in action.

Joe looked up from his files and rubbed his eyes. The Boeing 737-900 commercial airliner was in its final approach. He thought about his partner, Captain Brown. He'd learned a bit about her in the early part of the flight when they were trying to get acquainted. He found her to be very serious and business oriented. She wasn't much for small talk and she didn't reveal much about her hobbies or ambitions. She was quite beautiful and was in excellent shape from what he could see. That wasn't much since she was wearing her Marine uniform blouse and skirt. Her brown hair was short and trimmed and formed a tight curl above her forehead. In the back an almost imperceptible ducktail hung in the center at the base of her skull. She obviously worked out if not daily, then at least 5 days per week. Her neck exposed the tendons that stretched the skin taut from her head to her shoulders. No fat anywhere to be seen on this young woman. Joe put her age at about twenty-seven years old but he'd probably never know. She wasn't rude when asked a question that was off limits but she matter-of-factly avoided the question and went on with another topic. Joe appreciated that since he didn't like wasting time on small talk when there was business to be conducted.

Captain Brown was gathering her files and placing them in a soft bound leather case. She zipped the case closed and tucked the case between her left hip and the seat's arm rest. She glanced over at Joe with a raised eyebrow as if to ask a question, but she remained silent. Joe didn't know whether he was supposed to offer his opinion or simply wait to hear if she had formulated a plan yet. After a few awkward seconds, Joe said, "Ma'am, do you want to discuss any other details before we land? Per the Captain we have about 15 minutes before we touch down."

The Captain, without a trace of emotion said, "Sergeant, please call me Captain or Captain Brown. I'll call you . . . "

"Joe or Sergeant. Joe is fine with me."

"Great, Joe. I am floored by the crass nature of these crimes. I can't believe that there are Americans who would take advantage of young soldiers and sailors like this. These are the worst kind of scum." Joe nodded his head in agreement. She continued in a terse tone of voice that made Joe believe that this woman meant business. "We are going to put these bastards away when we find them and we are going to find a way to quickly identify and prosecute anyone else who thinks that military personnel are easy prey for scams like this." Joe was nodding. He was impressed by her direct manner and confidence. He could see that she believed in what she was saying.

"Captain, do you have a course of action in mind?"

"Not yet, but when we get settled into the office at the base, I want to start with interviews of the local detectives from the Grand Forks Police Department. I also want to talk with the brass at the base and find out why the hell they refused to cooperate with the detectives. We have a staffed Air Force Office of Special Investigations Detachment at the base. Why would they snub the local police? From what the files say, the body was found in the city of Grand Forks, in a private residence. They should have allowed the local police to do their job and provided whatever assistance they needed. Not cooperating was a blunder. We lost valuable time and information by not exchanging information right away. Worse yet, if there was any foul play, there may be more than just the local police and the AFOSI involved. If the widow and her brother were involved, and they have crossed state lines, then the FBI could get involved. Then this will really become a screwed up mess. We want to act quickly and decisively while drawing the least amount of attention possible."

Joe thought for a moment then said, "I agree with everything that you've said. You know that we may run into some of the same roadblocks from both our own people and the locals. If we do, how much authority do we have to step on toes to get what we need?"

She thought about Joe's question for a moment then answered. "From what our orders say, we can rattle as many cages as we need to get to the bottom of this. That includes the top dog at the base all the way down to Joe Shit, the rag man." In military speak, that meant the newest military recruit. "We'll get what we need. We may not get promoted any time soon but I'm not worried about that. Are you?"

"Considering that my tour is a matter of weeks, I don't expect a command promotion. I'd just like the satisfaction of nailing some of these bastards. I guess we'd better tighten our safety belts. It looks like we're about to land. I hope this captain's an Air Force Pilot. Navy Pilots are usually rough on their landings. They're used to dropping these things on aircraft carriers. They come in hard and short. Air Force guys use the whole runway."

"Well hold on to your lunch. The pilot's name is 'Pop' Rigor, as in retired Lieutenant Commander 'Pop' Rigor. 'Pop' is his nickname because he got a reputation for shearing a number of the arresting wires on board the air craft carrier Abe Lincoln. This could be interesting."

Joe leaned back into his seat a little tighter. He wasn't afraid of flying, but he wasn't too thrilled about the landings. *Bummer.*

He was amazed at the view of the landscape as they'd approached the runway during the 737's descent. The ground was pretty baron. The color was dark tan to nearly dark brown. The farmer's fields were mostly squared off except where washes cut the land. These normally dry gullies made the land look like the surface of Mars where water drained after rain storms or after a long winter snow melt. There was no snow visible from Joe's vantage but he was told to prepare for cold weather and breezy conditions.

The landing was not as rough as Joe had feared. They retrieved their checked luggage and headed for the front door of the airport terminal. The cold attacked Joe immediately as he opened the front door of the terminal. He'd been told to prepare for cold weather but he didn't expect that his teeth would be chattering. He thought about the 70 degree days that he left behind in Orlando and for a moment wondered what possessed him to accept the call up, though, in reality, he didn't have a choice. He followed Captain Brown to the National Car Rental desk where they rented a full sized Mercury Grand Marquis. They loaded their bags in the trunk and Nancy got in the driver's seat. Joe didn't mind. He wanted to work the heater and get the car warmed as soon as possible. The car sped out of the parking lot and headed for Route 2 West. The base was less than ten miles from the airport so the heater barely had time to warm the car before they were turning right onto Route 3 then left on Steen Avenue at the base entrance. Joe was still freezing.

They showed their Military IDs to the guard on duty who logged their names on a check in sheet. The guard gave them directions to the headquarters building.   Nancy headed west on Steen then right on Holzapple Street to the base Headquarters parking lot.   Joe and Nancy entered the base headquarters where they were greeted inside the entrance by a female Air Force Major.   The major was pleasant but businesslike. She was a fairly attractive woman.   She was about 5'7" tall and had a flat stomach but no muscle tone to her arms or legs.   She had sandy blond hair that had some dark highlighting.   It may have been long but Joe couldn't tell because it was made up in a bun at the back of her head.

"Welcome to Grand Forks Air Force Base.   I'm Shawna Hull, aid to Colonel Chester the base Commander.   I hope your flight was smooth."

"Hi, I'm Captain Brown.   The flight was fine but long."

Joe extended his hand and shook Major Hull's.   "Hi.   Sergeant Joe McKinney."   Joe was anxious to get through the introductions.   He had several phone calls to make and he wanted to get to those as soon as he could.   Through much of the flight, his concentration was broken by his dad's heart attack and worries about his recovery.   He was also thinking about Lisa and her dad.   He had no idea how she was dealing with her father's condition.   She also had the emotional baggage of a brother who was apparently worthless and only concerned with himself.   The only thing he wanted from his family was money.   Joe was also concerned with Lisa's state of mind.   Would this change her feelings for him?   Would she be so wrapped up in her family issues that she'd be forced to move back to Ohio and leave their relationship behind?   Joe had to get some privacy so he could use his cell phone to try and reach Lisa.   He wasn't even sure if his phone would work this far west.   If not, he figured he'd be able to use an office phone soon enough.   He needed to talk with Lisa soon or these questions were going to continue to wear on his mind.   It would also impact his ability to concentrate on the mission.   He wouldn't let anything interfere with his commitment to the Marine Corps.   He took an oath and he would perform his duties to the best of his ability; nothing less.

"Sergeant, can I help you with something?"   It was Major Hull's voice that brought him out of his deep thoughts.

"Ma'am, we need to know our arrangements as soon as possible.   I don't mean to rush you, but can you show us where we'll be working?   I believe that the Captain and I will be working into the early evening."

"No problem, Sergeant.   We have you set up in an office in the AFOSI building.   There is an office with separate private rooms off to each side of the central room.   I can take you there now if you'll follow me."   They walked behind Major Hull to the parking lot then followed her car to the Air Force Office of Special Investigations.   When they entered the common area of their office, the Major said, "The office is equipped with telephones in each office; all lines are secure.   There is internet access so you can send and receive e-mails.   I see that you each brought your laptops.   These are not secure so you should use caution in what you transmit.   We have a skilled Information Technology Department on base if you need any type of assistance." They slowed as they approached the open office door on the left side of the hall. She continued, "Airman Adam Goff will provide whatever office supplies you need. Just ask. Oh, and you have a local directory. Actually, the directory covers most of the state of North Dakota. We have also provided the names and telephone numbers for the detectives in Grand Forks Police Department. You'll also want to speak with Major Roland Geers. He is the Commander of the AFOSI Detachment. His office is at the end of the hall on the left."

Joe turned and addressed Major Hull. "Major, thanks very much. One last item before we get settled in. What about our quarters?"

"Oh, yes. We've made arrangements for you to stay at the Warrior Inn. Airman Goff will provide directions. The rooms are side by side for your convenience. Also, the units are near the base exit so that you can head into Grand Forks or anywhere off base that you need to travel. You have parking privileges in any spot on the base except hose marked reserved for specific officers." She paused for a moment, looked from Joe to Nancy then asked, "Is there anything else that I can do for you at this time?"

Both Joe and Nancy shook there heads and said in near unison, "No Ma'am."

"Then I'll leave you to your work. Again, if you need anything, Airman Goff will assist. If you need anything to eat he's your man. He knows every restaurant in the area. He'll be with you in a few minutes."

With that, Major Hull turned and headed back down the hall towards the main entrance. Joe and Nancy watched her leave then entered the center office that was to be their shared work space for at least the next few weeks. The office had walls painted in bright white and had some rather good pictures of a number of jet fighters and support jets. Many of the pictures depicted fighters being refueled by the larger fueling tankers from many different angles, including two from the refueling station aboard the tanker. You could clearly see the fighter pilot looking up at the fuel supply line connected to his jet. The pictures vividly showed the skill that was required to successfully complete an in-air refueling.

Joe turned to Nancy and said, "It's your choice, Captain. Which office would you prefer?"

"I don't know, let me look." She took less than a minute to choose the left office. Joe moved his files and his laptop into the right side office and began to unpack. He walked back to the door and said, "Captain, I have to make two personal calls. I should be less than ten minutes. Is there anything you need before I start?"

"No, Joe. It'll take me a few minutes to get unpacked and get oriented anyway. Let's meet in my office at 4:30 and we can pick up where we left off on the flight. First thing I need is a good white board. That's Airman Goff's first mission."

Just as the words left her mouth, they heard a slight rumbling from the hall outside. It was a large man in an Air Force uniform rolling a large portable whiteboard down the hall.

"Airman Goff at your service, Ma'am."

Joe noticed the slightest curl of Nancy's lips. It was the closest thing to a smile or any emotion that he'd seen on her face. Goff rolled the white board into Nancy's office and they started to exchange introductions. Once Joe had finished introducing himself, he ducked into his office and pulled out his cell phone. He shook his head as his phone searched for service but found none. He picked up his desk phone then paused. He thought for just a moment, trying to decide who to call first. He pulled out his wallet and extracted the small piece of paper with the number for St. Vincent's Medical Center in Toledo, Ohio.

* * *

When Joe asked the head nurse for the phone number in Lisa Goddard's father's room, the nurse said that the room was empty. She could not pass out any information regarding Mr. Goddard's condition but that she would try to locate a member of the Goddard family. Joe waited on the phone for four full minutes before a voice came on the line and said, "Mr. McKinney, I have Lisa Goddard here." The next voice that Joe heard was Lisa's. She had obviously been crying. Her voice was hoarse and she had to stop every so often to blow her nose.

"Daddy's gone, Joe," and she began to cry again. Between sobs, Lisa told Joe that her dad passed away within the last hour from a massive stroke. They'd removed all life support from her father at 2:45 PM and he drifted off to his calm death within 35 minutes. "Mom's in shock. She doesn't know what to do right now. My idiot brother couldn't be bothered to come to the hospital to see his own father."

"Lisa, I am so sorry. Please tell your mom that I'll say a prayer for her."

"I will. Joe, what will she do now?"

"You have to be strong for her, Sweetie. You can do it. First, just be with her. Don't let her out of your sight and comfort her. You can help each other. Try to talk with her about all the good times that they had together. You may have to go back a while from what you've told me but I think that it will help. Just don't let her sink into depression. Is there a chapel at the hospital?"

"Yes, I passed it on the way up here." She blew her nose in Joe's ear without thinking. Then realized what she'd done and said with a short laugh through the tears, "Sorry."

Joe had to smile a sad smile and said, "That's alright, Babe." He paused then said, "Has your mother said anything about funeral arrangements?"

"It's pretty much all taken care of. While they were having money problems, that was one thing that they figured that they'd better take care of or I'd have to bear the entire cost. They knew that Gary wouldn't be any help."

"That's good," Joe replied. "That's one less thing that you have to be concerned with. I think that your biggest job is your mom's mental state." Joe took a deep breath and went on, "Now, how are you holding up?" He put extra emphasis on 'you' to make sure she knew he was concerned about her well being.

"I'm kind of a mess but I'll get it together. Just hearing your voice means a lot to me. I am so glad you called. I haven't had time to think about anything else but Dad and Mom since I got here. I really miss you."

"I miss you, too. Listen, Lisa, how are you doing for cash? Do you need any money?" Joe looked at the wall directly across from his desk as he listened. He concentrated on a picture of an F-16 fighter jet that had just released its starboard air to air missile. He didn't know what kind of missile it was because he had no training in that area. He heard Lisa's voice.

"Well, I have enough for now and I have my charge card but the limit is $500 and I know I have about $365 charged already. We're alright for now, I guess." Joe heard her sniff once then blow her nose again, this time holding the phone away from her face.

"If you need any money at all at any time, you call me at the number I am going to give you. If you can't reach me, you call Pat and Diane right away. Don't hesitate even for a second. Understand?"

"Yes. Thanks." She paused for a few seconds and Joe was about to speak when she said, "Joe, I love you for this. I love you for everything."

Joe's throat got a little tight, then he replied, "I love you, too Lisa Goddard. You take care of your mother. Have you got something to write on?" Joe gave her his new office number and his brother Pat's number. He promised to call her at her mom's later and see how things were going. They said their goodbyes and hung up. Joe hung his head for a few minutes and thought about Lisa, her mother, and her now deceased father. He wished that things had been different for her family, that her brother hadn't been such a jerk and ruined Lisa's family's lives. He wished that he could have made it all better, but he couldn't. This chapter was coming to a close for them. Now they had to deal with the pain and move on. He wondered if there was anything that he could do to help. Then a thought crossed his mind and he looked back at the fighter jet, releasing its missile. *There is one thing that I can do. Her brother has caused enough pain.*

Chapter 13

Jim Hollis sat in his cubicle on the 8th floor of the NatFed Life Insurance Company in Richmond, Virginia and read the memo sent to all claims processors. He was indignant. No way could he 'look for signs of fraud' in the forms that were crossing his desk with the volume of claims that he had to process daily! He couldn't count the stack of folders in his in-basket and each day that stack grew taller. He was expected to meet his daily quota of 75 claims processed, which included verifying the data on the claimant, ensuring that the claim met the requirements for a payout, and ensuring that each 'i' was dotted and every 't' was crossed. The official guide for processing a claim was on its seventy-ninth revision and was now a whopping 629 pages long. Worse, the new approved changes that had not been incorporated into the latest revision were in a separate three-ring binder that sat next to the official guide. That binder was now at 59 pages. *How in the hell do they expect me to keep up with all this crap?*

Jim leaned back in his chair and stared up at the ceiling for a few moments. The white ceiling tiles stretched as far as he could see. The only thing he could see from this angle were sprinkle heads, fluorescent light fixtures and utility wire poles that ran computer lines, phone lines and electricity down to each cubicle where his counterparts were busy processing paper to keep the company profitable. He noticed the small square holes where other utility poles had been. Since the last reorganization, the poles were removed but the holes in the ceiling tiles remained. It was a grim reminder of the plight of the middle class service sector employee. Work your way up to middle management in a company the size of NatFed and what can you expect? A pink slip; A one way ticket out the door with not so much as a *thanks for all your time and effort to make the company what it is today.* He'd survived the last reorganization but there were certainly more to come. A couple of years ago, they called the personnel reduction a 'right-sizing'. Two years before that the reductions were due to the synergy achieved by gobbling up a smaller insurance company. Lucky for Jim, NatFed was the acquirer in that transaction. The acquired company took the lion's share of personnel reductions in that round of cuts. But rumors were starting to build again. This time, NatFed was rumored to be the target company. He couldn't afford to lose this job regardless of how much he hated it.

He was 48 years old and on his third marriage. His first two marriages ended up in divorce because his ex-wives had complained that he spent too much time at work and too little time with them. He was 5'7" tall with thinning brown hair that was graying at the sideburns. His face was pocked with acne holes from his youth and he had an extraordinary amount of hair growing out of his ears. He always looked like he needed a shave. His white golf shirt with the NatFed company logo was too tight over his torso. He wore black slacks that were a slight bit too short. His fellow employees called them his high-water pants. He had the bad habit of snorting when he laughed and his co-workers made jokes about him behind his back. Unfortunately, they were a bit too loud with their remarks and Jim overheard most of the comments. He hated them for it but what could he do?

His cubicle was like most others except that he was not well organized. A few weeks back, he lost several folders. His supervisor asked if he knew where they were and he'd said that he processed them a few weeks before. When he found them under a stack of papers, he was so afraid that he'd lose his job that he took the folders home and destroyed them. They had to be reworked the following week but at least he didn't get caught.

Jim stared down at the folder opened before him, an SGLI claim. That stood for Serviceman's Group Life Insurance; a government policy for active duty military. When one of these crossed his desk, it was an easy job. The military administrators who processed these forms were good at their jobs. Private Edward Eugene Sharp was KIA, Killed in Action, in Afghanistan, April 2 of this year. Claimant is Laurie Sharp, same home address and phone number as the decedent. Jacksonville, North Carolina, right near Camp Lejeune Marine Corp base. No issue here. He read each line of the form to look for any discrepancy that would hold up the claim for a period of time. His supervisor had explained to him and his co-workers that the longer they could hold up a claim, the longer that money could work for the corporation and add to earnings per share. More earnings per share meant more profit sharing for the employees. That was good for the employees and good for the shareholders. It was a great line to tell the new employees who would swallow that crap hook, line and sinker. Jim had been around long enough to know that profit sharing actually became reality only once since the program's inception 5 years ago. Jim's profit sharing check came to a grand total of $375.53 after income tax withholding, Social Security, Medicare, and health insurance deductions. But delaying the claims sucked even worse for the poor wives and kids who needed the money. It used to bother him that his company actually instructed their employees to stall delivery of claims to widows and widowers. Now he was numb to it. He never knew the people who would ultimately receive the money so he never put a face to the misery. It was like watching TV or a movie. It wasn't real to the claims processors at NatFed.

He had to make the call to Mrs. Sharp to verify the information but he was pretty confident that this was a slam dunk. He dialed the number on the form. The phone rang, three, four, five times. He was about to hang up when a woman answered. There was loud rock music in the background, and the voice on the phone was giggling as she answered. "Hello?"

"May I speak with Mrs. Laurie Sharp, please?"

There was a pause. Then he could hear a muffled command to turn down the stereo. "This is Laurie Sharp." The music in the background stopped and a man's voice asked the woman, "Who is it?"

"Mrs. Sharp, this is Jim Hollis from NatFed Life Insurance Company. First off, I am sorry for your loss. But I need to verify some information that is on the claims form for your husband's policy. Are you able to do that for me?"

In a voice that sounded more like a teenager answering a radio show quiz for a chance at a free pizza, Laurie Sharp said, "Sure."

Jim Hollis went through the standard set of questions to which Laurie answered perfectly. He explained to her that his company would be processing a check and she should expect to receive it by next week.

"Great!" Laurie exclaimed and hung up the phone.

Jim pulled the receiver away from his ear and looked at it for a few seconds in disbelief. Laurie Sharp didn't sound like the grieving widow. She sounded more like she'd just won a cash prize on a game show. He placed the receiver in its cradle and sat for a moment. He wondered if he should report the strange incident to his boss. This was an SGLI claim, a military policy for $100,000. If he reported it and the company investigated, he might be able to save NatFed the payout. Maybe he'd be recognized for his efforts, maybe get a raise or a bonus. Then he started to think about his profit sharing and the downsizing again. He looked around his cubicle and shook his head. *It isn't worth the trouble.* He had a quota to meet and he was already behind. He'd spent about 20 minutes on the phone with his own wife who was hounding him to spend more time at home and quit giving the company free overtime. "They are stealing from you just as if they take the money out of your pocket," she'd said. He gave the form one last look, signed it, stamped it with his official seal of approval for final processing and placed it on the stack in his out-basket. In an hour or so, a mailroom clerk would deliver the paperwork to the accounts payable department for cutting of the check.

His phone rang and it was his wife again. This time she needed him to stop at the store on his way home to pick up some things she needed before she could start supper. When he hung up the phone, he knew it was going to be a long night because he'd leave work late, get home with the supper supplies late, and get to bed late. Then it started all over again the next day. Maybe a layoff wasn't such a bad thing.

* * *

Laurie Sharp, aka Rebecca Lippert, turned from the phone, ran to where Bobby Garrett was lying on the couch and jumped on him. She stripped off the blue tank top and threw it across the room. She unclipped her bra and tossed it on the ceiling fan. Bobby looked up at her breasts as she lowered them to his face. She smiled as he took one nipple in his mouth and started to suck lightly. "Oh that feels real good," she said in a sexy tone. "You know what else feels good? Next week, we're going to be rich. That's what the insurance guy said on the phone."

Bobby stopped sucking, grabbed her by the shoulders and pushed her to a sitting position. His face took on a serious look. "That was the insurance company? Which one?"

"NatFed. I'm Mrs. Laurie Sharp." She put on a mock sad face and said in a poor imitation of a mourning wife, "My poor husband died fighting for freedom in Afghanistan." Then she smiled again and lay down against Bobby's chest.

Bobby looked away for a second. He was calculating the time from when the claim was filed to today's date. "That was quick." He looked back up at her, still serious. "It only took them a little over three weeks to process the paperwork through to the claims adjuster. When we get that check, we're going to celebrate. Who's your next husband going to be?"

"I kind of like that Wilson Brush guy. He seemed really nice and exceptionally gullible. The only thing I don't like about him is his friend. You know, you really shouldn't have brought attention to yourself at the bar. We don't need the publicity."

"Look, you do your job, I'll do mine." He had his hands on her shoulders and his grip was getting tighter. He saw the pain start to show on her face, though she didn't cry out or whine. He loosened his grip and the tension in her face relaxed. His smile finally returned as he looked up at her breasts again. "Okay, we have to get out of here until the check arrives. We can stop back in a little over a week. That should be plenty of time for the check to arrive. We can get in and out of here in a flash." He pulled her to him and again began to lightly suck on her nipples, one to another. She responded by reaching back and stroking his crotch through his blue jeans. It was the start of a very hot afternoon in Jacksonville, North Carolina.

* * *

Private Edward Eugene Sharp stood at attention in front of his unit commanding officer in a tent at the US Marine Corps makeshift base on the outskirts of Kabul, Afghanistan. He had no idea why he'd been called in from his patrol to the Colonel's tent. The tent was tan to try to match the desert floor as much as possible. The air was hot and dry and the sun beat down with no mercy. Even in the light-weight desert battle dress, the heat was oppressive. All he knew was that his squad was out doing a house to house search for some pretty bad characters and he felt like he should be there with them. His coming back to the base had left them short handed. His commanding officer was looking at a file folder when he entered the tent, saluted and stood at attention, awaiting whatever bad news he was to receive. Being summoned like this never meant good news. But the news he was about to receive was a bit beyond anything that young Private Sharp could imagine.

"Private Sharp, I have some bad news." The stern-faced Colonel paused to get the reaction of the young Marine. "You're dead."

Private Sharp remained at attention but his face contorted into a confused, twisted look. He stared at commanding officer, Colonel Larry Jenkins in utter disbelief. Why would the captain pull him from his duties to make this sick joke?

Finally, he cleared his throat and asked, "Come again, sir?"

"According to this memo, we're to forward all of your belongings to your wife in Jacksonville, North Carolina because you're dead." Colonel Jenkins got the reaction that he expected, though he was as dismayed as the young private. The communication came in via secure telex to the communications center, which was another tent a few meters to the south of the captain's tent. The radioman who'd received the message was as shocked as Sharp's Colonel and Sharp, himself. He knew Eddie Sharp well and spent the night before playing cards in the mess tent with him and half a dozen other Marines. He was quite alive. Eddie Sharp was half expecting to be reprimanded for the card game. The troops weren't supposed to gamble while in Afghanistan and young Eddie had cleaned out a couple of his buddies. He thought that word might have gotten back to the captain that he'd left a couple of his buddies without any money. This was far more serious.

Private Sharp continued his look of dismay until Captain Jenkins finally broke the silence. "I guess you're not dead, son. But we have a problem none the less. I have orders to send you back to the states while this whole thing gets straightened out. We can't have dead guys over here fighting the war for us. You need to contact your wife and family and let them know that you're alive and well. You also need to get packed because you leave at 1900 hours on a flight to Germany, then to the states. I hope to see you alive and well back here when this mess is cleared up."

"What about my squad, sir? I should be there with them. They're on a house by house search for that Ali Mousef guy. I can't leave them without finishing the mission."

"You've already been replaced, son. Your job now is to get this straightened out so you can get your mind back in the war. You're no good to your squad if your heads not in the right place. People get killed that way. Private Harris will see to your paperwork for your departure. Dismissed."

Sharp gave a crisp salute, did an about face and exited the tent. He headed for his own tent and quickly packed the few belongings that he had. Physically, he was ready to leave in less than twenty minutes. Mentally, he was on patrol with his squad, cautiously moving from door to door of the clay houses. He could clearly see the women and children's faces as they burst into a home and, without permission, searched the premises for the very dangerous Ali Mousef. *I should be out there!* He jumped when a hand touched his shoulder. He spun around and was ready to attack the person attached to the hand.

"Private Sharp, please follow me. We can head out whenever you're ready."

"I guess now's as good a time as any."

Eddie Sharp looked around the tent one last time, hoisted his pack and gun and headed out into the late day sun. The temperature was brutal. As Eddie Sharp tossed his gear into the helicopter, his thoughts were already shifting to Jacksonville, North Carolina and his sexy wife. He knew that she'd be thrilled to see him home, alive and well. Then he worried about his mother. If she heard about his death, true or not, she'd be devastated. Calling his mom would be the first order of business when he found a phone.

Chapter 14

"I don't have enough money to live on for the next three weeks! I'll be flat broke." Charlene Hall Wallace was pleading with claims adjuster, Jim Hollis, at NatFed Life Insurance Company. She was doing her best to sound distraught with fake sobs and as much dread as she could muster. "I've got to get a check as soon as possible or I'm going to have to go to a homeless shelter! I don't have anywhere to go! My parents are dead! I don't have any living relatives! My poor husband's parents are broke themselves. I can't impose on them! What am I supposed to do until I can get a job? Is this what I get for my husband giving his life for our country? I deserve better than this!"

Jim Hollis rolled his eyes as he listened to this woman who'd just lost her husband in Afghanistan. He hated these calls. Every word still tugged at his heart even though he'd heard these stories a hundred times. How can a company whose bottom line grows every day be so heartless to these poor souls who need a tiny fraction of this money just to live? When he was first promoted to the position of claims adjuster, he would get sick to his stomach when he received pleading calls like this. Over the years he'd become hardened to them, but he still couldn't understand why NatFed drug their feet on claims that were a slam dunk as this one appeared to be. This woman's husband had been killed on active duty in the Army hunting terrorists in a foreign country. How could they delay payment if they had a valid claim? All the paperwork was in order and signed by the appropriate military authorities. The claim had reached his desk because it had passed through the screening process. He was the last person besides his section Manager who had to review the paperwork before a check was cut for $100,000. That seemed like a lot of money to many folks but to a company with a book value of nearly $5 billion, it wasn't even a blip on the radar screen.

He thought about the consequences of approving this claim without the usual stalling of five to six weeks in which the claim was passed to a temporary storage area for no purpose but to stall the payout. More money left in the investment portfolio, the more profit the company posted per share. 'Remember, that money is also used to fund the profit sharing plan.' At least that's what the company executives told them. Jim Hollis laughed to himself as he looked around his cubicle at the clutter that he'd allowed to build up over the years. As he half listened to Charlene Wallace continue to cry about the dire straights that she was in, he looked at the dust balls building up between his desktop computer and the ancient monitor to which it was attached. *If only I didn't have all that alimony to pay, I could tell this company to stick this job up their collective asses and walk out of here. How many more years can I stand this before I die of a heart attack from stress?* He snapped back to reality when Mrs. Wallace asked, "Are you even listening to me?"

"Yes ma'am. I am and I understand that you are in a tough situation. I also am sorry for your loss. It's because of brave men like your husband that we're able to live in a free country." The standard company line came out so smoothly that he surprised himself.

"Are you trying to play me, Mr. Hollis? If you are, I am going to have you and your supervisor for lunch." She started to yell at Jim Hollis in a voice that was free from mourning and sorrow and full of venom. At that moment, he thought he recognized the voice, but he couldn't place it. Just as quickly as her attitude changed to anger, it changed back to a sorrowful wife. "Please, Mr. Hollis, help me through this tragedy. You can do it. I know you can."

Jim Hollis finally said, "Fine Mrs. Wallace. The check will be mailed out to you by the end of the day tomorrow. You should expect to have it within 5 working days." He could hear Charlene Wallace almost giggle over the phone. He thought that was very odd. This woman's mood changed almost instantaneously. In the span of 5 minutes she changed from a grieving wife to an angry, aggressive . . . what . . . bitch, to a whimpering, sorrowful widow to a giggling teenager. *Should I report this?* Then it hit him. It can't be. Could this be the same woman from the other day; what was her name? He couldn't place the name but he remembered having a similar reaction to his approval of her claim; almost giddy. But how could it be the same woman? "Mrs. Wallace, I have to verify your address and a few other facts and we'll be all set here."

It took Jim Hollis exactly 2 minutes and 15 seconds to complete the final verification of data on the claim. He wished Charlene Wallace well and again offered his condolences for her loss, to which she replied a cheery, "Great." Jim was once again in a real quandary. Should he report this woman's behavior to his boss or should he process the claim and move on. He looked at the stack of files in his in basket and shook his head. Then he thought about his two ex-wives and his current, demanding wife. He needed the job, the money, the retirement someday and the time away from the women who were feeding on him. What he didn't need was the stress of situations like this. Once again, Jim Hollis applied the appropriate signatures in the approval blocks of the various forms and placed the file in his outbox. He placed an express sticker on the outside of the folder which might net him a trip to his boss' office to explain why the situation warranted express processing. He already had his book full of reasons to choose from in cases like these. He shook his head, stood up, picked up his highly-stained cream-colored coffee cup with the NatFed company logo and headed for the coffee. He needed a break from his files, even if only for five minutes.

* * *

Charlene Wallace, aka Laurie Sharp, aka Rebecca Lippert was already thinking about what she was going to buy with her 'dead' husband's settlement. A new car would be nice. The clunker Toyota that she and Bobby were driving around was on its last leg. It appeared to be ready to break down any time they started the poor thing. She thought that a Cadillac would be nice. She wanted one of those smaller, sporty jobs with heated, leather seats. If they kept scoring payouts like the one they were about to get, they could get matching Caddies. That would be cool. She heard the door to the apartment shut, snapping her out of her daydream.

"Becky?" Bobby's voice boomed down the hall from the living room into the bedroom where she lay on the bed wearing nothing but a long nightshirt and a wicked smile. The bedspread was off the end of the bed on the floor. One pillow was on the floor by an old nightstand, the other was at the foot of the bed. Becky lay flat on her back on the sheets.

"In here, Babe. I've got great news. It's really kind of sad. I'm a widow again and poor Private Wallace, rest his soul, won't be seeing his new bride anymore. The insurance company is putting a rush on payment of his life insurance." The look on Bobby's face turned from a cold stare to an evil smile.

"I don't know how you do it but I'm glad you're on my side you nasty little bitch. You deserve a spanking."

"Oh, please Mr. Garrett, don't hurt me too bad," Becky said faking a fearful look.

"I can't believe this. You haven't even gotten over your last husband, Private Sharp. Hell that was just a few days ago, now Private Wallace? You should get an officer next time. I think you get a bigger payout."

"We don't need bigger payouts as long as we can keep playing these suckers. Sweetie, we're going to be rich in no time at all. You just keep that paperwork moving and we'll be fine. By the way, we need to head back down to Georgia. My next husband is waiting."

Bobby's grin grew wider. "You mean that Wilson Brush? You should have him at the altar in a couple of weeks. We have to watch out for his friend. I don't trust him." Bobby looked around the apartment at the mess. Dirty clothes were strewn around the bedroom and the bathroom was a mess. Wet towels were thrown on the floor and hair covered the sink. The apartment was cheap and trashy. The old bathroom fixtures were rusted in spots and the chrome on the faucet handles was worn off and rough, showing the brass foundation underneath. The porcelain of the sink was stained brown from years of drips from the iron deposits in the water. The more clutter and filth Bobby saw, the angrier he became. He needed an outlet for his anger and he turned towards Becky.

"Becky, what have you been doing all day? Why is this place such a damn mess?"

Becky knew that Bobby was getting tense. She had to do something quickly to settle him down. They were on the verge of their largest payoff yet and he couldn't relax. He had a short fuse and Becky still hadn't figured out what triggers set him off.

"I'm going to clean up and do the laundry right after I take good care of my man. So you just come over here and lay down on the bed and I'll give you the best back rub of your life, if you know what I mean. Come on Sweetie." She looked at him with the most seductive eyes then slowly leaned back on her elbows. The move effectively lifted the long bed shirt that she wore to expose her neatly trimmed pubic hair. Bobby was taking notice. His eyes stared right between Becky's legs, then up to her breasts which were barely hidden by the thin material of the night shirt. Her nipples were erect and this made her pose all the more sensual. Bobby slowly raised the tee shirt over his head, kicked off his shoes, and moved closer to the bed. He quickly reached out and grabbed Becky's ankles and pulled her to the side of the bed and rolled her over onto her stomach. This effectively put her legs over the edge of the bed and had her rear end fully exposed. He grabbed Becky's wrists and roughly pulled them behind her back, pinning them to her lower back with one hand. With his right hand he gave her right butt cheek a crisp smack. She gave out a yelp at the stinging. Bobby gave her three more swats in quick succession. Each slap on her butt was met with a high pitched "ouch" from Becky.

"So, you've been bad. You haven't cleaned up the apartment since we've been here. You sit around doing what, watching TV, listening to the stereo? Are you calling guys on the phone talking dirty to them?" He gave her another swat on the butt. He was getting aroused now at the rough play. He moved his hand down the crack of her butt and stopped to feel the moist spot between her legs. "So you like your punishment? You're gonna like it a lot more, too. Turn around here and get my pants off." He released her and she moved off of the bed on to her knees in front of him. She knew what was coming next. She'd played out this scene before. If this was punishment, then she liked being bad. She was very good at being very bad.

* * *

When Becky woke from her sleep, it was nearly 9:00 PM. Her rear end hurt where Bobby had spanked her repeatedly for one made up reason or another. It was a real afternoon to remember. Their sex was always remarkable and she wondered where he'd learned all of his tricks. She was no rookie either. She knew a few tricks of her own. But when she teamed up with Bobby, he taught her the things that men like and how they like it, which only made her wickedness even more dangerous. She noticed that he was becoming more and more physical and that was starting to worry her.

But she was experienced and she knew that she could get back at him easily if she had to. She sat up in bed and looked down at Bobby who was still sleeping soundly. She knew he would sleep for several more hours. They had to plan their next move when he did wake but there was no hurry. They had to get to the apartment of one Private Wallace and pick up their check. That shouldn't be too tough. The check should be in the mail, as they say. Then they would make the trip down to King's Bay, Georgia and seduce her new husband, Petty Officer Wilson Brush. That would be a bit tricky since Petty Officer Brush had a deployment date in two and a half weeks. They had to work fast if she planned to have him in a wedding chapel before then. *Plenty of time as long as Bobby doesn't bruise my ass. It's going to be hard to convince any man to marry me if I have hand prints all over my ass. I'll have to let Bobby know that the fun and games are going to have to be more controlled for a while.* She heard Bobby stir and kept an eye on him. *I wonder if I should go it alone? Bobby's becoming real possessive. That could be a problem. Besides, if we get these payoffs, maybe I could take my cut and his . . . hmmm. Food for thought.* Becky rose from the bed and walked into the living room. She was naked and felt the cool draft from the ceiling fan in the middle of the room. She walked over to the sliding glass door that led out onto the deck. She walked out onto the deck and surveyed the area below their apartment. It was a wooded area for about 120 feet before the other row of apartment buildings rose from the ground. It was a very dark night and it took her eyes a bit to adjust to the darkness. After a few minutes standing at the rail she could make out different objects in the wooded area. There was an abandoned bicycle and the animal shapes of the kiddy rides in the small park between the buildings. Movement from the kiddy park caught her eye and she thought that she saw a person move away from her apartment towards the buildings on the other side of the complex. She strained her eyes as she followed the figure. It was a woman, or so she thought. But what was she doing down there in the dark? She continued to watch the woman as she disappeared between two buildings. *That was odd. She's taking a hell of a chance down there, alone in the dark. This isn't the best neighborhood in Jacksonville, North Carolina.*

The breeze picked up and she felt a chill. She smiled to herself as she brushed her hands across her nipples then moved her smooth hands across her flat belly, touching her own skin lightly, causing goose bumps. She turned and headed back into the apartment and headed to the kitchen for a cup of coffee. When Bobby awoke, there were plans to be made.

* * *

When she reached the shelter of the two buildings she stopped and turned to look back up at the balcony of Bobby and Becky's apartment. She was pissed. *That little bitch stole from me and she is going to pay. It may not be real soon but it would be, just as sure as the sun comes up in the morning. The little bitch will pay. She thinks she can outsmart her own flesh and blood. She's got a real hard lesson coming, and not the kind of lesson that she's getting from Bobby. There won't be any pleasure mixed with this pain. I should really be pissed at Bobby, though. He's the one who started all this. He left me for a younger version of me. We'll see who has the last laugh.*

Chapter 15

It was just after 7:00 in the morning at the Warrior Inn; Nancy and Joe's first full day in North Dakota ahead of them. They were just finishing a breakfast of scrambled eggs, bacon, coffee and orange juice. They were thinking about the course of action for the day as the sun was just beginning to light up the eastern sky. Talk was sparse as their minds worked overtime. Independently they thought through a number of possible scenarios for the death of a young Tech Sergeant. They both had questions formulating about why the local Air Force Office of Special Investigations didn't cooperate with law enforcement at the City of Grand Forks. They hoped the answer would surface during interviews later that day. Joe knew that they would have to compare thoughts soon.

Nancy was an intensely focused person, much like Joe. She liked to keep things to herself until she had a plausible theory but she knew that she couldn't solve the case on her own. Major Hartnett told her that Joe McKinney was brought into this case because he had specific skills that she should use. He was good at analyzing complex situations and directing the right course of action, particularly during field operations. She remembered the Major saying, *"You listen to the Sergeant. You're his superior officer but you can learn a lot from him."* Nancy took that as an order but also as a challenge. She wanted to prove to Major Hartnett that she was more capable than Sergeant McKinney in the field. Since Major Hartnett and Griggs thought so highly of Sergeant McKinney, they'd be very impressed if she could prove more valuable than him.

After the long silence Nancy said, "This is how we're going to proceed. We start with the detectives at Grand Forks, get a look at the house where Staff Sergeant Reardon was found, then talk with the neighbors. In the mean time, we'll have Major Hull line up the Air Force Office of Special Investigation people for immediately after lunch and we can grill them. I can't believe that they dropped the ball on this." Nancy Brown was already headed down the path that there was negligence on the part of the AFOSI. She figured that there wasn't a whole lot of action for a group like that here at Grand Forks Air Force Base. What would they ever need to investigate? There's nothing on the base or around the base perimeter. The major attraction to this base had been removed some time ago as part of the Strategic Arms Reduction Treaty. The missile silos to the west of the base that previously held a major part of the United States land launched nuclear strike capability was less than one mile from the base perimeter. The missiles had been removed and the silos imploded. There was only one silo remaining and that one was slated to become a museum, *a stark reminder of a more dangerous time*, the official press release said. There was little this base had to offer as a threat for terrorist activities or internal plots. The most likely targets here were the fuel storage tanks used to load the tankers that were used during in-air refueling of fighter jets and cargo planes.

They stood and headed to the cashier. Joe said, "Airman Goff offered to drive us but I told him that wouldn't be necessary. I did tell him to be at the end of a phone so we could reach him if we needed anything.

Nancy replied, "We probably won't use him much except for errands. But we have to go by Headquarters building. Major Hull called my room early last evening and said Colonel Milton, the base commander wanted to talk with us."

Joe raised an eyebrow and gave Nancy a quizzical look. He thought *Is that normal?*

Joe and Nancy were heading into the front door of the administration building when Major Hull and a tall, slender, gray-haired, clean shaved man in an Air Force uniform approached. By Joe's estimation, he was about 6'6" tall and weighed about 200 pounds, give or take five pounds. He had light gray eyes and a squared chin, not unlike Joe's. But this man's chin lacked the distinctive dimple in the center. His gate was crisp for a man that appeared to be in his late 40's and it didn't look like he had an ounce of fat on his body. He spoke with a deep, booming voice. "Good morning, Captain Brown, Sergeant McKinney. I'm Colonel Milton Chester. I'm the commanding officer here."

Nancy spoke first. "Yes, sir. I recognized you from the picture in the building's entry." She stopped and waited for Colonel Chester to continue.

The Colonel continued, "I have instructed my staff to be cooperative with your investigation. If you run into any problems with any personnel on the base, you let me know personally. Major Hull has the authority to get you anything that you need. She also has the authority to summon anyone you need to question on a moment's notice unless they are involved in active operations. I do not anticipate that you will have any difficulty getting the information you need to bring your investigation to a quick conclusion. Do you need anything from me at this time?"

Nancy turned to Joe for a brief second, then turned to the Colonel and said in a firm voice, "No sir, not at this time. But we will need to question you at your earliest convenience."

This took the Colonel by surprise, based on the slight change in his demeanor. His right eyebrow rose slightly and he said in a very direct voice with no emotion, "See Major Hull and get on my calendar. I have a busy schedule tomorrow but I will make time. Is there anything that I need to worry about, Captain?" His face remained emotionless except the slightest upturn of his lips, almost a smirk, but not quite. Colonel Chester was a no-

nonsense officer. He wasn't about to let a female Captain get the best of him.

"No sir. We're here to gather facts about civilians taking advantage of military personnel who are deployed overseas or at sea. We're not on a witch hunt. But if there are any witches to be found, Sergeant McKinney and I will find them."

"I'm sure you will, Captain. Carry on." The Colonel turned abruptly and headed for his office where he would undoubtedly tell Major Hull to keep a close eye on the investigation and move it along at lightning speed if possible. Joe watched the colonel depart their company even as he and Nancy Brown headed out of the main entrance of the Grand Forks Air Force Base Headquarters Building.

The sun was bright and the air was dry but the cold was still there and the breeze was ever present. They headed for the Mercury Marquis parked in the nearest visitor space to the administration building entrance. Joe headed for the passenger side when Nancy pulled rank and tossed him the keys. "You drive, I'll navigate."

"Yes, Ma'am; I mean Captain." He smiled, and she gave a slight smile back. "Grand Forks Police Department?"

Nancy was buckled in her seat and Joe started the car and headed out towards the base entrance. "Yep. We have a meeting with two detectives, William Banks and Reid Hansen. They were the lead detectives on the case. When Major Hartnett called here from Camp Lejeune, he spoke with Detective Banks. According to Hartnett, they were real anxious to have any military assistance that they could get. It was mainly because they tried to get help from the base and no one would open up. The Sergeant died in their jurisdiction so there was no need for them to turn the case over to the military. And from the sound of it, the military just wanted to declare it a suicide and be done with it." She opened the manila folder that contained the case file on Air Force Tech Sergeant Kevin Reardon, now deceased. She started to leaf through the details of his death. She also read through the information on his widow. She was glad that she brought sunglasses because the glare from the low trajectory of the sun was a problem. At 7:45 in the morning the eastern sun was just over the horizon.

"You know, if this isn't a suicide, someone tried to make it look that way. From everything that I read in that folder, it sounds like a case of a lovesick military man coming home to an empty home. But if everyone thought he was already supposed to be dead, why would they kill him and why make it look like a suicide? If these are the same two that scammed the other soldiers in that stack of folders, then there are more Kevin Reardon's out there. Do we have forensics reports yet?"

"Banks and Hansen said that they would have that when we arrived at the police station. There was one thing they found that was odd. A pen was found outside the back door of the house. It had blood on the tip."

They rode in silence for the next ten minutes. Nancy reviewed every detail of the case file while Joe looked at the countryside. North Dakota was a flat baron looking land this time of year. Planting of some of the fields occurred before the winter snows and the seedlings had just started to break through the soil. The land looked light brown to gray. It was as dreary looking as the case that they were investigating.

Joe thought about Lisa. He missed her terribly. He wished he could be there for her but duty had called and he had answered. *It will work out*, he told himself. He thought about how devastated her mother must be feeling. What a tragedy to lose a life long partner at such a relatively young age; only fifty-four years old.

Then he thought about his mother. What would she do now? She lost one son to suicide and now her husband was in the hospital knocking on heaven's door; all this in a few short months. How would she deal with this crisis? Joe was glad that Pat was there for their parents. It would have crushed him to leave them all alone to deal with the crisis. Joe knew that his dad wouldn't follow doctor's orders but with Pat able to help her, she might be able to keep her husband under control, at least until he was healthy enough to take care of himself again. He was a pretty hard-headed guy when he wanted to be.

As they approached the city of Grand Forks on US Route 2 from the west, Nancy told Joe to take a right on 5th Avenue. He drove for a dozen city blocks until the station was in site. He pulled into a visitor's space, killed the engine and turned to Nancy. "Our main objective is to get as much information as we can about the widow and her brother. Anything else we should concentrate on or is there anything that we should try to avoid?"

Nancy thought for a moment as she gathered the folders and placed them into her brief case. "We really should try to stay open minded about how he died. I don't want to assume that he committed suicide before we see the evidence. I don't want to rule out anything but everything has to help lead us to the widow or her accomplice. I also don't want to assume that the man that she was with is her brother. That's just what she told everyone. If she's the lying cheat that we think she is, then we can't count on anything that she's said as being the truth." She took a deep breath then turned to Joe again. "Are you ready?"

"Yes Ma'am." She narrowed her eyes at Joe and waited for him to change his response.

". . . I mean, Captain."

They entered the Grand Forks Police Station building through a set of double glass doors and were about to ask the desk sergeant where they could find Detectives Banks and Hansen when two men in dress shirts and ties approached. Both were in their mid to late forties and both had close cropped hair. One was muscular and had a light complexion and blond hair.

The other was also large but not as physical looking as the blond. "Captain Brown and Sergeant McKinney I presume." Nancy and Joe nodded and extended their hands in greeting. Bill Banks and Reid Hansen introduced themselves and led them to the detective bureau. They led Nancy and Joe to a conference room where a timeline had been established. They noticed that the timeline was pretty scant on details but they'd obviously put some time into gathering as many facts as they could.

Joe spoke up and said, "I think that we're going to add some detail to your timeline but there are a few things that we'd like to talk through first."

Joe and Nancy proceeded to talk about the various cases that they were investigating that had similarities to the Reardon case. As they talked, Reid filled in the board with relevant details about the previous cases where soldiers were abandoned by their supposedly faithful wives. As the timeline filled in prior to the Reardon case, it became apparent that the cases didn't overlap. On the contrary, the cases seemed to be in series. One case would end, there would be a five to six week period of no activity, then another case would start. In all, there were six such cases just prior to the Reardon case. If the pattern continued, they could count on at least two more cases turning up in the next few weeks. Joe was certain the young woman was already busy with her next victim.

"The differences in the Reardon case from the others is that this is the farthest north that this has occurred and none of the other cases resulted in a death. Are we certain that the death is a suicide?" Joe's question was met with a frown by both detectives.

"Actually, we just got the coroner's final report on that today. It surprised us because we were working under the assumption that it was a suicide. But the coroner told us that it wasn't."

"That surprises us but why did it surprise you?" Nancy's question appeared to be directed at the timeline rather than the detectives.

"The position of the body, the debris field from his head wound and the fact that he had the gun in his hand when the body was found made it look like a suicide. It looked pretty straight forward." At the end of the board were several 4" X 6" crime scene photos of Sergeant Reardon's body. "But take a look here," Bill Banks pointed to one photo of the right side of the sergeant's head where he entry wound could easily be seen. "The bullet entered here, just behind his right ear. That didn't seem odd to us at the time until the coroner explained that Reardon had a rotator cuff problem. That's why he'd come home from his tour early. He'd had an operation in Germany when he was injured playing softball, of all things. The coroner saw the scar and looked at his records. Fact is he'd have had one hell of a time raising the 9mm to his head, especially at that angle."

Nancy looked quizzically at the detective. "What do you mean 'especially at that angle?'"

Bill continued and used himself as the example. "If I were to commit suicide, I'd raise the gun to my temple in the vicinity of my ear towards the front side of my head, like this." He placed his finger directly in front of his right ear as if pointing a gun to his head. "As you can see, if you look closely, the angle of the gun, it's slightly towards the back left side of my head. The exit wound would be behind my left ear. As you can see, the entry wound is behind the sergeant's right ear, meaning that he would have had to place the gun at an angle like this." The angle of his hand making the fake pistol was at an awkward angle. Banks continued. "At this angle, it would have been difficult for a person without a shoulder injury to aim the gun at themselves. With the sergeant's injury it would be nearly impossible."

Joe and Nancy both looked at the pictures of the head wound and had to agree with Bank's and Hansen's assessment. Joe asked, "Could he have been on pain medication, enough so that he could have raised the gun to his head and done this on his own?"

"No. We asked Dr. Rice, the coroner, about that. It wasn't physically possible for him to raise that gun with the extent of his shoulder damage. Even with pain medication it was still very painful for him to move that arm much at all. In addition to the injury and the angle of the shot, there was a shadow effect on the gunshot residue on his hands and wrist. So his hand was in close proximity to the gun when fired, say within a foot or two, but the pattern of residue is not consistent with a person who fired a gun. Whoever shot him did so at close range, nearly point blank."

Both Joe and Nancy raised their eyebrows at this. Their minds were working overtime trying to analyze this new piece of information. Joe asked, "Did any of the neighbors see his widow or her brother on the day of the shooting?"

Reid Hansen spoke up, "No. His wife and her brother, if that's who he is, had already left town a week before. They hadn't been seen since the day they packed up and left, supposedly for Pensacola, Florida. We suspect that they didn't really go there. We checked with the local police and county sheriff but they haven't had any reports of them or their car anywhere in the county down there."

"Did anyone see anyone who was out of place? I would think that it would be easy to spot someone who didn't belong around here. This is a pretty small town by most standards. People in close knit neighborhoods tend to notice when anything unusual happens." After Nancy said this, she realized that she was making a pretty broad generalization that maybe these guys wouldn't appreciate. "What I mean is . . ."

"Captain, you don't have to apologize." It was Reid Hansen who spoke. "We realize that Grand Forks isn't New York City or even Charlotte, North Carolina, but it isn't quite as small as you might think. We did question the neighbors about all this. The only activity around the house the day Sergeant Reardon was killed was the electric company read the meter and the cable company pulled the cable box from the house. That was the one thing that was just a bit out of the ordinary because a cable company serviceman came back two days later and was surprised that the cable had already been removed. He guessed that the previous service man had done the work but forgot to turn in his log sheets. That's what the lovely Lillian Weickoff had said."

The group gave Reid a questioning look.

"Lillian was the next door neighbor to the Reardon's. She spoke with the second cable guy when she saw him pull up. She thought it odd that the cable company would come out a second time and she started up a conversation with him."

"Did you guys follow up with the cable company?" Joe was leafing through one of their reports on the Reardon case as he asked the question.

"Yes. The story was different than what the second serviceman said. There was no job order for the Reardon house on the day Kevin Reardon was killed."

That brought a quizzical look from Nancy Brown. Joe just kept looking through the report. There were a few moments of silence while the four tried to digest the possible connection between the cable guy and the shooting. Then Joe asked, "What was the time sequence of the arrival of the cable guy in relation to when Kevin Reardon showed up.?"

Bill Banks fielded this question. "The cable guy was there about an hour before Sergeant Reardon. He was already gone at least 45 minutes by our estimation, when Reardon showed up. We've tried to locate this guy but by the description that we gave the cable company, only one guy comes close to the description given by Lillie Weickoff and it isn't that close. Plus the guy was across town at another call at the time the neighbors heard the shot."

Nancy asked, "Can we go to the house now? I'd like to see the . . . I guess it's a crime scene now, right? Is it still sealed off?"

"Yep," both Reid and Bill answered in unison as they nodded their heads. Bill went on, "We're ready whenever you are. It isn't too far. Do you want to follow us or would you like to ride with us?"

"How about we split up?" Joe then suggested that Nancy ride with Bill and he would drive the rental with Reid. "That way we can talk more. Maybe something will click." They all agreed, gathered their files and other materials and headed for the parking lot.

* * *

The trip to the house took less than ten minutes even with some mid morning traffic. As they entered the house, they noticed that there was no indication of decomposition, which surprised Nancy and Joe.

"Why no decomp odor?" Joe asked as he moved around the empty house. "I would have thought the closed up house would still smell bad."

"The heat had been off for a week or so before Sergeant Reardon was killed. It was like a meat locker in here and he wasn't dead that long before we were here on the scene, maybe twenty-five minutes. We'd have been here sooner but the neighbors were a little slow to call the station after they heard the shot. They didn't know what it was at first. The house was empty and so the shot didn't sound like you'd expect. The closed up doors and windows acted as kind of a silencer of sorts to anyone outside the house."

The debris field, the contents of Kevin Reardon's head, had been cleaned up and treated with an odorless antibacterial soap. There were still areas of stain on the tiles but there was little else to look at in the house. It wasn't as cold and empty as when Reid Hansen and Bill Banks had seen it on the day of the shooting but there was still a chill on this late April morning.

Nancy asked, "Was the gun Sergeant Reardon's?"

Reid answered, "No. We're still tracking that down. It was definitely not his though. The serial number is still intact so we should be able to trace it. I expect that we'll have that information possibly as soon as this afternoon."

The rest of their time at the house was spent reenacting the shooting and going through possible scenarios on how a shooter could get into the house, shoot Sergeant Reardon and get out without any of the neighbors seeing anything. They even tried to simulate the cable guy coming back in, shooting Sergeant Reardon, and leaving through the back door to the alley. None of the scenarios appeared to spark a lot of enthusiasm. Even worse, Nancy and Joe thought that they were going to concentrate on the widow and her brother taking advantage of the sergeant. Now they were looking at a full fledged murder investigation. They took one last look through the house, talked to Hansen and Banks about specifics of the case then headed back to the base to set up interviews with base personnel who knew Sergeant Reardon. It was going to be a long day.

* * *

They talked about the case on the twenty minute drive back to the base. It sure had taken a wrong turn. They had no experience in homicide investigations and now they were dealing with a possible murderer instead of a deadbeat wife trying to screw a gullible young soldier. They had to report this new twist to Majors Hartnett and Griggs. Maybe they needed new faces on the case, someone from the JAG office at Camp Lejeune or someone more local to Grand Forks. Nancy wondered aloud if they should be considering a consultant or a reputable private investigator. Joe thought of Johnny Poleirmo, a detective with the Orange County, Florida Sheriff's Department. Johnny had helped Pat and Joe with a problem that they had in Florida just months earlier. He was bright and he had a background in homicide but he was currently working in vice. Joe wasn't sure that he'd be available to assist. *It's worth a shot*, Joe thought as he made his way to his temporary office.   He closed the door behind him, walked to his desk, immediately picked up the phone and dialed his brother, Pat's number. Diane picked up the kitchen phone on the second ring.

"McKinney's."

"This is Sergeant Joe McKinney, Ma'am."   Joe smiled as he listened to Diane's reply.

"What can I do for you, you dork?   How in the heck did you get roped into another hitch in the Marines?"

"Just serving my country, Ma'am.   Has dad caused the nurses to strangle him yet?"   He chuckled at his little joke.   "All kidding aside, how's he doing?"

Diane smiled at Joe's remark.   They both knew how difficult a patient Joe and Pat's dad could be.   Fortunately, he was being pretty low key so far. The heart attack had really taken a toll on his body and his mind.   "Believe it or not, he's been pretty calm so far.   Maybe it's the drugs.   When they wear off, look out.   Pat's right here if you want to talk with him."

"Great.   Thanks Diane."   Joe heard a muffled, *It's your brother* as she handed the phone over to Pat.

"Hey Sergeant Dickhead.   Where in hell are you now or is it top secret, code red stuff, whatever the hell that means?"

"Very funny.   A million comics out of work and they're all funnier than you.   I called because I have a serious question for you.   First, I am supposed to be investigating some people taking advantage of soldiers and sailors who are deployed overseas or at sea.   What has been happening is that these young kids are meeting a young hotty and marrying her in a rather quick ceremony before they get deployed.   When they get back from their deployment, their dearly beloved has cleaned them out and skipped town with their money and belongings, or sold them to the nearest pawn shop or flea market dealer that they can find."

Pat said, "That sucks and that's pretty nasty but it's not unheard of.   I ran into that a couple of times when we came back from a patrol on the sub. My shipmates tracked down their spouses and it was usually a young girl who'd been overwhelmed by living away from home.   It all worked out, usually.   What's the big deal here?"

Joe replied, "These cases are a lot more than that.   It appears that we may have a repeat offender, multiple times.   The cases that we're looking at have the same pattern to them and they're happening in succession.   The description of the woman involved is not identical, but very similar.   The problem is that our last victim wound up dead in his empty house."   At the other end of the phone in Dunnellon, Florida, Pat's forehead wrinkled and his face turned a light shade of red.   He was still a Navy man at heart.   He hated to hear of a soldier or sailor dying, especially when it sounded so senseless.   Joe continued, "The kicker is, at first glance, it appeared to be a suicide. Now we know it was murder. He was shot in the head at point blank range." This made the red on Pat's face turn a much darker shade, and he started to grit his teeth. Across the kitchen, Diane was watching with interest as she could see Pat's anger rising, even though there were no other outward signs other than his facial expression.

"Do you have a plan of attack yet?" Pat was getting very interested in this case as he and Joe continued to discuss details.

"We did until the local cops dropped this 'murder' bomb on us. The reason for my call is to see if we can talk to Johnny Poleirmo about this. He's got some background in homicide, right?"

Pat thought for a moment. He did remember that Johnny had been a homicide detective for a stretch before his vice squad assignment. He was a great detective and would probably have some good advice for Joe and . . . who did he say? "Hey Joe, who are you working with? Do you have a partner?"

"Yep. A Captain from the JAG office at Camp Lejeune. She doesn't have any background in homicide though. We're trying to . . ."

"Wait. Stop. Hold on. *She?* Your partner is a female? Oh boy, are you in trouble. Does Lisa know?"

"No and now is no time to tell her. I didn't have a chance to tell you but her dad passed away yesterday. Her mom is devastated. His funeral is tomorrow and Lisa is going to stay in Ohio for at least a couple of weeks. She wants to make sure her mom's emotionally stable. She said her brother couldn't even take the time to see his dad in his dying hours. He was too busy," Joe said with disgust and a fair amount of contempt. "He'll be real lucky if we never meet. I'm ready to kick his ass 'til his nose bleeds, the punk-assed creep. Back to business or I'll be pissing myself off thinking about him. Can you have Johnny Poleirmo call me at this number?" Joe gave his office number to Pat. They exchanged a few more comments about their dad's health and Lisa's dad's passing. Pat wished Joe luck with the investigation and hoped that it would go quickly. He also told Joe to be over-supportive of Lisa. Joe replied that he would and they disconnected.

Half an hour later, Johnny Poleirmo called Joe and immediately said how sorry he was for the streak of bad luck that had befallen the McKinneys and their friends. He'd met Lisa at Pat and Diane's a few months earlier and was really impressed with her beauty and brains. "You take good care of her," Johnny told Joe before they got down to business.

As Joe sat in his office chair with the file open in front of him on the desk he told Johnny all the details of the horrible death of Sergeant Reardon. He described the forensics and the angle of the bullet. He also went over the house layout and how the neighbors heard the shot and called the police almost immediately. He described Belinda Reardon and her brother. Finally, he described the general nature of the other cases that appeared to have the same characteristics as the Reardon case and how they seemed to line up, one after another.

"Joe, where did the other robbery cases take place?"

"Most of them were in North Carolina, Virginia, and Georgia. All of them were in close vicinity of a military base. A couple of the cases were near submarine bases and happened while the sailor was at sea. The others were with either Army or Marine soldiers. All the cases involved young men in their late teens or early twenties." Joe waited while Johnny digested the information.

"Any idea why they would all of a sudden pack up and head from a warm weather area to damn near the North Pole?"

Joe thought about that for a minute. He couldn't even hazard a guess why anyone would voluntarily be here in North Dakota especially after spending a lot of time in the mid south. He was sure that if he hadn't been ordered to come here, he'd be in Florida or maybe Ohio right now. "Maybe they needed a change of scenery."

"Joe, a change of scenery from Florida would be the Caribbean or Hawaii. I think that these two were running from something, or maybe your Sergeant Reardon was transferred to Grand Forks and they had to follow him there to finish the scam. I'm sure they didn't go there because of the choice of military personnel awaiting deployment overseas. They probably followed your guy up there for a specific reason." Johnny and Joe were silent for a moment trying to piece this possibility into the equation.

"You said that the house was freezing cold and that the neighbors heard 'the' gunshot. Are they sure it was a gunshot or could it have been some other noise like a gunshot? In other words, maybe the phony cable guy that was in earlier did the killing and left. Then the neighbors heard a car backfire, or a trash can being knocked over, or any number of loud noises. You never know." Johnny was just trying to keep Joe from falling into the trap that just because things seem like they happened in a logical sequence doesn't mean that's how they actually happened. He'd been involved in too many cases where assumptions were made and the perpetrators got away with murder. Some detective or crime scene processing team saw things in the logical order that fit the way they thought it should fit only to find out too late that they missed key evidence. "Look Joe, what I'm going to say next is not meant to be personal, but your sister-in-law's case is a perfect example. The crime scene folks thought the case was a slam dunk when they found the video tape of her murder. They stopped processing and basically destroyed the crime scene. When the tape came up missing and they tried to recover the crime scene, it was too late. Everything was contaminated. So the best advice I can give you is to go slow and don't assume anything. Okay?"

Joe felt the pain of Julie McKinney's murder like a knife wound to the heart. It might as well have been a double murder because Mike never recovered mentally from the trauma of that day. Joe remembered it all too well. He still felt sick when he was reminded of that horrible crime.

"Point well taken, Johnny. I wish you'd have used another example but maybe this will make it more real to me."

"It's that important, Joe. Please be as thorough as possible. If you have any questions, need advice, or just need to do a sanity check on your theories, call me anytime. I mean anytime; understand?

"Thanks Johnny. I appreciate it. I'm sure Nancy will, too."

"Nancy?"

"She's my partner and the officer in charge of the investigation. I'm just hired help."

"Does Lisa know?"

"Look, I already told Pat, this isn't the time to tell Lisa anything. It's strictly business."

"Right." With that, Johnny and Joe said their goodbyes and disconnected.

Joe thought back on their conversation. *What if the time of death was much earlier than thought? Maybe our first cable guy was involved. Maybe he had help. Maybe he was Belinda's 'brother.' Maybe . . . Maybe . . . Maybe. Too many 'maybes' for one case.* Joe looked up at the standard military issue office clock. It was nearly time for the AFOSI interviews to start and he hadn't had lunch yet. He wondered if Nancy had thought about lunch. *Probably not.* She was on a mission. Ever since it was determined to be a murder, she was more focused than ever. Joe got up and crossed the central office to Nancy's office. She was combing through the case files with a concentration so intense that she didn't hear him walk into her office.

"Excuse me, Captain." She jumped as if startled. "Sorry. I didn't mean to interrupt you but did you want to break for lunch before we interview the AFOSI people?"

"I ordered in. Airman Goff is on his way to get it. I hope you like Chinese."

"That'll be fine." He hated Chinese.

Chapter 16

"This fucking phone isn't working. Nothing in this God-forsaken country works. The damn thing keeps telling me my phone is disconnected. That can't be right." David Wallace was pissed. He'd dialed the number a half dozen times and got the same response; a recorded voice that said his home phone was disconnected. His young wife, Charlene, should be home right now. He looked out the open tent at the dessert beyond. All he could see was light brown sand and heat waves.

"Hey Dave, you got a line waiting for that phone. Can't you speed it up some? If you can't get through, then try a different number. Maybe she went home to her folk's house or something. Are you sure you left enough money for her to pay he phone bill?"

"Not funny and you can wait in line all day for all I care, you prick." David Wallace had just one hour before he had to be back on patrol with his unit. They were scheduled to take over for another Marine unit that had been in a house to house search for insurgent fighters in central Kabul, Afghanistan. They'd been at it for hours and were in desperate need of a break. The physical search was tough in full military dessert fatigues in the 110 plus degree heat, but the tension of going from one clay house to another and confronting families in their homes took its toll. The young soldiers were exhausted. They needed to get out of the heat, out of their uniforms and into a shaded area. David Wallace knew that this task was going to be rough and he was ready, except that he couldn't reach his new wife. He needed to talk to her. He knew that hearing her voice would calm his nerves. He needed the contact; to imagine her face, her hair, her body.

"Hey Dave, come on man. We have wives and parents, too, ya know."

He just gave an annoyed look over his shoulder. Finally he dialed his parent's phone number. It took a few seconds to go through the satellite connection and relay back to ground circuits in the United States, but his mother answered before the second ring was finished. In a weak, sniffling voice, his mother said, "Hello."

"Mom, is everything alright? I can't reach Charlene."

His mother's response was so loud that her voice was distorted and he had to hold the receiver back from his ear. "Mom, calm down, I can't hear you."

"Oh David, you're alive!" she exclaimed. "You're alive," she said with a tone of absolute amazement. He heard her yell away from the receiver. "Dick, David's alive! He's on the phone!"

"Mom, what's going on? Of course I'm alive." He heard more shouts from his mom to his dad. "What's going on?" he repeated.

His dad came on the line. "Dave, it's really you son?" His voice exuded genuine surprise.

"Yea, Dad. It's really me. What in the hell is going on? Would you please tell me?" He was becoming angry and confused about the reception that he'd just received.

"Well, son, the insurance company called Charlene and told her that you'd been killed in action. She said that she received an official notice of your death a few weeks ago, less than a week after you got over there. Are you hurt? Were you injured?"

Dave was even more confused now. He had seen some combat action but he hadn't been shot or injured in any way. His parent's reaction was amazing to him. How did this story get started? Why did the Marine Corps tell his wife and family that he was dead? He hadn't been able to reach his wife for well over a week now and he couldn't understand why. But where was she? Why wouldn't she be at their apartment? Did she just up and leave when she got the news? "Dad, have you heard from Charlene in the last few days?"

"No, son. She said that she was going to visit her folks. The Corps told her that they wouldn't have your remains back in the states for nearly a month. Oh my God, son. We're just so happy that you're alive. This is all a big mistake. Do you know Charlene's parent's number? We can get in touch with her and let her know the good news."

David Wallace was starting to put a few things together and he wasn't a happy guy. "Dad, I don't know her parent's phone number because her parents are supposed to be dead."

Richard Wallace's face twisted with concern then started to flush with anger. He looked at his wife and mouthed, *that little bitch!* The Wallace's didn't like Charlene from the start. They thought that she was moving a bit too fast when Dave met her about six weeks ago. They were adamant about David not rushing into this marriage. They could see trouble coming from a mile away. But David was of age and he could make his own decisions. "Dave, we'll do what we can to find her. I'm sure that it's a big mix up and that she's just off grieving, relying on friends."

"Thanks, Dad. Look, I have to go. I'll contact my Captain and see what I have to do. I'm sure that they can look into this and find out what's going on. I'll call you next chance I get. If I can, I'll get home on the next flight out of here. If not, it'll be soon, I promise. "

"Okay, son."

"Let me talk with Mom for a second."

"Here she is. Dave, I love you, son, and no matter what, we're proud of you."

David's mom got on the line. "David, you just don't know what this means to us to hear that you are alive and well. You stay safe, you hear me? I love you."

"I love you, too, Mom. I'll get home as soon as I can. Goodbye." He hung up the phone hard. The guys behind him were afraid that he would break the receiver before they had a chance to use it but they didn't complain. They could see that his call home wasn't a happy call. Whatever it was, David Wallace was pissed. His comrades knew that these calls were treasured and they were usually happy calls mixed with lots of emotion, usually feelings of joy at being able to talk with loved ones. When a call didn't go well, fellow soldiers allowed space to let the feelings settle before any words of comfort were offered. In the end, the constant need for attention to detail or the mission always snapped a Marine back to reality. That reality was that you had to pay attention to the mission or you and your partner got killed. There was no time for grieving or sulking in the field. He turned and walked directly to his Captain's tent and requested that they talk.

Captain Samson, a muscular dark-skinned black man with a 4 year degree in Mechanical Engineering looked up at Private David Wallace. One look told him that this was trouble. "Private Wallace, you look like you could chew nails and use them for bullets. What seems to be the problem?"

"Captain, apparently the government thinks that I'm dead." This caused Captain Samson's left eyebrow to rise in an exaggerated angle that made his face take on a look of disbelief. "Come again, son."

David Wallace, Private in the US Marine Corps, explained the whole telephone call fiasco to his Captain. By the end of their conversation, he was getting watery eyes, but not crying, because that wouldn't do for a Marine to cry over a woman, especially in front of his Captain. You could shed tears for a fallen comrade once the fighting was over, but not for a woman, especially one that may not have had honest intentions. Captain Samson had seen this scenario before, but not to this extreme. Usually it was just a soldier coming home from a deployment and the apartment is cleaned out or the bank account is empty and the young bride has moved back in with her parents. This was potentially much more serious. He gave Private Wallace the pep talk, told him to get his gear ready for the patrol and be mentally prepared to fight. He was a soldier first. After soldiering was done, they'd fight this new enemy together. He wasn't about to let an enemy at home defeat his soldiers while they were overseas protecting their country's interests. Anything further, Private Wallace?"

"No Sir!"

"Dismissed!"

In a crisp reply, Private David Wallace shouted, "Yes Sir!" He pivoted in a snappy about face and headed to his tent for his gear. Captain

Samson headed immediately to the command tent and asked the base commander to do some inquiring into the young bride of David Wallace. He wanted to know who was screwing with his men at a time when their heads needed to be on straight.

* * *

David's dad, Richard Wallace drove for three hours to Jacksonville, North Carolina. It was nearly three in the morning but this had to be dealt with now. His wife didn't want him to make the trip but there was no reasoning with him. Their daughter-in-law was up to no good, he was sure of it. David was off fighting a war in foreign country and couldn't stand up for himself. "He's my son. It's the least I can do," he'd told his wife as he walked out their front door in Hickory, North Carolina. There wasn't any protest from her until she saw the gun in the holster under his jacket.

"Why do you need that?" She'd asked.

"Because we don't know what kind of people we're dealing with here. You know what a little tramp she is. Who knows what kind of guys she's hooked up with?"

"I don't like this one bit. We should call the police or the FBI or something. You can't do this on your own."

He just looked back at her without a word. He had to do this alone. The reason their son was in the Marines in the first place was because he'd badgered David into joining. 'You'll never amount to anything if you keep hanging out with all your loser friends. You need to get out of Hickory.' As David always did, he drove off fired up mad at his father. This time he stormed into the Marine Recruiter's office, took the tests and signed the papers. Within three weeks, he was at Paris Island, North Carolina in basic training. At first, his parents thought that it was the best thing that could have happened to him and it was making a positive impact on his personality and decision making. He was starting to gain control over his slap-shot decisions and had an entirely different outlook on life and on his country. He'd actually said to his dad, 'This is my country. I'm proud to fight for it.'

Richard broke out of his trance when his wife said, "You're as hardheaded as your son. Do you know that?" Again, he just looked at his wife. "If I can't change your mind, you be damned careful. If you find that little hussy, slap her once for me and tell her if she ever sets foot on our land again, I'll kill her myself."

"I will."

As he drove east on Interstate 40 in his Ford Tempo, he thought back on the times he'd wished that his relationship with David had been more civil. As it was, they'd fought like cats and dogs over everything from how he talked, to how he dressed, to the friends he hung out with. When David told him that he was joining the Marine Corps, he was even critical of that decision. "Are you sure about this, son? This is a hasty decision.

Shouldn't you think this through?" As David left to catch the bus for boot camp, he turned to his dad and said, 'You can't even be proud of me for making a decision like this. I can't do anything right. You'll never be happy.'

Richard wanted to say, 'That's not it, son. It's just that I'm afraid for you. War is a dangerous business.' But in the end, he kept those thoughts to himself. Now, as he drove alone down the interstate, he wished that he hadn't been so confrontational with his son. He was proud of him and what he'd accomplished. He only wished that he wasn't so quick to make decisions without asking for advice or thinking the idea through. But that was David's personality and that's why he was headed to Jacksonville, North Carolina. Maybe he'd find that Charlene had really run out of money and the phone was off for a good reason. *Fat Chance.*

* * *

Becky Lippert and Bobby Garrett were in room 209 of the Econolodge in Jacksonville, North Carolina. It was just one half mile from the apartment of David and Charlene Wallace. They picked this hotel because it was so close and they needed to get in and out before being spotted in the morning. The mail at the apartment complex was usually delivered early, around 9:45am. By then, most people were at work. This would work well for them since they wanted to be invisible to Becky's old neighbors. They knew her as Charlene Wallace. It would not be good for them to see her with Bobby Garret looking all happy picking up the mail.

"The check should be in the mail tomorrow morning. We have to get in and out of the apartment before anyone spots you. Then we deposit a small amount in the bank and get the bulk of it in cash. Then we can get the rest using an ATM card. Then we head for Georgia and find you a new husband." Bobby Garrett was smiling from ear to ear. By noon tomorrow he was going to be a rich man. Within a week he was expecting to get another windfall and possibly a week after that, he would get the third check from the NatFed Life Insurance Company. Finally, their 'hard work' was paying off.

"Becky, do you realize that by tomorrow afternoon, we could be holding $100,000? Have you ever held that much cash? And think about this baby. By next Friday, you could be holding nearly $200,000. Does that make you wet? I am about to cream my jeans just thinking about it."

Becky knew that she better calm him down a bit or she was going to be in for a long night. When Bobby got excited, she had to endure his appetite for dominating, rough sex. She usually enjoyed the high excitement herself, but lately he was carrying things farther than she wanted to go. He could hardly hold back his excitement which translated to more and more acts that bordered on perversion. Until recently, she could take control of most situations and satisfy his needs. It was getting harder for her to maintain that control.

"Hey baby, let's talk about what we're going to do with that money." She smiled her biggest, sexiest smile. "How would you like to get a nice, new car and dump the Toyota? We could get one of those little Lincoln LSs or maybe a Cadillac CTS. Or how about a BMW? Haven't you always wanted a BMW? I hear that they are the hottest, fastest, smoothest running cars on the road. What do you say to that?"

"How big is the back seat in a BMW?" Bobby asked with a devious grin. He was still in the gutter. She had serious work to do here.

"It's big enough for the both of us. What do you say we get some rest tonight so we can get that cash and go car shopping tomorrow afternoon?" Becky was trying to get him to seriously think about something that wasn't related to sex. With her last suggestion, she thought that she was making headway.

"What color do Beamers come in?" Bobby was thinking that a jet black Beamer would fit real nice around his body. His dark hair and eyes would look great through the windshield of a BMW. His pale skin would contrast the black surfaces. Add dark black sunglasses and he would look like a movie star, he thought. "Yea. I think that I like that. Let's go car shopping tomorrow."

Becky was in control now. That was easier than she thought it would be. "Lay down, baby. I want you to relax so you can sleep tonight. We have a big day tomorrow and I want you to be fresh when we go to the bank. We have lots to get accomplished before we can get you that black Beamer."

Bobby took off his shirt and lay on the couch. Becky straddled his butt and began to rub his shoulders and back. She worked on him for about 15 minutes. Then she heard him snoring. *Mission accomplished.*

At that very moment, Richard Wallace was parking his car at the Valley Forge Apartments in front of apartment 2D. That's where his son's wife should be. The apartment was dark. Either no one was in the apartment or whoever was there was fast asleep. Richard Wallace knew that he could wait. He needed to catch a few winks before he could check out the apartment in the morning light. He thought about Charlene and how she had done his son wrong. He was going to catch her at whatever game she was playing. He looked at his watch in the faint parking lot light; 3:23 am was his last thought before he dozed off.

At 7:10 am, Richard awoke to the sound of a car door shutting close to his car. He looked around the lot and saw that people were heading off to work. A number of spaces were already empty. He must have slept through those car doors slamming and engines being started. He stretched as much as he could, his legs pushing the car's firewall behind the gas and brake peddles. He reached under the arm rest and felt the .38 caliber pistol with a fully loaded magazine. He was ready if need be. He relaxed again and watched as the complex came to life around him. He picked up the spy novel that he brought along and started to read in the 13th chapter. He chuckled to himself as the character in the book was sitting in a car in an apartment complex, waiting for a terrorist to emerge from the apartment, supposedly with a detonation device for a nuclear warhead. *I hope she isn't into nuclear warheads . . .*

After three chapters and a number of curious looks from several tenants, Richard's patience finally paid off. He crouched down in the front seat of his car as a beat up Toyota pulled up several parking spaces down from where he was parked. A tall, pale man with dark black hair got out of the driver's side and moved to the sidewalk. He looked around the parking area then nodded to someone in the passenger seat. A sandy blond-haired young lady got out and walked up next to him and said something that Richard couldn't hear. It was his daughter-in-law, Charlene. He reached under the arm rest and pulled the pistol out, checked to make sure that the safety was on and tucked the gun into his pants at the small of his back. He watched as the two made their way up the stairs to the apartment, put the key in the door, and walked in. He was about to get out of his car to follow when he noticed a police car in his rear view mirror. He took his hand off the door handle and slowly settled back into the driver's seat and waited. He watched the car move slowly past. He worried that one of the tenants had called to cops on him. *That's the last thing that I need right now.* The police car turned down the next turn in the parking lot and headed away from apartment 2D. Richard again waited until the car was out of site. He looked up and saw Charlene and her . . . what . . . lover . . . boyfriend . . . walking down the steps of the apartment, both looking at the contents of an envelope that the man held in his hand. *That's my son's mail. Why is this guy looking at my son's mail?* He again started to get out of the car. He opened the car door and put one foot on the pavement. He felt a thud hit the back, left side of his head. It was his last conscious thought. The 9mm slug tore into his head and shredded a portion of his brain. The bullet exited his right eye socket and scattered bits of brain and blood throughout the inside of his car. He slumped over bumping his head on the steering wheel causing the car horn to sound one brief honk. Bobby was briefly startled when he heard the horn. They both looked up and saw the white Tempo and the man slumped over, leaning towards the passenger side of the car.

Bobby moved in front of Becky's view so that she couldn't see the car. He saw what appeared to be blood splashed on the interior of the windshield. He quickly looked around the grounds of the apartment but no one else was within sight. He was nervous and afraid. He didn't hear a gun shot, only what sounded like a thud. He knew that he didn't have time to worry about the poor guy in the car. He and Becky had to move quickly and get out of the complex.

Without hesitation, Bobby grabbed Charlene's arm and quietly but sternly said, "Get in the car." The confused look on Becky's face made

Bobby grab her arm tighter. "Move it!" They quickly jumped into the Toyota and sped off, Bobby being careful to avoid the Tempo and not race from what was now a crime scene in more ways than one. They headed out the way that they came in and headed for east bound Interstate 40. Becky apparently didn't see the blood because she didn't say a word about it.

She asked, "Why'd we have to get out of there so fast?"

Bobby took a deep breath and said, "I got nervous when I heard that horn. That guy must have been reaching for something in his glove box and hit the horn with his elbow. I just got jumpy, that's all."

Back at the apartment complex, a burgundy colored utility van slowly pulled away from the parking spot four spaces down from where Richard Wallace's body lay in his white Ford Tempo, the gray interior now decorated with a crimson spray with some brain and bone fragments mixed in.

Chapter 17

Joe McKinney was in Nancy Brown's office at the headquarters building of Grand Forks Air Force Base. They were comparing notes from the various interviews they'd held over the last few days. There was still not much to go on in the case of the murdered Air Force Staff Sergeant. Nancy had raked the AFOSI personnel over the coals but got no information that had any impact on the case. She was angrier after those interviews than she was before they began. One member of the AFOSI commented that the Grand Forks Police Department was being uncooperative. He also said that Colonel Chester requested a quick resolution to the investigation. He found the Colonel's interest in the case odd, but figured he was up for a promotion and didn't want any waves to rock that boat.

The single most important piece of information they got was from a neighbor of Kevin and Belinda Reardon, Mrs. Lillie Weickoff. They'd interviewed most of the neighbors. The stories were like a replay of the information they read in the case files provided by Detectives Banks and Hansen. The one revelation that was new was that Mrs. Weickoff thought that she had seen Belinda Reardon a week after Belinda and her brother had packed up and moved for Florida. As she talked, all four investigators scribbled the details in their notepads. She saw the woman at the local Wal-Mart store. At first she only saw her from the back. When she approached to ask her how she had been the woman turned around. It wasn't Belinda Reardon, but this woman resembled Belinda so much that Lillie thought it might be her mother or an older sister. Joe remembered Lillie's comments; 'She turned and looked at me with a scowl, a real angry look, as if I'd insulted her. It really upset me at the time. Then I got busy and forgot about the whole incident until the other day when I was going over all this mess in my mind. I remember the date and time because I saw Colonel Chester in the Wal-Mart parking lot the same day. You almost never see him away from the base. When I say she looked like an older version of Belinda, I mean it's what I expect her to look like in about 15 years.' That conversation stuck in Joe's mind. But could there really be a connection? He and his brother Pat looked quite a bit alike. So much, in fact that they'd used it as a ploy to fool the police within the last year. Joe took Pat's place at a convention in Jacksonville, Florida and no one knows even to this day that they'd traded identities. But that seemed like a lifetime ago. He looked up to see Nancy, pen held to the right side of her mouth, looking at him, apparently wondering what was on his mind.

"So what has you in a trance?" She asked.

"Those comments from Lillie Weickoff about seeing someone that looks like Belinda, only older. It may not be significant, but we don't have much else here that's new. Anything that you see different than what was in the original case files?"

"I was just trying to think if we're any closer now than we were when we arrived. It's been almost four weeks since Kevin Reardon was found dead and we're no closer to finding his wife. We have people watching for any credit card purchases. We have the cops in the panhandle of Florida with her description. If she is the perpetrator in all these cases, chances are she's scoping out another victim as we spin our wheels in this freezing-assed state. We're losing ground here. The trail's going cold." Nancy stopped, stood and stretched.

"Do you want to take a break and get lunch? Maybe a break will clear our heads a bit and we can start from the beginning, walk through the timeline again, and see if we can fill in some of the holes." Joe looked at the table in Nancy's office that was covered from end to end with papers, pictures, and file folders. On the portable whiteboard, they had reconstructed the timeline from the Grand Forks Police Department. They pledged to keep their board in synch with the board that Detectives Banks and Hansen were keeping. Joe leaned back in his chair, rubbed his chin then asked Nancy, "What if this older woman is involved somehow?"

"Are you talking about the lady that Lillie Weickoff saw? How would she be involved? If you knew that Reardon was murdered and that you might somehow be implicated in some way, would you hang around? I don't see how she comes into play at all. I think it was just a coincidence that this woman looked like Belinda Reardon."

"You may be right," Joe said, not fully convinced. He left the subject alone for now. But he wasn't planning on forgetting Lillie Weickoff's words or her description of the feeling she had; this woman was somehow related to Belinda Reardon.

"Are you ready for that lunch?" Joe asked. Nancy was about to answer when her phone rang. She waited until the second ring and answered, "Captain Brown." A short pause followed by "Yes sir, Major Hartnett." There was another longer pause while Nancy listened to her supervisor on the phone. Her eyes widened and her face became more animated as she scribbled down a few notes. She took a separate piece of paper and scribbled a quick note then passed it to Joe. In large letters on the 8-1/2 by 11 inch paper, the note said, "Another murder, missing spouse. Jacks. NC." As best Joe could make out, there'd been another murder in a case involving a spouse who'd left her husband. "Jacks, NC' must be Jacksonville, North Carolina. He couldn't wait until Nancy got off the phone.

* * *

The fax machine pumped out the report so slowly that Joe wanted to reach in and rip the papers out. The 23 page report was a detailed description of all that the Jacksonville, North Carolina police could determine as of 1:30pm, Eastern Standard Time. The report was an hour old as it was now 1:30 Central time. The victim was Richard Wallace, 46 year old father of David Wallace, USMC, deployed in Afghanistan. Richard Wallace was married and lived in Hickory, North Carolina. The police contacted the Hickory Police to question his wife. Mrs. Wallace was admitted to the hospital with a possible stroke. All she kept saying before she was transported was 'I told him to call the police and let them handle it.' No other questions were asked because of her condition.

The shooting took place at about 9:40 to 9:45am. The coroner had not ruled on the cause of death but there was a hole in the back of Richard Wallace's head and an exit wound out of the right eye socket so Joe and Nancy already figured out what the coroner's report would say. The cause of death was that he had his brains blown out. There was no robbery. Mr. Wallace had over $300 in his wallet when his body was found. He had been dead only twenty minutes to half an hour when the coroner arrived on the scene. The crime scene was fresh and was roped off quickly. A patrol car had been on the scene possibly as soon as five minutes after the shooting took place. There were no eye witnesses. Most of the residents in the apartment complex are working class people and were at work. The few that work the night shift were already in bed. Private Wallace would be notified as soon as he returned to base. He would be on a jet home immediately after that.

Nancy was looking at the faxed images of the crime scene. Her mind was racing as she tried to piece together the events that led to Richard Wallace's death. They expected to get an e-mail with better quality pictures of the scene but they couldn't wait for that. She asked Joe in a quiet voice, "What was Mr. Wallace doing at his son's apartment if his son was in Afghanistan? From this report it doesn't look like he ever went up to the apartment, but someone had been there. The mail was in two stacks; one was less of a pile than a random toss away from the door. The second pile was in front of the door where the mail slot is. The pile was moved only when the door was opened. There were pieces of an opened envelope left in between the piles. The crime scene guys said that it looked like only one envelope had been opened. The rest were untouched. No bills were opened. Even a personal letter from Private Wallace's parents was left in the pile of discarded mail." She paused. "It says that they found a cheap pen in the car on the driver's side that might have blood on it. Not surprising because there was blood all over the inside of the car. They're going to do DNA on the blood and see if it's the victim's."

"Whoever was in that apartment had only one thing in mind. They picked up a single envelope and didn't bother with anything else. It looks like the Reardon house. The rest of the house is cleaned out. No furniture, no personal effects, nothing. Here, look at this shot. The living room is empty; just carpet, dust, and cob webs." Joe stopped talking and squinted his eyes to look closer at the picture of Richard Wallace slumped over in his car. He saw the chain around his neck that held the symbol of the US Marine Corps and a pair of dog tags. "He was a Marine Veteran," Joe said to Nancy. "He was wearing his dog tags." Joe's jaw tensed as his anger grew. One of his fellow Marines was shot in the head from behind in the country that he fought to protect, probably by a citizen who enjoyed the freedom for which Mr. Wallace would have willingly given his life. Joe's clenched fist came down hard on the photo of his fallen comrade. "We are going to catch whoever did this. When we do, they had better hope there's someone there to restrain me."

Nancy saw the red color and the tension in Joe's face. Calmly, but with conviction she said, "We'll catch them, whoever they are, you can count on that, Sergeant McKinney. But right now, we have orders to wrap things up here and head for Jacksonville. I'll contact Banks and Hansen and let them know when and where they can reach us. You need to get your gear together and get ready to fly. We'll grab a bite to eat before we head to the air strip. We're flying out at 1530 hours. That's less than two hours, so let's get moving. We can talk more on the plane."

Joe nodded without a word, stood and returned to his own office. His mind was swirling with information, none of which was in a logical order. There were bits and pieces of timelines and random facts. His brain was on overload, partly because of the volume of information and partly because there was a sprinkling of anger thrown into the mix. He took a deep breath to try to clear his head but it would take some time before he was totally under control. *What would Pat do if he were in my shoes? He usually can keep a level head. I'll call him and see if he can make sense of this whole mess.* Before he could sit at his desk, his phone rang. He answered, "Sergeant McKinney."

"Joe, its Lisa."

"Oh, Hi Babe. How are you holding up?"

"I'm not too bad but Mom's a mess. The funeral was today and she's been crying on and off almost all day. She's on sedatives to try to help her sleep but she just won't stop. She's cleaning up the house now." Lisa paused to see what Joe would say, but Joe's mind was still racing. The case was at the forefront of his mind and he barely heard what Lisa said. "Joe? Are you still there?"

"Yes. I'm sorry Lisa. It's been a long, bad day today. Is your mom okay?"

Lisa held the phone away from her ear and gave it an exasperated look. She said, "I just told you that she's a mess. Are you listening?"

"Yes. Yes. I'm sorry. She needs to rest. Try to slow her down if you can. I'll be flying to North Carolina today. There's been another problem similar to the one we're working here. It just happened."

"Joe, when are you going to be through with this? It sounds like it's going to go on for a long while yet."

Joe's hesitation was just a bit too long and Lisa's patience was short. She said in a short and angry tone, "I have to go. Call me when you can think straight!"

"Lisa, I'm sorry," Joe said as the phone clicked in his ear. He pulled the receiver away from his head and looked at it for a few seconds then set the receiver on the cradle. *What the hell is wrong with me? I better call her back. But I have to call Pat.* Joe pulled out his chair and sat as he picked the receiver back up. He dialed Pat's number and waited for the connection. As he waited, Nancy walked in and set another fax on his desk. It was confirmation from the crime lab that a 9mm was used in the shooting. As Joe quickly scanned the report, it was clear that whoever did the shooting was a very good shot. The report said that the shooter was at least 45 feet from the victim. With a pistol, that is tough to do, especially a moving target.

"Hello," Pat's voice came over the receiver. "Hello," he repeated when Joe, still staring at the fax, didn't say anything.

Finally Joe said, "Hey, Pat. Sorry, I got a little side-tracked."

"I guess so. I was about to hang up. What's up, little brother?"

"This case is what's up." Nancy turned and left Joe's office, but not before she pointed to her watch and tapped a couple of times letting Joe know that they were under some time pressure. Joe nodded his head to Nancy and continued his conversation with Pat.

"We just got a call from Camp Lejeune. There's been another death associated with a case similar to the one here at Grand Forks. We're flying out of here in less than two hours, headed for Jacksonville, North Carolina. I'll just give you the thumbnail sketch about that case. A Private Wallace is deployed in Afghanistan. He has a new, young bride. She turns up missing and not answering his calls from over there and he gets worried. He calls his folks and his dad drives over three hours to their apartment to see if the young Mrs. Wallace is home. Apparently Mrs. Wallace or someone close to her takes exception to Private Wallace's dad butting in and they blow his brains out."

Pat winces as he hears the last detail. His mind briefly flashes back to a view he once had through the scope of a sniper rifle. The view was of the head of a guy named Danny Vallero. He gets a chill that runs the length of his spine as he recalls seeing the contents of Danny's head splatter all over the wall behind him. Pat shakes his head. He asks, "When did all this go down?"

"About two hours ago. The dad's probably not even cold yet." Both Joe and Pat briefly think about their own father and his recent health issues. Joe continued, "There's more. The apartment was empty, like the house in Grand Forks, but the mail was stacking up. Somebody was in the apartment going through the mail. They left after opening just one piece of mail, as far as we can tell, anyway. There were scraps of torn paper that looked like what would be left from an envelope that had been hastily opened. The scraps were left next to a pile of unopened mail."

"Any idea what mail they may have been looking for? It must have been important if they were searching for one specific piece of mail. I mean, this woman's husband supposedly had been killed in Afghanistan, but really isn't. Was there anything like this in the other cases?" Pat asked.

"Nope. All the other cases ended up in empty apartments, for the most part. The exception was the Reardon case here in Grand Forks. But, in all cases, the couples were in rentals. That's not real unusual because most new, young military families move around a lot, depending on the 'needs of the military'. You remember that clause, don't you? I'm living proof." Joe said.

"I guess with an empty apartment there's no way to tell if Private Wallace had anything of value like a gun collection, coin collection, stocks or bonds, or substantial savings. What else is there?" Pat asked.

"I don't know. Maybe this chick is just hocking all of her spouses stuff. I know it wouldn't be much, but at the rate she's hooking these guys, she could almost make a career of it."

There was silence on the phone while both brothers thought about the various cases. Pat asked, "Is there anything different from the earliest cases to the most recent ones?"

"Well, yea. In the most recent cases the parents were notified that their sons were killed in action. We don't know if the reports came from this lady or if they came from an official source. But we do know that the parents of the last two, Reardon and Wallace, were told that their sons were killed in action. Nancy and I will look into that to see what else we can find."

"So, you're on a first name basis with your superior officer? What's that all about?"

"It's nothing. It's like a professional courtesy. She doesn't want me to call her by her first name in front of our fellow military brethren but in the privacy of the office we use first names. It's strictly work related."

"Watch yourself. Fraternizing with officers is serious stuff. You can get your pee-pee whacked."

"Knock it off, Pat. It's not like that. Anyway, I may need your help on sifting through some of the information that we're getting. Is it possible that you could come up to North Carolina for a few days? I think that you could help us."

Pat paused for a minute, thinking what was on his schedule for the next few days. He had a few business contacts that he had to make for his consulting business but they were going to be telephone calls. They could be completed from anywhere. "I'll have to check with the boss and see what's going on. Diane may have some reservations about this but I think that I can convince her that it's important. I also have to check in on Dad and see how his rehab is coming. He's getting stronger every day, by the way. I think that he may be back to about seventy-five percent real soon."

Joe felt a twitch of guilt. He hadn't thought about his dad for the last couple of days he'd been so tied up with the case. He asked Pat, "How's Mom holding up? Is Dad giving her a hard time?"

"Actually, he's been pretty decent. I guess he figures that he's lucky to be alive. He's been pretty civil to Mom so far. But it's still early. After he gains his strength he may be a real grouch. I'm real sorry to hear about Lisa's dad. She must be devastated."

"Yea. She is."

"Have you talked to her lately?" Pat asked.

"Right before I called you. I have to call her back. I was a little preoccupied when she called. I really should get away from the case and call her back."

Just then, Nancy came to the door of Joe's office and looked in. She tapped her watch again, this time with a look of annoyance. He nodded in her direction, then said to Pat, "I've gotta cut this short. I'll call you when I get set up in Jacksonville. Let me know if you're able to get up there."

"Okay, Joe. Later." The phone disconnected.

Joe looked down at the open file of Private Wallace in front of him. *So what is so important that a guy has to get shot in the back of the head? From the way he was slumped over in the car, he probably didn't know what hit him.* Joe shook his head, gathered the file folder and tucked it into his briefcase. He had a plane to catch.

* * *

Lisa Goddard was staring at the phone, tears streaming down her face. She was in her old bedroom in her parent's house in Oak Harbor, Ohio. What a horrible week this had been. Her dad was dead. Her mother was a wreck. Her brother was a jerk . . . no . . . a complete asshole. Now her boyfriend was blowing her off. She felt abandoned, alone, and in despair. Her eyes wandered around the room, looking at family photos, pictures of kittens, and her one Kinkade painting hanging on the light pink wall. She looked at the ceiling fan that would not be needed for a few more weeks. Then she lay back on her bed and stared at the rosebud-textured ceiling for a few minutes. She was tired but not sleepy. Her mind told her to get up but her body said no, not right now. She wanted to go out into the living room and console her mother but feeling like she did, she wouldn't provide much comfort. She sat up and pulled a tissue from the box on her night stand and blew her nose. She threw that one in the trash can next to the night stand, pulled a second tissue out and wiped her eyes. Her thoughts were almost all about Joe McKinney these days. She was so in love with this guy but what kind of baggage came with a guy like him? She wasn't absolutely wild about his past. In fact, it was the one thing about him that really bothered her. But at least he had the decency to tell her and not hide it like his brother, Pat, had done to Diane. She would probably have hated him for that had he not come clean and she found out later; especially knowing what problems she and her parents had gone through with her brother. She wasn't sure what to do. Could she call someone? *I think I'll call Diane. She'd said to call her any time. Now is as good a time as any, I guess.*

Lisa picked up the receiver and dialed Pat and Diane's number. Pat answered on the first ring. "Hello?"

She hesitated then said, "Pat, this is Lisa."

"Lisa! Hello. My goodness. Are you holding up alright?"

"Well, not really. I was hoping to talk with Diane. Is she home?"

"Yes she is. I just talked to Joe. He is such a jerk. I mean that in the nicest way. He mentioned that he talked to you but said that his head was in the case. He feels pretty stupid. But trust me; he's going to call you when he gets to North Carolina. Did he mention that he was leaving North Dakota and heading closer to home?"

Lisa was sniffing a bit, but managed to say, "Yes, he did mention it. That's about the only thing he said. He was real distant when we talked."

"He's like that when he is concentrating on something. You should have seen him in high school. He would study for tests until he got headaches. What a head case he can be. He'll make it up to you. You can rest assured." He wanted to tell Lisa that Joe was going to ask her to marry him but he figured that Joe would kill him for that. "Here's Diane."

"Pat . . . thanks."

Lisa waited while Pat handed the phone over to Diane. "Lisa, dear, are you okay?"

"Diane, I really don't know." Tears poured down her cheeks as a flood of emotions opened up. Just hearing the concern in Diane's voice triggered a much needed release of pent up fear and isolation. She wasn't alone anymore. "I'm afraid I'm a real mess."

With a soothing voice full of compassion and reason, Diane said, "Let's talk."

For the next hour, Diane and Lisa talked about the recent tragedies that had befallen their families, about the McKinney brothers, Pat, Joe, and their recently deceased brother Mike. They talked about Mike's wife and what she was like. They talked about hate and love, the past, present, and future, and of things that could happen. Diane said, "I know that you love Joe very much. He's a great guy, much like my husband. But they do come with some issues, both past and present."

"Tell me about it. I couldn't believe it when Joe told me that he was being recalled and that he didn't know what he'd be doing. I can't believe that he didn't even question it. He just dropped his existing life and reentered his old life in the Marines. He is so damned intense." Lisa proceeded to tell Diane about the first time they'd met in the weight room at their apartment complex. Joe's workout was so extreme that she thought he was having a heart attack. Then they had a race swimming laps at the pool and he was concentrating so hard that he did several laps after the race was over.

"That's Joe," Diane said. "He gets his mind on something and that's all he thinks about. He zones in on the subject and tunes out everyone and everything else. You have to decide if you can put up with that for the rest of your life."

Diane's last comment hit Lisa. What did she mean? Did Diane think that Joe was that serious about their relationship? She and Joe had talked in generalities about the future but they hadn't made any commitments; nothing serious anyway. "Diane, I shouldn't ask this, but has Joe said anything to you about how serious he is about our relationship?"

"Listen, if you want Joe all for yourself, all you have to do is take him. You just have to decide if that's what you really want. I can tell you this much; you'd be hard pressed to find a better man than Joe McKinney. But, and this is a big 'but', he has his moments. You have to be willing to work at it. You're getting a taste of the tough times right now. If you can make it through this, especially with your dad passing and everything that goes with that, then you can make it work. I know you can."

Lisa smiled as more tears streamed down her face. These tears were not like her tears from an hour ago when she felt her world was falling apart. These were tears of joy and hope for the future. Diane had helped her see through the tough times and see a brighter future. She knew what she wanted now and she knew that she could get it. *You'd better look out now, Joe McKinney. I've got you in my sights.*

Chapter 18

Bobby and Becky left the parking lot from Savannah, Georgia's Fairway BMW in their new car. Compared to the beat up Toyota, the 3 year old black BMW was a luxury car. It had a six cylinder engine, an AM/FM stereo with a CD player, air conditioning, tinted windows, and heated leather seats. It had a new car smell, look, and feel, especially when compared to the Toyota's stale cigarette and burned oil smell. The seats in the Beamer were comfortable and could be adjusted to several different positions, all with the touch of a switch. The car had real low miles. The previous owner was an elderly man who only drove it to the grocery store and the senior center. The dealer said that the car rarely was driven over 45 miles per hour. He'd sold the sports car to the elderly gentleman years earlier. He'd tried to talk him into something less sporty and more luxurious but he wouldn't have any of it.

They were on Interstate 95 headed for King's Bay and Becky's date with Petty Officer Wilson Brush. Becky was still giddy. For the tenth time since the previous day, she took out the zipper pouch of money and counted it. They had over $75,000 left from their first big payday. It was intoxicating to her to see that much cash. She couldn't believe they went into the car dealership and plopped down cash for the car, then stopped at Outback Steakhouse for a great dinner. She was already thinking about shopping for new clothes. She didn't really need anything but the fact that she could afford whatever she wanted was all the excuse she needed to get something new.

At first, when Becky counted the money, Bobby shared her excitement but after the third and fourth time she counted it, he was getting irritated. Now, on the tenth time, he was angry. "Damn-it Becky, put the money back in the pouch and leave it alone. It hasn't changed since the last five times you counted it. Someone's gonna see you with it. We don't want to lose it to some dope head mugger. We have to keep our heads on straight or we're gonna screw it up. If you're this goofy over a hundred grand, what are you gonna act like when we have half a million?"

Hearing Bobby say half a million almost made Becky wet her pants. She screamed out loud, "Half a million bucks? Oh . . . My . . . God! I will be such a perfect little wife to my big, strong husbands. It's too bad that they have to sacrifice their lives for us."

Becky broke out into a laugh as if she were high on pot or drunk in a comedy club. Bobby could hardly stand it any longer so, while still driving down the interstate at 75 miles per hour, he reached over, grabbed Becky by the arm and said in a firm voice, "Look Becky, you need to calm down. I am not fucking joking with you. We can enjoy this as long as we're not in prison. I do not intend to go to prison so get your shit together." He stared at her for a few seconds too long and coasted into the passing lane, almost clipping a car that had been passing them. That was bad news because the Georgia state trooper that was about 1000 feet behind them saw their car as it jerked back into their own lane. The trooper moved quickly in behind their BMW and ran the temporary tags. Bobby saw the trooper and released Becky's arm. He slowed to about 68 miles per hour and told Becky not to look because a trooper was behind them. She quickly straightened up and slowly dropped the zipper pouch with the money under the passenger seat, all without moving her head and shoulders. The trooper, seeing the report come back that the car had just been purchased, put on his flashers and sounded his siren briefly, signaling that they should pull over, which Bobby did.

Before the trooper approached the car, Bobby said, "Be on your best behavior. Don't say anything stupid."

Becky was pissed at his remark and said, "You mean something like, 'Officer, this man's a pervert child rapist and I am in grave danger.' You mean something like that?" She smiled at Bobby in one of her sarcastic, don't-mess-with-me smiles.

"If you fuck this up, you'll be real sorry. This is your fault. Make sure the pouch stays under that seat and out of sight." Bobby looked in his side mirror and noticed that the trooper was getting out of his car and approaching the driver's side of their new car. "Remember . . ." was all Bobby said as his window glided down to greet the trooper.

The trooper leaned over and looked into the Beamer at Bobby and Becky. He had his right hand on his sidearm as he assessed the situation and relaxed slightly when he saw the two of them. He said, "Good afternoon Sir and Ma'am. Sir, I saw you swerve and almost hit the car in the passing lane. That is why I stopped you. Can you tell me why you swerved at that moment because there were no cars immediately in front of you?"

Bobby replied in a calm voice, "Sir, I was distracted for a second. I didn't see the car that was passing me. He was in the blind spot in my side mirror and I have to admit I didn't look back over my shoulder."

"Okay, sir. I still need to see your license and registration."

Bobby produced his driver's license from Virginia and handed over the temporary registration from the car dealership. It would have to do since they just purchased the car within the last hour. He was nervous. He knew that Becky was good at surprises and he didn't need a surprise right now. He was afraid that she'd try to seduce the cop or something equally insane to get out of the ticket. She'd done worse, he thought to himself, but that was mostly before they met. Some of the stories that she'd told Bobby were of a wild young woman. She still did weird things now and then. He was sure that her stories were true. As the trooper headed back to his car, Bobby turned to Becky. "Just stay cool and we'll be on our way soon." Becky thought for a minute. She was thinking ahead to a time when Bobby would no longer fit into her plans. She needed him now but that wouldn't last for long. He was getting too uptight for her liking. Why get all this money together if you couldn't enjoy it. If it makes you all uptight, what's the point? She had to think of a way to get Bobby to loosen up or the time to dump him would come sooner rather than later. He was also getting too demanding when it came to sex. Sure the intensity of their games was a lot of fun, but he was getting close to hurting her. There was only so much that she would endure and they were quickly approaching the limit.

The trooper was back at the car window. "I'm going to give you a warning for failure to yield. Please pay closer attention to what you're doing, sir. You wouldn't want anything to happen to your pretty passenger, now, would you?"

"No, sir. Thanks officer. I'll be more careful." Bobby pulled out and left the trooper sitting at the side of the road, lights still flashing. As soon as they were safely out in traffic Bobby said to Becky, "That was too close. See what I mean about screwing around? If we're not careful, we'll lose it all. You can't keep thinking that this is a big joke. It's serious."

Becky was ticked off at Bobby's remarks. It was his fault that he almost ran into the car in the next lane. She didn't have any control over the situation. Just because he couldn't keep his cool didn't mean that it was her fault for his temper. She said, "That was totally your fault back there. You get all jacked up because I'm having fun. Lighten up, Bobby. If we're going to be all serious all the time, why bother getting rich. We can be miserable and be poor."

"Don't talk to me that way. That was your fault for getting me pissed off. We can't afford to have you acting like a child in a candy store." He was silent for a minute then said, "Awe, forget it. We have work to do. Just remember, we have to be back at the other apartment in Jacksonville in two weeks. Mrs. Sharp's check will be there by then. So you have to make quick work of this Brush guy. So when do you have to meet your new fiancé?"

"I'm supposed to be at my apartment ready to go tomorrow night at 7:30. I have to be nice and pretty and rested for my future husband, even though he doesn't know it yet. What do you have in mind?" She said with a big smile.

"I was hoping for some animal-like sex but I guess I'll have to settle for a blow job. That'll give you practice for your date." He said this with an evil smile. She didn't like the idea of him demanding whatever he wanted whenever he wanted it. She was the one doing all the work here.

She was getting the guys to fall in love with her which wasn't a whole lot of work for her but she had to endure the evenings playing kissy face with these gullible guys, most of them too young to know about real love. She had to share the rewards with Bobby and he didn't even like for her to see it, touch it, or count it. He was becoming a liability. She would miss the high energy sex but there were others she could teach to play that game.

"Bobby, I've got a headache. Maybe we should just rest tonight. I have to make sure that you didn't bruise my ass too much the other night. Remember, my future husband may see me naked tomorrow night. I can't have a bruised ass or bruises on my arms, like where you grabbed me a little bit ago."

"Headache, huh? We'll see. Take something so you get rid of it by tonight. You'll be ready."

Becky just turned her head and stared at the salt marshes on the side of Interstate 95. When they got to their motel room, she would have to leave for her apartment and make sure it looked lived-in for when Wilson came to pick her up tomorrow night. She would then be Tanya Walters. She had to tell Wilson about her nice visit with her Auntie Jenn and Uncle Walt. They're getting old but they really enjoyed her visit, she would say. It was all part of the plan. Wilson would eat it up. He was so young and gullible, and perfect for her next husband. She was already visualizing the next $100,000 check. She could see the teller counting out the cash and turning it over to her. She saw herself counting the cash over and over again. She imagined herself lying in bed looking at the mirror hung from the ceiling, naked as the day she was born, with hundred dollar bills thrown all over her. She didn't see Bobby anywhere in her daydreams.

* * *

A maroon van barreled down Interstate 95 and passed a Georgia State Trooper on the side of the road. He'd just turned his flashers off and was pulling back out into traffic. Up ahead of the van, a black BMW was taking it a little slower than before. That would make it much easier to follow, though it really didn't matter. The van's driver knew where Bobby and Becky were headed. There was no hurry. The van sure did guzzle gas. One more stop was in order before the final stop for the day at St. Marys, Georgia. There was a cheap motel room waiting, very close to Bobby and Becky. The van traveled at just over the speed limit. *No reason to get a ticket now, is there?*

Chapter 19

Petty Officer Wilson Brush and Tanya Walters were married within two weeks of her arrival at St. Marys, Georgia. Wilson was head over heals for his new bride and couldn't wait to show her off to the world. Of course, Tanya was a bit shy about that and would rather have kept a low profile. They were married by the Justice of the Peace at the Camden County courthouse in Woodbine. Wilson's best man, Doug Farrell, tried to get Wilson to slow down the relationship but Wilson would have no part of it. He was deeply in love with this woman. 'Doug my man, I deserve this,' Wilson had said before he and his new bride headed for a 2 night honeymoon in Boone, North Carolina. It was spring and the air was very cool up in the Blue Ridge Mountains but that wasn't going to be a problem. A two night honeymoon meant they didn't do any hiking in the mountains.

After their brief, torrid honeymoon, Wilson was back at King's Bay starting turnover of the USS Nevada from the blue crew. It was rumored to be a short turnover with a long shakedown cruise. Normally, after turnover, the on-coming crew performed maintenance activities for a few weeks then took the ship out to sea for a few days to perform routine testing and drills. Then if major problems showed up, there was still time to make repairs before the real deployment began. This go around was going to be different. The Nevada was headed down to Port Canaveral, Florida to prepare for some weapons testing the crew was asked to perform as a demonstration for some big wigs from Washington, D.C. Having this much attention always made a ship's captain nervous. When the captain was nervous, the Executive Officer was under the gun to get the crew in shape as quickly as possible. That meant more than the normal ration of drills which meant very little sleep. That also meant more than the normal amount of field days, the extra cleaning and shining that the ship needs to impress some group of politicians. Wilson was already exhausted when he got to the ship and it showed. His eyes were bloodshot with extra large bags under them. His shoulders sagged and he walked a little bowlegged. That netted him a number of high-fives and a few lewd comments from his shipmates. Once he was off watch, he hit his bunk and he was out. But it usually only lasted for an hour or so and a new drill would start. That meant he was rousted from his bunk to man his drilling station, whether it was for a battle station missile, or battle station torpedo, or an engineering drill. Within a few days of being back at sea he was whipped. His division officer caught him sleeping on watch and warned him that if he was caught again, he'd be headed to captain's mast. That could cost him a stripe and some money. He was coming down with a cold and he was lonely. He missed his new bride already. He missed the many talents that she had in bed or beside the bed on the floor, or on the couch, or the living room floor. The USS Nevada had been at sea for about four days and Becky figured it was time to take care of business. One of the things that she loved about her new husband was that he was a collector. He didn't collect junk either. He had a classic 1964 Ford Mustang, a gun collection and a coin collection. She'd been admiring his gun collection ever since he left for the ship nearly a week ago. She thought that it would net about $500 but she talked to a collector before she made a move. To her surprise, the collection was worth nearly $12,000 and sold quickly. Next was his coin collection which was another $4500. Finally, he had nearly $6500 cash in his bank account which she cleared out in two withdrawals. She was very thorough and soon she was selling their furniture. Some of the wives in the apartment where they lived were suspicious when they saw furniture being carried out the apartment door. She told them that Wilson wanted it all replaced before he came back from sea. 'He is such a wonderful husband. I am so lucky to have found a man like him.' She was right about that. She and Bobby hit the gold mine when Becky got her hooks into him.

Bobby was busy, too. He readied the paperwork to have Petty Officer Wilson Brush declared KIA, killed in action. That would be icing on the cake since they'd already netted some $25,000 from his various collections and personal belongings. As soon as Bobby received word that the Nevada cleared Port Canaveral for the longest part of their cruise, he submitted the paperwork. He was getting very good at his handy work now. He was able to use differing pen strokes and different types of pens to forge signatures on the appropriate lines. The insurance company was oblivious to the positions, names, and ranks of the administrative personnel and the officers that were required to sign off on the payout of Serviceman's Group Life Insurance policies. Bobby knew that and he was counting on that to continue. He figured that he and Becky could pull off about two or three more of these scams before they needed to lay low for a while. By then they'd have nearly half a million dollars between them. Thinking of this, he began to wonder just how long he needed Becky Lippert. He started to think that maybe he could pull this off on the women being deployed overseas. After all, this was an equal opportunity military these days. He could find himself a young female soldier just out of boot camp. She'd be horny as hell from being cooped up like a prisoner. She'd need some serious lovin' and he knew how to please. Just as quickly as the thought came, it went away. He knew that Becky was the real pro at this game. Besides, he'd made a promise to take care of her; a promise that even Becky didn't know about. That was a problem that would have to wait for another day and that day was a ways down the road.

Bobby and Becky were fast asleep in their hotel room with money thrown all over themselves and around the queen sized bed. Becky had convinced Bobby to have a little fun and lighten up for a few hours. She knew he was going to be sore in the morning but that was okay. As long as he was sore in the right spots, he'd be less likely to try and get into her pants and play his little rough sex games for a few days. She had to think ahead about her next 'husband'. It couldn't be near Jacksonville, North Carolina or St. Marys, Georgia. They had to pick a new base in a new area of the country away from the places that they'd already scored. They couldn't risk running into anyone they knew. They both decided that it had to be warm, too. Their stint in North Dakota was no fun at all. The brutal cold turned them both off and they swore that they'd never go north of the Mason Dixon line again. Becky couldn't believe it when Bobby nearly demanded that they go that far north and west to Grand Forks. She'd spent most of her life in the southeast where it was warm most of the year. Becky took out the atlas and started to leaf through it looking for military towns. She looked along the coast of Florida and saw the panhandle and Pensacola. *That might work. But that's where we said we were headed when we left the frozen tundra of North Dakota. They might be looking for us down there.* Then she swung her fingers up along the Atlantic Coast. *Hmm. Norfolk, Naval Base in Virginia. Right near Virginia Beach. That would work.* Becky started thinking about how to sway Bobby into heading that way after their business was finished here. She was confident that she could convince him to make that their next target area. Besides, he'd been stationed there. *He knows his way around and the area is huge. There's plenty of night clubs where sailors hang out. This would be easy pickins'. I could probably pull two scams at once.*

Bobby stirred, then rolled over and fell back to a sound sleep. He was a satisfied man. But he was happy to have such talent on his team. As he slept, he dreamt about his cash machine and the things that she could do. *Sleep tight, big boy. You have some driving to do tomorrow. We have to get back to North Carolina. There's a nice paycheck waiting for us in Jacksonville.*

* * *

A maroon van pulled back into the parking lot at the hotel. *They're staying at fancier places. They must be doing well. I'll see how well in the morning. I need to get some sleep.* She moved to the back of the van and lay down on the makeshift bed next to her sleeping son. Sleep was difficult. There were just too many thoughts spinning around in that head. *The girl has to be protected. She is just too precious. She always has been even when she went through all those foster homes and was abused. She came out alright. I have to get some sleep.*

* * *

Interstate 95 heading north near the Hilton Head interchange was very busy with traffic this morning. Bobby and Becky didn't realize that it was graduation weekend for many of the universities and colleges. Students and parents in minivans loaded to the brim with dirty clothes, furniture, mini-refrigerators, stereos and TVs were screaming by their BMW. They were in no hurry, in fact Bobby planned to get to a rest area and take a long break. They didn't want to get to Jacksonville before nightfall. He wanted some darkness to use for cover. The last time they were in this city, they witnessed a murder and he wasn't sure that they weren't seen. They wouldn't be anywhere near the apartment complex where Becky and her husband lived but there was no sense taking chances.

Becky had purposely left the atlas in the front seat so that she could work on Bobby and get him to agree that Norfolk would be a good next move. Before she could bring up the subject, Bobby said, "You know, Norfolk would be a great next stop for us. I know the area and the base. I know many of the spots where sailors hang out. Hell I used to hang out there myself."

Becky outwardly didn't show any emotion except for a slight upturn in her lips. Inside she was almost screaming "Yes." Now Bobby thought that it was all his idea and she wouldn't have to fight with him about it. After a moment she asked, "What makes Norfolk such a great choice other than the fact that you know your way around?"

"Well, for one, it's easy to get to the highway and head in any direction. Plus there are lots of things to do within a few hours of Norfolk. Virginia Beach is really great. The summers here are hot but not scorching like Florida. If we went to Florida, we'd have to go to Jacksonville or Tampa or Pensacola. I really don't care for any of those bases. We don't want to go near Pensacola since we mentioned that to your old neighbors in Grand Forks."

"You're probably right. No sense taking a chance like that. What about Norfolk? Would anyone still be there that might recognize you?"

"Nope. That was such a long time ago that all the guys I knew are gone."

They sat in silence for a while as they moved up the tree lined interstate. Bobby moved his legs once in a while and made little groaning sounds as if he was in pain, which Becky knew to be true. Then Becky asked, "What's the plan for tonight?"

"We're going to go to the apartment, grab the check from the mail and get the hell out. Then we'll get back on I-95 and head in the general direction of Norfolk. We can get an apartment near the base, within a few miles anyway. It doesn't have to be real close. I'll get a hotel room close by and we'll get to work; within the next few days, that is. I can show you around the area so you can get used to the size of the city. It's much larger than the places we've been working."

Bobby had the cruise control exactly on 65 miles per hour. He had no desire to draw any unwanted attention. He passed a South Carolina State Trooper who was sitting in the center medium timing drivers heading north. *No more close calls.* They had a check to pick up and he didn't need the aggravation. He figured that they had about 4 more hours in the car, give or take a half hour. He knew that there was a Shoney's restaurant at the Walterboro exit. That would be a good place to stop, eat and rest for a while. They could do a little shopping, too. They needed toiletries and some snacks for the rest of the trip. He also knew that there was a gun shop near the exit. He was feeling a little vulnerable without any protection. That was going to change.

Bobby looked over at Becky. She looked so beautiful and sexy sitting cross legged on the passenger seat. He couldn't imagine that she was comfortable in that position but he couldn't believe some of the positions that she assumed during sex. Sitting there in the passenger seat must have been easy for her. He asked, "Do you have your next identity worked out yet?"

"Oh yea. I am Julie Lippus. I saw the name in an obituary a few months back and did a little research. I have a Virginia driver's license and a Pennsylvania birth certificate all made up and ready to use. I'm a product of foster care since my real parents gave me away at birth. You know that they couldn't interrupt their college careers to take care of poor little ole me."

"You are a genius. How'd you know we were going to end up in Virginia?"

"I didn't."

"You're still a genius. A sexy, little genius."

Becky just smiled out the window and they fell into silence again.

* * *

It was nearly 9:30pm when Bobby pulled the BMW into the parking lot at the Arbor Arms apartments in Jacksonville, North Carolina. Bobby and Becky were both well rested but were a bit nervous about this pickup. Earlier in the day Bobby had stopped at a convenience store for drinks and picked up a newspaper for later in the evening. That's when he noticed a story on the bottom of the front page. The headlines said, "No Leads in Parking Lot Murder." The story took up two columns about 8 inches long. He read the story from start to finish before they left the store parking lot. Becky had been sleeping until he tapped her on the leg and made her read the story for herself. The article made mention that the local police had requested the assistance of the local military investigative unit at Camp Lejeune. There was little detail in the article but Bobby was agitated just seeing it.

"I don't think that we should go after this check. You know that they may have contacted Private Sharp by now. They have to know that he really isn't dead," Bobby said to Becky in a sullen, nervous tone.

"What, you getting scared? All we're doing is going into my mailbox and getting my mail. Remember, these apartments are different. The mailboxes are outside the ground floor apartments. We don't even have to go inside. I'll run up, check the box and run back. It'll take less than a minute."

Bobby thought for a minute. He was still concerned but maybe Becky was right and they could get in and out of there quick so he agreed.

Now they were sitting in the parking lot about two buildings down from the apartment where she and Private Edward Sharp lived for less than two weeks. They had a plan this time. They didn't want any surprises like the one at the Wallace apartment across town. "Okay," Bobby started, "you walk casually along the walkway and turn in to the apartment group prior to yours. Take a minute to make sure that you're not followed and then move on to your apartment and do your thing. Just get all of the mail, stuff it in this bag, and bring it back to the car. Don't take time to look at it. There may be a lot of mail since it should have built up for the last three weeks at least." Becky looked bored with all the spy routine. Bobby didn't think this was funny and grabbed her left arm. "This could be dangerous, so don't take this lightly!"

"Okay! I don't! I just don't get my panties all twisted like you!"

Bobby released her arm. She got out of the car and headed for the first apartment building just as instructed. After about ten seconds, she emerged from the shadows of the first building and headed for her old apartment and stood in front of the mailboxes. She quickly pulled the key from her pocket and inserted it in the box. When she opened it a few pieces of mail fell out on the ground. She unloaded the mail into the bag and bent to pick up the fallen pieces. She noticed that one of the envelopes on the ground was from NatFed Life Insurance Company. It looked like a check inside. Her face lit up like a child at a birthday party. When she picked up the envelope and stood she was facing a young man who'd silently walked down the apartment steps. It was Private Edward Sharp in the flesh. Becky's face went pale as she looked up from the mail.

"Hello Becky." Becky was silent. The moment seemed like an eternity. Her hands started to shake and she looked as though she might faint. "What are you doing? What's going on? Why haven't you called or come home?"

Becky could see the tears forming in the young soldiers eyes. He wasn't angry. He was simply heartbroken. For a brief moment, Becky felt sorry for this poor, young man. Then she was brought back to reality and she knew she and Bobby were in danger. She had a hard time clearing her throat, but said, "Eddie, I can explain. I was just so scared and alone when you left for overseas. I didn't know what else to do so I went and lived with some friends. I came back to get the mail and I was heading back to their house again."

As tears rolled down Eddie Sharp's face, he asked, "Then how do you explain the empty apartment? Why is the bank account closed? I just got back to the States yesterday and went to my folks. They said that you haven't called them or anything. What the fuck is going on?" His anger was starting to rise despite his broken heart and Becky knew that she had to do something or this would get ugly fast.

"Eddie, let's go upstairs and talk. Like I said, I can explain."

"Okay. This ought to be good. You go first." Eddie Sharp backed up and let Becky start up the stairs. Her breathing was controlled but she was on the verge of panic. As she ascended the steps ahead of Eddie, she heard two dull thuds and a groan from behind her. She turned around to see Private Eddie Sharp spin and fall down the steps face first. His head hit the pavement at the base of the steps with a final thud. Becky covered her mouth to stifle the scream that would have raised the dead and surely would have awakened the apartment dwellers to the commotion in the complex. She dropped the bag of mail when she went to cover her mouth and it landed right on Eddie's now blood-soaked back. She looked down, still shocked to see him on the ground. She saw Bobby running towards her holding a gun and knew that she had to get it together or they were both going to get caught. She reached down, picked up the blood soaked bag, wiped it on Eddie's shirt and stepped around the body. She ran to Bobby and they both headed back to the car.

When they were safely on the road, both still breathing heavily, Becky yelled, "Why did you have to shoot him? I could have talked to him and let him know that it was over between us. We could have walked away."

"Becky. . ."

"You didn't have to . . ."

"Becky, I . . ."

"Why Bobby?"

"If you'll listen to me for a second, I'll tell you. I didn't shoot him."

"You're lying!" Her whole body was shaking as she looked at Bobby. She wanted to reach over and strangle him.

"No I'm not. Feel the gun barrel. It's ice cold. If I'd have shot it, the barrel would be hot or at least very warm. I didn't do it, Becky!"

There was silence. Becky looked down at the dashboard but wasn't seeing a thing as thoughts about the shooting raced through her brain. None of the pieces fit.

"Well if you didn't, who did?"

"I don't know," he said. "I don't know." But he had a real good idea.

Chapter 20

It was 7:30 in the morning. The Naval Criminal Investigative Service office on Julian C. Smith Boulevard at Camp Lejeune, North Carolina was buzzing with activity. Joe McKinney stood in front of the white board walking through what was known about Kevin Reardon's murder and the latest turn of events; the murder of Private David Wallace's father. The apartment where the elder Wallace was murdered was to the west of the base about four miles off US Route 17. The team planned to head to the crime scene for a review of what happened that day. Private Wallace had been placed on administrative leave because his mother lapsed into a coma after having a stroke. It would take a major disaster for Private Wallace to have a worse spring. His wife left him and took everything he had. His father was murdered, now his mother was in a coma. There was a real possibility that she would never come out of the coma and would die in the hospital. The fact that his military career, which had been going very well, was now sidetracked indefinitely seemed minor by comparison.

Pat McKinney, wearing his base visitor badge, shook his head as he read through the Wallace file. *Poor bastard.* Pat listened to his younger brother, Joe, as he walked through the timeline on the board in Nancy's office. The board contained the details of other cases, all color coded to easily identify where one case left off and others began. It was becoming clear that the cases were overlapping in a neat pattern. If these cases represented the same suspects, they were working fast, lining up one victim after another.

Pat had arrived late last night after driving all day from his home in Dunnellon, Florida. The drive had been pleasant enough. The trees had filled in with new, green leaves and the air smelled heavy with pollen. There'd been no rain and the temperature was in the high 80s while in Florida and South Georgia. It was closer to the high seventies now that he was in North Carolina.

Pat had offered his services for free but Major Hartnett had insisted on a contract. Hartnett and Major Griggs agreed that Pat and Joe's talents combined would be good for the investigation. They checked Pat's credentials with the Lake County Florida Sheriff's Department where Pat and Joe helped take down two major drug dealers in one sting operation. They were impressed with Pat and Joe's investigative skills. That sealed the deal with the Majors.

Diane wasn't thrilled that Pat was going to get involved in a military investigation regardless of whether it was with his brother. 'What skills do you have that can help the military experts?' she'd asked. He'd replied that he ran a consulting business and all he was going to do here was consult. He didn't know what he could contribute specifically but Joe thought he could help in some way. He knew that Joe was a pretty smart guy and that if there was anything that he could help with, he would. If it turned out that there wasn't any reason for him to stay, he'd leave. 'Besides, Honey, I'm going a little stir crazy here. I know my business is just getting started but the dead time between calls is killing me.' In the end, Diane gave her blessing, mostly because she trusted Joe's instincts, not Pat's. So Pat was with Joe in Nancy's office trying to take in all the details of the expanding case.

"We're pretty sure that there are at least two people involved," Joe said. "There is definitely a young woman, age 22 to 28. She is very pretty, blond hair, slender, about 105 to 115 pounds, blue eyes and well proportioned, probably 36" bust. We don't have any pictures yet but we're checking with the parents of her 'husbands.' The Grand Forks police provided these artist sketches made from the Reardon's neighbor's descriptions." He handed the three computer renderings over to Pat. "The Grand Forks connection is a bit weird, too. Most of the case files that we have with this particular pattern all happened here in the southeast. The North Dakota case seems out of place. We're trying to see if there's some reason for the one time, out-of-place occurrence."

Pat said, "That's screwed up. Let's just assume that there are two people, this brother and sister combination. What would possess them to make that trip?" Silence for a few seconds as Pat rubbed the scar on his chin. "Maybe they knew one of their victims before they went up there. Is it possible that they followed the guy up there because of a transfer? Maybe he got transferred before they could pull their scam."

"That's not possible. Reardon wasn't transferred right before his deployment and one of the scams occurred during the time Reardon was already at Grand Forks. It would make perfect sense except that he didn't have that much to steal," Joe said.

Pat asked, "What did he have of any value? Any collections; inheritance; a classic car? How about fancy furniture? Any investments?" Each question met with Joe shaking his head. Pat continued, "Some of these kids have trust funds that they can't collect on unless they join the military; kind of a tough love approach to getting their kids to grow up and take on some responsibility. You remember what it was like going through boot camp and all the training. It wasn't so much the skills training as it was learning how to be disciplined, learning respect. It sure taught us a lot that we didn't know."

"Yes it did." Joe thought for a moment back to Paris Island and some of his roughest moments. The physical training was hard but the mental games were the most difficult. But he knew he was training for a life and death mission that had nothing to do with the military. He shook his head clear again and thought about the current cases. "Kevin Reardon didn't have squat as far as anything of real value. We checked his bank account. He had less than $1000 in the bank between his savings and checking. He had some woodworking tools, furniture and a car, but that wasn't worth much. His wife sold his tools. That was the one thing he had that was worth something. They were worth a pretty penny but his wife sold them for a fraction of what they were worth." Pat raised an eyebrow at this. Joe continued, "We also talked with his parents. They said that he was just getting his feet on the ground financially. They said he had a good head on his shoulders and he had a plan until that 'little tramp' got hold of him. Their words, not mine. Then his plans were on hold for her. They said he couldn't stop talking about her. Everything shifted to center around Belinda. It's like she sucked the brains out of his head."

"I believe she sucked something out of his head, but I don't think it was brains and we're talking about the wrong head," Pat said, his lips curled into a crude smile.

Nancy Brown walked into the office and looked at Pat, then at Joe, then back at Pat again. Pat and Joe both stood. She said with a slight smile, "So, are you two twins? You look so much alike."

Joe answered, "No, I'm much better looking than this creep. Captain, this is Pat McKinney, my older brother." Pat shook hands with the Captain. Pat was impressed with her firm handshake and strikingly good looks. He had to work at keeping eye contact as his instincts wanted to look her over more closely. "We were just going over some of the details in the Reardon case. Pat's already reviewed several others."

Nancy walked around her desk and took a seat facing the brothers. Her facial features, once tight and smooth at the beginning of the case, were now showing signs of wear. The lines at the edges of her eyes were visible as were the slight bags under her eyes. Her energy level was also low as the details in the cases were coming in slowly. It seemed to both her and Joe that they'd gone over the timeline a thousand times. They both knew it by heart. When Richard Wallace was killed the Jacksonville Police were brought up to speed on the other cases. They had two detectives assigned to the Investigation Team but as with most police departments their involvement was limited by their caseload. Having the Jacksonville Police on the team did provide added resources, not just personnel. The Jacksonville Police Department had an excellent Crime Scene Investigations Team with new, high tech equipment. The problem they faced now was their services were now in demand by the Onslow County Sheriff's Office and every small town police department in the county.

Joe recommended bringing in a fresh set of eyes and that's when he called Pat. In turn, Pat suggested that they contact Orange County, Florida Sheriffs Detective Johnny Poleirmo again, to see if he could jar a few new thoughts from their tired brains. Pat had one other person that he thought might be able to help; William 'Radar' 'Hatch' Hatcher. Hatch was an old shipmate of Pat's from the USS Alabama. He'd helped out the brothers several months back when they were in a bind so Pat was a bit reluctant to ask for help again. He knew Hatch wouldn't mind but Pat didn't want to stretch that friendship too far. Hatch had secrets that Pat didn't want to expose. The possibility of adding him to the team would have to wait and only be done as a last resort.

The three were going over details again when the phone rang. They looked up at the clock before Joe reached for the receiver. It was 8:09 am. Nancy answered after the second ring. "Captain Brown." Silence. "Yes sir." Silence. "Yes sir." More silence. Nancy's forehead scrunched into wrinkles. "Yes sir, we'll get right over there." She hung up the receiver. She looked first at Joe, then at Pat and said, "That was Major Hartnett. There's been another murder. It looks like it may fit the pattern. It's here in Jacksonville, just down the street. The local police are on the scene and have the area roped off. They asked for our assistance."

Joe said, "We must have made a good impression on them when Private Wallace' dad was killed. Let's go. We've got work to do."

* * *

There was a small crowd at the apartment complex looking on as they approached in their rented Chevy Impala. Two uniformed officers were stationed to keep the crowd outside the taped off area. As they approached, the officer motioned them over to a spot away from the crowd where they could get through with little interference. He pointed them in the direction of a tall man wearing a dark sports coat. He had a crew cut and what little hair he had was nearly white. He appeared to be in his mid to late fifties. Near him, kneeling next to the body were several crime scene investigators. The body was still on the ground at the base of the stairs. It was difficult to see the body because there were overgrown shrubs hanging over into the sidewalk at the approach to the stairs. The apartment had six units per building; two upstairs, two about six steps up and two basement level apartments. The mail boxes were at ground level by the stairs that led down to the basement apartments.

An ambulance was just leaving the scene with its lights off and the county coroner's van was awaiting the release of the body from the scene. There was a distinct smell of blood in the air as they moved closer to the body. They could see the gun shot wound to the back and the contusion on the head, apparently from a fall. There was a pool of blood drying on the sidewalk next to the body and a smaller pool near the head.

The detective turned and greeted them. In a deep voice with a strong southern accent he said, "Hi. You must be Captain Brown." He shook her hand. "I'm Harold Pierce, Homicide." Joe and Pat each shook his hand and introduced themselves.

"We called ya'll in because this here young man is Private Edward Sharp, US Marine Corps. He was found here early this morning by the lady from the upstairs apartment. She works the morning shift at the base commissary. You are going to want to talk with her. She has quite a lot of information about Private Sharp, including that she heard rumors he was killed in action in Afghanistan. That's why she was real surprised to find his dead body outside her apartment."

"Seems to be a rash of that going around," Joe said. "Did she say anything about seeing a young woman in her mid to late twenties, blond, nice looking . . ."

"You mean Mrs. Sharp, by your description anyway. Yes she did. As a matter of fact, she thought she saw Mrs. Sharp last night, but said she was mistaken."

"What do you mean?" Nancy asked.

"She said she saw a woman who looked a lot like Mrs. Sharp but it turned out the woman was much older. She didn't go into any more detail. Is that important?"

Nancy replied, "Yes. Either there's an older sister going around or she's a very common looking lady. From the description, I don't think that's the case. We need to ask her a few questions about this older woman."

Detective Pierce rubbed a hand over the top of his bristle brush hair. His already wrinkled face showed the lines of stress as he squinted against the bright sunlight. "We'll question her again and you should accompany me. Sounds like you have some specific questions in mind."

Nancy nodded, "I sure do."

He changed the subject. "As best we can tell, the shots came from over there in the parking lot. There was either a person standing by the third parking spot or they shot from a car at about that same spot." He pointed a finger in the direction of several parking spaces. "The cars that were parked there were moved before we could secure the scene. I think that the shooter was in a vehicle. We can't find any residue or spent casings in the parking lot."

Pat asked, "Do we know the size of gun?"

"Yes. It was a 9mm. Whoever the shooter was, they're either very lucky or very good. From that distance, they put two slugs in his back, about 2 inches apart. That's about 50 feet. That's no easy task especially if Private Sharp was moving."

Pat, Joe and Nancy all raised their eyebrows at this. Joe said, "Same thing we thought at the Wallace scene."

Detective Pierce said, "That's right. That head shot that Mr. Wallace took was from a bit of a distance. We're dealing with a real nasty person here." He paused, then said, "We did find one thing that might be important. We found a pen in the grass over there." He pointed away from the scene. "It had dark red stains on the tip. At first we didn't think anything of it but then our crime scene folks determined that the red stain was blood. It wasn't completely dry. It may not be anything but we're checking it out." Joe made a note about the pen then glanced at Nancy and Pat. Detective Pierce continued, "You folks take a look around here. Let me know if you have any other questions. We can meet back at the department right before lunch."

They all nodded in agreement. The three of them moved around the crime scene and took notes. They approached the crowd and asked if anyone saw anything. Not one person admitted to seeing anything. After a few minutes of talking with the crowd, most of the onlookers dispersed. They didn't want to get involved. So the trio headed back to their own office to gather their newest timeline addition. This could be a break; two murders in the same city within weeks. Nancy said, "I think that we should set up a sting operation. It appears as if our killers have settled on a single location for a while. Let's talk with Major Hartnett and see if he'll support it. What do you think?"

"It can't hurt," Joe said. "It looks like they've settled in this area for a bit. There aren't that many bars but a sting operation is still a long shot."

Nancy came back with, "But we know that she hangs out at bars frequented by military guys. We can narrow it down based on that. That usually means pretty close to the base. I think that we can get an operation together quickly and get into several of the local bars. We need some young looking soldiers or sailors. You guys know anyone who might fit the description?"

Pat said, "I'll bet if you offered a job to some fairly new Marines that just finished boot camp and that job involved hanging out in a bar to try to lure chicks, you'd have no shortage of volunteers. Throw in that it's for God and country and they'd consider it their duty."

"Very funny, Pat," came Joe's sarcastic reply.

"Actually, that's a very good idea." Nancy was smiling wryly, her hand on her chin, thinking about how they could have more bars covered with teams of young Marines. "Let's talk with the Major and see what he thinks."

* * *

Nancy and Joe were in Major Hartnett's office at NCIS. They'd just explained their plan to the Major.

"Excellent. Captain Brown, contact Major Griggs and make the arrangements. I want this to proceed immediately. This is getting out of hand and it has to be stopped as soon as possible."

"Yes sir," Captain Brown and Sergeant McKinney said in unison. They turned and left the Major's office. They were joined by Pat in the hallway outside the Major's office.

"So . . .? How'd it go?" Pat asked.

"He jumped on it; said start immediately. I think that we can have our first team in place late tonight. We have to get some surveillance equipment lined up. We don't have a minute to waste."

They made their way to the office of Senior Chief Terrance B. Shephard. Shep, as he was called around the office, was an electronics genius. He had electronic gadgets stashed everywhere. "Captain Brown, how are you?"

"Great, Shep. How about you?"

"Doing just fine, thanks." He looked at Joe and Pat and extended his hand.

Nancy spoke up, "This is Sergeant Joe McKinney. Joe spent six years in the Corps, some of it in Iraq. This is his brother, Pat. Pat is a Navy veteran. He was a submarine sailor."

"Bubblehead, huh? Well I won't hold that against you."

"Thanks, I think." They both smiled.

"Call me Shep. But I guess we're on a tight schedule. I hear you'd like to get a sting operation together." They nodded. "You've come to the right place." They walked through a door in the office down a long corridor that was painted institutional green and into what appeared to be an electronics lab. There were two sides to the room separated by a glass wall. One side of the room had a number of countertops like a kitchen. The counters had several outlets for various types of electrical and electronic hook ups. There was also a small briefcase with what appeared to be pens, paper clips, and other assorted office supplies. On the other side of the glass wall was a clean area. A number of technicians were dressed in white lab coats with hair nets and dust masks over their mouths. They looked like a team of surgeons but there were no patients. Only electronic circuit boards, most the size of a quarter.

Over the next three hours the team was introduced to a number of electronic surveillance experts. The experts in turn showed the team the latest in miniature spy cameras. There were watches and pens and rings and eye glasses all with built in cameras, microphones and transmitters. The transmission distance on these tiny devices was well over three miles. Pat and Joe were impressed. Nancy had seen the demonstration before. They were also introduced to several young Marines. None of the bunch looked like they were old enough to shave. Each one had the look of a kid who was gullible; just what the doctor ordered. They held informal interviews with each candidate and were impressed by the knowledge and talent that each had for role-playing. Of the eight soldiers that the team interviewed, they chose two as their choices for the first go-around. The men were briefed on their assignment and told to report back to the NCIS office by 2000 hours for a final prep. The men were dismissed and left the building.

"I'm impressed," Pat said to Nancy and Joe. "This could actually work. If local law enforcement had these tools, they could really do some damage to civil liberties."

"They probably do have a lot of these tools but if they ever tried to use them without a court order, the evidence would get tossed out of court," Joe said. "Most judges in this country these days would never allow the sting op in the first place. Liberal pricks."

"In the wrong hands, these electronic gadgets are real dangerous. Can you imagine someone's daughter getting drugged and filmed by someone with these toys? She'd end up on the internet in some lewd, live performance without even knowing it." Nancy spoke as if she knew someone who'd experienced such a problem. Pat and Joe both wondered if that story had come from personal experience.

They chose the bar that they would target on this first night. Then they talked about the plan to have their young Marines move around the bar acting shy and gullible. They covered the means of gathering evidence and when they would move in if necessary. The young men would be unarmed. The team would be placed around the bar at strategic locations so that they could respond quickly in case of an emergency. After three hours of planning and re-planning, the three felt good about their course of action. Now they needed a stroke of luck.

* * *

It was 2310 hours in Jugheads Tavern. The smoke was thick and the music loud. The bar had a small stage at the wall opposite the main entrance. The main bar was to the left of the stage and a smaller bar was on the right far wall. The perimeter of the bar had raised platforms with booths along the wall and tables along the rail. The lights were very low except the stage lights which were switching between pink, purple, blue, and white as the Lynard Skynard cover band punched out popular tunes, one after another. The crowd was less than appreciative as just a smattering of applause rang out after each tune. This crowd wasn't here for the music; they were here for the skin.

The team set themselves up at strategic points around the bar on the raised platforms to provide a good view of their operatives on the bar's lower level. The two young Marines were dressed in night life golf shirts and blue jeans. Both men were in excellent physical shape and very obviously in the military. Even the most casual observer could tell that they were new recruits, probably recent graduates of Paris Island, waiting for their first set of orders. They were working independent of each other. Joe was in contact with Marine Private Jeffrey Steers via a miniature earpiece and microphone button on his golf shirt. Nancy was in contact with Private Leonard Skiff. Pat and two other agents were roaming the floor or standing at the bar, keeping an eye on the action. Pat couldn't believe the young girls walking around the bar floor. They appeared to be much too young for this scene. He thought of his own daughter, only three years old. *Is this what I have to protect her against? I'm really getting too old for this.* For the past hour, the action had been slow; no real prospects approached the two young Marines. Then a young, slender blond woman who fit the description of Belinda Reardon approached Private Steers. He said "Hi" and she stopped at his table. He asked her to sit and the conversation appeared to hold promise.

"So, how long have you been a Marine?" the young woman asked, then raised her glass and took a sip of her Tequila Sunrise. Joe listened and was impressed by the clarity of the voice transmission from the miniature microphone.

Private Steers played right along. "I just got out of boot camp. I just got my orders today. I'm heading over to Afghanistan in about three weeks."

"Are you scared? I mean, you don't look very old. What are you, eighteen, nineteen?" She asked.

"I just turned nineteen. My mom's a wreck. I'm more worried about her than I am about myself. She's been worried about me since I joined. See, my dad died when I was pretty young and she's all alone. She's okay financially 'cause she got a pretty good settlement when Dad died. He was killed in a train-car accident. The lights at a train crossing failed and he got hit as he tried to make it across."

Joe heard her wince as she heard the details of this totally fabricated story. He noticed the young woman put her hands on his as a show of comfort.

"Does your mom live close by? I mean, will you be able to see her before you get deployed?" *She's wasting no time,* Joe thought as he listened to this less than private conversation.

"I don't think so. She lives in Nebraska. She still lives in the farm house. She leases out the farm now but she doesn't like to leave the farm and property unattended. It's not like there's a lot of crime out there but it's a habit. We'll keep in touch though. What about you? What's your story?"

Joe thought, *This should be interesting. Let's see where this takes us.* "We're practically neighbors. I'm from Missouri, up north of St. Joseph. I didn't live on a farm or anything. My dad works for the state. He's an agriculture inspector. Mom works for the local library. It's mostly volunteer work for her, just to keep her busy. My name's Belinda. Belinda Rice." She extended her hand. Joe thought *Belinda Rice . . . Belinda Reardon. Pretty close. Too close for coincidence?*

"Jeff Steers." He smiled. "Come here often?"

"Not really. I just moved here a while ago. I got a job at the base working personnel files for civilian base support. It's a decent job. I hope that it will lead to something better."

"Sounds interesting. Do you have to interview people?" Jeff was doing a great job playing along. He wasn't being too obvious or pushing the conversation in one direction or another.

"No. I work with three other clerks. It isn't really that exciting."

"How long have you been in this job?" Jeff asked. *Don't push too hard, Jeff,* Joe said into his earpiece. Jeff raised his hand and grabbed his earlobe in a very natural looking move to acknowledge that he heard Joe.

"About four months. I just finished my probationary period. I got my first raise last week."

"Congratulations. Here's too many more." He raised his beer to her glass and they clinked.

The band switched songs to a quick tempo, loud, southern rock song that wasn't by Skynard. It sounded like a cross between .38 Special and Molly Hatchet; driving and rowdy. It was probably an original by the band and wasn't too bad. The crowd seemed to be getting into it. Jeff turned his attention back to Belinda. Joe said, *Ask her if she'd like to dance. We're going to check out her story. Don't let her see your earpiece.* Jeff immediately asked her to dance and they hit the dance floor. Joe relayed the question about Belinda's employment to a van in the parking lot. The technicians accessed the base computer and the database on current employees. Within seconds they had verification that Belinda Rice was in fact employed by one of the contractors at their personnel office and had been in that status for nearly five months. She had been stationed at Camp Lejeune for the entire period and could not have been in North Dakota at the time of the Reardon shooting. Even though this was a good test run, Belinda Rice was a dead end. Joe relayed the message back to Private Steers. He hoped Steers would be able to get away from her and try his luck with another young woman.

As Joe was relaying the information to Private Steers, Nancy noticed a woman approaching Private Skiff. She, too, fit the description of Belinda Reardon. She went right up to Private Leonard Skiff and asked if he'd like to dance with her. Lenny, being the gentleman that he was, obliged without missing a beat. As they hit the floor, the band switched gears. They started a slow easy listening tune. Immediately, Lenny Skiff turned into a charming, respectful young man and held his dance partner lightly. The young woman said, "I want to dance, not walk in the park," she said with a broad smile and pulled him closer.

He returned her smile. "My name's Lenny. What's yours?"

"Linda Walls. Where you from sailor?"

"Pardon me Linda, but I use sailors for dust rags," he said, his smile widening. "I'm a Marine. I'm stationed here at Camp Lejeune, at least for the next two and a half weeks."

"Where to then, Marine?"

144 P. J. Grondin

"I can't say for security reasons, but let's just say there's a bunch of rag hats where I'm going. I guess that's not PC but what the heck."

"You don't even look old enough to be out of high school and you're going overseas to fight? Have you got a girlfriend, Lenny Skiff?"

"Nope. Not yet anyway. You want to be my girlfriend?" He asked her in a playful way, his smile in a little, sly twist.

"Well I will be for tonight. I saw you across the room here and I thought, there's a guy who needs a woman for tonight and I'll be damned if I wasn't right."

"So Linda Walls, what do you do here in Jacksonville?" Lenny Skiff was a natural talker and appeared to be very at ease talking with this total stranger. He knew that there was an element of danger in this mission but that didn't seem to bother him.

Meanwhile, Nancy was listening in on every word between the two. She gave him no instructions as he appeared to have the situation under control. She watched closely as the two danced and talked, Lenny asking seemingly innocent questions, getting the information that they needed to find their woman.

Linda said, "I just got into town about three weeks ago. I was up in Ohio working at an auto parts factory when they up and closed their doors. So I sold a bunch of my junk and headed for warmer weather. My brother's stationed down here and he told me that there might be jobs available, so here I am. Still unemployed but I have enough cash saved to hold me over for a while." *I'll bet you do*, Nancy thought. "Anyway, I have several prospects. I have a second interview in a few days at the base with a contractor. If I get too hard up I can wait tables for a while. I'm not proud."

"I think that contractor would be nuts not to hire you. You sound like you have it together pretty well. Does your brother still live in the area?" *This could be the million dollar question.*

"Yes he does. We're sharing an apartment for right now. It's just up the road. Arbor Arms." *Bingo.*

Nancy turned to Joe and said, "I think that we can at least bring these two in for questioning. We might want to follow her back to the apartment and see if the 'brother' is there."

"I checked with the guys in the van. They have the conversation recorded. She's not admitting to anything but the timeline seems to fit and it would be a pretty big coincidence that they live at the same apartments as Private Sharp. Pretty ballsy though, don't you think? Could it be a coincidence?'

They both slowly shook their heads, convincing the other that they were on the right track. Nancy talked to Lenny Skiff through the ear piece, "See if you can get her to take you to her apartment. Once you get there let us know by a series of coughs that her brother is there. We'll follow you and take her and the brother in for questioning." Lenny gave the earlobe pull in acknowledgement. It only took him 15 minutes to walk out of Jugheads, arm in arm with Linda Walls. Nancy and Joe were certain that they had their suspects. They were wrong.

* * *

By the time the questioning was complete, the team knew they had erred. Linda and Richard Walls were indeed brother and sister, he was still in the Marines and stationed at Camp Lejeune. He was an infantryman back from his second tour of Afghanistan. He was respectful but pissed to be under suspicion of murder. He had all the proof that he needed to convince the team that he had nothing to do with any murders. His superior officers were called in the middle of the night to confirm it. They also were not pleased, especially Major Griggs, Joe's former commanding officer. Early the following morning, Captain Brown was called into Major Hartnett's office. He and Major Griggs were both there and they gave her the third degree.

Major Hartnett started. "Captain Brown, you jumped the gun on this one. We went along with the sting operation but you have to remember that these things are usually long shots. You have to get more solid information before you take personnel into custody and start dressing them down."

"Yes sir," was all Nancy Brown could say. She knew that the Major was right and there was no going back on that. She stood at ease and stared straight ahead. She took her verbal reprimand professionally without showing any signs of weakness. It was Major Griggs turn to speak. "Captain, you have a very capable Sergeant to help you. If you feel he is not providing all the support you need, let me know and he will be off the team." Major Griggs had all the confidence in the world in Joe McKinney but he wasn't sure if Nancy was using him to his full potential. "I'm sure that you and your team will regroup and get back on the right track but do not hesitate to stretch Sergeant McKinney's skills to their limit. He will only be with us for a short time. Use him."

"Yes Sir," was her only reply.

"Do you need any other resources to move this investigation along? You name it, we'll get it."

"No Sir. We have the talent we need. I just need a little patience. This will not happen again, sir. I will write a full report on the botched sting and have it to you by tomorrow morning."

Major Hartnett and Major Griggs looked at each other. Without speaking they came to the same conclusion; that Nancy Brown and Joe McKinney could handle the situation. Major Hartnett turned back to Nancy and said, "Alright then. Get back to work. Let's find these bastards. Dismissed."

Nancy Brown, in a firm, confident voice said, "Yes sir." She turned and strode out of the office. On her way back to her office she gathered her thoughts to revise the plan for the sting.   She made some wrong assumptions and was too impatient. *We made a mistake. We'll be smarter next time.*

When Nancy entered her office, Joe said to her, "We have some news. We have a better idea of who 'they' are.   We just got a fax of a picture of Belinda Reardon." Joe handed the letter sized fax from Grand Forks Police Department. It was a little grainy but it was easy to see facial details in the fax. There was one identifying mark on the picture that would be relatively easy to distinguish Mrs. Reardon from other women.   She had a birthmark on her neck below her left ear.   It looked like the state of West Virginia. Nancy looked at Pat and Joe and said, "Is this birthmark a blip on the fax or is this real?"

Joe said, "According to the detectives at Grand Forks, it's real. I can't believe that no one told us about this before. It'll sure help when we come across the real Belinda Reardon."

Nancy replied, "If there is such a person . . ."

Chapter 21

Bobby and Becky returned to the hotel at 7:15 in the evening from their brief tour of the area surrounding Norfolk Navy Base. The area was ripe with bars full of sailors. Bobby wanted Becky to see the bars in the daylight so that she could get a feel for the neighborhoods, parking areas, street access, and entrances and exits. He wanted to plan ahead. Becky thought that it was just a bit too dramatic. She just wanted to pick a bar, go and meet a guy and make him fall in love with her. She'd done it a dozen times already. It was second nature to her now. Bobby was getting nervous about each new target. He kept telling Becky that there was more at stake now that they'd made two big scores. He'd say 'we have to be more cautious' or 'we can't afford any mistakes'. Becky felt that she couldn't afford to be that cautious. Sure she had to be careful but if she appeared too uptight about every move, someone would wonder why she was always tense. In Becky's opinion they were more apt to make a mistake by being so mechanical about every little detail. She tried to get Bobby to understand that approach but Bobby would only get agitated and angry with her. So she decided that it was best to pretend to go along with him and just continue to do what came naturally to her. She already had her new name and life story figured out. It was all the detail that she needed. What these sailor boys wanted was in her panties and that's all the preparation she needed; a name and a story. The rest would come naturally.

Her eyes wandered around the hotel room with cheap furniture. There were a few starving-artist-style paintings hanging, crooked to one side or the other at odd locations on several of the antique white walls. The room smelled of years of cigarette smoke covered with lots of cheap air freshener. *Why do I have to put up with this? We have a lot of money, and half of it is mine. We should stay at better places.*

Her mind wandered to the face of Edward Sharp. She vividly saw the tears roll down his cheeks and the pained look in his eyes. She still saw the look on Edward Sharp's face as he fell, head first onto the sidewalk. She got a chill when she saw his blood-soaked back. She also remembered his blood on the bag of mail that she'd dropped on his back. The paper said he was killed by two gunshot wounds. It wasn't too difficult to explain the blood stain on the corner of the $100,000 check that they presented to the bank clerk for deposit when they'd opened the account at the Virginia Savings Bank. She'd explained that the check got blood from hamburger that was thawing on the counter near her stack of mail. 'The package was over the edge of the plate that I used. The puddle got on the envelope and

soaked through to the check. I am so sorry. The checks still good isn't it?'
The clerk had made a face but still deposited the check. Bobby and Becky
had already withdrawn most of the cash and were across town by the time
the account was a day old. It wouldn't be long before the police put the
murder and the check together but they'd be back in King's Bay by then,
collecting a check for her newest husband, soon to be declared KIA, Wilson
Brush.

Becky thought for a moment about the killings. There was more to
the killings than Bobby was telling her. Maybe that's why he was so tense.
If he did know more than he was willing to let on, then maybe he was right.
It couldn't hurt to be a little cautious. *But I sure can't get all uptight like
him. Why bother with this if you're gonna get all stressed out? Might as
well be poor and relaxed than rich and uptight. Maybe that's why rich folks
die of heart attacks so young.* The slap on the back of her head came out of
nowhere. Becky yelled "Shit! What'd you do that for, you prick?"

"You need to pay attention. Can you tell me anything that I've said
for the last five minutes?" Bobby paused for effect. Becky didn't respond.
She just glared at him and rubbed her head where his ring had hit the back
of her head. "I didn't think so. You've got to get it together, Becky. We
need to move fast so we stay ahead of the cops. I'm sure with that killing at
the apartment, if we're found they'll try to pin that on us."

"But we didn't have anything to do with it, did we Bobby?" She
paused. "Did you have anything to do with this? Is someone else involved?
I saw you talking to that lady in the parking lot at Tommy's at King's Bay."
She paused to gage his reaction. It didn't take but a fraction of a second
before she felt his temper.

He reached out and grabbed a handful of her hair and pulled her face
to his. He raised his other hand and quickly brought it down in a sweeping
motion. He stopped just before he would have made contact with her face.
Then he pointed his free index finger directly at her face. "I'm not going to
hit you because you have to look pretty for your next husband. You don't
know what you're talking about. There is no one else. Those killings had
to be a coincidence because I don't have any other explanation for them.
Maybe you're the one with the outside man killing these guys for real.
Maybe I'm the one who should be asking the questions here, making
accusations. You're the one who's out there shaking your ass in every guys
face. Maybe that's not enough for you anymore." His grip remained tight
on her hair and her face showed the pain of her head where hair follicles
were being torn out of her head.

"Bobby, you're hurting me." Tears were streaming down Becky's
face.

"He eased his grip on her hair some to give her some relief but he
didn't totally release her yet. He pulled her face to his and said in a stern
but quiet voice, "You have your job to do. I have mine. If you want to

keep making a lot of money, don't question me about my part. I had nothing to do with those killings and the police can't tie us to them. We want to keep it that way. So when I'm giving you instructions, you listen up and we'll both be rich someday. You got that?"

Becky nodded slightly, because Bobby hadn't released his grip.

"Are you going to be more careful when we do these jobs?"

Again, Becky nodded. Finally, after a few seconds of Bobby looking into her eyes, he let her hair fall free and he leaned back in his chair. He picked up where he left off in his planning for the next pickup as if nothing had happened between them.

But Becky was growing more fearful of his erratic behavior. She knew that Bobby was close to really hurting her. She had a lot of tools that she could use against him any time she pleased. Maybe that time wasn't so far off. *I'm not scared, but he should be.*

* * *

Pat and Joe were working late at Nancy's office at Camp Lejeune. They were both wracking their brains trying to piece together any leads that would complete the links in the human puzzle on the white board before them. They now had three dead bodies in two states that were linked only by circumstances. The circumstances were so similar that Pat, Joe, and Nancy believed the same people were behind all three murders and the cases of theft. The problem was they were always reacting to the killer instead of being able to predict the killer's next moves. The sting operation was their first attempt to get ahead of the game but that move only got them a reprimand from Major Hartnett and Major Griggs. They both knew that the reprimand was nothing more than a slap on the wrist but the real message was 'The team needs to produce'. With the failed sting there was added pressure to find these lunatics fast. That was a tall order considering what they knew.

Nancy Brown had gone back to her apartment for the evening. She had a migraine headache. She couldn't focus so she took a couple of pills and went to bed. She was wrapped pretty tight over the reprimand, but she was even more frustrated with the course of the investigation. It was accentuating the lines in her face and her mood swings were becoming legendary. One minute she was up, the next she was brow-beating herself and the team over details that, in the big scheme, didn't really matter. She said that she'd sleep off the headache and be in early the next morning. Pat and Joe told her not to rush it. The investigation would still be here when she got back.

Pat changed the subject away from the investigation to personal matters. "Hey Joe, when was the last time you talked to Lisa?"

Joe's face tightened. He looked down at his desk and rubbed his right hand over his face. "It's been a few days."

"Try over a week you insensitive shit-head! I'm going to leave the room in a few minutes after I beat your frickin' head in. What is wrong with you, man? You always do this. You get so wrapped up in crap like this investigation that you lose sight of the important things in your life." He was making exaggerated hand gestures in the air then pounded both fists on the desk. His face was getting red as he pointed a finger in Joe's direction, "Diane called me a bit ago and said that Lisa called her. She said she hadn't talked to you in a while. She was near tears. Her dad just died and her mother's a wreck. She needs you. Have I called you an insensitive shit-head yet?"

"Okay, okay, I screwed up! I get it!"

"No you don't. You need professional help. You get so insanely intense over this kind of crap. This stuff that we're dealing with here, it isn't our lives. We have real lives. Mine is with Diane. Yours could be with Lisa if you pull your head out of your ass!" Pat took a deep breath and stood. He walked around his desk, picked up Joe's phone and set it down hard in front of him. "Call her right now. Don't hang up until she clearly understands that you love her. You frickin' dope." Pat turned, walked out of the office and closed the door hard behind him. He re-opened the door and said, "Call her now!" He closed the door again.

Joe looked at the phone. *What am I going to say? I know I screwed up. She probably hates me.* Joe took a deep breath, picked up the phone and dialed her mom's phone number in Oak Harbor, Ohio. Lisa answered after the first ring. Her voice was weak. She sounded exhausted. It broke Joe's heart to hear her like this. He said in a quiet, almost apologetic tone, "Hi Lisa. It's Joe."

"Hi." Her reply was quiet, reserved, not like the strong, confident young woman that he knew from Florida; the same woman that whipped his butt handily in a fifty lap swim, worked out with him, spent hours talking with him, and spent nights making love to him. He knew that this was his fault. She already had tremendous pressure from her father's death. Her brother added to her stress by being a complete jerk. Now she had to deal with a fool of a companion. It was his fault alright and he knew he had to make this right.

"Lisa, I am so sorry for not calling you."

Quietly she replied, "It's alright. You're busy with theinvestigation and . . . "

Joe cut her off. "No. It's not alright and I want you to know that I know it isn't alright. I've been a jerk and a fool. This investigation is nothing compared to how important you are to me. I've let this consume me like I've let other things consume my life and I am not going to let this happen again."

On the other end of the line in Oak Harbor, Ohio, Lisa Goddard was crying into her tissue, and smiling at the same time. She longed to hear

Joe's voice just in casual conversation. But to hear him now with such emotion in his voice, it made her come alive again. She was still drained but she knew this was the start of her revival.

Joe continued, "Lisa Goddard, you are my life. If you hate me now because of what I've done, leaving you alone when you needed me most, I wouldn't blame you. But I know how badly I screwed up and I wanted you to know that." Joe stopped talking to give Lisa a chance to respond and he was worried when she didn't say anything right away.

Then Lisa, still sniffling and fighting back tears of happiness said, "Joe McKinney, I love you. Just tell me when we're going to see each other again. That's all I want to know right now. I don't care how long it takes, I just want to know when."

Joe said, "I'm going to tell Major Hartnett that I need a couple of days off and I'll see you late tomorrow. I have to see you. I have to make up for being such a jerk and make sure everything is right between us."

"You call me as soon as you know. Joe, I do love you. You call me, understand?"

"Yes, Lisa. I will. I can't wait to see you. When I do, you can tell me everything that's been happening and I'll tell you as much as you want to know about what I've been doing. I'll call you tomorrow with details about when I'll be there." There was silence except for the sound of Lisa's sniffles. They both said 'I love you' several more times then were silent. They stayed on the line a few seconds longer, then they both disconnected. Joe took a deep breath as his eyes were wet, but no tears would run down his face. He was a Marine, after all. He rubbed his eyes with the back of his hand to make sure no tears made it to his cheeks.

At the other end of the line, Lisa was sobbing tears of joy until her mother called out to her and asked her if she was alright. Her emotions immediately took a turn and she felt guilty. How could she feel such joy at a time when her mother was in mourning at the loss of her life partner? Lisa went out to the living room to give her mother the news about Joe's call and to continue to be with her at her time of need. They spent the rest of the evening talking about family. There were many tough times and many bad times, but they ended the evening talking about good memories. It lifted both their spirits. Lisa was glad that she was able to help her mother. Her mother was happy for her daughter and her new love, one that Lisa was sure she had lost. They both felt renewed.

* * *

Joe sat at his desk in deep thought, still abusing himself for being such an idiot regarding Lisa when his phone rang. It startled him at first as his mind was anywhere but at the office. To his surprise, it was Major Sharon Hull, Colonel Milton Chester's aid from Grand Forks Air Force Base. "Sergeant McKinney, Colonel Chester requested that I contact Captain Brown. Is she in?"

"No, Ma'am. She had to leave early today. What can I do for you?"

"The Colonel wanted to know what progress you've made in the investigation into Staff Sergeant Reardon's death?"

Joe hesitated for a moment before answering. He wanted to be cautious about what details he gave out to personnel not directly involved in the investigation. Colonel Chester should be updated on the investigation but Joe felt that it would be more appropriate if Nancy provided that update. He apparently took a while longer than Major Hull expected because she said into the receiver, "Sergeant McKinney, are you still there?"

"Yes, Ma'am. I would prefer that Captain Brown provide this update. It is her investigation. She has to decide what information is relevant and appropriate for . . ."

Major Hull cut him off. "Sergeant, you will provide me with the details of this investigation and now. There is no need to wait for the Captain. I'm sure she'll understand. The Colonel wants an update and you will provide that update. Now, let's get started. What progress has been made on the Reardon murder?"

Joe hesitated again, deciding if he should try one more time to request that Nancy provide the update.

"Sergeant?" Major Hull was becoming impatient.

"Ma'am, I'm sorry but I'm trying to do two things at once here. I cannot provide the Colonel with any information about the investigation. If you wish to take this up with Captain Brown she will be in tomorrow morning." He paused, waiting for a response.

The deep voice of Colonel Chester boomed in Joe's ear, "Sergeant, I want that report now. If I don't get it, I'll file a report with Captain Brown and Major Hartnett about your insubordination. Is that clear enough for you, son?" Major Hull, if still on the line, was silent.

"Yes, sir, I understand you. But you will still have to wait for the report from Captain Brown. If you wish to file a complaint or charges, that is your prerogative, sir." Joe stopped to see if Colonel Chester would continue his demands.

"Listen, son, you've had a short but distinguished career. Don't trash it over something as simple as providing an update on a murder investigation. I just want to know how close we are to wrapping this up."

Joe said in a calm but deliberate voice, "I understand, sir. Captain Brown can provide those details to you in the morning."

Joe was quiet. He wasn't intimidated. It only piqued his interest more as to why Colonel Chester would be so insistent that Joe provide this update now. What was in it for him?

"Big mistake, Sergeant. I hope you enjoy civilian life."

The line went dead. Joe just held the receiver for a moment longer then slowly placed it on the cradle. *Wow* was all Joe could think. He shook his head, trying to think of any reason that a Colonel would listen in on a conversation covertly.   He really didn't want to go back to North Dakota but there may be good reason to make the trip.   Maybe they could ask the local detectives to look into anything that might link the Colonel to Kevin and Belinda Reardon.   It was almost too far fetched to consider but he'd seen and experienced stranger things than this in his young life.

As he stood, Pat opened the door and walked in. "Did you call her?"

"Yes I did. I am going to see her tomorrow. I don't know how and for how long but I am going. I might stop there on my way to North Dakota."

"Say what?" Pat's dumbfounded look was priceless.

"You're gonna want to be seated before I tell you this," Joe said.

"This ought to be good."

It was. Pat also found the Colonel's behavior out of place. Pat's brain got to work trying to analyze the facts for a tie, however slim, that might involve Colonel Chester. As Pat sat and thought, he rubbed his chin scar, feeling the texture that was distinctly different than the rest of his face. Joe could tell that Pat thought he was close to a breakthrough, but it just wasn't coming out.

"What is it, man?" Joe asked.

"I'm not sure. This North Dakota connection is so different than the rest of the cases. There's got to be a logical connection. I just can't place it. It'll come to me."

Joe leaned back in his chair, looked up at the ceiling and closed his eyes.   He knew Pat was good at coming up with obscure facts and remembering things that happened years ago.   When they were kids they would watch Star Trek every afternoon.   Pat got to the point where he would say the actor's lines before they had a chance.   Joe and his youngest brother, Mike, would get mad as hell, telling Pat to stop it, but he just kept on. He could also remember sports statistics. He'd memorize the backs of baseball cards and get Joe and Mike to ask him questions. They finally told Pat that they didn't want to play that game anymore. They were tired of him showing off.

When the brothers got into their teen years, they started their experimentation with pot and Pat's memory started to falter. He could no longer remember details that had previously been easy for him to remember.   It took a major travesty in the family to get them to stop smoking grass, but in the long run, Pat's memory regained some of its recall, but not all. Pat was sure that those few years of smoking grass had impaired his mental capacity at least a little bit.

Pat shook his head. "Let's go over the Kevin Reardon file again. Maybe it'll jar a detail or two loose."

Joe chuckled to himself and leaned forward in his chair again. He looked over at Pat and said, "Would you stop rubbing that damn scar? You're gonna rub a hole in your chin.

"Sorry?" Pat said as he sat on his hands.

They went over the Reardon file again. They both came up empty. Pat said, "Nancy will be in tomorrow morning. We'll talk with her about this. She's gonna go through the roof, having a colonel trying to butt in. She'll be loaded for bear by the time she gets her morning coffee. I'll bet five bucks that she's on the phone with Hartnett before the clock strikes 0800 hours."

Pat was off by six minutes. She was furiously punching in numbers by 7:54 am.

Chapter 22

When Nancy Brown got off the phone with Major Hartnett, both men were smiling at her as she turned to face them. She leaned back against the edge of her desk and asked what they were smiling about. They both said in unison, "Nothing, Ma'am." Nancy crooked her lip into a half-smile. She was trying to unwind from her anger. She'd actually managed to calm herself down about mid-way through her call with Major Hartnett. She finally realized that she was raising her voice to a superior officer. This usually wasn't tolerated, especially when the officer doing the yelling had just been reprimanded the previous day. But Major Hartnett liked the Captain's grit. Plus, she was right. Colonel Chester crossed a very clear line and was trying to apply pressure on members of his investigative team. He offered to call the colonel but Nancy explained that they intended to do a little covert work back at Grand Forks. She also intended to provide the requested update but with limited information. Major Hartnett approved.

Joe hadn't told Nancy yet about his plans to take a side trip through Ohio. That would be the next task of the day but Joe wanted to wait until Nancy was totally calmed down and she had her first cup of coffee. Pat helped by asking Nancy if she had any thoughts on how Colonel Chester might be involved. She said that maybe he wasn't trying to protect himself. Maybe someone else close to him was involved. That was one possibility Pat and Joe hadn't considered. Maybe the Colonel had family members or close friends that he was trying to protect. Pat wrote some notes from their brainstorming on the timeline board about the Colonel and about his possible connection to the killings. Just as Nancy finished her first cup of coffee, the phone rang on her desk.

"Captain Brown."

"Good morning Captain. This is Bill Banks, Grand Forks PD."

"Good morning Detective Banks. You're up awfully early. What is it, 5:00 am out there?"

"No Ma'am. We're only an hour behind you here. So it isn't that early. It is awfully dark though. The sunrise here runs a bit late since we're so far west. But I didn't call to chat about time zones. We have something that you're going to want to see." Nancy's eyes widened as she looked at Joe, then Pat. She put her hand over the receiver and mouthed 'good news.'

"What is it, Bill?"

"Several things. We have a very clear picture of Belinda Reardon, much better than the one we faxed earlier. We also have a stack of obituaries from deceased girls and women, ages 15 to 25. Somehow

Belinda Reardon, or whoever this woman really is, got social security numbers for each of the dead women listed in the obits. It looks like it's an identity theft toolkit. We found some drivers licenses that looked like they had flaws. And some pretty authentic looking birth certificates. The licenses and birth certificates we recovered looked like they were used for practice but they could have fooled me. She has everything she needs to switch identities whenever she wants. As long as nobody checks dead person files, she has an identity that is pretty much foolproof. I can e-mail a copy of the photo and copies of some of the birth certificates and drivers licenses to you. We'll keep the originals here. One of the women in the obituaries is named Belinda Lockart. We think that this is the identity that she used when she married Kevin Reardon. We're trying to verify that now."

Nancy and Bill exchanged more information including details on the murders in Jacksonville. They hung up after agreeing that they needed to continue to work these cases together.

Nancy turned to Pat and Joe and said, "We just got a lot more information to work with. Bill Banks has a photograph of Belinda Reardon. He is e-mailing a copy now along with a list of names that Belinda may be using as aliases. Also, Bill thinks the same as we do that there is one accomplice, no more. He has the remnants of an identity theft kit. The kit had old obituaries, names and addresses of family members of the deceased, personal information about hobbies, schools, degrees, boyfriends' names, and a lot more. They're trying to get prints from anything in the case but so far only smudges, nothing useful. It appears that our grieving widow has a lot more marrying planned." Pat and Joe both leaned forward in their chairs. Nancy continued, "One of us needs to go look at the evidence in North Dakota, the stuff that they can't copy and e-mail. Plus we have a little more work to do up there. We need to find out why they were up there. It's just out of place. Like we've said all along, it doesn't fit the pattern."

Nancy continued, "Once we receive this stuff from North Dakota, we need to comb the local case files to find where these aliases were used. We may be able to determine a possible list of names that might be used in the future. This could be a huge break."

Joe took the opportunity to offer his services to go to North Dakota. He planned to take the scenic route through North Ohio. "Nancy, I'll go to Grand Forks. I have to take a personal day anyway so I'll do that on my way up there. I'll fly into Cleveland, take half a day to take care of my personal business then fly back out to Grand Forks the next morning." Joe waited to see Nancy's reaction. He was surprised when she said, "Sure. That would work fine." She even started to smile. That worried Joe.

"So, what's the smile about?"

"I think that Colonel Chester needs to sweat a little after what he tried to pull. We'll cut off all contact with him but drop hints in strategic places that you're heading up there to continue the investigation. We'll also let it be known that we've discovered some pretty significant evidence. We won't publicize anything about the nature of the evidence. That might rattle his cage a bit. If there's no connection then we'll know that by his actions. What do you think?"

"How are we going to watch him if Joe's the only one up there?" Pat asked.

"We can use the new Marine recruit graduates from the other night. They did a great job, don't you think? Maybe we can get them to do a little scout work for us in Grand Forks. Or better yet, why don't we set up a surprise site inspection? We could get a couple of seasoned inspectors and have our guys work with them to make the Colonel nervous."

Both Joe and Pat scratched their heads. They weren't sure where Nancy was going with this but it was interesting to watch her as she developed a plan. They just wished it was clearer to them.

Nancy said, "Joe, when you get to Grand Forks, I want you to get caught up on any new interviews Detectives Banks and Hansen have had with the Reardon's neighbors. I think we missed something there. Now that we have a picture of Belinda we can show it around the local department stores and . . ."

Pat jumped out of his chair with his arms in the air. "That's it," he exclaimed. "I knew it would come to me. The one neighbor, chubby lady, Lil . . . "

"Weickoff." Both Joe and Nancy said it in unison.

"Right." Pat was getting more animated the more he tried to continue. "She said that she saw a lady that looked like Belinda, but older at the Wal-Mart a few weeks after she was supposed to have left for Florida."

Joe said, "So what? She saw some lady. Big deal."

Pat continued, "She said the reason she remembered so well was because she also saw Colonel Chester at the Wal-Mart near where this woman was standing. Maybe there's some kind of relationship there. Maybe Colonel Chester knows this woman and maybe this woman and Belinda Reardon are related somehow."

"Well that was one shit load of 'maybes. If we throw in a few more, maybe we can accuse the Wal-Mart clerks of being Belinda's sisters because they have the same colored hair as her." Joe's remarks were soaked with sarcasm.

"I know it's far fetched but maybe there's a connection. What if this woman is Belinda's mom or older sister? What if Colonel Chester had an affair with this woman? Maybe that's the reason for Belinda and her accomplice to go to North Dakota. Have we checked that out?"

"Okay, let's capture all those questions and we can start looking into possible connections." Nancy said, "Let's get Joe's travel plans together. Pat, you and I will go over the latest information from Grand Forks and see how it fits our timeline. Let's get the Jacksonville Police and the rest of the team in here when we get the e-mail from Grand Forks and exchange information. We're starting to get more intelligence so we're going to have to work fast. Make sure that you're thorough as you sift through the evidence. I want to start to distribute the pictures of Belinda Reardon and the sketches of her brother to bar owners near all the bases from Kings Bay to Norfolk. I also want to get teams into those bars if only for an hour or so each. We know that they favor bars frequented by soldiers and sailors. Maybe with this new information we'll get lucky. I feel like we're close to a breakthrough."

* * *

Over 200 miles away in Norfolk, Virginia, Becky Lippert was fast asleep in the beat up queen sized bed of their newly rented apartment while Bobby Garrett finished lacing his shoes. He was headed out to get breakfast and have a covert meeting with an older woman. He looked in on Becky one final time then quietly made his way out of the apartment. He drove north on US route 460 and found the small, dingy diner. The woman had said to meet her there at 8:30 and be alone, without Becky. He was doing as instructed because he knew she meant business. He reached inside his light weight windbreaker jacket and made sure he had the wad of cash; $10,000. She'd demanded $20,000 but Bobby told her he didn't have that much to spare, that he and Becky hadn't pulled that much cash out of the account from the one check that they'd received. She'd called him a liar, but what did she know? There was no way that she could know that they had nearly $190,000 in cash at the hotel since they'd made two scores, not one. He had no intention of ever letting her know. He knew that she was not stable but he felt it was better to try to appease her with a little cash rather than turn her down. That could send her off the deep end. He was pretty sure that she'd already committed murder at least three times. The victims were total strangers to her. Who knows what she was capable of doing to people that she knew who'd crossed her. He knew he was on that list.

He parked at the diner, went inside, and found the booth near the back corner as she'd instructed. From this vantage point, Bobby could see the entire west parking lot. In the distance he could see the booms of the large loading cranes used to load and unload massive equipment and stores for the destroyers, frigates and aircraft carriers at the Norfolk Naval Shipyard. The booms were different colors but the predominant color of everything on the base was gray. As he looked out over the western skyline of cranes, ship radio towers and support buildings, it seemed fitting that the sky was also a light gray, with a slight chill in the air. A waitress approached and asked, "Coffee?"

"Yes. Black."

"You need a menu?"

"Yes."

"Are you expecting company?"

A little more impatiently, Bobby answered, "Yes. Just leave one menu."

The waitress said nothing else as she laid a menu on the table and poured his coffee, being sure to spill some on the table around his cup. She turned quickly and left.

After several minutes passed, a woman entered the diner. She wore sunglasses even with the overcast sky and she had on a baseball cap with a Navy emblem. She wore a dark blue windbreaker jacket similar to the one Bobby wore. She strode with a purpose directly to Bobby's booth and sat across from him. She had what could best be described as a scowl on her face as she sat and looked across the table directly at Bobby's eyes. She started to speak until she saw from the corner of her eye that the waitress was approaching. Before the waitress was within 10 feet of the booth, she said, "Coffee, black." The waitress nodded and grabbed a cup off the coffee station, set the cup in front of her and poured.

"Will you need a menu?"

The woman said, "No, now please leave us alone."

Without another word, the waitress turned and headed for the kitchen. She looked back over her shoulder only once with a facial expression to show her disdain for the two of them.

In a near whisper, but with a tone that had force behind it, the woman asked, "So Bobby, did you bring my money?"

"This isn't your money, Abbie. We earned it, Becky and me. The only reason I'm giving you this is so you'll get the hell out of here and leave us alone. We're happy and we don't need you following us around the country like some mother goose. I'm taking real good care of her and she's taking care of me."

This brought a wicked smile to the woman's face. "I'll bet she is, you son-of-a-bitch. I wasn't good enough for you but she is. I could be doing this for you right now, you know. I can't believe you think she's better than me. You left me like a piece of trash, like I wasn't worth nothing. Well you're gonna pay for that move, mister. Today's just the down payment. I want 20% of everything the two of you make. I can't punish her because she doesn't know what you did to me. If she knew the truth, she'd kill you. Do you know that? She'd cut you open like a pig." Her face was becoming more twisted and menacing as she spoke. She was getting louder with each sentence and Bobby was worried that the few other patrons in the diner would hear her. She went on. "Another thing, you haven't earned a thing.

I know that Becky is doing all the work. If it wasn't for her, you'd be broke on your ass. You're like a leach."

"Look, Abbie, we had a good thing, but it's over. Just get over it and move on to someone else. You made me fall for you easy enough. Find some other poor bastard and suck the life out of him."

She took off her sunglasses and her hat. He saw her eyes tear up as he spoke these harsh words. When her hair fell around her shoulders, he saw the resemblance to Becky immediately. But the years had been hard on Abigail Jean Glover. She spent too much time in sea side bars drinking hard with sailors. She also spent too many nights in bed with those sailors; sometimes more than one. Bobby felt sorry for her, but he knew he couldn't help her the way she wanted to be helped. She was only forty-one but hard living zapped another 10 years from her appearance. *Is Becky going to look this old in just 14 years? It can't be possible.*

Bobby reached inside his jacket and pulled out the envelope with $10,000. He laid it on the table in front of Abbie. "This is it, Abbie. You put this in your pocket and get out of our lives. You're bringing us too much attention. We can't work this way." He paused. "You can use this to get yourself on your feet and find a place to settle down. There are plenty of truckers out there who'd love to have a companion like you." He took a long drink of his coffee. He set the cup back on the table and said, "Becky and I are planning to settle down after the next two scores. We'll have enough money to buy our own place and we can stop racing all over the country. Maybe we'll get a condo in the mountains."

"Bobby, you're never gonna settle down. Scheming is in your blood. You'll always be looking for a way to screw somebody over. Mark my words; the only place you're going to settle is in your grave. It's too bad you have to take my sweet Becky with you."

With that, Abigail Jean Glover picked up the envelope, stuffed it in her jacket pocket and walked out. She walked around the parking lot and disappeared from Bobby's sight. He hoped it was the last time he'd ever see her, but he was pretty sure that it wasn't to be. That was a problem he needed to remedy. He hated the thought that he would have to kill his former lover.

* * *

Becky Lippert awoke from her deep sleep and looked around the unfamiliar apartment bedroom. She had a hard time clearing her head as the plain walls came into view. Slowly, she remembered that she and Bobby had rented an apartment in Norfolk near the Navy Base. She hated the smell. It was like someone else's dirty laundry. She hated the way she and Bobby lived now, but Bobby promised that they'd get a new place soon with the money that they'd made. *He means the money that I made. But he does know how the insurance forms work so I guess he should earn something. But I give him enough rewards. Things better improve soon or*

I'm finding a new man. She threw the covers back and rolled to one side. She had a view through the gap in the curtains that covered the six foot sliding glass door of the bedroom. She got out of bed, naked, walked to the curtains and looked out through the opening. The balcony overlooked a common area between several apartment buildings to the west. She could see the Lafayette River in the distance between the buildings. The neighborhood was mostly apartments, many occupied by sailors and their families and many low income civilian families. It appeared to be a rough mix of folks and had the potential for trouble if one lived here for long. It was like many of the apartment communities that Becky and Bobby had occupied before. They never really lived at any of the apartments for long, using them solely for the purpose of having a base of operations for staking out their targets. Bobby liked this particular apartment complex because of the high population of Navy personnel. It would almost certainly be petty officers with lower ranks which meant recently graduated recruits or men that had a difficult time making rank. That meant they were in trouble or weren't too bright. For Bobby and Becky, that meant that they were easy targets.

Becky didn't see anyone outside the sliding glass door so she opened the curtain and looked out at the wider view. No one was in the common area and she couldn't see into anyone else's apartment windows. The sun was shining, with just a few wisps of cirrus clouds above. The morning looked good and Becky felt good in all her naked glory, exposing herself to the world outside. She smiled at nothing in particular and lifted her hair with her hands and tossed it back. She ran her hands down across her breasts, then across her flat stomach. She shook her head, tossing her hair from side to side. She wondered where Bobby went but figured that he'd gone out to get doughnuts or some other breakfast supplies. That was fine. She enjoyed her time away from him. At least she didn't have to worry about performing any sexual acts for him. She looked at her arm where he'd grabbed her the day before. Sure enough, there were bruises made by his fingers where he gripped her arm. She'd have to show him those. He had to control himself better. He was damaging the merchandise. *Maybe not for long.* She turned, went into the bathroom to take a shower. *I'll feel better after a long shower. Maybe Bobby will be back by then. If not, I'll go out for a walk and meet the neighbors.*

Bobby still wasn't back when she finished her shower. She threw on a long tee shirt and panties and went into the drawer where Bobby said he kept the cash. *There it is; the prize money in two envelopes.* She counted the cash in both envelopes. She loved to see it and feel it in her hands. But there was something wrong. *There's only $178,000. Maybe I counted wrong.* She counted again with the same results. Her forehead wrinkled and her face twisted into a frown. Then she relaxed. *Maybe Bobby went out to get me something special. I deserve it after all. I'll just let it pass* *and see if he surprises me.*   She smiled to herself.   She looked around the apartment again.   *Soon, we'll get a decent place.   We'll get new furniture, all our own.   We'll be driving fancy cars.   I'll be wearing nice clothes.   Real soon.*

Chapter 23

It was nearly 10:30 PM when Pat unlocked the door and entered the apartment that he and Joe shared in Jacksonville, North Carolina. A thin streak of light shown through the curtains that covered the patio sliding glass doors at the back of the living room. The curtains didn't quite meet in the middle and allowed the glow from a street light to trace a thin line of light on the green carpet. He looked around the dark living room and noticed that the light on the answering machine was blinking bright red, alerting Pat that there was at least one unanswered message. He flipped a switch just inside the door that turned on a table lamp at the end of the couch. The lamp was on the lowest of the three settings and at 50 watts, there were many shadows cast on the walls from other furniture in the living room. As he approached the phone, he could make out the number 4 in the red LED display. *I should get a shower first. But if one of these is Diane, I should probably get back with her. I'll call her, get a shower then listen to these.* He picked up the receiver and dialed his home phone number in Dunnellon, Florida. The line was busy. He pressed button to disconnect his first attempt and hit the redial button. The line was still busy. Pat put the receiver on the cradle and headed for his bedroom. Before he could get out of his clothes, the phone rang. It was Joe.

"Hey little brother, how was the trip to Ohio?"

Joe said, "The flight was fine. The drive to Oak Harbor was okay. The temperature in Oak Harbor is about seventy degrees but it feels cool. Did you get the message on your machine?"

"Not yet. If it's seventy in Ohio, it should be about fifty in Grand Forks. Man, you get all the cherry assignments. How do you rate?"

"You're hilarious, Pat. At least I'm with Lisa for tonight."

"How is she holding up?"

"She seems to be alright, really starting to come around. I think I really screwed her up by not calling this past week. I'm such an idiot. Her mom's also feeling stronger. She told Lisa to get back down to Florida and get on with her life but Lisa told her that she'd stay a while longer."

Pat said, "Is Publix going to let her stay away from work this long?"

"If they don't she can always find another job. It's not a career. Besides, I have an idea that she may not want to go back to work. She'd really rather go to school full time. I've got something in mind that might convince her." Joe paused for a moment. "I'm going to ask her to marry me tonight."

"It's about time! What's taken you so long?"

"I already told you, I'm an idiot. Hopefully I can keep my wits about me long enough to ask her."

"Just ask her! Quit wasting time, man! All she can say is yes . . . or no. Don't pass up on the chance again. Some local farmer boy will come by and scoop her up. Maybe her old boyfriend is waiting for the right moment to pop in and steal her from you."

"Get hosed, Pat. I told you, I'll ask her tonight."

Pat heard a quiet voice over the phone. It was Lisa. He heard her say, 'Ask what?' Joe quickly said, "I've got to run. I'll call you tomorrow."

"Okay man. Later." Pat put the receiver on the cradle and again looked down at the number 4 blinking red on the answering machine. He started to turn down the hall to his bedroom but something told him that he should listen to the messages. His body tensed as he leaned over the machine and lightly touched the button to play the first message. The number 1 flashed as the machine prepared the first message for playback. It was Nancy Brown. She said she went back to the office after dark. Her headache was gone and she was planning to stay a while if Pat needed to get in touch with her. She said that she received a call from Private David Wallace. He'd heard that they were investigating cases like his. He wanted to come in to their office and talk. Nancy asked Pat to call her at the office no matter how late. *That's interesting.*

The machine flashed number 2 as it moved to the next message. It was Diane. She asked Pat to call her when he had a chance. Nothing urgent, she'd said.

Message number 3 was from Joe. He wanted Pat to know that he made it to Oak Harbor without incident. He said he'd call when he got to Grand Forks. The message ended.

For some reason, Pat didn't want to listen to the last message. He wasn't sure why, but as the machine beeped and the number 4 flashed, signifying the last message was being cued up, his heart felt heavy. Somehow, he knew that this message bore bad news. The message started. It was Diane again. This time her voice was tense and her message tentative. "Pat. If you're there, please pick up. If not, please call home the moment you get this message. Pat, it's your dad. He's had another heart attack."

The phone went dead and the answering machine reset, the number 4 turning solid signifying that all four messages had been answered. Pat collapsed in the couch next to the end table. He shook his head then rubbed his right hand over his head. His forehead furled into wrinkled tension lines as horrible thoughts consumed his mind. How could his dad survive a second heart attack so soon after the first? He was still early in his recovery and the damage to the heart couldn't have been repaired in this short amount of time. He rubbed the scar on his chin as he sat motionless except for his finger against that patch of rough, white skin. He wondered how his mom was holding up; not well, he knew. She had to be a wreck by now. She wasn't very strong after the first attack. She certainly would fall to pieces now, especially since no one was there to help her. He felt as helpless as he'd ever felt in his life. He missed Diane now more than ever. She always knew what to say to comfort him in tough times like this. He reached for the phone and dialed his home number in Dunnellon.

Diane picked up the phone on the first ring. "Hello."

"Hi Babe. How's Dad?"

"I just got off the phone with your mom. He's in the ER now but they'll be moving him to the cardiac care unit as soon as they can stabilize him. Your mom said that they haven't told her much yet but the doctors and nurses appear to be much more concerned this time. That may just be Mom talking. She really sounded bad. I don't know how long she can stand to be alone down there."

"Did she leave a number with you?"

"Yes." Diane read the number to Pat and he wrote it down on a note pad by the phone. "How long ago did he have the attack?"

"About half an hour, maybe forty-five minutes." Diane paused. "I'm worried about Mom, too. She sounded much more fragile this time. She was in tears the whole time I talked with her. I tried my best to console her but she's beside herself."

The line was quiet for several seconds which seemed like minutes. Then Pat said, "I'll check flights and try to get out tonight but I can't guarantee that I'll be able to catch a flight until morning. I'll call Mom and tell her to try to stay calm. I'll get there as soon as I can."

"What about Joe? Can you call him?"

"I'll do that later. He's up in Ohio with Lisa. I just talked with him a few minutes ago. He's gonna pop the question if he can get the frog out of his throat. I'll wait until I'm relatively sure that he's already done the deed. I'll call after I talk with the doctors at Ft. Myers."

"Wow. I can't believe this is happening. Dad seemed to be doing so well. I'll say a prayer for him."

Pat asked, "Do the kids know, in particular, does Sean know?"

"No, he's already in bed. They're both fast asleep. I'll wait until morning to tell Sean. I'll know Dad's condition better by then. I'll have to figure out how to break it to him in a way that he can understand. He's too young for the details."

"You might be surprised. Listen, I have to get moving if I'm going to get out of here tonight. I'll call when I know the flight details. I'll try to get a direct flight to Fort Meyers. I have to figure out the nearest commercial airport. Wilmington, I think." Pat thought for a moment how he would get to Wilmington. Then he said, "Hell. It'll be days before I get down there."

"Pat, don't rush and get hurt. That won't do any of us any good. Now get moving. I love you."

"I love you, too. Kiss the kids for me." The phone went dead.

He held down the button to get a new dial tone then cradled the phone in his shoulder with his chin. He pulled the phone book from the end table drawer and looked up Airlines in the yellow pages. He dialed the 800 number for the first airline in the short list and got a recording. If you are checking on the departure and arrival times for a flight, press 1; if you are . . . . Pat held the phone away from his mouth and cursed technology. After 8 minutes of walking through the phone call maze, he reached a real person in flight reservations.

Without waiting for the standard greeting from the US Airways clerk, Pat jumped right in and said, "I need to get to Fort Myers, Florida as soon as possible. When is the soonest departure and are there any direct flights?"

The attendant informed Pat that there were no flights that went directly to Fort Meyers from Wilmington, which was the closet commercial airport to Jacksonville. She said all of the commercial flights made connections through Charlotte or Atlanta. Pat's heart sank. She continued and explained that the flight that arrived the earliest in the morning would land at 11:30 AM. Pat's heart sank a little more. He looked around the apartment as he tried to think of a question that he could ask to change reality. The room started to spin as his thoughts were running into each other. Then the clerk said, "There is one other option." Pat waited for what seemed like an eternity. "You could hire a charter jet out of AJ Ellis." Pat's first thought was that this was going to cost a fortune. The clerk asked, "Sir, are you still with me?"

"Yes. Where is AJ Ellis from Jacksonville?"

"It is just west about 10 to 15 miles. Take Highway 258 to Highway 111. It's on the left side of the road. There are two or three pilots that I know of that will fly on short notice. It is a bit expensive but if you are in a hurry, I can call and find out their availability."

Pat thought for a second then said, "Please call and check. Can you do this while I wait on the line?"

"Yes sir."

Pat had visions of paying $20,000 cash for the hop to Florida on a chartered jet on such short notice. He thought for a second. *Hell, what am I worried about? Money is no object. So what if it costs twenty grand or even thirty grand. I have to get down there.* He was worried sick about his dad. He was even more concerned about his mom and her state of mind. Then he had to call Joe and give him the bad news. How was Joe going to react to having to drop out of the investigation? Was he even going to be able to do it? Joe was active duty. The US Marine Corps owned him, at least for now. The clerk asked, "Sir, are you still there?"

"Yes."

"I have a pilot for you. His name is Rupert Hillsdale. You will have to talk prices with him. We don't get involved with that. I'll give you his number if you like?"

"Please." Pat took down the number, thanked the clerk for her time and dialed Mr. Rupert Hillsdale. The phone rang three times and Pat started to wonder if Mr. Hillsdale was available.

At the end of the fourth ring, Rupert Hillsdale answered in a thick southern drawl. "Hillsdale Transport."

"Mr. Hillsdale?" Pat asked.

"Speaking."

"I need a pilot to take me to Fort Meyers, Florida tonight. Are you available?"

Pat tensed as Mr. Hillsdale responded. "Yes, sir. I'm available. What time do you need to get there?"

"As soon as you can get me there."

"Let me see. I have to file a flight plan, prep the aircraft, fuel up and all, but I can be ready in about twenty-five minutes to half an hour. It'll take us a couple of hours to get down there."

"What's your price?" With this short of notice it could have been a million dollar question, Pat thought.

"Fort Meyers? That's a pretty good clip. The flight'll cost you $2800 one way, $3200 round trip, plus expenses. Do you want me to wait and take you back?"

"Yes I do but it might be a few days.

"My expenses include hotel and meals if it's an overnighter. I charge an additional $75 per hour on top of expenses if I have to stay longer than twenty four hours. Expenses include a rental car. So if you're staying a full day, you're looking at about five grand. You can do the math after that. If I get a charter in the middle of an extended stay, you may get hit for additional charges. You want to think about it and call me back?"

"Nope. You get ready and I'll be there in about half an hour. It's a family health issue and I need to get down there. Mr. Hillsdale, thanks."
Pat gave Rupert a credit card number and his phone number.

"Alright then. I'll get moving." Mr. Rupert Hillsdale hung up the phone.

Pat called Diane and let her know the arrangements. She was surprised that he was able to get a chartered flight. The price seemed very reasonable considering the time and expedience of the trip. They shared a few more comments about concern for Pat's dad, said their goodbyes and disconnected. Pat's next call would be more difficult. Joe had no idea that his father was in the emergency room. He dialed Lisa's mom's in Oak Harbor. Lisa answered with a rather cheerful "Hello."

"Lisa, this is Pat. How are you?"

"Pat, I'm great. I just accepted an offer from your brother. We're going to be in-laws."

Pat tried to respond with as much cheer and surprise as he could muster, "That's fantastic, Lisa. I figured that you two would get it together. It's been tough with all the health problems in both our families." His last statement reminded him of the reason for his call. "Lisa, I need to speak with Joe for a few minutes."

The switch in Pat's voice tone surprised Lisa. She said, "Is something wrong Pat?"

Pat hesitated for a fraction of a second. "Yes, but I should let Joe tell you." Pat hesitated again then said, "It's our dad. He's back in the hospital."

"Oh, no. What this time?" Lisa's voice showed genuine concern and bore the weight that she'd been feeling over the past few weeks. Pat could hear the dread as she called to Joe.

"He's had another heart attack. I'm so sorry to tell you this news when this should be one of the happiest times in your life. You've been through so much with your dad."

"I know. It's been rough. Here's Joe. I'll talk with you soon." She handed the phone over to Joe.

"Hey, Pat. What did you say to Lisa? She looks like she just lost her best friend."

"It's Dad, Joe. He had another heart attack. He's back in the ER at Fort Meyers. I'm flying down tonight. I hope to be there before 1:00 in the morning."

"Oh shit." Joe sounded defeated. He wasn't expecting to hear anything like this. His mind was racing as he tried to take it all in. "How bad is it?"

"We don't know yet. It just happened within the last hour. Look, I've gotta run. The pilot is prepping the plane now and it's about a twenty minute drive to the airport. I know you've got a lot to think about but can you call Nancy and tell her what's going on?"

"Sure Pat. Go get your flight. Call me in the morning unless something happens tonight that I need to know about. I have to fly out again tomorrow late in the afternoon."

"Aren't you coming down here?" Pat asked a bit surprised and perturbed that Joe wasn't planning to immediately change his plans and join him in Fort Meyers.

"I don't think it's necessary, do you?"

Pat response was quick and sharp. "Yes I do, Joe! You need to get down here and be with Mom!"

Joe's temper was now on the rise. He thought that Pat was being a bit presumptuous, thinking that he could drop all of his obligations and go wherever he pleased. He had a job to do and that was that. "Pat, isn't that what you're going there to do? We both don't need to be there. I have a commitment that I have to keep. That's what I signed up to do and that's what I'm going to do. I'll be down as soon as I can get there."

Pat's face was red with anger. He wanted to reach through the phone and throttle his brother. "You can't be serious. You're not in combat, man. You're an investigator. They'll let you go, but you have to ask first. Are you going to do that or not?"

"No, I'm not. I'll let Nancy know the situation and she can lay out my options. We have a plan in place. If she believes that it can wait, then we'll change the plan accordingly."

"Dad could die, Joe! Do you want to risk not seeing him again?"

"Listen, Pat, don't lay that shit on me! We all could die at any minute. I could die on my way to the airport."

"Look, I have to go! You get your ass here as soon as possible!" Pat's words were laced with anger. "Mom needs us now! Put your macho, jarhead bullshit away! Be on the next available flight to Fort Meyers. Let Nancy know that you're needed elsewhere now. You can get back to work on the case as soon as Dad's condition stabilizes. Joe, I'm not fucking joking!"

"Me either Pat. Catch your flight. Later." Joe hung up.

Pat slammed the receiver down, picked up the phone and started to hurl it towards the far wall, but the phone rang before he could release it. It was Diane again.

"Pat, your mom just called. Your dad is in grave condition. He may not make it until morning."

Pat collapsed into the couch as the room swam around him.

Chapter 24

Private David Wallace sat in the waiting room of the Frye Regional Medical Center in Hickory, North Carolina, just outside the intensive care wing. There were dozens of magazines to choose from sitting on the end table to his right. A nineteen inch television played a show that droned on and on. It was an old comedy, one David didn't recognize. The room had two hanging baskets, one Spider plant, one Wandering Dew, and a tall Norfolk Island Pine that sat in the corner. The walls were the same institutional off white that must be used at every hospital and nursing home in the country. It evoked no emotion for the patients or anyone visiting or waiting to hear news of a loved one.

The wait was over for David. The Doctor had just given him the news that his mother had passed away from the aneurism in a vessel in her brain. It was that aneurism that caused her to lapse into a coma after hearing the news of her husband's murder. She came out of the coma only briefly then relapsed into the mindless calm where she succumbed to death's grasp. David was told several days prior that there was little hope of her recovery and that she probably would be better off if she would continue her journey to the other side. He was grateful that her suffering was only the emotional torment that briefly went along with learning of her husband's murder and the brief pain of the initial break in the blood vessel in her brain. The doctor assured him that, after that she felt no pain at all. Of all the possible ways to go, the doctor said this was the most peaceful.

Now David had to decide what to do next. A couple of weeks ago, he was happily married to a beautiful woman, had a promising career in the US Marine Corps, and both his parents were alive and healthy. Now, his wife was nowhere to be found, his military career was in question, and both his parents were dead. He leaned forward on the dark red, vinyl couch and buried his face in his hands. He felt like crying but that was never his way. He'd never shed a tear in his adult life. His father told him that men didn't do that. He wanted to break something which was a more typical response for David but he couldn't do that here in the hospital. That would only get him in trouble. He didn't need trouble right now. He needed clear thoughts. He needed to gather himself and decide what he was going to do next. He was all alone and that would never do. A nurse walked up to him as he sat in deep thought. He looked up at her as she approached. She was a pretty woman in white pants and a multi-colored smock. She had a pleasant face with a slightly dark, olive colored complexion but the face bore a look of concern. She asked him if there was someone that she could call for him and he responded with the shake of his head. She said if there was anything that she could do, to let her know.

One thing that he did know is that he had to take care of funeral arrangements for his mother. She would be laid to rest right next to his father whose grave would still be mounded high with dirt and no vegetation. The floral arrangements would barely be wilted when the crews began to dig his mother's grave. All the same friends and extended family would be recalled to the site to mourn yet another who was taken away much too young. His parents were both in their mid forties and looking forward to living well into their golden years. Now that was dashed out like a cigarette.

How had this happened? How did his life that seemed on track get derailed so quickly? Only God knew for sure, but there was one person who knew something. Her name was Charlene Hall Wallace. Before his father's murder, he'd heard that there was an ongoing investigation into servicemen getting ripped off by their spouses while they were deployed overseas. He remembered thinking how foolish those guys must have been to get suckered like that. Now he was one of them; one of the gullible masses that were sucked in so easily. But he wasn't going to give up. He was going to get to the bottom of it no matter how long it took. His first order of business was to make the proper arrangements for his mother. Then he was going to contact whoever he needed to make sure he was involved in the investigation. He was a Marine. No enemy, especially one from his own country, was going to defeat him. No one was going to get away with making him look weak and defeated. He stood and walked over to the nurse's station and spoke to the nurse who'd approached him earlier. Her name tag said Elana Vargas. She had only slight Hispanic features but he could see her ancestry in her dark brown eyes and light olive skin. He said, "I want to thank you for taking care of my mother. It must be difficult to work around patients who have little chance to survive. You have a special gift. I just wanted you to know how much I appreciate it."

Elana nodded and said, "Thanks. I wish we could have done more."

David reached out his hands and lightly held Elana's and said, "You did fine. From what her doctor said, there was nothing more that could have been done." He nodded, gave her hand a light squeeze, turned and left the nurses station as tears trickled from Elana's eyes. She watched David as he headed for the elevator down the hall, then grabbed a tissue and wiped the tears from her face.

An hour later at his parent's home, he sat and stared at the fireplace in the great room. The home was a nice place, nothing fancy but very comfortable, especially for a couple coasting in the middle of their lives towards retirement. He was still in shock, wondering how his life had fallen apart at the seams in such a short stretch of time. But his shock was starting to fade. He stood, then went upstairs to his old room. His weight bench was still in place with 200 pounds attached for his workouts. He took off his dress shirt and shoes and lay down on the bench. He lifted the bar bell off the rack and started repetitive lifts. As he pushed the weights up, he became more energized. With every little boost in energy he became angrier. His adrenaline started to purse through his body and his mind became more focused. He sped up his lifts and the sweat started to bead on his forehead, arms and chest. He continued until he could barely lift the bar bell back onto the rack. He struggled with the last two inches but managed to get the weights in place before they would have dropped onto his chest. He got down on the floor and assumed the sit up position and started doing sit ups. He continued to think about his misfortune but he began to focus on the reason for that misfortune. All he could think of was one name. Charlene. She was the reason for his troubles. Everyone had tried to warn him to slow down but he was too far gone, too in love, blinded by that love to see what was apparently right in front of his face. Charlene was a fraud. She didn't love him. She loved what she could take from him. He continued to pump up and down, his face turning bright red, the sweat dripping from his face and body now. *Charlene. Charlene. Charlene.* He heard himself repeating her name with every sit up. Finally, he stopped abruptly and screamed, "Charlene!" He put his face in his hands and, for the first time he could ever remember in his life, he wept. He stayed there for ten full minutes before he got up, took a hot shower and dressed. He knew what he had to do. He knew who to call. He dialed the number for the Camp Lejeune JAG office. The private on duty transferred the call to the office of Captain Nancy Brown.

Nancy was working late. She'd just gotten over a mega headache and was now wide awake. When she took the call from David Wallace, she was excited but saddened. She was heartsick that this young soldier lost both parents so close together. She thought that they should be worrying about him being an active duty soldier who until recently was in a hostile country. Now they were the victims of a war, but this war was a domestic conflict. The enemy was less visible than the enemy overseas in the desert and the mountains of the Middle East. At least over there you were expecting to be the target of the enemy. Here in your own country you weren't supposed to have to worry about that. You were supposed to be safe. Your parents were supposed to be working towards a long and healthy retirement. *I'll have to remember to call Mom and Dad later.* Nancy turned her attention back to the notes that she was taking while on the phone with Private Wallace. He was planning to drive back to Camp Lejeune in the morning. He said that he would be at the office by 10:00 AM. He had pictures of his wife, Charlene, and may have some things with her fingerprints. Nancy asked if he had anything with her hair on it like a hair brush or a lint roller. He said he would try to find something. Charlene hadn't been to his parent's house but he had some luggage that they'd used on a trip to Grandfather Mountain in North Carolina.

"That would be great, whatever you can find." She paused for a moment then said in a confident, sincere, even voice, "Private Wallace, we are all very sorry for your loss." She paused again. "We will find Charlene. I promise you that we will make her pay for what she did to your family."

A choked-up voice filled with anger mixed with sorrow said, "Thank you, Captain." The line disconnected.

* * *

Petty Officer Wilson Brush was tired and cranky but he was looking forward to a reunion with his new bride, Tanya, courtesy of a broken Main Sea Water pump shaft on the USS Nevada. The Engineer decided that the crew needed a break and the work would be performed by contract workers who would be flown in to Kings Bay Submarine Base. Before the Electricians Mates had shore power hooked up to the ship, Electric Boat personnel were already working on removing railings and other interference to remove and replace the broken pump shaft. The work would take about 3 days so each duty team would get one full day off the ship. One lucky duty team might even get a second day but that was unlikely. The Captain would want the crew back on board in plenty of time to prepare the ship for getting underway. That meant the Engineering guys, the Nukes, would be back on the ship going through a reactor startup far in advance of the forward guys, like Missile Techs, Torpedomen, Radar and Sonar Techs. The ship would be ready to set sail before the completion of the pump shaft replacement. As soon as the last Electric Boat employee was off the ship, they'd cast off the mooring lines and they'd be back out to sea again, protecting the United States from Communist aggression.

Wilson Brush thought that was just fine because he was on the Port Duty Team. They had the first 24 hours off. They'd pulled into port at 0430 hours, or 4:30 in the morning. The ship was on shore power by 0520 and the reactor was in the process of being shut down to hot standby. With any amount of luck, he'd be to his apartment by a few minutes after 0600. He was anticipating having his first orgasm by 0630.

The Engineer asked to speak to the port duty team on the pier before they departed so after the reactor was shut down, members of the off duty Engineering Divisions climbed the aft hatch ladder. Wilson took a deep breath as he exited the hatch and got a whiff of decaying vegetation and dead fish, compliments of the Crooked River which wound its way to the sea from the Southern Georgia salt marshes. It smelled wonderful compared to the stale, musky air of the submarine after being closed up and under water for two weeks. The air is periodically re-circulated with fresh ocean air while underway but not nearly enough to clear away the stench of dirty clothes, bed sheets and body odor. Add to that the smell of industrial machinery with oil and grease and dozens of other chemicals used to keep equipment lubricated and clean and you had a foul soup that you inhaled with every breath. Then there was the smells from the galley. The fresh food smelled pretty good. But after the scraps and waste started to build in the cooler before being discharged out the trash ejector, the odor also started to build. So smelling fresh air, or even air tainted with decaying vegetation and dead fish was a welcome aroma. Wilson looked across the Crooked River at Crab Island which was little more than a shadow this early in the morning. He looked back to the west at the lights glowing from the buildings, parking lots and other facilities around King's Bay Submarine Base. He couldn't wait to get off the pier and head towards his apartment. He could picture Tanya in bed, still asleep, unaware that her husband had a surprise for her. The wives had little warning that they would be there and no one knew whether they would have any time off so there was no cheering crowd to greet them this early morning. A number of his shipmates had cars parked on the base. He had offers of a ride home from two friends but Doug Farrell said that it wouldn't be a problem. Wilson waited at the top of the hatch as Doug poked his head up through and looked around at the ship's missile deck. He made his way out of the hatch and they headed for the gangway to muster on the pier.

After the Engineer gave his words of wisdom to the departing duty section, Wilson and Doug headed for Doug's car. It was a good fifteen minute walk which gave them time to chat. Wilson's mind was on one thing; getting home to Tanya. Doug was thinking about getting home to sleep. He hadn't had a lick of sleep for the last 26 hours so all he could think about was getting to his bed. On the pier, there were high intensity 480 volt lights set approximately forty-five feet apart. The walkway was bright enough to see but not so bright that you could see every little object along their path. Doug got a little close to the walkway's edge and his boot caught the edge of a large cleat. He fell in a heap on the pier, skinning his left elbow and the palm of his right hand.

"Son-of-a-bitch!" he exclaimed as he got up to one knee, then back to a standing position. "That hurt like hell!" A couple of their Engineering buddies were behind them and they broke out in boisterous laughter. Doug turned and looked back at them, intending to ask them what they thought was so funny, but he only succeeded in starting to laugh himself. He was too tired for a fight.

"Are you going to make it to my apartment?" Wilson asked.

"Yea. I'm fine. I just need to get some sleep. Let's get you home to that sexy wife of yours."

They made it to Doug's car without further incident and drove off the base towards Wilson's apartment in Saint Marys. On their way, Doug asked Wilson, "So, does this mean your bar hopping days are over?"

"Probably. I don't see any reason to go fishing if I've already got the trophy fish at home. I've never been so happy to get off the boat in my life. This is the first time that I've ever had something to really look forward to since I've been on the Nevada. Can you believe it? I'm married. I've got a woman waiting for me at home. I've never had that before." Doug was yawning about every ten seconds but Wilson kept on talking about his new bride and how he couldn't wait to make plans for their future. They were nearing the apartment complex entrance but Doug was having trouble keeping the car between the lines and away from the curb. Wilson shouted, "Hey! Wake up, man. You almost hit the curb."

"I'm okay," Doug replied.

"The hell you are. You're staying here today. We have a spare bedroom and an extra bed. We can't have you getting yourself killed or arrested."

"Really, I'm okay. Maybe I could get a drink of ice water or something. That's all I need. It's only a couple of miles to my place. I'll be fine." Doug turned his car into the complex entrance and nearly took out the brick sign that announced you were entering the Grand Neptune Apartments.

"Dude, you are staying here today. You can get up around noon. I'll have Tanya make you a nice lunch then you can be on your way. Pull into that spot." Wilson pointed out an empty parking spot directly in front of his apartment. Doug had a time maneuvering into the slot but managed to do so without hitting the cars on either side. He turned the ignition off then belatedly shut off the lights. The sky in the southeast was beginning to brighten as the sun approached the horizon. The clouds were a mixture of bright pink and purple and made a spectacular painting on the canvas that was the sky. Wilson took in the site briefly, then opened the door and looked up at the windows that were his and Tanya's apartment. There were no lights on at this hour which didn't surprise him. He knew that Tanya was a late riser which suited him fine. He preferred that she be in bed this morning. He turned to Doug and said, "Come on sleepy. Get your ass out of the car and get up here. You're not driving another block."

Doug shook his head to clear the cob webs then exited the driver's side of the car. He and Wilson headed up the short flight of stairs of the three story apartment building. Wilson and Tanya's apartment was on the second floor above the basement apartments which were half underground. The dark green wooden siding above the brown brick surrounded them as they moved towards the door to apartment 822, which stood for building eight, second floor, apartment number two. Wilson already had his keys in his hand but he rang the doorbell once to make sure he didn't startle his wife. She wasn't expecting him home, after all, especially at this hour in the morning. He inserted his key, unlocked the deadbolt. He then inserted the other key into the door knob and unlocked the door. Doug was nearly asleep leaning against the wall next to the door when Wilson finally turned the knob and pushed the door open.

"Hey baby, I'm . . ." His words stopped short as he looked around at the living room. It was completely empty. Wilson stepped into the room slowly. Once inside the door, he looked to the right where the dining room table should have been. The spot was blank. He continued his slow walk through the apartment which was as empty as the look in his eyes. Doug followed his friend and shipmate around the apartment. He was so tired that at first he thought he'd fallen asleep and was dreaming. But after a few moments, he realized he was now as awake as he could be, considering he'd had no sleep for the last day. Wilson made his way into the master bedroom and stared at the spot where his king sized bed had been. The only thing left were indents in the carpet from the bed legs. He turned and looked over his shoulder at the wide open bi-fold closet doors. His coin collection should have been on the shelf. It wasn't. He also looked at the floor in the closet where his gun cabinet had been, the square indentation in the carpet easy to see. The rest of the closet was completely empty. Wilson collapsed to his knees then sat back on his haunches. The only thing that was empty more than his apartment was his heart. He was crushed.

Doug sat down on the floor next to him, exhausted by the lack of sleep. He said, "Hey buddy. Let's get over to my place and we can both get some sleep. We'll get up about noon and talk about what we need to do next. Sitting in here staring at this place isn't doing you any good."

Wilson turned and looked at his friend. "What am I going to do? She's gone. She took all my guns and my coin collection. Maybe there's something wrong with this apartment and she had to move. Could she have moved us into a better place?"

Doug was too tired to listen to his friend's ramblings. He knew what happened. Wilson had been set up then cleaned out and there was nothing he could do about it. He was too quick to fall for the charms of a beautiful, sweet, but not so innocent woman. Doug remembered how quickly Tanya wanted to get married and get her name on everything before they left for sea. He told Wilson to slow down but he was too blind to see it. He stood and nearly fell over from exhaustion. He extended a hand and said, "Let's go, man. There's nothing else for you to do here. You have to get some sleep. After you do, you can think more clearly and we can figure out your next move."

Wilson looked up at Doug, his face red with anger now. His mind raced with possible explanations but the more he thought, the more he accepted that Tanya had taken him for a fool. He would start this morning talking with neighbors and see what they knew. Then he would get some sleep and start fresh with a clearer head as Doug had suggested. "Doug, here's what I'm going to do." He explained to Doug what he intended to do. Doug agreed as long as Wilson dropped him off at his apartment first.

Wilson would then come back to his apartment to talk with neighbors and the apartment manager. He'd get as much information as he could, then head back to Doug's and get some sleep. At noon, they'd get up and get a plan together. Doug agreed. They locked up the apartment and Wilson dropped Doug off at his apartment, took his car back to his own complex and started knocking on the doors to all the apartments in his building. He was floored by what he discovered. His loving bride, Tanya, had moved out, telling the neighbors that they were moving into a condominium. She had a male friend helping her move. They described the friend as a tall, slender man, about 30 years old with dark black hair nearly to his shoulders, very dark brown eyes, and pale skin. Tanya said that the man was her brother but he bore no resemblance to Tanya at all. Her neighbors were all suspicious but there was nothing they could do to stop her. They couldn't prove she was lying and several said it was none of their business or they didn't want to get involved. The woman that lived in the apartment across the common landing said that Tanya's 'brother', using her fingers in the air as quotes, was really obnoxious. She was watching him struggle with a large metal cabinet when he turned to her and said, 'you want to take a picture or something? Why don't you mind your own business?' She said his face was twisted in an angry, menacing look.

That's when the lights went on in Wilson's head. His neighbors were describing the guy at Tommy's Bar outside the sub base at St. Marys, Georgia. The descriptions were consistent especially about his nasty disposition. Tanya and her brother were in this together. Wilson's mind raced, jammed up with information as he thought back to the minor scuffle at Tommy's. He hadn't seen any evidence that Tanya knew the guy but it was obvious now that she did. He thanked the woman for her time and headed down the steps and back to Doug's car. He was about to start the car when he thought that he should check the mail box. Maybe there was mail that might help him find Tanya. He retrieved the mail and returned to the car before he scanned the pile. Much of the stack was junk mail; advertisements for magazines, charge cards, a solicitation for a timeshare condominium tour, and a free razor. Among the other pieces were a letter from his parents to Tanya, a couple of bills from the power company, cable company, and phone company. There was also a letter from NatFed Life Insurance Company to Mrs. Tanya Brush. He figured that NatFed was trying to sell them life insurance so he tossed the envelope on the seat in the pile with the junk mail and continued to look through the rest of the stack. When he finished, he decided to head to Doug's. He was yawning about every 30 seconds and he didn't want to wreck his friend's car. Before he hit the road, he had another thought. He needed to talk with a friend from the Nevada; William 'Hatch' Hatcher, from Moniac, Georgia. Hatch was a country boy, through and through. He was slim and talked with a deep southern accent. He'd inherited a large tract of swamp land from his parents who'd been killed a few years ago. His younger sister had also been killed, but not before she was raped and beaten. The local sheriff couldn't get any evidence to prove the murders but Hatch wasn't satisfied. Rumor has it that Hatch tracked down the perpetrators, tortured them, just like they'd tortured his little sister, and killed them. The sheriff's department didn't lift a finger to find out who had killed the bastards. Everyone suspected, but no one cared in this Southern Georgia town. In fact, most folks were glad to be rid of the bums. But, that was all speculation.

When Wilson got to Doug's apartment, he dialed Hatch's number. It was a long distance call to Moniac but Doug didn't care. He was fast asleep, dead to the world. Hatch picked up on the fifth ring.

"Yup?"

Hatch's greeting caused Wilson to pull the receiver back and give it an odd glance. He put the phone back to his ear and said, "Hatch, is that you?"

"Yup," came the reply.

"This is Wilson. Can I talk with you about a problem I've got?"

"Shoot."

This dude is a man who doesn't waste words. "My wife, Tanya, took off with all my stuff. She took my collections and furniture. I haven't checked yet but I'm sure she cleaned out my bank account." Hatch didn't say anything when Wilson paused. Wilson continued, "Can you help me find her?"

Hatch took a moment to think before answering, "Wilson, you know we have to be back to the boat by 0600 hours tomorrow, right?"

"Well, yes. But I just can't sit around without doing anything. I have to find her."

"You do know that I have to be there, too, right?"

"Yes Hatch. Can you help me or not?"

"Yup. But I can't do it myself. I have to have a friend help us out. He used to be on the Alabama with me. His Name's Pat McKinney."

"What can he do to help?"

"Plenty," was Hatch's reply. "Now, tell me all about little Miss Tanya."

Wilson spent the next twenty-five minutes telling Hatch everything he knew about his missing bride, including Doug's altercation at Tommy's Bar with the guy his neighbor's said was Tanya's brother.

Hatch said, "This guy ain't real smart if he's tangling with Dougie Farrell. He's a big boy. Now, this is where you met Tanya? How long ago was that?"

"About three weeks before we deployed."

"Which patrol?" There was silence on the line. "This patrol? Are you kidding me? You married this girl in two weeks? I have a solution for ya. You need to have your nuts removed because they've taken over control from your brain." Hatch chuckled for a second but he stopped and said seriously, "Look, Wilson; shit happens and it happened to you. This chick must be a real pro so don't be too hard on yourself. I'll get Pat looking into this and we'll see what we can do. Okay?"

"Alright. Call me at Doug's and let me know if Pat can help me."

"I don't have to call. I know he can and he will."

With that, Hatch disconnected and immediately dialed the home of Pat McKinney. Diane answered on the second ring. "McKinney's."

"Well Miss Diane, your voice is like a songbird in the morning on the Okeefanokee Swamp."

She recognized the southern twang and charm of William Hatcher immediately and smiled. "Hatch, I sure hope there's a compliment in there somewhere."

"Oh yes ma'am. How are your lovely chillins?"

He mispronounced children so badly on purpose that Diane had to think about what he'd said. "Oh, the children . . . they're fine except Sean may not take too kindly to being called 'lovely.' He's a bull-headed six year old now. He's got a hard head like his father."

"I'm sure he does. The acorn don't fall too far from the tree, if you know what I mean. Speakin' of Mr. McKinney, is he home?"

"No he's not. We have a bit of a crisis. Pat's dad had a heart attack, the second in a few weeks, and Pat's down in Ft. Meyers at the hospital with his mother. I can give you his number if you like?"

"That would be a great help, ma'am. I really hate to disturb him at a time like this. Is his brother, Joe with him?"

"Joe's up in Ohio with his fiancé. Did you meet her when you visited?"

"Yes I believe so. She's very skinny if I recall." This made Diane chuckle. "So you have some very emotional things going on right now. Some very bad, some very good. Life sure can be funny and cruel all at the same time. Is everything else okay? Pat treating you okay because if he's not, I can come down there and whip the snot out of him. I hate to do that with his dad in such a state and all. But I'm willin'."

Diane laughed, "No. Everything else is fine. He was up in North Carolina working with Joe for a few weeks before his father's attack. His business is going well but between clients he really isn't too busy. Too much free time. I told him to get out of the house and help his brother."

"If you don't mind my askin', what are the brothers working on?"

"Some case about some soldiers and sailors getting ripped off by some young female hustler."

Hatch's eyebrows raised. He was now very interested. "Tell me more about this case, if you can. Is the bride stealing these guys blind while they're deployed out to sea?"

"That's exactly what's happening." Diane was amazed that Hatch figured it out just by her brief description. "How did you know?"

"A little birdie named Wilson told me. It's actually a coincidence. That's why I'm calling. A friend of mine just had everything stolen except the shirt off his back. We came home early because of problems on the boat and he went home to an empty apartment. Why don't you give me their number in North Carolina, too?"

She gave Hatch Pat's cell phone number and the number for Nancy Brown's office at the Naval Criminal Investigative Service at Camp Lejeune.

"Diane, I wish I could chat more. It is always a pleasure talking with you. You are one terrific southern lady."

Diane smiled. "Hatch, I'm from Ohio."

"Don't tell anybody and I won't hold that against you." They both laughed and hung up.

Hatch immediately dialed Pat's cell phone number. There was no answer. He left a voice-mail message with a few details about Wilson Brush and his runaway bride. He also let Pat know that he would be heading back the USS Nevada by 0500 hours in order to get on board ship by muster time at 0530 hours. He hoped that they could connect before then. Hatch ended his message with "How in the hell did you get so lucky to marry a woman like Diane. You are clearly blessed by a higher power."

Chapter 25

Joe McKinney was in Lisa's bedroom in Oak Harbor, Ohio. He'd just finished packing his suitcase when Lisa walked in carrying the cordless phone. "It's Pat," she said. She handed Joe the phone then reached up and kissed him lightly, but sensuously on the lips. She lingered for just a second then withdrew. She turned and walked from the room to give the brothers some privacy. She sensed that Pat had something important to discuss and she didn't want to intrude.

Joe stared at Lisa as she walked away. When she was finally out of site he held the phone in place on his shoulder. "Hey Pat. I'm getting ready to head to Cleveland. What's up?"

Pat's voice was stern and loud, not quite a shout but close. "Dad's in grave condition, Joe. He's not expected to live. He could be gone in a week or he could be gone in a few seconds. The doctors give him virtually no chance of surviving this time. You really need to get down here, no bullshit. We have to be here for Mom."

Joe didn't have to think about it this time. He knew he couldn't continue on to Grand Forks. He had to let Nancy and Major Griggs know that he had family obligations to tend to before he went on with the case. They would just have to understand. "Okay, Pat. I'll get my flight changed when I get to Cleveland. When I get there I'll call you to see if anything's changed. I'll get the earliest flight available."

When Joe hit the 'end' button on the cordless phone, he sat on the edge of the bed with his head in his hands. He didn't want to tell Lisa but he knew he had to tell her. She'd already been through so much with her own father's passing now his father was at death's door. Last night, life was grand. He'd just asked his beautiful girlfriend to marry him and she'd said yes. They were madly in love. In less than 12 hours, life had thrown him another bag of crap. He had to tell the woman he loved that he had to make the torturous trip to Florida to watch his father die. That was if he was lucky enough to make it there in time. Lisa knocked quietly on the door frame to her bedroom and took a tenuous step towards Joe. He looked up, raised his arms to welcome her into them. He remained seated as she wrapped her arms around his neck and drew his head to her chest. He moved his muscular arms around her waist and held her there for a long while before either of them said a word.

Joe finally pulled his head up and looked Lisa in the eyes. "I have to go to Florida. Dad's back in the hospital. He had another heart attack. He isn't expected to live this time."

Lisa's eyes started to overflow. "Oh Joe," she said in a sad groan. She leaned down and kissed him lightly on the lips. "If you want me to go with you, I will. I can be packed in twenty minutes."

"I would love nothing more than for you to be with me but your mom still needs you here."

"Needs who here for what?" Lisa's mom was in the doorway of Lisa's room. "What's going on, Joseph?"

Nobody had called Joe by his full name in at least ten years, but Joe didn't protest. He didn't really know how to tell Lisa's mom about his dad without just telling her the truth. "Dad's had another heart attack. He isn't expected to live more than a few days. I have to get to Florida immediately. I just thought that Lisa should probably stay here with you, considering the circumstances."

"That's very thoughtful of you Joseph but how about this idea? I think that I can help your mother. I know what she is going through right now. Why don't the three of us fly down to Ft. Myers. That's if you don't mind me tagging along. I think you two have been apart long enough and I really need to get out of this house for a while. Maybe it would help me clear my head." Joe thought he saw a slight smile form on her lips but just as quickly as it formed, it disappeared. She moved in closer to the two love birds and put an arm around each of them. "What do you say? Is it a deal?"

Joe gave Lisa a quizzical look to which she nodded. He looked back at Mrs. Goddard and said, "It's a deal on one condition. The trip is on me; airfare, hotel, car, whatever. I'll make sure you get everything you need."

Mrs. Goddard's smile returned. "That sounds like a deal. When do we leave?"

"Let me call and make flight arrangements and I'll let you know." Joe was off the phone ten minutes later and said, "They just have to do a couple of changes once we get to the airport and we'll be all set. You two have twenty minutes to pack. I'll get the car loaded as soon as you're finished packing and we'll be on the road."

Lisa thought about her brother. She looked at her mother and asked, "What about Gary? Shouldn't we tell him?"

"He'll know when he stops by the house, sees we're gone and he can't get in. I'm having the locks changed while we're gone. I already have the new keys. He's in his twenties. It's time he grew up."

Lisa smiled. Her mom was coming out of her mourning period in style. Her character was growing stronger by the minute. Lisa had her doubts when she first arrived back home whether her mom would recover. Now she knew she was going to be just fine.

* * *

The change of ticketing for Joe went smooth, an amazing feat in modern flying. He was able to get the additional tickets for Lisa and her mom, the seats in the same row as his. It was near boarding time when Joe called Pat. There was no change in his Father's status so Joe, Lisa and her mother boarded the flight to Southwest Florida International Airport at Ft. Myers.

The flight was uneventful except some minor turbulence over the Gulf of Mexico. They sailed through the airport lobby to baggage claim and to the rental car agency and were on the road within 35 minutes of touchdown.

The drive from the airport to Lee Memorial Hospital took almost 20 minutes, though the actual distance was less than 10 miles. Traffic was bumper to bumper heading north on Cleveland Avenue. Once inside the hospital, they were directed to the Open Heart Intensive Care Unit. When they got off the elevator and turned the corner to the waiting area, Joe immediately knew that they were too late. Pat was kneeling in front of their mother, holding her in his arms as she sobbed on his shoulder. They must have just missed the doctor delivering the news that their father had passed away. Joe was sick to his stomach. Lisa and her mother stopped short and hugged, crying quietly to each other. They knew what Emma McKinney was feeling at this very moment and they wept for her. They kept their distance for the time being not wanting to disturb her grief. They knew that this was something she needed to do for her own health, both physical and mental. After what seemed like an eternity, Pat turned and saw them standing in the hall. His face turned in a series of emotions, from recognition, to grief, to anger, then back to grief again. He stared at Joe, locking eyes, trying to convey a message between just the two of them. But Lisa knew that Pat was angry with Joe. She knew he was angry with him for not being there. She felt guilty that she'd kept him in Ohio with her while his father was dying in a bed in Florida. She didn't know the circumstances at the time, but she felt guilty all the same. She turned away and tried to focus her thoughts on Joe and how he must feel at this moment. She looked at him and was surprised at the lack of emotion. He was stone faced, looking back at Pat with no apparent emotion. How could he be this cold at a time like this? She didn't know Joe extremely well but she remembered what Diane had once told her. *Joe is focused and not real emotional. Sometimes I can hardly believe that he and Pat are brothers. Pat is at the other end of the spectrum. He's very emotional.* Lisa could see it now as if the words were written on each of their foreheads.

Pat and Emma separated and she slumped over, covering her face with her hands, still crying. Lisa's mother walked over and sat next to Emma who looked up to see who'd sat down next to her. "Emma, my name is Ann Goddard. I'm Lisa's mother. I'm so sorry for your loss." As she said these words of comfort she put her arm around Emma's shoulder.

"Thank you," was all she could manage before she continued to cry.

Pat stood and walked towards Joe and Lisa. When he was about 6 feet from them, he growled at Joe, "You're too late. He's gone. If you'd have been here 15 minutes ago, he was still here and you could have said your good-byes."

The shrill sound of his voice carried through the hall of the hospital wing and caught the attention of everyone within earshot. Heads jerked towards Pat's voice just as he lunged at Joe. Lisa jumped back to avoid being caught in the middle of the attack. Joe was much stronger than Pat and he was a trained Marine. He grabbed Pat by the wrists and held him at bay.

Joe gritted his teeth and said, "Pat, get control of yourself! This isn't helping." Pat worked his left hand free and took a wild swing at Joe who dodged the sweeping fist as it whistled by, inches from his chin.

The head nurse was reaching for the phone to call security when Emma McKinney stood and shouted, "Patrick! Stop this instant!" Everyone turned and looked in surprise as Emma, the grieving widow became the mother of her remaining sons. "We've had enough tragedy in this family for a lifetime. I will not allow you to disgrace your father's memory like this! His death, like that of your brother, should make us closer and stronger!" She looked first at Pat then Joe and continued, "It has to or it will destroy us."

Pat's arms went limp and Joe released his other arm. They walked together over to their mother and hugged, sharing their grief together, still experiencing that grief in their own way; Emma and Pat wearing theirs on their sleeves, Joe allowing his to eat away at the interior of his body and soul.

Emma said in an unsteady voice, "We all knew that your father would never follow the doctor's orders. He was bull headed, like the two of you. He had to prove he was over his first attack so he decided to do something special for his grandchildren. I found him face down in the yard with a shovel by his side. He'd planted a tree. On the way to the hospital he said he wanted to plant it so we could watch all of our grandchildren play in its shade when it grew taller." She put her head down, took the tissue that she held and wiped an errant tear from her face. "He'll have to do that from heaven but we'll be able to enjoy the shade of that tree. I want you to remember that your father had you and your children," she looked at Joe, "or future children in mind when he did this. Remember to tell them when they are old enough to appreciate it."

After a moment, Lisa and Ann Goddard joined the group. They stood there for over ten minutes before they sat and talked about what to do next.

* * *

Wilson Brush had fallen asleep on Doug Farrell's couch after trying to figure out what to do next. He called his parents earlier. They told him that they hadn't heard a word from Tanya since he left port. They tried calling her on several occasions but she never answered the phone. They sent her two letters but again received no reply. He told them that if they heard from her to get as much information from her as they could and let him know. They knew that they wouldn't hear from her and so did Wilson.

When he hung up the phone, he'd fallen asleep. He had a dream that he was on the ship leaving port and Tanya was on the pier waving as they pulled away. Then a tall, dark haired man appeared and grabbed her from behind. He cupped her breasts with his hands then began ripping her clothes off. Instead of resisting, she turned to him and began to press her body into his. As he ripped off the last shred of clothing, she turned towards Wilson and winked. In his dream, all his shipmates were around him whistling at her and shouting words of encouragement for her to keep going. Then they turned and laughed at him, taunting him, telling him what a slut for a wife he had. He was getting more and more angry. He ran and leapt off the missile deck and began swimming towards the shore but he started to sink, his boots feeling like lead weights around his feet. He awoke on the floor next to Doug's couch, writhing around as if in the ocean. He felt as if he hadn't slept a wink. Now he was wide awake. He looked around the apartment living room. Except for his heavy breathing, there was dead quiet. It was eerie in a way that he couldn't describe. He looked into the kitchen and saw an empty coffee cup and decided that coffee was a good idea so he started to brew a pot. At the kitchen sink, he splashed water on his face and looked out over the parking lot. Few cars were in the lot as most of the residents were at work. He noticed the two stacks of mail on the counter, one Doug's and one that he'd brought from his own apartment. He leafed through the stack as he'd done in the car but paid more attention this time. As he found junk mail, he tossed it in Doug's kitchen trash. He opened the letter from his parents to Tanya and read it. They were inviting her up to East Liverpool if she felt the need for company. It was a nice letter, not too invasive and warm. He put that aside and continued to sort the junk from the few good pieces. He opened the first bill but left the other sealed. He knew what was in them. Then he got to the envelope from NatFed Life Insurance Company. He waved his arm as if to toss it in the trash with the other junk mail but this letter had an official look to it. *Probably just trying to disguise a sales pitch.* But his curiosity got the best of him. Better safe than sorry, he figured. He ripped the envelope open and extracted the single page form letter. He expected the letter to say how important it was to have adequate insurance. He read the first paragraph and had to grab a stool at the counter and sit while he read it again.

> *Mrs. Brush,*
>
> *We're sorry for the loss of your husband, Petty Officer Wilson R. Brush. We have received the notice from the Department of the Navy regarding his death while on active duty with the USS Nevada. After we verify . . .*

He read the letter a third time, still in disbelief. How could this be possible? He felt detached from his body as if he really was dead. He dropped the letter on the counter and put his hands flat on the counter as the room spun around.

When Doug heard the thud and the apartment shook as if a car had run through the building, he jumped out of bed from a deep sleep. He ran out of his bedroom and looked into the spare bedroom then around the living room. He turned to head back into his bedroom when he saw Wilson on the floor in the kitchen. There was a little blood from a cut on his head but he knew that Wilson was alive. He was breathing.

"Wilson!" He shook his friend's shoulders trying to wake him. He figured that he'd just fallen asleep while on a barstool. "Wilson, are you hurt? Come on, man. Snap out of it." He started to stir. Doug reached into a kitchen drawer and pulled out a clean dish cloth, wetted it down with cold water and wiped it over Wilson's face. The cloth smeared some of the blood from Wilson's head wound but Doug didn't care about that. The cold cloth got the young man moving. "Wilson!" Doug said again. This time he got a response.

"What happened?"

"You must have fallen off the bar stool buddy. Have you been up this whole time?"

Wilson still didn't have his bearings down and was trying to collect his thoughts. Then he remembered the letter. "I'm okay Doug. Help me up." When he was sitting back on the stool he picked up the letter and handed it to Doug.

As Doug read through the letter his eyes widened and his jaw dropped. He looked up at Wilson with a look that was part anger and part disbelief. He looked back down at the letter just as Wilson had done and reread the letter. "Is this for real?" he asked still in shock.

"I think so. How could this be? I'm alive. Could the Navy have fucked this up?"

Doug shook his head. He didn't believe that the Navy, as screwed up as some things might be, could screw this up. He had a feeling that this all had to do with his little lost sweetie. Over the next fifteen minutes Wilson told Doug all the things that he learned from his neighbors. He made special mention of the dark haired guy with the attitude. "Sounds like the guy from Tommy's doesn't it?"

"Exactly. I think that you'd better get this to the X.O." The X.O. was the ships Executive Officer. He was in charge of all personnel matters on board the USS Nevada. "He's going to want to investigate this. We'd better get moving. Maybe they can get a team to track her down. This is big shit my man."

Yea. Big shit. And I'll be at the bottom of the pile.

* * *

By dinner time, the letter had been brought to the attention of the King's Bay Submarine Base Commander, Admiral Wesley Alberts. He immediately contacted BUPERs, the military's Bureau of Personnel. They tried to contact NatFed Life Insurance Company but the office was already closed. The contact would have to wait until morning. Petty Officer Brush was ordered to get his gear off the ship. They would find a replacement for him or the ship would sail with a man short.

Captain Nancy Brown learned of the incident by 1830 hours. She received a faxed report detailing the new case. She read through the report and wished that Pat and Joe were there to help ensure that she didn't miss any details. She knew that their father's death took precedence for the time being but she needed their experience to boost her confidence that she was on the right track. As she read, it was obvious that the case fit the profile of the previous cases. But how was this woman getting from one state to another in such record time. They thought that she was here in Jacksonville, North Carolina and she ends up with a guy in South Georgia. After she read the report, she took a bite of the turkey sandwich and a sip of coffee. She stood up and pieced the details of the new case onto the white board. She used a red marker to differentiate the new information from the old. As she pieced in the new details, it became apparent that this couple was on the move from state to state. They were in one place only long enough to make contact, get their hooks into some poor young kid and move on. Then they were submitting the paperwork to collect on the insurance. It had worked well until now.

She wondered how many claims for SGLI were submitted each week. She wrote a note to herself to check this out when she called NatFed in the morning.

It was now 10:30 pm and Nancy was starting to tire when the phone rang. It was Joe. Pat was on the phone as well.

"You're working late. We kind of figured that you would be with the new case and all."

"How did you guys know that there's a new case? I just found out about it after dinner this evening."

"We've got friends in low places, Captain," Pat said. "Actually, I have a friend who is on the Nevada. He called and told me. Wilson Brush is the victim, right?"

"Yep. Wife, Tanya, left him high and dry. Took all his stuff including a coin collection, a gun collection, cash, and other stuff. He's really pissed and wants to find her bad. He won't be sailing with the ship when it leaves in a few days. Oh, this is a secure line on this end. Is yours?"

"Sorry. We're at our mom's house. Our line is not secure. No more talk about deploy dates. Anyway, how does this fit on the timeline?"

Nancy went over her theory about the perpetrators hooking up with a poor soldier or sailor and taking them for a ride then moving on quickly.

"They come back and pick up the check later after the insurance company payoff is complete. Now all we have to do is get ahead of them. Find out where they're going to strike next. Sounds easy, right?"

Joe said, "Sure Captain, whatever you say."

Chapter 26

The crowd at Dee's Pub on Little Creek Road was lively at 11:30 PM thanks in part to twenty-five cent drink night. Plans were to have a Naughty Mamma contest and everyone was anticipating seeing them strut their stuff. If you were a good looking mamma and could prove that you left your kids in good hands, you could win a night of free drinks. There were lots of takers for the contest and many of the women were dressed, or barely dressed to win. The crowd was thick with horny sailors from Norfolk Naval Base. The crowd was a near fifty-fifty mix of sailors and locals which made the bar staff nervous. They had as many bouncers on hand as possible, all wearing dark black T-Shirts with bright white letters identifying them as bar security. Their aim was to maintain control over any developing situation before it got too rowdy. So far they were doing a good job and everyone seemed to be enjoying themselves. The music was loud. Most of the tunes were country but there was a fair amount of country rock and classic rock mixed in. The dance floor was crowded and lively. There was a lot of body grinding going on. The barroom was dark except for the low lighting in the server's area behind the bars and the colored lights illuminating the dance floor. There was a haze of smoke from cigarettes and the distinct smell of some illegal form of smoke. The three bars in Dee's were placed at the north, south and west walls and were manned by several bartenders each.

Becky Lippert and Seaman Dean Gray sat at a table tucked away in a corner of the bar. They'd been dancing for nearly twenty minutes and needed a break and a drink. Becky set her whisky and 7Up on the table as Dean was taking a long pull on his beer. "So sailor, where are you from?" Becky's seductive manner was alluring even when she talked to men who were alert and defensive. When a man had a few drinks under his belt, she was like a prize fighter cornering her prey. She had her eyes on Dean Gray and she was moving in for the kill. She wore a low cut white tank top and no bra. Every time she leaned over she revealed a good part of her ample cleavage. She was leaning over towards Dean, acting like she couldn't hear him well with the loud music in the background. The view was not lost on Dean as his eyes strayed almost continuously.

"I'm from Ankeny, Iowa. It's just north of Des Moines. Do you know where that is?"

"I know about where Iowa is. That's about it. Lots of corn up there, right?"

"Yep, lots of corn," Dean said as he adjusted the collar of his bright green golf shirt. All that was missing from the shirt was a John Deere logo. He looked as if he could be a John Deere tractor salesman. He wore black wingtips and tan, pleated pants. His close cropped hair was well within Navy specs. He had a slightly rounded face with a few freckles and one scab on the right edge of his chin where he must have cut himself shaving. He barely looked old enough to shave but his manner was more mature than his looks. He had the verbal skills of a young salesman. "We have a John Deere plant that makes the machinery that picks corn. There are a few other businesses but most everything has to do with farming. That's why I'm here. I don't want to farm." Dean Gray seemed like a real talker. He was anxious to tell his story; one that Becky was pretty sure would be boring. It might be a challenge for her to stay interested even though Dean seemed like an interesting person. She just hoped that he wouldn't talk about Iowa the whole night or she was certain that she'd fall asleep and end up on the bar room floor.

"Wow, a John Deere factory. I wondered where they made all those fancy farm machines. Do you know how to drive one?"

"No. My dad doesn't farm. He sells insurance; does pretty well, too. He's been Mid-States Insurance Company's number one salesman in the region for a couple years running. That says a lot because they have a large territory."

"Wow again. What about your mom? Is she a stay at home mom?"

"Mom passed away about 7 years ago. Breast cancer. It happened real fast. They discovered it and in less than two months she was gone."

"Oh, I'm sorry. I didn't mean to . . ."

"That's okay. It's been a long time. I've learned to deal with it. She was great and I miss her but time heals. Dad met a nice lady and recently remarried. She's a bit younger than Dad but they seem to get along alright. She's been great to me and my brother. It's not the same as Mom, though. It never will be."

"I can't imagine what that must be like. Tell me about your brother? Is he older or younger?"

"He's three years younger. He's still in high school, a junior this year. He's my best buddy. We leaned on each other a lot when Mom got sick. We helped each other through some rough days. But it happened so quick that we hardly had time to grieve. I'm sorry. I didn't mean to go back to that again. So, Julie, tell me something about you."

Becky made a mental note to remember her alias. She thought for a moment before answering Dean. She wanted to make sure she didn't screw up her story. Tonight she was Julie Lippus from Beaver Falls, Pennsylvania. With juggling so many identities it was getting more difficult to keep her current identity straight. "Well, I'm from Beaver Falls, Pennsylvania. My parents have lived there all of their lives and they figured that I'd stay there, get married and have grandkids for them. I really wanted to get out 'cause there isn't much happening in Beaver Falls. I want to see more than just little rolling hills and I want to hear more than people yelling 'Steelers' at each other." As she yelled 'Steelers' she picked up a napkin and twirled it around, made a long face and exaggerated deep voice. She smiled at Dean who was laughing at her imitation of a Steelers fan. "Anyway, I decided to come down to Virginia 'cause I heard there were jobs at Virginia Beach. When I got there, they said there were jobs here near the Navy base so here I am. They were right. I got a job with a civilian contracting firm that works with the Navy on ship repairs. It's a small firm but they may be getting larger contracts soon." She leaned back stretching her top over her breasts which made her nipples stand against the thin fabric. She picked up her drink and finished it. Dean's eyes didn't miss the show. He flagged down a waitress and ordered each of them another round. She leaned forward again placing one elbow on the table. Resting her chin on the palm of her hand she smiled seductively and asked "So, Dean Gray, do you have a girlfriend back in Iowa?"

"Nope. I did go out with a few but nothing serious. I haven't met anyone I really like yet. How about you?"

"Same here." Becky folded both arms on the table and leaned forward again. Dean's eyes dropped to her chest on queue. "If I met the right guy I might fall for him. Maybe that'll happen some day." She stared into his eyes which met hers on their way back from between her breasts.

"Maybe," he said, smiling.

Across the bar, Bobby Garrett watched as Becky performed her magic. He was amazed how she could hook a guy and reel him in so quickly. She was a pro at picking out the vulnerable ones. He drank his beer and listened to the band as they played a terrible rendition of the newest hit on the radio by Brian Purcer and the Hot Licks, *I Know You Better Than You Think*. He was starting to get that familiar feeling of jealousy as she leaned closer to the young sailor. Her breasts were just about to pop out of her top. She really didn't need to pour on the charm like that. She could accomplish her end of it without looking so much like a slut. He would have to tell her to not bring so much attention to herself. The guys at the tables all around her were looking over her charms as much as the guy she was trying to seduce. Hell, she was attracting a pack of horny dogs. He could tell they were all sailors with their short haircuts and short attention span. He remembered when he got back from sea all he thought about was getting laid. He knew what these guys were going through. They couldn't help but stare when a hot chick like Becky showed her wares. He thought about going over to her and telling her to cool it a little but he had to trust that she knew what she was doing. He saw her reach her hand up and caress the young sailor's cheek. Then she leaned over and lightly kissed him. He could feel the heat rise in his cheeks as his temper started to fire up. His stare intensified and he was about to get up when a barmaid asked if he'd like another round. He looked up at her. She had a nice smile and she wore a loose fitting pink tank-top. He looked at her eyes. In the reflection of the changing stage light, they looked green but it was hard to tell. His face remained emotionless as he said, "Sure. I'll have a Bud. What's your name?"

"Lucy. What's your's?

"Bobby. Bobby Garrett."

"Bobby, I'll be right back with that beer."

Bobby watched as Lucy headed towards the bar, her behind swaying as she walked. He enjoyed the view for a few more seconds but when he turned back to see how Becky was doing with her newest mark, the table was empty. He quickly scanned the area around her table but she and the sailor were nowhere in sight. He stood looked around at a wider area of the bar but could not see Becky anywhere. He began to get agitated and started to walk towards her table when he spotted Becky and Dean back on the dance floor. Bobby made his way back to his table and settled down to wait for his drink. He was getting more agitated as he watched Becky grind away at her male companion. His role in this scheme was getting harder to stand. Becky was having all the fun while he did all the grunt work. He had to find the best locations for their hunting. He had to fill out the paperwork for the big scores. He had to protect Becky in case any of these guys turned out to be violent or perverse, though that hadn't happened yet. But it could and Bobby had to be ready to jump in and save Becky in case it did happen.

He was deep in thought when Lucy returned with his drink. She set it on the table and said, "That's $2.75, Bobby."

He frowned and said, "You've got a pretty good memory if you can remember my name out of all the people you serve."

The frown struck her as odd but she said, "I try. I go to school and one of the things that I do for mental exercises is memorize names. I try to remember what people wear and their faces. It helps to keep my mind working. I haven't seen you in here before. Are you new in town?"

His frown remained as if she was annoying him but he said, "No. I just haven't been here before; wanted to see what the rave was about. Friends of mine told me I should check it out. The hired help is sure nosey." He made a half smile to make sure that Lucy got the point. He laid three bucks on her tray. When she went to give him change, he said, "Keep it," as if it were the biggest tip she would receive all night. She turned without a word and headed back towards the bar again. He watched as she stopped at another table to take orders. He wondered if her memory were really that good. That might be a problem if she was questioned about a guy with dark black, shoulder length hair. He made a mental note to look into ways to become less conspicuous.

He turned his attention back to the dance floor and watched as Becky was really turning on the sex appeal. She was really grinding into her man. Bobby's jaw started to tighten once again. He was really stressing out. He turned his attention away from Becky on the dance floor and noticed Julie the barmaid talking with two men at a table that was on the outer edge of the bar. She was deep in conversation and it didn't appear that she was taking their drink order. He watched as she looked across the bar in his direction. Both men followed her gaze. He quickly lowered his head to try and get out of their line of sight. He pushed his chair back, got up and moved away from the table. He slowly moved among the crowd and made his way to towards the dance floor, moving among the other patrons so as to not draw attention to himself. When he was within a few feet of Becky on the dance floor, he made one final look around to find the man and woman who'd looked his way. They were moving towards the table where he'd been sitting. He moved passed Becky and acted as if he'd accidentally bumped into her. When he did, he said quietly in her ear, "We have company. We have to go."

She turned to him and said loud enough for Dean to hear, "You're excused."

Bobby made his way slowly through the dancers and headed for the door. He pulled a nylon skull cap from his pocket and tucked his hair up under the cap. He quickly changed his appearance enough that whoever was looking for him would not recognize him, especially in the dark bar. He made his way outside to their car in the parking lot and waited for Becky to appear. It was a full ten minutes before she hopped into the passenger seat.

"Where have you been?" he growled.

"I was trying to make sure we didn't lose this guy. I've got him hooked. I'm supposed to be in the lady's room right now. I'm heading back in a second."

"The hell you are. We're getting out of here. There's a guy and a chick in there looking for us. I saw them head for where I was sitting. It looked like they knew me or at least knew who I am. We can't stay here."

Becky was adamant. She knew she could make a big score with this newest mark and she wasn't about to cut and run. She raised her arms and wrapped them around the head rest of the passenger seat. The effect was to push her breasts out hard against her tank top. She was turning on the sex appeal again, this time to win Bobby over. In her most sexy voice she said, "Bobby, you head back to the apartment and wait for me to call. If they know who you are it's okay because they don't know who I am. I'll tell you where to pick me up later. I promise I'll make it worth your trouble."

Bobby's gaze was where most mortal men would look. Becky released the head rest and moved her hands across her breasts. She stroked her nipples through her shirt then folded her arms across her chest, effectively pushing her breasts together tightly. He was getting turned on more and more with every move she made. He started to reach his hands across to grab her but she put out her hands and stopped him.

"Not so fast," she said in a sing-song manner. "We have business to take care of yet tonight. When I've got Mr. Gray on the hook we can celebrate. Till then, hands off the goods." She smiled seductively, which only made Bobby want her more. But he backed off without saying a word.

"This guy has some bucks and we can make this a quick score." She paused for it to sink in. "When we have this score in the bag, we can take a break and enjoy the money for a while. Maybe we can head out to the west coast and try the bases out there. What do you think?"

Bobby wasn't thinking about anything except getting into Becky's pants later that night. But he managed an almost inaudible, "Great. West Coast. Right."

Becky leaned over and gave Bobby a kiss on the cheek before heading back into Dee's.

* * *

Inside Dee's Pub, Private Jeff Steers, Private Leonard Skiff, and Lucy the Barmaid walked to the table where Bobby Garrett had been sitting. There was nearly a full beer still sitting on the table but Bobby was nowhere to be found. The noise level in the bar was rising to unbearable levels due to the band turning up the amplifiers at the request of an obviously well lit crowd. The quality of the tunes was getting worse as the volume went up which made it more difficult for the three to communicate.

Lucy shouted to Jeff and Leonard, "The guy fitting the description was sitting right here a few minutes ago. He couldn't have gone far. He just paid me for this beer. What a jackass, too. He tried to look tough at me as if he was a big shot or something. He had a real crappy disposition."

Jeff yelled over the music, "Did you see anything that stood out about his face, hair, or skin?"

Lucy shouted back, "Yes. He was real pale looking. His hair was real long and black, almost looked dyed black. His eyes were dark, too. He's a real strange looking guy; almost . . . what is it called? Gothic. If you put one of those armored suits on him, he'd of fit right in back in the middle ages, except he's real skinny, too." As she shouted the words 'real skinny, too' the music stopped and there were few applause. A few people close to the trio looked their way and chuckled as the words came out loud. "Sorry," Lucy said.

"Don't worry about it." Jeff pulled out a sketch of a man with long hair. He showed Lucy the sketch and asked her, "Did he look anything like this sketch?"

Lucy looked at the sketch and without hesitation said, "Yes, that looks a lot like him. Almost dead on."

Jeff looked over at Leonard then back to Lucy. "Did you see him with a young woman at all this evening?"

"No, not at all. He said this was his first night in here. He said that a few friends had recommended the place and he wanted to check it out."

Next, Jeff took out a picture of Belinda Reardon and handed it to Lucy. "Have you seen this woman here tonight?"

Lucy looked at the picture for a moment then shook her head. "Nope. I'd recognize her. She has a number of features that I'd remember. I work at recognizing people as a mind exercise. I try to remember names, faces, and clothes. I'm getting pretty good at it and I would definitely recognize her."

Across the bar, Belinda, aka Julie Lippus, made her way back to the table where she and Dean Gray were camped out. Dean smiled brightly as she approached. Her hair was recently colored a light red and clipped to above her shoulders which made her appearance totally different than the picture that Lucy now held. It would have been difficult for anyone who didn't know her personally to pick her out in a crowd unless they got a look at her West Virginia shaped birth mark.

As Becky sat and reached for her drink, her gaze caught a face staring directly at her from across the bar. . She stared directly at the woman who maintained eye contact for several seconds. It was the woman from the parking lot at Tommy's in St. Marys, Georgia. Dean noticed the look on her face and followed her stare. "Do you know someone here?"

She broke her eye contact, turned her attention to Dean and said, "No. I thought that I knew a woman a few tables over but now that I see her, it isn't her." She looked back again and the woman was gone. Rather than raise Dean's curiosity, she turned her attention back to Dean and the task at hand. "So, Dean, do you have an off base apartment where we can go and talk in a more quiet setting?"

Dean's eyes lit up. "Yes I do. Let's blow this pop stand."

* * *

Lucy told Jeff and Leonard that she had to get back to work. They thanked her for her time and gave her a card to call in case she remembered anything new or if Bobby Garrett returned. She assured them that she would and moved off. Jeff and Leonard scanned the bar for any sign of Belinda Reardon. They noticed a woman with blond hair moving towards the woman's room that fit Becky's description. They couldn't get a good look at her face because she was walking away from them. They followed, closing the distance between them. As she reached the door to the woman's bathroom she turned and looked out at the dance floor. The woman bore a remarkable resemblance to the picture of Becky, but she was clearly much older. Jeff and Leonard both let out a breath and gave each other a look of disappointment.

As they turned to scan the bar, Julie Lippus, and Dean Gray walked out the front door of the bar to Dean's car. Dean was already anticipating a hot night. Julie was looking beyond that to a big paycheck. Both wore broad smiles at the thought of screwing each other in entirely different ways.

* * *

Private Jeff Steers called Captain Nancy Brown on her home phone. It was 11:45 pm. He and Private Skiff stopped searching for Belinda Reardon and her brother at Dee's Pub. They were nowhere to be found. One thing was clear; Belinda's brother was at the bar and they were afraid they may have tipped their hand.

Captain Brown instructed the soldiers to return to the bar the following evening and continue surveillance. Maybe they weren't seen.

"Be as inconspicuous as possible. In a bar full of sailors, that shouldn't be too difficult." Nancy was unaware that she'd just insulted the soldiers.

After he hung up the phone, Jeff turned to Leonard and said, "She just insulted us, Len. She said we look like squids."

Leonard said, "Damn."

Chapter 27

Daniel Ryan McKinney was buried three days after his passing. Emma felt that there was no need to drag it out and wanted closure as quickly as possible. Her new friend, Ann Goddard agreed the sooner she had this sad event behind her, the sooner she could get on with her life. She was, after all, a young woman. She had a lot of living ahead of her. 'We both do' Ann had said following the grave side service. Family and friends met at Emma's home in Ft Myers, gave their condolences and offered words of support. The whole affair left Emma McKinney drained of emotion and physical energy. She told her company that she was going to lie down and take a nap.

Pat and Diane's children, six year old Sean and three year old Anna went to the family room and played. Anna seemed oblivious to the fact that her grandpa was dead. Sean was very sad. He thought that his grandpa would be healthy again. He had his first lesson in mortality and he was scared. He was afraid that his dad and mom would suddenly die and leave him and his sister without parents. Pat talked with him about life and death and assured him that neither he nor Diane was going to die anytime soon. This seemed to allay his fears. Diane, Lisa and Ann went about cleaning the house to make sure that it wasn't left to Emma. While the women were busy cleaning, Pat and Joe retired to their late father's office. They closed the door and dropped into the comfortable chairs, Pat behind the desk, Joe on the love seat along the wall. They didn't speak for five full minutes.

They were both deep in thought on diverse but related topics. Pat was at it again with his finger, rubbing the scar on his jaw. The habit was annoying to Joe but he was too preoccupied himself to notice. Pat was thinking about all the times he'd let his parents down while growing up. He knew that his father had suspected they dealt drugs. He didn't know that it was limited to marijuana but it didn't matter. In Daniel McKinney's mind it was all illegal drugs. He had no proof so he didn't confront his sons. He was equally proud of them for their legal business dealings, but Pat knew that he'd deceived his parents for years and now with his father's passing, he felt genuine remorse in not having the courage to tell his dad the entire story.

Joe's thoughts were of his future and how it was off to a rocky start. The first two times he'd attempted to ask Lisa to marry him were marred by the death of a parent. Was it an omen or just coincidence? He couldn't dwell on that. He knew how much he loved Lisa. She'd stolen his heart and his heart gave up without a fight. He'd never met a woman like her.

She seemed to have a plan and the same kind of drive that kept Joe going. All she lacked was the financial means and he could help her with that. The small fortune that he'd amassed when he and his brothers were in business together was just sitting in boring investments. This was a chance to have that money work for something positive. He didn't want to use his wealth to bribe her into a relationship but he did want to seal that relationship; to wrap it up in a tidy package and have it for the rest of his life.

Then he thought about Mike and Julie McKinney. Their joyous marriage and brief life together was snuffed out by evil men. Those men were dead now but how many other men were out there ready to spread death to unsuspecting victims. His thoughts were going to a dark place where no good could be found until the gong of his father's mantel clock broke him and Pat out of their thoughts.

Joe broke the silence. "I have to get back to the task force. I have to call Nancy and Major Griggs and let him know that I'll be heading back to Jacksonville tomorrow. They've been pretty gracious letting me slide like this."

Pat gave Joe a look of annoyance. "You mean attending your father's funeral is gracious? That's why I never did fit in with the military mindset. They act as if they're doing you a favor letting you do things that normal people take for granted. You've been brainwashed to think like them."

"I am one of them. I took the oath and I will live up to that oath. You were a squid, you wouldn't understand." Joe and Pat were silent for a few seconds as they allowed their brains to process the events of the day and each other's comments. They were in two different worlds. Pat was all civilian and Joe was in that state between civilian and military lifer. Joe's Active Reserves commitment to the Marines was only for another year and a half. His mental commitment to his country was for life. If he ever was asked to defend his country even after his official discharge from the reserves, he'd gladly take up the call. Pat knew this was true and he didn't fault Joe for his commitment. Maybe when he has a wife and children to care for he'll back off of this thinking, but then again, maybe that's why he's so gung ho Marines. He wants to protect his country for our way of life. Who knows, maybe he's right?

Pat asked Joe how everything went with Lisa and his marriage proposal.

Joe said, "It must have gone well. She said yes."

Pat smiled, stood and walked over to Joe who stood to greet him. Pat grabbed his hand and threw his other arm around his brother. "Congratulations. Have you set a date yet?" They sat back down and continued.

"No. With all that's happening, we haven't had time to talk about it. Since you and I are heading back to North Carolina tomorrow, I don't know when we'll have time. Maybe we can talk tonight. Should I get her out of here for a while? I don't want to leave her mom alone."

"Diane and I will keep Mom and Ann company. You and Lisa get out of here and spend an evening alone. There's a ton of restaurants and hotels here that you can choose. Pick one on the beach and have a nice evening together. You need it and you deserve it."

"That's a good idea. Toss me that phone book."

Pat tossed the large, yellow business directory and Joe leafed through to the restaurant section. He picked out a restaurant that had a large display add with a variety of seafood and steak entrees. He stood and made reservations for 6:30 PM. Then he booked a room at the Marriot on Ft. Myers Beach. He was all set except to tell Lisa of his plans. He wanted to surprise her but he also didn't want to wait until she made alternate plans with her mother. Pat said, "Let me go and make sure that you and Lisa are going to be free. I'll make dinner plans for Diane, Ann, Mom and me. You go practice your lines in the mirror so you can impress Lisa."

With that, Pat left Joe in their dad's office and headed back into the kitchen where Diane, Lisa and her mom were just finishing off the last dishes. Ann said, "Your mom's refrigerator is full. She won't have to buy groceries for a week."

Pat looked at Diane with a smile. She knew something was up when she saw his face. She gave him a look that he recognized as *what are you up to now*? Pat said, "Diane, how about if you, Mom, Ann and I go out for dinner after Mom wakes up. That way nobody has to fool with dinner this evening. I know Mom would appreciate getting out of the house. You and Ann sure don't need to do any more work around here. We'll have time to visit and maybe the change will cheer Mom up a bit. What do you think, Ann?"

"What about Joe and Lisa?"

Joe walked into the kitchen.

Lisa walked up to Joe, put her arms around his neck, looked into his eyes and asked, "Yea. What about Joe and Lisa?"

Joe turned a bit red in the face before clearing his throat then said, "Well, uh, how about if you and I go out to dinner alone? Uh, I have a few things that I'd like to talk with you about."

Ann Goddard laughed out loud causing the others in the room to laugh as well. She walked up to Joe and looked up at him. "Joseph, you and Lisa go out and have a wonderful evening." She reached up and kissed him on the cheek. Joe's cheeks flushed a bright red.

She turned to Lisa and gave her daughter a big hug. "Have a good time. We'll see you when you get back here, whenever that is." The message was clear. *I'll be fine. Go with each other and start your life plans.*

Lisa whispered to her mom as tears filled her eyes, "You are the greatest. I love you Mom."

Pat said, "That's settled then. I'll make the arrangements for dinner and we'll plan to leave about 6:30. Anyone have any specific requests?"

There were none so Pat made reservations for four adults and two children at Chef's Garden. Pat's mom and dad had never been there and Pat didn't want any old memories to spoil their evening.

* * *

Joe called Major Griggs later that afternoon. He wanted to touch base with the Major before he left for North Carolina the next day. Major Griggs was pleased to hear from Joe. He hadn't expected to hear from him for at least another two days. Joe had been called to Active Duty status but he wasn't in a combat situation. Investigations were less demanding, manpower-wise than combat deployments. But this investigation was getting hotter by the hour and Gus Griggs wanted Joe's mind in the game. Nancy Brown had just reported some positive developments in the case and Joe needed to get up to speed with these new pieces of the puzzle.

Major Griggs said in his low, gruff voice, "Captain Brown is doing a great job, Joe, but she needs you here to help her with the details. She's determined as all get out, like you. She doesn't have the benefit of the analytical skills and field experience that you have. Before you go to North Carolina I want you to stop at King's Bay. Is your brother, the squid, coming with you?"

Joe chuckled to himself at Major Griggs characterization of Pat's former service branch. "Yes he is, sir. He knows Petty Officer Hatcher and briefly met Petty Officer Brush so he'd like to talk with both of them."

"Well, Hatcher is back on the ship and at sea. Brush was left ashore. They felt he'd be a burden on patrol under the circumstances. I can see why, poor bastard. Stop in and see that Brush kid and pump him for all the information that you can get. He's distraught but Captain Brown said now he's angry, not love sick. Apparently he wants to get back at this woman for stealing his life's collections."

"Will do, Major. I'll get in touch with the Captain and get the details from her. Is there anything else, sir?"

"Yes, son. I am very sorry about the loss of your father. I lost my dad to the Korean War. I think that I know what you're going through. Give my condolences to your mother and brother."

"Yes sir, I will and thank you sir."

"One more thing, Joe. You keep your mind clear, your chin up and your head down. Just because you're not on a battlefield doesn't make this enemy any less dangerous. There've already been three people killed. Let's keep it at that and get these bastards off the streets."

"Yes sir!"

* * *

After dinner, Joe and Lisa checked into their room at the Marriott on Ft. Myers Beach. They spent the evening in bed exploring each other's bodies, talking very little, taking cat naps between love-making. At 12:30 AM, they finally started talking about their future together. They decided on a late spring wedding the first week in June. They figured that there were no real drawbacks since work schedules were not an issue with their mothers or other family. They also decided to have the wedding in Ohio so that the weather would still possibly be somewhat cool. Of course that could change in a heartbeat with Ohio weather that time of year. Lisa said that she would take care of color selection. They decided to have the wedding at Saint Boniface Catholic Church in Oak Harbor. That's where Lisa went to church until she moved to Florida and stopped going altogether. That's also where Lisa went to grade school for a short while. Joe agreed since he hadn't attended church in some time, which could present an issue during their preparation for their marriage. As they talked things through, Joe was agreeable to most everything that Lisa proposed. He did insist on paying for everything regardless of whose side of the family traditionally paid. He said it was the very least he could do considering her family's recent loss and the difficulties that her brother had put her family through. She was reluctant but agreed.

Then they came to the subject that Joe dreaded the most; his current obligation to the Marines. She asked Joe when this obligation was up and he told her that he had another year and a half. She said, "Do you plan to extend your reserve time?"

He took a while to think about his answer because he hadn't really decided. He started to answer her but she cut him off. "If you decide that you have to commit to more time, can we at least talk about it before you sign any commitments? Please promise me that you'll do that first?"

Joe slowly nodded his head. "Yes I will. I promise."

They snuggled closer together and kissed long and deep. They stayed that way for several minutes then Joe said, "I'm driving up to King's Bay Submarine Base tomorrow with Pat. We have to question a former shipmate of Pat's. This guy's wife left him and took everything that he owned. We're looking to see if it's the same people that have been doing this to others over the last year or so, maybe longer. I think that we're heading out about 4:00 pm. It'll take us a little over seven hours to get there. We'll question him first thing in the morning then we'll head for North Carolina after that. I'll call you when we arrive at King's Bay and again when we get to Jacksonville. I wish you could go with me."

"Me too but you'd never get any work done. I'd have you in bed every waking hour."

"It'd be worth it." Joe paused. "Seriously, what are your plans for getting back to work at Publix or have you thought that through yet?"

Lisa turned her head and looked at the hotel room ceiling. She thought about Joe's question and it dawned on her that she really didn't know. She'd been so tied up with caring for her mother that she neglected to take care of her own problems. Finally she said, "I don't know. I probably should get back to Orlando and see if I still have a job. It's been almost a month. They've probably given up on me."

"Why don't you call them before you decide on anything? Maybe they're holding a position for you. If not, that makes your decision easier. You move into my apartment. We'll cancel the lease on yours and we'll get your stuff out of there. We can decide what to store and what to keep later. For right now it'll fit in the spare bedroom. If you're out of a job, that's okay because you really don't need a job. You can start looking at course materials for your college career. What do you think?"

For the first time in her life, Lisa realized that she had choices. She didn't have to work, pay her bills then figure out whether she would make it to her next paycheck. She could get serious about her school and a possible career. She smiled in spite of herself, then turned to Joe and kissed him hard on the lips.

* * *

Joe and Pat loaded their suitcases into Pat's car and made the rounds of the four women and two children that were there to send them off. There were plenty of tears and promises of returns home and lots of pledges of love. Ann told Lisa that she planned to stay in Florida for at least another week. During that time she planned to go shopping and spend time with her new friend, Emma. Diane was driving back to Dunnellon later in the day. She had to get to the store early the next morning to shop for school supplies and clothes for Sean, who would start first grade in the fall, and Anna who was looking forward to pre-school.

Lisa called her boss at Publix who told her that her job was filled, that he was sorry that they just couldn't wait for her return. He promised to hold the next open spot for her if she would be available but she declined. He wished her well knowing that she would be better off pursuing a different career path, one that really used her talents. He knew that she wouldn't be standing at a cash register her whole life. She was planning to leave later in the week and start looking at colleges. She planned to see the guidance counselor at University of Central Florida when she got back to Orlando. She also took Joe up on his offer and cancelled her lease. She got his apartment key and planned to move into Joe's apartment as soon as she could. Joe already called the apartment manager and let him know that Lisa's name was to be added to his apartment and that they'd take care of the particulars upon his return in a few weeks. The apartment manager didn't have a problem with the arrangements.

During the drive to King's Bay, Pat and Joe reviewed the information they received from Major Griggs along with the events that had occurred before their quick departure for their dad's funeral. They were amazed at how quickly the perpetrators were going from one base to another, hooking young men into marriage and stealing them blind. Just in the last six to eight weeks there had been three known cases. Could there be more than one group of individuals committing these crimes? If not, how could they be moving this quickly? By the time they set up operations in the town where the crimes were taking place, the perpetrators were already in another town setting up another scam. They both agreed that they needed to get better at anticipating where the next move was to be made. That would be tough because there didn't appear to be enough of a pattern to see where the next victim would be. The sting operation had been a good idea. It didn't work but maybe with what they learned from the first attempt they could be successful the second time around. They rode in silence for a while as they each tried to formulate the next course of action. It really didn't matter what they thought because they had to run any ideas past Nancy Brown. At this point, she was looking for any plan that would work. Then Major Hartnett had the final say on any operation.

According to Major Griggs, she needed their input and analytical skills. They hoped to get new information when they talked with Petty Officer Wilson Brush, the latest victim. Maybe he could fill in some of the missing pieces. When they got to King's Bay, they would call Nancy and get the latest information before questioning Petty Officer Brush. Maybe then some of the pieces would fall into place.

Chapter 28

Pat and Joe pulled into the parking lot at the Submarine Support Facility, Kings Bay, Georgia, well rested after a night at the Holiday Inn Express. The drive from Fort Myers had only a single glitch as traffic was backed up on Interstate 4 through Orlando. The drive took eight hours to reach the hotel at St. Marys just north of the Florida-Georgia border. They faced the early morning sun as Pat parked the car in a visitors slot near the large, red brick building. The pine trees towered above the surrounding buildings, shielding the area from the sun coming in at a steep angle. The shade from the trees at this modern military facility helped keep some of the sun's rays from heating the blacktop in the parking lot even at mid-day. The heat and humidity during the summer were unbearable at times and the shade from the pines helped provide some relief. As Pat looked around the lot, he noticed that more than fifty percent of the cars had cardboard sun protectors in their windshields. Since it was early in the morning and the angle of the sun was blocked by the trees, Pat decided to not use the protector that he kept in his car. In addition to the many pine trees, several stands of palm trees were placed around the facility. They added a tropical theme to the grounds that enhanced the pleasant appearance of the base. The facilities at Kings Bay were relatively new and modern.

Pat had many memories of his time stationed on the USS Alabama, some of them were even fond memories. All of them were good now that they were in the past. He'd made seven deterrent patrols and he hated every one of them. His favorite memory was his last step off the gangway after his last patrol. He saw Diane, Sean and Anna waiting for him on the pier as he made his way away from the sub and onto solid ground.

"Hey, man. Wake up. Are you reliving your glory days as a protector of freedom and the American way?" Joe was smiling as he jabbed Pat in the ribs. He could tell Pat was in a nostalgic funk.

Pat retreated from his brother's good natured jab and accompanying remark. He turned and said, "Yea, I was. I had a good time or two here. I'm even happier that it's over and done with."

"So where are we supposed to meet Petty Officer Brush?"

"He's supposed to meet us here at the Submarine Support Center. We can start here. Then we're supposed to talk with a counselor at the Fleet and Family Services building up near the Stimson Gate. They have a file started on him and his so-called wife. They have a few statements from friends and neighbors. Then we have one other stop. Petty Officer Brush would like to stop in at legal services. They're trying to see if they can track down some of his collections. They figure they've probably been or will be sold to a pawn shop."

They stepped out of the car onto the sidewalk. The smell of the pine trees filled their nostrils. There was a faint odor of fish in the air from the Crooked River that was some 400 hundred yards away. Pat looked around for the entrance to the building. Like most military buildings the entrance was marked by the American Flag and the associated military branch flag; in this case a Navy flag flew below the American flag on a single pole. A sailor in 13 button dress blues, or 'cracker jacks' was standing at the entrance looking their way. They started towards the young sailor. When they got within ear-shot of the sailor Pat said, "Looks like our welcoming committee."

"Yes sir. I'm Wilson Brush."

"No reason to insult us by calling us 'sir', Petty Officer Brush. I'm Joe McKinney. This is my brother, Pat." They exchanged handshakes.

"Call me Wil, please, sir, I mean Joe. You two look like you're twins."

"Strike one, Wil. I'm much more handsome than Pat." They all smiled.

Petty Officer Brush said, "Let's get out of this heat. We can talk in the office just inside the door. I've been authorized to talk as long as you need me. Since I'm supposed to be on board the ship, I'm listed as support staff so I'm not real busy. The Engineer personally told me to provide all the support I could to make sure that Tanya, or whatever her name is, gets caught. I can't believe that she totally had me fooled. I mean, I really believed that she loved me."

They entered the office, closed the door, and each took a seat. The office appeared to be designed for interviews of new arrivals to the sub base. On the wall opposite the door were pictures of the President of the United States along side the Commander, Naval Submarine Base, King's Bay. On the other walls were pictures of submarines in various positions, from underway at sea to sitting out of water in dry-dock, to being constructed at the Electric Boat production facility in Groton, Connecticut. On a display table on one wall was a scale model of a trident with part of the hull removed for viewing the interior of the sub. Several miniature sailors and a number of other model trucks and buildings were next to the sub for size comparison. Pat marveled at the model that showed the relative size of the Trident Submarine, which, out of water, was taller than a 5 story building if you included the sail. He shivered as he thought about the destructive power of just one Trident Submarine, which could carry as many as 192 individually targeted nuclear warheads, each with the destructive power far exceeding the bombs dropped on Hiroshima and Nagasaki.

"Pat, we'd like to get started if you don't mind?" Joe's comment brought Pat out of another trance and he realized that he was again rubbing the scar on his chin. *I've got to break this habit.*

"Right. Have you got the picture? We might as well start there."

Wilson pulled out a picture of Tanya Brush and handed it to Pat. The picture was a digital camera shot that had been printed out on a standard sheet of printer paper. It was unusually good quality for not using photo quality paper. The young woman in the picture was in a sexy pose on a couch, probably at Wilson's apartment. She was fully clothed but had one shoulder of her tank top hanging down low on her arm. She had a sensuous look on her face. Pat could see the sex appeal that roped young, unsuspecting sailors and soldiers into her web. He wondered about her personality and the lies that she must be able to tell without missing a beat. There was no doubt about it; she was a dangerous woman. Pat handed the picture to Joe who pulled out a different picture from the file folder that he'd laid on the table in front of him. He compared the two shots and said, "No mistake. She's the same woman." He turned to the young petty officer, "Wil, this is a picture of Tanya, except we got it from a soldier, Private David Wallace. This is his wife, Charlene."

Joe slid the pictures over to the young man for his inspection. His eyes welled up but did not spill over onto his cheeks. His face turned a bright red, at first from embarrassment then from anger as the level of her deception became obvious. Wil asked, "How long ago was this picture taken?"

Pat answered, "About 4 weeks. Dave Wallace took the shot just before he left for Afghanistan. We believe that she was already working on you then. Would that be right?"

Wilson thought for a moment then said, "Yes. We met at a bar south of the base. Tommy's. She was just so damned nice and innocent. At least that's how she presented herself. She said that she was brought up by her aunt and uncle 'cause her parents were both dead. Do you know if that's true?"

Pat again answered, "We're not sure because we don't know her real identity."

Wil said, "She charmed the pants off of me. What I am seeing and hearing, it's like we're talking about two different people. It's just hard to believe that she could be so . . . evil."

The three sat in silence for a moment letting Wil's last statement sink in.

Pat finally spoke. "You need to know that there have been three people murdered. Two were married to Tanya or Charlene or whatever her name is. She may not be the shooter but people who've had contact with her are being killed. If you see her again, you need to contact our office and your command immediately."

Wilson didn't know about the murders. He immediately wondered if Tanya's brother was involved. From his encounter with Wilson's friend Doug, at Tommy's, he seemed like he had a temper and an attitude. Wilson told them in detail about the guy who'd scuffled with his friend Doug at Tommy's. They asked him if he'd seen anyone else with Tanya that he didn't know or recognize but he said no. They asked a few more mundane questions that didn't land any significant comment. They asked Wilson if there was anything else that they should know or that he could remember, regardless of how insignificant.

"There is one thing that I never could figure out. Right before I deployed, I was getting ready to leave for the sub. She'd gone shopping that morning. While she was in the bathroom, I started to unpack the groceries. At the bottom of one of the bags was hair coloring. You know, like in the commercials." Pat and Joe gave each other a sideways glance. Wil continued, "It was odd because it was a shade of red. Tanya had blond hair. I wondered what she was doing but figured that maybe she wanted to experiment with it. I never gave it a second thought until now. Do you think that she's trying to disguise herself?"

* * *

Seaman Dean Gray's apartment was neat and orderly. He had a number of expensive art décor pieces on the dresser and end tables as well as in the living room. He had art work that was above the norm for an apartment dweller. He'd mentioned to Julie that a number of the pieces were serialized reprints of expensive originals. He'd told her that the collection was worth over $5000. He was a young man with above average taste and self control when it came to finances. He had no video games lying around. He did have a computer where he said he did some trading in stocks. 'Not much, just about $15,000 worth, depending on the market,' he'd said. "My dad taught me the value of money and how to take advantage of it, make it work for you instead of against you."

"Julie, I know we just met, but I feel like I've known you my whole life. It's so weird how comfortable I feel with you." Dean Gray looked directly into Julie Lippus' eyes, then faltered and looked down at her breasts. They were naked under the sheets that were covering them both in Dean's bed. He looked back up at her face and asked, "Will you marry me? I know this is quick and . . . "

"Yes. Absolutely yes!" She threw her arms around his neck and crushed her body into his. Within minutes she had Dean Gray aroused and moving inside her. She was going to make sure he didn't forget what he'd asked her to do. As they made love for the third time that morning, she said, "I'll . . . marry . . . you. You're making me . . . so . . . happy!" She moaned loud with sexual pleasure, so loud that Dean was afraid that the neighbors were going to hear and call the police. Then he figured *what the hell. I'm making her happy and I'm happy.* He began to respond with noises of his own. Pretty soon they were humping and grinding and shouting as Dean climaxed and Julie faked her third orgasm of the day. *There are plenty more where that one came from.*

After they both rested from their 15 minutes of intense sexual activity, Dean said, "I don't have to be back to the boat for two days. Let's have a pre-honeymoon. I can get my folks place down at Tybee Island. It's only about a four to five hour drive. We can spend the day on the beach and have a blast. There's a lot to do and you could make that hot tan even hotter."

Julie smiled broadly and said, "That sounds great. We can set a date for our wedding while we're there and figure out how we want to set up our home. I have to get my stuff moved in while you're out to sea. I have some money but I don't know if it will last the entire time you're gone."

Dean made the fatal error that sealed his future. "You don't have to worry about that. We'll get your name added to my checking account right away. We also have to make sure you're on my insurance policies, like my car and life and renter's insurance. It won't take too long. We can handle that on Monday. I have to report back on Tuesday so it should work out perfect. We're not scheduled to leave port until the following week and I should have time off on several of those days."

"I love you," Julie said with an ever widening smile as she snuggled ever closer to his body. She did love him, or at least his wallet and bank account.

* * *

The pre-honeymoon at Tybee Island went smooth as creamy peanut butter as far as Julie was concerned. They set a date for their marriage for the Friday following their return from Georgia. Dean hadn't had this much sex in his entire life prior to meeting Julie. He wondered how she could keep up the pace. He also wondered how long he'd be able to keep it up. She was wearing him out. But he figured that she was just a woman in love and they'd both have plenty of time to recharge their batteries while he was deployed. They'd finished taking care of all the important matters like his checking account and life insurance. She even deposited all her savings and checking money into his account, so she'd said. It totaled $776.48. That brought the account up to $2,435.92 with what Dean already had on deposit. He instructed her to make sure she paid all the bills on time and pointed out that he had a paycheck that would be automatically deposited on the fifteenth of this month to cover upcoming bills. She assured him that he needn't worry about the bills. She would take care of them.

Dean also mentioned that his father and step mother would like to meet her parents. His dad had an insurance convention in Pittsburgh and that they could make a side trip to Beaver Falls. Julie asked when the convention was and Dean had said in about two weeks. Julie agreed, knowing full well that she would be gone by then. She smiled her most assuring, alluring smile. "Maybe I'll make the trip up there myself and meet your folks. I'd like that."

"I'm sure they'd like that, too. Do you want me to arrange a flight for you?"

"Dean, that's not necessary. I can handle it. You don't have the time right now. There's enough money to cover a ticket if I need one, isn't there?"

"Sure and if you run short, the savings book will be in the strong box." Dean looked at Julie again with a gleam in his eyes. "I'd say let's do it again, but I afraid that it would fall off. You're killing me."

"With love. At least you'll die happy."

"That's for sure."

* * *

All the paperwork for their wedding was completed and authenticated. They lined up witnesses and a few flowers. Dean dressed in a nice sports coat. Julie had to buy a new off white dress that was pretty low cut with a sexy split up the side. The marriage went off without a hitch. Mr. and Mrs. Dean Gray retired back to Dean's apartment for their final love fest since they didn't have time for a real honeymoon. They spent the evening in Dean's and now Julie's apartment.

The next morning, Dean had to report back to the Nimitz for duty. The mighty air craft carrier was set to leave for a deployment in the Eastern Mediterranean Sea. The duration of the deployment wasn't known but was suspected to be for about 4 months. Dean was quickly becoming depressed. He'd just been through a sexual cyclone that left his mind in a fog and his penis nearly on the disabled list. But he was happy in knowing that he'd be returning to a beautiful wife and more wedded bliss. He was glad to see that Julie was in tears as he left, but she promised to be strong while he was gone. She also promised that he'd be a happy sailor when he came home. Dean felt like the luckiest man alive when he left his apartment to report to the Nimitz. Julie Lippus, aka Becky Lippert, also felt like the luckiest woman alive. Then she corrected herself. *I'm the most skilled woman alive. They're like puppy dogs, so cute and cuddly. Then you can spank them with a newspaper and they just come back for more.*

As soon as Dean left for the ship, Becky Lippert dialed the phone. Bobby Garrett picked up on the second ring. "Yes."

"We're in business. I'd say that within the week we can have this place cleaned out and be on our way to the next gravy train."

Bobby smiled and said, "Excellent!" They both disconnected.

Chapter 29

"Joe, I think this might backfire on us." Major Griggs words stung Joe because he thought that he had a good course of action laid out to help find the woman who was victimizing young military men along the East Coast. "This could cause these folks to turn and run before we can nail them. We don't want that to happen."

Major Hartnett studied Gus Griggs, Nancy Brown, and Joe as he thought about the potential consequences of taking the action that Joe was proposing. The four of them were in Frank Hartnett's office behind closed doors. The lighting was lower than Joe liked as the window shades were drawn. The room was made up with dark trim and dark green wallpaper. Everything about the room was dark, including the paintings on the walls and the scale models of various weapons systems on the Major's desk and near the book case. The room had the odor of a recently smoked, fine quality cigar though there was no smoke visible in the air. Major Hartnett instructed his aid that they were not to be disturbed. They'd been discussing options for nearly an hour, along with details of each of the case files. Major Hartnett wanted to apprehend the perpetrators but he also wanted to stop the killing. If they got scared off and the killing stopped, he was happy at least for the time being. They could then concentrate on identifying and apprehending the 'perps', whoever they were. That was the root of the problem; they didn't know the identities of these low-lifes. All they had were pictures of the woman and some false identities. If they knew their real identities, it would be much easier to find and arrest them. Hell, they weren't even sure how many people were involved.

Nancy chimed in. "I like Sergeant McKinney's plan except that it does have the real possibility of chasing the bad guys away. Is there any way to do this quietly? If we limit the policy order to announce the terms only upon a request for permission to marry that would lessen the possibility that the perpetrators would find out. Everyone in uniform has to get permission, right? So only upon receipt of that permission they are directed to get counseling. That would slow them down for a week or two. Right now it looks like this woman meets these guys and within two weeks they're married. If we could add a couple of weeks to that process maybe we can weed through the requests and identify our woman. How many requests can there be each month at the Southeastern Bases?

Gus Griggs said, "I think you'd be surprised."

Joe was listening to everyone's points regarding his idea. It was hardly a proposal. He thought of it on the last leg of the drive to

Jacksonville from Kings Bay. His initial thought was that when a request came in, the team could review the information provided and might be able to identify key information that would point right to the killer. It seemed simple enough. He didn't think that there'd be more than a handful of guys getting married after only knowing a woman for a few weeks. That there might be more than just a handful of couples in that much of a rush seemed ludicrous to him. But as he listened to Majors Hartnett and Griggs and Nancy Brown, he wasn't so sure of himself any longer. He also agreed with the majority in the room that they didn't want to scare them away. That would defeat the whole purpose of the investigation.

Joe said, "I'd like to recommend that we try this at three bases. That way we limit the potential to chase these folks off. The three bases would be the same ones that they've been working here in the southeast; Norfolk, Kings Bay and Camp Lejeune. It also limits the number of people that know the nature of the operation. Captain Brown and I can work out a detailed operations plan and have it to you in the morning. We could start the operation within a day or two. The only other question is do we have any other possibility of increased manning? Can we keep the young men who we're using on the sting operation with us during the day as well as the sting operations at night?"

Frank and Gus looked at each other. They appeared to be contemplating the pros and cons of the operation. Frank had the final decision on any operation and he said, "You two get to work on that plan. Once we see the final plan, we'll decide then whether to initiate the actual operation or not and how many resources we will use." Gus nodded his agreement. Frank continued. "Captain, Sergeant, we have to make this work. We're getting a lot of pressure from above. We don't want this to hit the press. If it does, we're out of business and these freaks get away with murder." He looked from Nancy to Joe, to Gus and back to Nancy. "Get moving. Dismissed."

Nancy and Joe left Frank Hartnett's office and headed for the parking lot. When they were safely in Nancy's car she told Joe, "I think this is a good plan but if we don't execute it, I'm sure I'll be replaced."

"This will work but we're going to have to have a certain amount of luck no matter how good of a plan it is. We keep getting more and more information but they're staying one step ahead of us. We can't seem to get out front and be waiting for them." Joe stopped, then said, "It didn't help that Pat and I had to leave for these past few days. I never did get to Grand Forks."

"That's going to have to wait. If we can pull this off, it solves the Grand Forks case, too. While you and Pat were in Florida, Private Dave Wallace and I went to a bar in Norfolk. We spotted a woman that looked like our woman but it turned out to be an older woman, not David's wife. A barmaid also said that she served a guy who looked like the guy from the bar by the submarine base in Georgia. Before we could get a good look at him, he was gone. He left a full beer that was still cold. We're afraid we spooked him. I didn't want to say anything in front of the Majors but we may be getting close. The problem is they may know it."

"Don't worry about that. These two or three seem real greedy. I think they're going to get careless. I think the takedown is going to happen real fast. We really have to be on our guard. We have to keep reminding ourselves that these folks are very dangerous. We have three dead bodies as proof."

Nancy put the car in gear and they headed back to their off base office.

* * *

The next day, they handed over the 28 page operational plan to Major Hartnett's aid and headed back to the office to wait for their instructions. They were already getting space ready to receive the forms from base chaplains on couples requesting permission to wed. They also briefed their young support team on what to look for in the forms that would raise red flags. The forms were designed to be simple and non-intrusive but had a couple of key questions that could weed out potential suspects. The biggest question was simply 'How long have you known each other?' The chaplains were also instructed to provide a few key pieces of information that would help cut the list of potential suspects even further. These questions were not seen by the marriage candidates but were answered after the candidates left the counseling session. The two key questions were 'What race is the prospective bride and the same question for the prospective groom?' and 'What are the bride's physical characteristics such as weight, height, eye and hair color, and build.'

Several of the base chaplains voiced their protest of the new directive but they were informed that this policy was not an option. They were also instructed to request and provide information in a manner that would not arouse suspicion about the reasoning for the battery of questions, just that it was part of the requirements for approval of their request. It was, in fact a requirement since it was directed by the Commanders of each of the three bases involved in the operation.

Within one day of the directive, forms started arriving at the task force office. They continued to come in throughout the day and well into the next. By the end of the third day, they had twenty-six forms, eleven of which could not exclude the bride to be as a possible suspect. The team realized that the investigation was not going to be easy.

Joe finished looking through the files of the eleven women still in the 'possible' stack. There were a couple of files that were likely not their target but Joe didn't want to eliminate any that had even the slightest possibility of being their woman. He felt a twinge of despair. When he first thought of this plan he thought that they'd be able to find this woman just by looking at the data from the chaplains' interviews. He was quickly realizing that it wasn't going to be that easy. He wanted to talk with his brother Pat, but he wasn't in the office. He'd talked with Nancy but she was busy studying the operations plan. He didn't want to disturb her. She already had enough weight on her shoulders.

He called Major Griggs. Gus picked up the phone on the second ring and said in a loud, gruff voice, "Griggs."

"Major, this is Sergeant Joe McKinney."

"Joe, how's the op going so far? Any hits?"

"That's what I wanted to talk with you about sir. We're getting lots of information and we expect to get lots more tomorrow. I'm not sure that we have the manpower to chase all these leads down, sir."

Joe could hear the Major sigh at the other end of the phone. "Listen son, I know this seems hopeless and each time another one of our brothers gets taken or killed, it hurts like hell. You feel like we're letting them down. We're not the ones doing this. You saw combat with me in Iraq. The reason you're here is because you have a special talent at analyzing situations and taking the best immediate action for the situation. This op that you and Nancy put together is a good op. It will work but the operative word is work. If you have something, however remote, go with your instincts. Take action. You'll know soon enough if it was the right course. If it was, you win. If it wasn't, you make a correction and take action again. In the end, we'll get these bastards off the street. I have all the confidence in the world in you, son. I have that same confidence in Nancy. You two are a winning team. All you have to do is execute." He stopped, seeing if his pep talk had the desired effect.

Joe let the words sink in then said, "Major, I believe the plan will work, too. We just have a pretty good stack of suspects already and it's just going to get bigger."

"No it's not because you are going to go out, starting this evening and talk with each one of these couples. You have pictures of the perp, right? Contact the chaplains and show them the pictures. It shouldn't take any time at all to determine if one of these young women matches the pictures. Just remember, Joe, these folks are dangerous. You need to have a good reason for knocking on their doors at night. What was the name of that Jacksonville Police Detective?"

"Harry Pierce. We have to talk with him about any evidence that he found at the Private Sharp murder scene anyway."

"You ask Detective Pierce if he or anyone in his department can help with knocking on doors."

A thought clicked in Joe's head. "If they could supply a couple of uniformed patrolmen, we could show them the pictures of our perp and they could knock on the doors and see these women. They could easily say that the neighbors heard noises or that there was a reported prowler in the area of their homes. I think it might work if they'll help."

"They have every reason to help and none to hold back. I think you have something, son. Now get to work."

"Yes, sir. Thanks Major."

The phone went dead before Gus could say "My pleasure" to the dial tone in his ear.

Joe immediately called Detective Harold Pierce who was glad to help. He even recommended the line that his patrolmen should use when they approached the various women's apartments and homes to arouse the least amount of suspicion. Joe then told Nancy what he had planned. She asked a few questions then officially approved the actions. Within the hour, Detective Pierce had 4 patrolmen knocking on doors and looking at the young brides-to-be. It was working well. Over the next four hours the field was narrowed from eleven to three.

* * *

Pat McKinney hung up the phone from his wife, Diane, and tapped his pen on the desk. His face bore the look of a man who'd been under pressure for an extended period. The lines were more visible on his forehead and the bags were dark and pronounced under his eyes since returning from their dad's funeral. He was worried about their mom more than ever. Having Lisa's mom visit and talk helped quite a bit, but now Ann Goddard was packing to head back to Ohio. Lisa planned to fly with her but she was planning to only spend a few days then get back to her and Joe's apartment. She had a lot of leg work to do before starting school in the fall semester. So their mom was going to be alone down in Ft. Myers. He decided to call her with the offer that he and Diane just discussed. Pat wouldn't have considered it except Diane insisted that he make the offer for Emma McKinney to move in with them, on a temporary basis, of course. Pat was reluctant to proceed with the offer to give Diane time to think this through. It wasn't easy having anyone move into your home, especially an in-law. Pat wanted Diane to be sure that she was ready to handle the intrusion. He told her that there would be times when Emma would butt in where maybe she shouldn't and that this would cause tension. 'I'm talking about simple things that you wouldn't expect to bother you but they will'. Diane assured Pat that she could handle it. 'This is temporary. We all have to keep that in mind,' Diane said. *Right!*

So Pat picked up the phone and called his mom in Ft. Myers. "Hello."

"Mom, how are you holding up?"

"Patrick. I am doing much better today. I've only cried a few times and managed to eat a little at breakfast and again at lunch. I'm still at a loss without your father here to direct things. You know how he ran the household but I'm sure I'll get the knack for living alone. It's so quiet here without him. This place is really big, too."

"Mom, that's why I'm calling. Why don't you sell that place and move closer to Diane and me? For the time being, you could move in with us. We have a spare bedroom and lots of space. We wouldn't invade your privacy when you need it and you'd be able to spend lots of time with your grandkids. In the mean time you could start to look for a place of your own. You wouldn't be rushed to buy a place or sell your place down there. You could take it as slow as you want."

"I could never impose on you and Diane. What would she think, me barging in like this?"

"We already talked, Mom. She said that she would love to have you move in." That was a bit of a stretch but close enough. "I can come down anytime and help you get packed and get the house ready to sell. We could have it listed by the weekend. What do you say?" Pat stopped talking to let it sink in. Emma had just lost her husband. He was pretty controlling and Pat didn't want her to feel that she was being pushed into moving. But he also thought that she probably needed a little coercing since she never had full control of her life before.

After a few minutes, Emma said, "Patrick, I think you're right. I need to get away from this place. It holds lots of good memories but with your father being gone, I'm afraid if I stay here I'll lose them. When will you be here?"

"I'll catch the first flight to Ft. Myers. I should be there by tonight. I'll call and let you know the time. Do you know a realtor that you can contact about listing the house?"

"Well, there is a nice man in our neighborhood. He works for one of the national companies, I forget which one. He was at the graveside service. I don't know if you remember Dick Hargrove?"

"Yes I do. He was a real personable guy. I think he'd be a good choice. We'll call him tomorrow." Pat paused. "Mom, I'll see you tonight. I love you."

"I love you, too, Patrick." The dial tone sounded while Pat held the phone to his ear. He felt drained.

He looked over at Joe who was listening to one side of the conversation. "It sounds like she's going along with it. That's good. She needs to be with family. I really appreciate this, Pat."

"It's the least I can do after everything we put Mom and Dad through. I just feel sorry for Diane. Having another woman invade her home isn't going to be easy."

Joe smiled. "You know Diane better than I do but I'll bet she'll handle Mom just fine."

"I hope you're right. My marriage depends on it." They both smiled. Pat got up and packed his briefcase. He let Nancy know that he would assist in any way he could from long distance as time permitted. He said his goodbyes and headed for the door. Before he left he turned and asked Joe and Nancy, "Who is the next person on our list to check out?"

Joe said, "Lady's name is Julie Lippus Gray. She just married Petty Officer Dean Gray, Navy Nuke who was just deployed on the Nimitz. She didn't meet the pre-marriage criteria, strictly speaking. She and Dean were married a few days ago. One of the chaplains said he included the couple in the list because the marriage happened so fast. He was concerned that he was too young and there was about a six year age difference. She's older than he. But, according to the chaplain, they insisted that it would work and they did appear to be truly in love. Technically they didn't have to get his permission. He got his commands' approval and that was all they really needed. They went in to talk to the chaplain voluntarily."

"Interesting. Well, watch your back and good luck."

Pat turned to head out the door when Nancy said, "Call when you get in and have a few minutes. I want to make sure you stay up to speed on the cases. Things may start to happen pretty fast if we can continue to narrow the field of suspects."

"Will do."

* * *

The flight to Ft. Myers had a short layover at Atlanta's Hartsfield International Airport. Pat had to go from Concourse A to Concourse D which was no small feat in the time allotted. But he managed to get to his connecting flight in time for boarding. The rest of the trip was smooth and for the third time in a few short weeks, Pat was back at Southwest Florida International Airport. He was surprised when the car rental clerk knew him by name but he guessed that they were good at recognizing repeat customers.

By 8:30 pm, Pat was at his mother's house having a glass of decaffeinated iced tea. They made a list of tasks that had to be accomplished in the morning. By the time their planning was done, it was near 10:15 pm. Pat kissed his mother goodnight then called Diane to let her know that he arrived safely and fill her in on the plans for the next few days. They both knew that what they were doing was the right thing, but both drew a deep breath when Pat said that Emma would be moved in with them by Sunday. It was temporary, but temporary is relative.

Then he called Nancy and Joe who were still at the office. He hoped that they were working on the case. He didn't need anything else to worry about.

Chapter 30

Dee's Pub was loud with southern rock and thick with smoke. The lights were down pretty low and much of the illumination was from the band's stage lights. It was difficult to see much. It was especially tough when you were looking for a person based on a couple of photographs and most of the patrons were in the shadows. The dance floor was hopping with gyrating bodies. It wasn't the kind of bar where two guys could get away dancing with each other. But two women would be more than welcome. Much of the crowd was from Norfolk Naval Station meaning there were lots of horny sailors in the bar. For them, two women dancing would be a welcome site on the dance floor.

The band was better tonight than the previous night. They still played southern rock but they appeared to have the songs down pat. The amps were not turned up full blast either so the noise level was tolerable, even pleasant to some. They played an array of favorites from Lynard Skynard and .38 Special to Allman Brothers and Charlie Daniels. They were getting a good response from the crowd, too.

"Joe, check out the lady at the table along the west wall. I'm talking about the one with the white blouse and reddish-blond hair, about shoulder length. She looks like Charlene Wallace. Can you get a better look at her from your angle?" Nancy was trying to talk quietly into the microphone that was in the top button of her blouse. It was a silky pink top with a small collar. The problem was that the button was lower than it should have been to capture her voice cleanly. There was a lot of background noise and Joe was having a difficult time hearing her through it all.

Nancy listened for Joe's reply to come into her earpiece when a young man approached her and asked her if she wanted a drink. "No thanks. I'm with someone."

"I don't see him around," the man persisted. "Maybe we can disappear before he gets back?" His smile gave him away as a bar predator and Nancy didn't have the time to waste. She was trying to concentrate on the woman across the bar. She said in a voice that was near contempt, "Look, buddy, I said I'm with someone now beat it."

"Lady, I like when women play hard to get. I'll just sit down here . . ."

A hand gripped his shoulder hard. Another grabbed his hand and twisted it so that it was at a painful angle. Then a voice whispered in his ear, "The lady said 'beat it.' I recommend that you do exactly that and don't come back if you want to keep that hand of yours attached to your wrist. Got it?"

"Sure man. I got it."

"I'm gonna release your hand. When I do you walk away without a scene." Marine Private Jeffrey Steers relaxed and released the man's hand and shoulder and he walked away only looking over his shoulder once to sneer at the young Marine. It was harmless and Jeff knew the guy wouldn't be back. He saw the fear in his eyes through his tough-guy façade.

"Are you alright, Ma'am?"

"I'm fine, Private. Sit here for a minute and look over at the table, number four from the left side of the room. Tell me if the woman seated there looks like our target."

Jeffrey looked across the room and zoned in on the table in question. The woman sure did bear a striking resemblance to Charlene Wallace, Tanya Brush, and Belinda Reardon, all who were the same woman. But Private Steers couldn't be sure. He started to tell this to Nancy when she held up her hand indicating that someone was talking to her over her earpiece.

"Nancy, she sure looks like our gal. Let me know and I'll strike up a conversation and see where it goes."

"Use your best judgment but keep your mic on. If someone is keeping tabs on her, we don't want this to get ugly. We'll watch you from here."

"Roger that," Joe said. Nancy Brown and Jeff Steers watched as Joe moved across the bar to the table where the young woman sat alone. As he approached, a young man, probably a sailor in civilian clothes, sat down across from her. She smiled at him as he made some comment to her. She shook her head no. He made another comment and she again shook her head. He paused for a moment then got up and left. Joe had stopped about ten feet from the table and looked out over the dance floor. Once the young man was gone, Joe moved towards the table, leaned over and asked "May I join you?"

She looked up at Joe and smiled. She looked Joe up and down then said, "Sure. What's your name, sailor?"

"I'm Joe. But I'm not a sailor. Do you want to guess again?"

"If you're not a sailor then you're a Marine. Am I right?" Her smile was intoxicating and her manner was easy going. He could see immediately why men would fall for her quickly. She had a perfect complexion and beautiful eyes.

"You're very good. I'm a Sergeant in the Corps. I'm doing a little R&R, visiting friends up here. How about you? What brings you to Norfolk? You're not in the military. Am I right?"

"You're pretty good yourself. No I'm not. I moved here with my husband who is in the Navy. Well he was my husband when we got here. Now he's my ex. He's deployed on the Nimitz right now, not that it matters." She smiled the entire time she talked about this person that didn't exist. "He left me high and dry for some female officer he met while on duty."

In Joe's earpiece he heard Nancy say to probe a little more about her hometown and her family. She thought that they might be able to match her story up with one of the stolen identities from the kit that they'd found in North Dakota. Joe smiled and said, "So what's your name and where are you from?"

Becky Lippert thought that she'd try something different; the truth. Joe seemed to be analyzing her. He was a no-bullshit, calculating kind of guy. She could see that there was more to this guy than a night out on the town. She thought it might be fun to try to match his wits and see what kind of game he was playing. "I'm Becky. I was born out west in Colorado Springs. My mom was a flyboy's girlfriend, from what I've heard. I've never met my real dad. I spent a lot of time in foster care growing up."

"No way. Foster kids are ugly and they grow up scarred and mentally unstable. You're downright beautiful and you're pretty self assured. From what I can see, you shouldn't have any problem meeting guys."

Becky laughed. "Meeting them is one thing. Keeping them happy is a whole different story. Most guys are pretty naïve. Most have a lot of growing up to do. I mean, the younger ones are only thinking of one thing. A long term relationship isn't it. I need a guy who's willing to commit something real to a relationship. I don't want a one night stand. Maybe three or four as long as it's an attempt to be something more meaningful."

Nancy was listening in to the conversation as best she could. She hoped that the recording being made in the surveillance van outside was getting better quality sound than what she was hearing. She couldn't make a move on what she was hearing now. There just wasn't enough evidence to warrant taking a chance and scaring her off. So she listened patiently as Joe tried to say something that would give them cause to take her into custody. At the same time, the team was combing the bar to try and locate the tall, skinny, pale guy that was supposed to be her accomplice. So far they weren't having any luck. They continued to scan the bar while Joe and Nancy concentrated on Becky Lippert.

"Ask here if she's ever been to Jacksonville, North Carolina or St. Marys, Georgia." She watched as Joe moved his hand to the back of his neck, letting Nancy know that he heard her but that he didn't agree with the idea. She said to him over the headset, "Okay, let's wait and see where this goes." This time Joe casually grabbed his right earlobe. He was okay with that.   He apparently had an idea where he wanted to go with the conversation so she let him go and listened in as the conversation continued. He asked Becky questions about her schooling and if she'd ever been to college. He asked her if she worked in the area and where. She gave answers that were both credible and smooth. When she answered, Joe couldn't tell whether she was lying or telling the truth. She didn't bat an eye when talking. No blinking or any other indication that she was deceiving him. She finally said, "Hey, you know almost everything about me, what about you? Where are you from?"

This threw Joe off balance a bit. He had to decide quickly whether he would tell the truth or make up a story as he went. He wasn't real good at lying so this was going to be a challenge. He decided the truth was best since he wasn't prepared with a good story. "I'm from Ohio originally, a little town called Port Clinton. My folks moved me and my two brothers to Indiana and then Florida. We spent a lot of time north of Orlando. My two brothers and I started a nursery business when we got out of high school but it didn't go real well so we joined the service. That's how I ended up here."

"Did you see combat anywhere?"

"Yes, a little time in Iraq. Nothing special."

"What about your brothers? Are they in the Marines, too?"

"Well, my younger brother died." He broke eye contact and lowered his head a bit. He felt real pain at this very real part of his story.

"I'm sorry. Were you close?"

"Yes, we were and I still am with my older brother. He went to the Navy. He spent some time on Submarines. He was stationed at Kings Bay. Do you know where that is?" Joe's questions caught Becky off guard a bit and for the first time in their chat, he could see her searching for an answer.

"Um, yes I do. I was there once with my husband."

"Why'd your husband go there, it's a sub base? He's a skimmer sailor."

"Yes, but he went there to meet some friends that are sub sailors." *Nice recovery. What a pro*, Joe thought. "We stayed overnight there at a hotel right off the base." Becky casually looked around the bar and was surprised to see a couple staring right at her and Joe. She continued to move her head as if she were looking for someone but watched the two from the corner of her eyes. They continued to look at her and Joe. She turned her head and looked directly at them. When she did, the couple abruptly turned their heads away. Becky was spooked though she didn't show any outward signs that she felt like she was being watched. She scanned the bar a little more but didn't see anything else out of the ordinary. She looked back at Joe who was talking about his brother, *what did he say the name was? Pat, that's right.* She looked at Joe as he continued his story. She wasn't really listening but she appeared to be engrossed. As he talked, he reached up and touched his ear. He'd done this a couple of times. She found this odd and wanted to know why. She casually looked towards the center of the dance floor and suddenly smiled brightly and waved to someone. Joe followed her gaze but didn't see anyone return her wave. While he had his head turned, Becky could see the listening device in his ear as plain as day. She knew it. She was under surveillance. She figured that Joe and the two from across the bar were the surveillance team and there might be more. She had to think fast and get out of there before they cornered her.

Joe asked, "Someone you know?"

"Just a guy I met the other night. He was pretty nice but it looks like he's moved to another lady for tonight. He wasn't that interesting. Not like you anyway. So Joe, how long do you have left in this country's Marine Corps? Are you going to make it a career?"

"Probably not. I have a few other things that I want to try before I get too old to do them."

"Like what? Do you have any examples, like jumping out of a plane or rock climbing?"

He shook his head and smiled, "No, nothing that exciting. I'd like to go deep sea fishing and adventure skiing."

"You can tell me about adventure skiing when I get back from the lady's room." She stood and picked up her purse. "Do you mind?"

"Not at all." Joe smiled as he stood to pull her chair out.

"Save my seat, please." Joe turned and watched as she walked the thirty feet to the lady's restroom. It was in clear line of sight from where Joe sat. There was little interference and Joe saw her enter. He spoke low trying to move his lips as little as possible so he didn't look too crazy talking to himself. "She's definitely our target. Any luck finding her sidekick?"

Nancy could hear Joe clearly. "No. She may be flying solo tonight but I wouldn't expect it. How long can you keep up the small talk? You seem to have a pretty good rapport going with her."

"She's an easy woman to talk with. We could be best friends if I didn't know anything about her. I better keep my eyes on the rest room door. I don't want her to see me chatting away with myself. She'll think I'm nuts."

"We'll keep looking for pale face. Clear your throat when she comes out of the rest room so we know that you're about to be back in business. If we don't see her partner within the next fifteen minutes, we'll move on her."

"Roger that," Joe responded.

Becky was busy in the woman's restroom. She found an empty stall and removed her blouse and bra. She tucked those into her pants pocket for a moment. She reached into her purse and pulled out a bright red, silky tank top and pulled it on. She then pulled out a short wig with dark brown hair. She pulled her reddish-blond hair up into ball then flattened it out as best she could. She pulled the wig over her head making sure that her hair was tucked up under the dark wig. She pulled a silk flower from her purse and attached it to the wig over the top of her ear. Then she took out a pair of glasses with narrow lenses that were slightly shaded. She smoothed her blouse, hair and pants then exited the stall. She looked at herself in the mirror and pulled out a tube of bright red lipstick which she applied and touched up with her fingernails. She looked again from side to side and was pleased to see that she looked nothing like the woman who entered only a minute or two before. She wanted to exit as quickly as possible before the surveillance team got worried and came in looking for her. She walked out of the restroom and walked casually right passed Joe who was still sitting at the table looking towards the restroom door. She waited until she was past him before she smiled a big, broad smile. She walked right out the front door of the bar and headed for the BMW. Bobby was in the driver's seat with the seat laid back, resting. When she knocked on the window, he unlocked the door using the button on the driver's side. She got in and said, "Hey baby, are you relaxed?"

With still sleepy eyes and a yawn Bobby said, "I must have dozed off there for a minute."

She said, "Well you better wake up because there're some folks in there looking for us. This guy was talking to me and another guy and a lady were watching me everywhere I went. Let's go in and I can show you."

Bobby was alert now. He looked Becky in the eyes and asked in a tone laced with disbelief, "Are you sure about this?"

"Hell yes I'm sure. The guy who was talking with me had an earpiece and it wasn't a hearing aid. It had a small wire that ran down inside his shirt. His two friends were looking directly at us as we talked. I could tell they were keeping an eye on us."

"Let's go."

Bobby got out of the driver's side and Becky joined him as they headed back towards the door. She stopped him before they got to the entrance and said, "You need to do something with your hair. If they know what I look like, chances are they know what you look like, too."

He went back to the car, grabbed a ball cap and tucked his hair underneath. He turned and asked Becky, "How do I look?"

"Like a dork. Even in the dark you look like a skinny dork."

"But do I look like Bobby Garrett?" He cocked his head back and smiled.

She gave him a sideways look with her lips moved to one side. "Nope, I guess not."

"Good, then let's go. We have our own surveillance to do." They turned and walked back to the main entrance of the bar, Bobby with his hair under his hat and Becky with her dark wig, bright red lipstick, and glasses. They looked like a couple of punk rockers headed for a party.

Inside, Joe was getting worried. He thought that Becky had been in the woman's restroom for quite a long time. He said into his microphone, "Nancy, she's been in there a while. You should go in and see what's going on in there. It's probably nothing but she should have been out by now."

"Give it a couple more minutes. Maybe she's freshening up for you."

"Okay, your call, but I wouldn't wait too long."

"Understood." The line went silent again.

Becky and Bobby were scoping out the bar. Becky already pointed out Joe. Bobby wanted to get a better look at him but didn't want to risk being seen so he stayed back against the wall in a dark spot in the bar. Becky pointed out Nancy and Jeff Steers across the bar. They were obviously panning their view across the bar looking for someone. Becky was sure that that someone was her. They turned their attention back to Joe who was putting his hand to one ear then talking. They saw his lips moving but no one was anywhere near him. He stood and began to scan the bar. He looked right at Becky, stopped for a brief moment then went on scanning the bar again. He didn't recognize her. They were in the clear.

Becky whispered to Bobby, "Do you believe me now? Let's get out of here."

"Wait a minute, baby. The fun has just begun." With that Bobby slowly walked towards Joe. As he walked he reached in his pocket for his cigarettes and pulled one from the pack. He walked right up to Joe, looked him right in the eyes. He paused and stared at Joe for a minute. Joe was about to say something to him when he stuck the cigarette in his mouth and asked, "Got a light?"

Joe replied, "Sorry, don't smoke."

"No problem. Have you seen my friend? She's about 5'2", dark black hair, and blue eyes. She was wearing a red tank top. He looked past Joe with an expression of recognition and said, "Never mind. There she is. Didn't mean to bother you pal."

"That's alright, partner." As Bobby started to move away Joe turned his attention towards the bar again, looking at Nancy and Jeff. He shrugged his shoulders as if Becky had disappeared. He said into the microphone, "Maybe you should make that trip to the Lady's room." He heard a voice from behind him,

"What did you say?" It was Bobby again.

Joe had a surprised expression on his face as he turned to face Bobby. "I didn't say anything." He turned away. As he turned, he felt a burning sensation on his arm and every muscle in his body contracted. The pain running through his body was excruciating. He blacked out and collapsed. The next thing he remembered was several people standing over him asking him if he was alright. It took several minutes before he could speak coherently. Nancy and Jeff were questioning him but he couldn't really tell them anything. One minute he was talking with a guy about lighting a cigarette, the next thing he knew he was on the floor in pain. He touched his arm which hurt like a cigarette burn. The skin was raw, but not bleeding. He reached into his pockets. He still had his keys. Then he reached for his wallet. It was gone.

Out in the parking lot, Bobby was starting their BMW, laughing so hard that his eyes were watering. "Did you see him drop like a ton of bricks? His eyes actually rolled back in his head." He laughed harder and louder.

Becky was not amused. She thought that he'd taken too big a risk. "Bobby would you settle down and get us the hell out of here? What if someone saw you and followed us? We're sitting ducks. Come on, let's get going."

Bobby's laughing fit started to subside as he thought that Becky may be right. He still had a broad smile on his face when he put the car in gear and headed out of the parking lot and onto East Little Creek Road and towards their apartment. He felt good. He sent these investigators a message that they shouldn't fuck with Bobby Garrett. Next time maybe someone would really get hurt. The stun gun packed a 900,000 volt punch. It would knock any man to his knees. Bobby made sure that he got solid contact on the guys arm. As they moved down the highway, he pulled the driver's license from the guy's wallet. *Joe McKinney. Here all the way from Orlando, Florida. Well, Joe McKinney, you should head back to Orlando before you really get hurt.* He continued to look through Joe's credit cards, his military ID. *Marine Corps Reserves. He wasn't such a bad ass. Wasn't real bright either.* He looked through his pictures. He came across a snapshot of Lisa in a tank-top and shorts. *Hmmm. Who's this? Pretty hot. Maybe she'd like a real man?*

"Bobby!" Becky shouted. He looked up and braked just in time to keep from ploughing into the back end of a Jeep Wrangler. "Put that shit away and get us back to the apartment in one piece!"

Bobby reached over, grabbed Becky by the arm, and pulled her close. "You don't ever yell at me like that. I decide what we do and don't do. If we'd have done what you wanted we'd still be in the dark about who's watching us. Now we know. Now we have the upper hand." He released her arm. She rubbed the spot where he'd grabbed her. She knew it would bruise. She was angry but she was also scared. Bobby's temper was at a boiling point and he'd snap at the least little comment. She also knew that when he was in this kind of mood, she was in for another night of rough sex. She wasn't looking forward to that. The time was getting closer when she would disappear but she wouldn't leave without her money. The good news was that Bobby wasn't keeping the money locked up so when she decided to pull up stakes and run, it would be easy. She just had to make up her mind when enough was too much.

Bobby put the wallet aside for now. He'd get back to that later. Now he was thinking about the woman in the bar. He didn't know her name but that wouldn't be too difficult to find out. One call to BUPERS, the personnel office at Norfolk Naval Base and he'd have his information. He still had his connections. Having Joe McKinney's name was the key to his new offensive strategy. He hadn't thought it all the way through yet but he had the beginnings of a plan to get these guys. They were going to be very rich and have fun in the process. "We have to make a stop at your new apartment. We have to work fast and get as much stuff out of there as we can. They won't expect us to do anything else tonight so now's a great time to get the most important stuff out." He smiled at Becky. "This is going to be so much fun. Let the games begin."

* * *

Joe, Nancy, Private Jeff Steers, and Private Leonard Skiff were back at the makeshift office at the Holiday Inn trying to piece together the events that led to Joe's assault. Joe was still light headed and had a terrible headache as well as a whale of a burn. The brief stop at the hospital emergency room confirmed that there was no serious damage from the shock of the stun gun. The Doctor recommended some pain medication and plenty of fluids. Joe declined the drugs but was hitting the water heavy.

Joe described the guy in the ball cap that asked him for a light but couldn't remember any details about what he was wearing other than the ball cap. "It happened so fast that I didn't get a good look at his clothes or face. I was trying to get turned around to watch the bathroom doors at the bar when the lights went out."

Nancy said, "All we saw from our table was a crowd gathering around you. One minute you were standing there looking around the bar, the next minute the crowd was over you. We got to you in less than a minute. We didn't see anyone suspicious, no weapons."

Jeff Steers said, "It was a stun gun, probably pretty high voltage. You can tell by the burn pattern. It looks like the prongs of the gun were about 1 inch apart, maybe a little more. We had some training on these things when I was in training for the police department back home."

"Well it hurts like a son-of-a-bitch. That was some serious pain." Joe moved his arm back and forth and rubbed the burn.

Nancy looked around the room. She was beginning to feel like the team was losing ground now. If the attacker had Joe's wallet, they had information on his real identity. He was compromised and that was a real problem for the team. It was also a real problem for Joe and his fiancé. These people knew where Joe lived and Lisa had just moved in with him. "Joe, you should call your fiancé and tell her to be real cautious. You can't tell her exactly why but I would recommend that she not move in yet. It might even be better if she got you moved to a different apartment. Remember, these people have killed before. There's no indication that they'll stop now."

Joe sat down at hotel room table and leaned back in his chair. "This all sounds terrible but the real question is what do we do next? They always seem to be one step ahead of us. We thought we had them tonight and they got away. How? We were so close, I know it. So let's stop worrying about me and Lisa. I'll take care of that. Let's start planning our next move. We know these two, at least we think it's two, are here in Norfolk. Or at least they were tonight. What time is it?"

"Just before 0100." Leonard Skiff looked at the clock to confirm his statement. Just before 1:00 am. "It's been just over an hour since you were stunned."

Joe said, "They can't have gone far but we don't know what they're driving, if they're driving, or where they're staying. We need more information on them."

Steers asked, "Do you think they'd risk going back to Gray's apartment?"

Skiff said, "She wouldn't go back there. She'd have to be a complete fool." Jeff and Leonard looked at Joe, then at Nancy. ". . . unless she left something at the apartment. Would she risk it though?"

"Norfolk Police have surveillance set up in the parking lot. If there's activity, we'll know it." Nancy looked around the room. "Unless we hear something in the next five minutes, we'll call it a night and gather at 0700. Private Steers, are you and Private Skiff going to relieve the Detectives on the Gray apartment surveillance?"

Jeff Steers said, "Yes Ma'am. We're heading over there at about 0200. They'll relieve us again at 0800."

Nancy said, "After you get finished, get some sack time and call me at 1400. Everyone else, get some rest. We can't afford to be fatigued if we get close again."

Everyone on the team nodded and headed for the door. It was going to be tough to get rest this morning. Too much had happened and Joe still had a headache from the stun gun attack. *It could have been worse. It could have been a 9MM instead of 900 kilovolts.*

Chapter 31

Dean Gray's apartment building was typical; three stories with 12 units in each building. Dean's apartment was on the sub floor meaning his apartment was halfway underground. His windows were just above ground level. Shrubs on either side of the windows for the bedrooms and the living room provided a narrow view to the grounds outside. That view was usually of the front bumper of a car in the parking lot. That was fine for Bobby and Becky as they scrambled to find his most valuable possessions. Bobby stood in the living room looking at all the art work and miniature sculptures on the walls and end tables. He thought that Dean Gray must be gay to have all this frilly stuff in his apartment. But it was good for them because these works were probably valuable to some collectors. On the other hand all of the furniture was department store grade, pressboard with laminated surfaces. They held little or no value. There was no room for furniture in the BMW anyway.

The table lamps were low and didn't illuminate the room well, leaving shadows behind the furniture. The carpet was a multi-shade of brown to tan, designed to hide stains of careless tenants. Bobby moved into the kitchen and systematically opened and closed the cabinets looking for anything of value. So far he was striking out. He opened drawers in the cabinet next to the refrigerator; nothing but cheap silverware. The next drawer had dish towels and dish rags. He lifted the stack of dish towels and discovered a key that appeared to be for a strong box. He yelled, "Becky, do you know what this key unlocks?"

Becky came into the kitchen and looked at the key. "Yes. It's to a strong box back in the bedroom."

"Is it a safe, I mean, does it need a combination to open?"

Becky answered that it wasn't, that the key should open the box directly.

Bobby took the key and said, "I'll take care of this." Becky nodded and followed him to the bedroom. As she made the turn in the hallway, the doorbell rang. She stopped in her tracks. She eased her way back into the living room from the hallway and looked at Bobby for direction. She raised her hands and made a face asking, *what should I do?* Bobby quietly walked her way. When he reached her he said, "Answer the door and act normal. If they want to know what's going on, tell them that you and your sailor boy husband are going to be moving. Remember, I'm your brother." The doorbell rang again. He whispered, "Go."

Becky took a deep breath and made her way to the door. She had to put on her Julie Lippus Gray persona. She looked through the peep hole and saw Dean's next door neighbor, Gerald Jamison, standing in the doorway. Gerald was a sailor, too but not on the same ship as Dean. Gerald was on the USS Estocin, FFG-15; a Fast Frigate. He was home quite a bit lately because his ship was in for an overhaul. She left the chain on and opened the door a crack and greeted Gerald, "Hi Gerry. What's up?"

"Hi Julie. I was going to ask you the same thing. I heard some racket in there and thought that someone might be breaking in. Are you alright?"

"Yea. Everything's fine. I'm just trying to find something that I misplaced. I might have been getting a little carried away with opening and closing drawers. I hope it didn't wake you. Were you sleeping?"

Gerry was trying his best to look past Becky to see if he could see anyone else in his friend Dean's apartment. He didn't care if this was his wife or not. He and Dean had a mutual agreement to watch out for each other's apartment when either of them was deployed. He knew he'd heard a male voice coming from the apartment. "You have company? I thought I heard someone else."

Becky was a bit flustered, which was unusual. She was pretty calm and quick witted. She smiled and said, "Yes there is. My brother is here to help me get things organized. Dean said that we should get a new apartment a little farther from the base in a better part of town. We're talking about starting a family and he wants us to be in a place that has more of a family atmosphere." The lie flowed from her lips like water over the falls. She was in her element now.

Gerald tried to keep the look of surprise from his face but he wasn't a practiced liar. "Really? Congratulations," he said with no emotion. He didn't know what to say. "Have you decided on a place yet?" He was fishing for information now.

"Not really. I just started looking and I can't decide on my own. When Dean gets back I want to have a few choices ready." She paused then said, "Anything else 'cause I really have a lot to do yet." She looked at Gerald with her pleading eyes, trying to dissuade Gerald from further conversation.

"No, I need to get some shut eye anyway. If you can, please try to keep the noise down. That would be a big help."

"We will. Thanks for looking out for us, Gerald. It's nice to know we have a good neighbor." She closed the door.

Gerald stood outside thinking about what he should do next. He had information that he knew was bogus. He knew that Julie was lying and that Dean wasn't about to have a family. He'd said that he didn't want kids any time soon. He wanted to build up a sizable nest egg before he ever considered it. Dean and Gerald were in an investment club together and had discussed family matters and their hopes for the future many times. Dean may have been the marrying type but he wasn't ready to be a father so he wasn't in any hurry to move to a family oriented apartment complex. He planned to buy a house next. Gerald went back inside his apartment and sat on the couch against the wall that was common to his and Dean's apartment. He could hear muffled voices coming from Dean's place and wished he could hear what was being said. Then he remembered the stethoscope he had in his closet. It was an old one that his mother had given him when his father had passed away. His father was a paramedic on an ambulance crew and his mother gave it to him as a reminder to be like his father and always help people. He retrieved the stethoscope and headed back to the living room wall. He placed the pad of the instrument on the wall and listened. The voices were still a bit muffled but he could hear Julie talking to someone about him. *'That's Dean's nosey neighbor. He and Dean talk a lot. I don't know how close they are but he talks about the club they're in together. He didn't say what kind of club.'* Then the male voice said, *'Maybe they're gay and it's a gay swap club. Or maybe it's a wife swapping club. Maybe you should stick with this guy.'* She replied, *'Very funny, you prick. Let's get moving. We have a lot of stuff to look through.'* The voices stopped and all Gerald could hear was muffled noises and the opening and closing of drawers and doors. Then he heard a distinct word. *'Bingo.'*

In Dean's closet, Becky had opened the strong box. It contained Dean's savings account book, his stock broker's account and a sheet with pin numbers. When Becky looked at the total in the stock account, she nearly lost her breath; over $65,000. Add to that an additional $5000 in his savings account and they were looking at over $70,000. Becky also found two charge cards inside plain envelopes with the credit limits listing an available credit line of $18,000 between the two. Then Becky read the name on the cards in the envelopes; Julie L. Gray. The security strips were still on the cards instructing the card recipient how to activate the cards. It was all she could do to keep from screaming for joy. Then she thought for a moment. Bobby hadn't seen these yet. Maybe I should keep this little discovery to myself? She tucked the envelopes with the cards into her pants pocket and continued to search the strong box for any other valuables. She found a few rare coins and other mementos that were probably of personal sentimental value to Dean. She left those since there was no real monetary value. As she walked out of the master bedroom, Bobby was carrying a guitar and amp out of the second bedroom. He also had a bag of wires, pedals, and other gadgets used for an electric guitar. The guitar, Becky knew, was a vintage Gibson Les Paul that his father had bought for him when he graduated from high school. Dean had said it was worth at least $3500. Bobby could barely handle the guitar case and amp. Becky grabbed the bag from him and said, "Leave this crap. It isn't worth anything compared to that guitar. Leave the amp, too."

"No. I want the amp and at least one cord. I'm playing this bitch tonight."

Becky just looked at Bobby with disgust. "You're going to get us caught for a guitar amp? You're a fool."

She knew she'd made a mistake as Bobby's pale face turned bright red. He dropped the guitar case and amp and raised his hand as if to smack Becky. Then he stopped short. Instead he grabbed her and pushed her hard against the wall. "You are going to pay for that remark. Now help me get this stuff to the car." He picked up the guitar case and amp and headed for the front door. She picked up the bag of cords and followed. He turned around and said, "Did you get all the stuff from the strong box?"

"Yes. We're going to be pretty happy about our decision to come here tonight." Her face twisted into a wicked smile. His frown turned to a smile that was more menacing than the angry expression he wore only moments before.

He motioned for her to get the door. She did and they headed up the stairs to the parking lot.

Gerald moved from the couch and looked out his peep hole to see the duo heading out to the parking lot with a few of Dean's most treasured possessions. He backed away from the door to think about what he could do to stop them but he was frozen with indecision. He decided to call 911. He reached for his phone then hesitated again. *What if they tell me that they can't do anything about it? Dean and Julie are married. Fuck it. I know their ripping that stuff off. He's my pal. I have to stop them.* He picked up the phone and dialed 911.

The operator came on, "What is your emergency?

"I want to report a robbery in progress."

* * *

The lighting in the apartment complex parking lot was poor at best. The orange colored glow from the mercury vapor lamps failed to cover much of the lot. Much of the lot was in darkness. A number of the bulbs were nearing the end of their life and would blink out before trying to restart. This caused even more of the lot to be in temporary darkness as the lamps heated up and snapped back on before going dark again. The night air was humid with a temperature staying near 85 degrees. Outside the apartment, Bobby and Becky were struggling to haul the guitar, amp and other possessions to their car. They got to the car and had to set their loads down to rest while Bobby unlocked the car and opened the trunk.

Jeff Steer and Leonard Skiff were just about to call off the surveillance job when Jeff tapped Leonard on the arm, "Hey. It's hard to see but someone's coming out of the stairway in front of Dean Gray's apartment." They watched as a man and a woman approached a Black

BMW no more that 100 feet from their car. "Call it in then we'll approach."

Leonard made the call to the hotel room and alerted Nancy who was already asleep. She assured them that'd she'd get the police back up and as many of the team as she could muster.

Jeff said to Leonard, "Are you ready?"

"Yep. Say the word."

"Let's go."

The two Marines exited their dark Suburban and slowly walked towards Bobby and Becky as they loaded the guitar and amp into the trunk. When Bobby heard footsteps he stopped and turned to see who was approaching. He saw two muscular men about 75 feet away, walking with purpose directly towards them. He whispered to Becky, "Just keep loading. Remember, this is your husband's stuff. You heard that there were some break-ins at this complex and you wanted to move the stuff to one of those storage places where they'd be safer." He didn't have time to say more as the two men were within 10 feet now.

Jeff Steers said to Bobby and Becky, "Good evening sir, ma'am. Please keep your hands where we can see them. We're working for the United States Marine Corps Military Police. We're investigating a series of robberies in the area and we'd like to see some ID please."

Bobby was not about to allow a couple of jarheads push him around. He knew that they had no legal jurisdiction at the complex and neither he nor Becky was in the military. He turned square to Jeff Steers and said, "What kind of ID are you looking for because we don't have military IDs. What authority do you have to question us about anything? My sister's husband is out to sea and she's trying to protect their stuff while she's at work. She heard about the robberies and she's afraid that these bastards are going to steal her husband's stuff."

Jeff spoke again. "Sir, we really don't want a scene but we really do have jurisdiction here and we need to see some ID."

Becky tried to act like the mediator. She said to Bobby, "Come on, big brother, let's just show them our driver's license and let them get back to their car and look it up. They can verify with the base that I'm Dean's wife and that will be the end of it."

"We don't have to do that, Julie. These guys are blowing smoke and we don't have to put up with it. We're not in the fucking Marines or the Navy or the Army. They can fuck themselves."

Jeff and Leonard looked at each other and rolled their eyes. It looked as if they were going to have to get physical with this guy and they really didn't want it to come to that. As they turned back towards Bobby and Becky, the nearest streetlight blinked off. They were standing in near total darkness. Bobby turned away and picked up the amp and set it in the trunk of the car. Jeff took a step towards Bobby and started to tell him to turn back around and keep his hands in view. As he did, he heard a sound like an air burst and he immediately felt an impact in his back that knocked him to the ground. He rolled on the pavement and looked up as Leonard Skiff's neck opened up and started spewing blood in spurts. Leonard fell to the ground and jerked involuntarily. Jeff looked around and saw a small cloud of smoke coming from the window of a dark van. He heard a woman screaming. He knew that his partner had been shot in the neck and there was no hope for him. The blood leaving his neck was being pumped out with great force. He looked up in time to see Bobby reaching down towards him but he couldn't do a thing about it. The slug from the gun had hit his Kevlar vest and knocked the wind out of him. The man pressed a hand to Jeff's neck. He felt every muscle in his body contract. Pain shot through his entire body and everything went black as if every light in the parking lot blinked off at that very instant.

* * *

Private Jeff Steers woke to multiple sirens approaching. He tried to open his eyes but they wouldn't cooperate. There was a man standing over him yelling, "Are you alright? Oh my God! Are you okay? This is my fault! I should have called sooner. Oh my God!"

Jeff opened his eyes enough to see the young man standing over him. His hand felt warm and he looked at it. It was discolored and felt sticky. He watched Leonard Skiff's blood drip from his fingers. He shook his head slightly but it hurt to move. He slowly looked around and saw his partner lying on the pavement. He said with slurred speech, "Lenny, you have to get up. We've got to get these guys."

"He's dead," the guy standing over him said. "He was shot in the neck. He took one in the vest but the one in the neck hit a vein. He bled to death before I got here. Are you shot? You act like you've been shot."

"I must've . . . taken one . . . vest. Knocked . . . wind outta me. Who are you?"

Multiple sirens could be heard approaching now as police and medical personnel responded to Gerald

"Names Gerald Jamison, Navy. I know Dean Gray and his so called wife, the bitch. She ripped him off. Someone's gotta catch her. Someone's gotta tell Dean what's going on."

The first police car arrived on the scene. Two officers exited the car, drew their weapons, and pointed them directly at Gerald. He turned white as a bleached sheet. The officer from the driver's side yelled, "Put your hands on your head and get down on your knees now!"

With wide eyes and a freaked out, pale expression, he did as he was told. He started to tell the officers that he was the one who called 9-1-1 but he couldn't clear his throat. The officers approached the three men who were down on the parking lot. More sirens approached the entrance to the complex and another squad car screeched to a halt by the first. An ambulance followed seconds later. One of the first officers on the scene covered the three while the second looked for a spot on Leonard Skiff's neck to check for a pulse. He said to the first, "No need to check this guy. His jugular is blown out of his neck. He bled out in seconds."

The cop holding the gun said to Gerald and Jeff, "What happened here??" He still held his gun leveled at the two who were still alive.

Gerald said, "A guy and a lady were robbing my next door neighbor. I called 9-1-1. I was watching out my living room window and saw shots fired from a van that was right over there." He nodded in the direction behind the officers keeping his hands on his head, still kneeling. His knees were starting to ache as the gravel dug into his knees.

"Did you see a gun?" The cop with the gun was taller and older. He was well built and wore less gadgets that the other officer. The younger officer had to be fairly new. He was about the same age as Gerald, about twenty-two. He wore a side arm with extra clips, handcuffs, a baton, a can of pepper spray, and a number of other devices that Gerald couldn't identify.

"No. It was dark. This street light blinked off." Just as he said it, the light blinked off as if he'd just commanded it as part of a magic show. Darkness covered the entire section of the lot where they stood. Other officers came up to the group followed by three paramedics. They took one look at Leonard's body and knew to not waste any time on him. They turned their attention to Jeff Steers who was still trying to get his bearings straight. They told Jeff to lay back and let them take a look at him. They asked him what happened and he told them about the impact to the vest on the left side of his back. They turned him on his side and felt the hole in his shirt and felt the slug still stuck in his Kevlar vest. One of the paramedics told him he was lucky to be wearing a vest. If he'd have been without a vest, chances are he'd be dead or fighting for his life.

The light was starting to come back on. Gerald was getting braver as the pain in his knees worsened. He looked at the name tag on the older cop; Harris. "Officer Harris, can I stand up?"

"Sure." Harris holstered his 9MM then got on his radio. He told whoever was on the other end of his radio that there had been a shooting, potentially one fatality, the shooter still at large, possibly in a dark full sized van. He said more details would follow but they needed homicide and crime scene support. The uniforms asked Gerald a few more questions about how he knew Dean and his wife. They got a great description of Julie and the conversation that took place between Julie and her supposed brother. He told them about the Black BMW. He told them that they loaded the equipment into the car before the shooting and that they sped out like race car drivers. The van turned left when it left the entrance, the Beamer turned right.

"Hold it a second. There were two vehicles? Were they together?"

"I don't think so. It was weird. Julie screamed when she saw the man get shot. I would think that if she and her brother were in it together with the shooter that she would know someone could get shot. Why would that freak her out if they were all in it together?"

Gerald looked at Officer Harris who was thinking about that question. He looked back to Gerald and said, "Tell me more about the van; things like color, year, make model, plates, condition, anything peculiar or out of place. Take your time." Gerald told Officer Harris all he could think of and it wasn't much. He remembered that the van was an older model, probably an Econoline but he couldn't be sure. It was dark but so was the parking lot so distinguishing a color was impossible. It could have been dark blue or maroon, but not black. It did have a lighter rectangle on the side where an advertisement or company logo might have been painted at one time. That was about it. Harris asked about the BMW then. Gerald said it was black, fairly new but they all look the same for several years running. That was all he could remember. Harris thanked Gerald, got his phone number, gave him his card and told him that the detectives would be along momentarily and would ask him most of the same questions and more. "Don't get too impatient, it's going to be a long night."

Then Harris went over to Jeff Steers who was standing now but leaning against a car. "Sir, can I ask you a couple of questions?"

Jeff was feeling better but was still a bit groggy from the stun gun blast, at least that's what the paramedics said it was. The bruise on his back from the gun shot was throbbing. Then he remembered that Joe McKinney had been the victim of a stun gun attack and his mind became a little clearer. He turned his attention to Officer Harris. "Sure."

"What is your name, son?"

"Private Jeffrey Steers, United States Marine Corps, Sir." His answer was crisp but not snappy as if he were addressing an officer while standing at attention. He was still recovering from the stun gun jolt and he wasn't yet at 100%.

"What were you and your partner doing here this evening?"

"We were investigating the woman and her accomplice for robbery, extortion, falsifying government documents, fraud, grand larceny, and about a dozen other charges."

This caught Officer Harris' attention. His face tensed a bit more and he asked, "What authority do you have to conduct this investigation?"

"I am a military police officer working under the direction of the Navy Criminal Investigative Service at Camp Lejeune, North Carolina. The Officer in Charge is Captain Nancy Brown. We're working with Detectives in your office. Contact Detective . . ."

Steer's head ached and he couldn't remember the names of the Detectives that he and Leonard Skiff had relieved earlier. When he said Nancy's name he knew that he had to call her as soon as possible. This was going to be one of the most difficult tasks in his life but he knew it had to be done. "Officer Harris, this is the fourth murder associated with this case. All of them except one have been military personnel. That's all I can say. If you want more information, you'll have to speak with Captain Brown. I am not trying to stonewall you but she is the Officer in Charge of the investigation."

"All right, Jeff. Where can I reach Captain Brown?"

"If you can get me a phone line, I'll call her and you can talk with her then." He was taken to a squad car where they patched him through to a telephone line. When he told Captain Brown about Private Skiff, he could feel the energy drain from her even through the phone lines and radio signal. This investigation was wearing her down. Unfortunately it was her job to inform his parents of his plight. It would push her almost to the breaking point.

* * *

Back at Bobby and Becky's apartment, the pair totaled the take from Dean Gray's apartment. They walked away with nearly $7500.00 cash and over $60,000 in combined checking, savings, and investment accounts. All Becky had to do was cash them out and they'd be home free. They would have to move fast, but Bobby figured by mid morning they would have Dean's accounts stripped of all cash. Bobby was in the mood to celebrate. Becky looked worried. She saw another murder right in front of her eyes. This time she witnessed a man's neck appear to explode and spew blood all over the parking lot. It made her sick and after she screamed she'd vomited right on the spot. When she and Bobby left, she got sick again. She barely had time to open the car window and stick her head out when she let loose. Back in the apartment they had money, stock account papers, and a few expensive men's watches and rings spread out on their queen sized bed. Bobby had stopped counting and was now hooking up Dean Gray's vintage guitar and amp. He was in the mood to party.

"What are you doing? You can't play that thing. It's nearly 3:00 AM. The neighbors will be calling the cops and we've got all Dean's stuff in the apartment." Becky was talking to Bobby like he was a teenaged kid, mainly because he was acting like one. He tossed the guitar on the couch and glared at Becky. Then he turned back towards the amp and turned it on. It hummed to life. Bobby picked up the guitar and strummed a few cords. The guitar was loud and the cords sounded awful. Becky was sure that the cops would be there in no time. As Bobby continued to play she went over to the electric cord for the amp and pulled it out of the wall.

"Bobby yelled, "Hey, what the fuck are you doing?"

Becky turned and looked at him and said, "Look, if you want to fuck up your life by being a fool, you go ahead but you're not taking me to prison with you. You're the one who was so serious about keeping our shit together. Now look at you. We got a good thing going and you're determined to get us caught. There was a murder tonight and you act like nothing happened." She paused and stared at him. "If we're caught with this stuff, the cops will think that we did it and that's murder. I'm not going to prison for something I didn't do. Are you?" She looked him directly in the eyes and saw something that she'd never seen before. Bobby was thinking with a worried look on his face. He had an expression that told Becky that he knew something that she didn't. She was beginning to realize that he did know something about the murders. This wasn't just coincidence or if it was, he couldn't control whoever was doing the shooting. Now Becky was more nervous than before. Bobby knew the shooter, she was sure of it. She walked back into the bedroom and grabbed her purse and a wad of bills and a night bag. She threw a few clothes into the bag then went to the bathroom and tossed in her tooth brush, soap, shampoo, and her makeup pouch. She headed for the apartment door. When Bobby saw her, he yelled, "Where're you going? Don't open that door."

As she did, he got off the couch and watched as she walked quickly down the steps.

In a firm voice he said, "Stop!"

She kept going.

"I said stop!"

She kept walking, picking up her pace now. He ran down the steps after her but she was already to the BMW and had the doors locked by the time he got to the car. She wouldn't look at him. He pounded on the window and yelled at her, "Becky, you open this door or I'll break the window and drag you out!"

She ignored him, started the car, threw it into reverse and sped backwards, almost hitting the cars parked across the lot. She threw the car into drive and peeled out of the lot. All the while, Bobby was yelling at her to stop and that she better not leave, or else . . . They were empty threats and he knew it. He also knew that she'd be back. She had no one else and nowhere else to go. He was her rock and she had nothing else. She was a two-bit tramp when he found her in Key West and he knew that she didn't want to go back to that penny pinching life. They had real money now. Why would she throw that all away? She wouldn't and he knew it and she knew it. *She'll be back. She just has to calm down and see the reality in all of this.*

Bobby turned and went back to the apartment. He didn't see the dark van pull out slowly then accelerate to catch up with the Black BMW. His mind was occupied by the murders and what he had to do to stop them. Someone he knew thought they were looking out for him and Becky. They didn't realize that they were putting them in more danger by their reckless actions. He tried to stop it before but that didn't work. Now he had to stop it for good. It wasn't going to be easy no matter what he did to resolve this problem. At least one more person would have to die.

Chapter 32

Becky Lippert was still dressed in the blue jeans and red silky tank top that she wore to Dee's Pub. She'd taken the dark wig off and tossed it on the end table. She stared at the ceiling as she laid on the king sized bed. She couldn't get over the beautiful texture of the ceiling, painted bright white. She was in the bedroom of the suite she rented at the Holiday Inn Select on North Military Highway. She took deep breaths, something she wouldn't have dared in the sleazy motels where Bobby used to take her. This suite was properly cleaned and sanitized. She even liked the sound of the word; *suite*. It seemed so much more important than a hotel room. *I have a suite, not a room.* You could smell the chemicals that made the suite germ free, smelling like a bouquet of flowers. There wasn't a spec of dust anywhere. The bathroom was spotless, too. No rust stains from dripping faucets and no mildew anywhere, not even a hint of discoloration on the fiberglass enclosure. She liked that. The sheet and blanket on the bed where she lay was fresh and clean. No evidence that anyone had ever slept on this bed before she arrived in her room. She was staring up at the ceiling and the only light in the suite's bedroom was from the television. The picture was on but the sound was muted. She wanted silence. She wanted to hear the sounds of anyone outside the suite in case Bobby tracked her down. That would be impossible, she thought, but she wanted to be sure so she listened for any evidence that he was around. She'd paid for the room in cash and she parked the car down several hundred feet at the other end of the hotel parking lot adjacent to rooms that were on the other side of the hotel. She wanted to be sure that she would be left alone. So far, after 35 minutes, it appeared that her precautions were paying off. She was alone in the silence. It was early in the morning, about 3:10 AM and very few people were up and moving around the hotel. She felt safe, so safe that she decided to go for a drink from the machine down the walkway.

She got up and slipped on her shoes. Before she left the suite she took another look around the living room and kitchen and admired the luxury with which she'd rewarded herself. The suite was equipped with a small kitchen with all the amenities. The cabinets were nicely polished. There was a coffee maker for in the morning. The suite had a full set of dishes and silverware. In the living room, an entertainment center had a decent sized flat screen TV. It wasn't a plasma TV or anything expensive, but it was larger than any TV Becky had ever owned. The carpet was dark green and thick, designed to take a large amount of traffic and not show wear. The living room had a sliding glass door that opened on to a balcony with a nice view of the city of Norfolk. Becky was smiling to herself. She was free, at least for the evening. She knew she'd have to face Bobby again in the next day or two, but for now she could relax and enjoy peace and quiet.

Her mind strayed to the parking lot of Dean Gray's apartment. She saw a young man and his partner approaching her and Bobby. Then his neck exploded and blood flew everywhere. She saw blood pulse from his neck. She saw him fall into his own blood on the parking lot pavement. She started to get nauseous and moved to the kitchen sink. She felt as if she would heave but the nausea passed.

She started to get a second image. This one was of her husband, Private Edward Sharp, as he approached her near the mail boxes at his apartment. She saw him fall forward, blood pouring from his back. Then she saw the bag full of mail that she'd dropped, but didn't remember dropping. She picked the bag up and Eddie Sharp's blood dripped from the bag. The wave of nausea returned, this time more quickly than before. She leaned over the sink and heaved. She hadn't eaten in some time so nothing came. She heaved again, still nothing. She grabbed a paper towel, dampened it and wiped her mouth. As she backed away from the sink, she grabbed a chair and sat. The vision of the two dying men was so vivid that she could see the jagged flesh in the areas of the wounds where a slug had either entered or exited the skin. She never imagined that she'd ever witness such things. She knew the men were both dead. There was no stopping the bleeding that gushed from the last guy's neck. She was no doctor or nurse but she knew that nobody could survive a massive wound like that.

She opened her eyes and shook her head. *I've got to get outside for some fresh air. I need that can of pop.* It was nearly 3:40 in the morning but she wasn't worried about that and she wasn't in a hurry. She planned to sleep in as long as she wanted, take a long, hot shower whenever she got up and get breakfast no matter what time she left the room. It was her decision. Bobby wasn't there to push her around and tell her that she needed to get up and get ready to meet another sucker. She was on her time now. Maybe she would keep it that way for a few days. She liked being her own boss.

Becky stood, grabbed her keys and the swipe key to the suite and headed out the door for the soft drink machine. She found it and got a Cherry Coke. As she turned to head back to her suite, a young man nearly ran into her as he turned the corner walking towards the machines.

"Excuse me," he said with a look of surprise. He was about a head taller than Becky and was several years her junior. "I'm sorry. I almost knocked the soda out of your hand." His Midwestern accent was unmistakable. He was handsome and had features similar to hers. His hair was sandy blond and wavy. It was over his ears. He had narrow eyes and a slightly narrow jaw. His face was rough with stubble. He looked as if he hadn't shaved for a couple days.

She said, "That's okay," and started to walk away.

He said, "Where are you from? You have an accent like mine."

She turned back to him and said, "I'm originally from Ohio. Akron. How about you? You have the Midwest written all over you."

"I'm from Sharon, Pennsylvania. I used to say 'Where yuns from but I lived most of my life in Michigan, near Toledo, so I learned to drop the 'yuns'. I guess the kids made fun of me enough that I just stopped saying it. Not to change the subject, but you're up awfully late or very early. Aren't you a bit wary about being out alone this late?"

"Not really. This seems like a real safe place. Besides, I can take care of myself better than most folks would suspect." She paused a moment then asked, "What's your name?"

"Ace Glover." Ace held out his hand and Becky took it firmly and shook. "My real name is Alex but most folks call me Ace."

"I'm Becky. Becky Lippert. Nice to meet you, Ace. What brings you to Norfolk?"

"I'm looking for my sister. She's here in town living with a guy. Mom and I don't think he's good for her so we're here to try and get her away from the creep. He's just using her." As he said this he looked right into Becky's eyes. His eyes were warm, convincing eyes. Becky thought that he could charm the pants right off her. She smiled at Ace as she thought of her own situation then said, "There's probably a lot of that going around. Do you know where she's staying?"

"Yea. She's at an apartment not too far from here. I forget the name but Mom's got it written down." As he talked, Becky heard footsteps approaching from down the hall. Ace was at the corner of the hall and Becky heard a voice say, "Ace, where have you been? I wanted that Coke about 15 minutes ago." As she rounded the corner she said, "Oh. I see. Found a friend to talk with." She smiled as she looked at Becky, first at her face, then down her body to her toes and back. "What's your name Sweetie?"

"Becky Lippert."

Ace said, "Becky, this is my mom, Abbie Glover." Abbie held out her hand as she continued to smile and look directly at Becky's eyes. As Becky looked back she felt as if she were looking into a mirror. This woman looked a lot like her and her features were similar to hers as well. She looked at the woman's hands and arms, then her face and eyes. The only difference was that this woman looked to be at least fifty. She looked like a lifetime smoker with leathery skin and pronounced wrinkles on her gaunt face. Her hair had streaks of gray mingled in with the sandy blond. Ace continued, "Becky's from Akron, Ohio. You can tell when she talks. She has that Ohio accent."

"Well you sure are a pretty young lady. You shouldn't be out late around here. The place is filled with horny sailors and you can't trust any of them. You have to watch out for them guys. They get back from sea and all the want is one thing." Her facial expression changed as if to say, *you know what I mean?*

Becky said to them both, "It was nice meeting you. I should get to sleep. Maybe I'll see you tomorrow. By the way, what is your daughter's name?"

Abbie looked directly at Becky, then said, "Same as yours; Rebecca." Abbie smiled showing straight teeth that were stained by years of cigarette smoke. At one time she must have had a beautiful smile but that was many years and many cartons of cigarettes ago.

Becky got a shiver that ran the length of her spine. She looked at Abbie, then back to Ace. She sensed for a moment that she'd seen both of them before but how could that be? Their faces were so familiar but nothing came to mind. She looked back at Abbie and smiled a nervous smile and said to both of them, "Good luck finding Rebecca." She turned and headed back to her suite, locked and bolted the door. She stripped off all of her clothes and crawled into bed, thinking about Abbie, Ace and their Rebecca. She hoped that Rebecca would get away and not be found. She thought that maybe Abbie and Ace were looking for her for their own selfish reasons. She had no basis for thinking this but she felt sorry for Rebecca, whoever and wherever she was. They were both very pleasant and nice to her and if they'd wanted to do anything menacing, they could have done it while everyone else in the hotel was asleep. They didn't but she was still troubled by the meeting. She had a difficult time falling asleep. She kept thinking about Abbie, Ace, and Rebecca. She dreamt about Rebecca and saw her as a little girl. She watched as baby Rebecca played with her friends at the park. She was having a wonderful time swinging on the swings and playing in the sandbox with a boy. They were getting along and playing when all of a sudden, Ace grabbed her from behind and lifted her to his shoulder. As he walked away with her, the mother of the young boy tried to stop him but Abbie went up to her and shoved her, knocking her into the sandbox with her young boy. Then she saw Abbie pull out a gun and point it at the woman. She saw her pull the trigger . . .

Becky awoke in a panic and soaking wet from sweat. She looked around the unfamiliar room for a few moments and finally recognized the bedroom of the suite. It was a horrible dream. She saw everything so vividly, but now the dream was starting to fade as the reality of the moment was sinking in. She was in her own suite, but people were still invading her world. She had to figure a way to get away from Bobby. She had to get away from the killing. She had to make a clean break and start over. But the first thing she needed was a hot shower. She hoped it would wash away her fears, but that wasn't to be.

* * *

Joe McKinney raised his arm over his head in a circular motion trying to loosen the sore muscles that had been involuntarily contracted by the charge from the stun gun. He was headed to the shower where he planned to stay for at least 20 minutes with hot spray on all of the sore places, which was pretty much every square inch of his body. He'd never felt such intense, widespread pain. The stun gun was quite a weapon. It could incapacitate a person for several minutes. Then it took several more minutes to recover to the point of functioning anywhere near normal. The least painful part of recovering from the stun gun attack was the two burns left on the skin from the electrodes, the electric contacts that allow the voltage to pump electric current into the body. The burns are small but painful, like two close cigarette burns. As Joe stepped into the hot stream of water, his muscles thanked him but the burns intensified as if a snake were biting him and grabbing hold. He winced at the increased pain but continued to allow the water to sooth his sore muscles. After 15 minutes of allowing the water to work its healing power on his muscles, he washed his body then his short hair, rinsed and stepped out. He toweled off, taking his time to stretch and bend, still trying to loosen up. He finished shaving, deodorizing, and brushing his teeth. Then he got dressed in his tighty-whiteys and jeans. He pulled his shirt on over his head and headed to the kitchen. He wanted to get breakfast but he had to call Lisa first. He didn't want her to hear about the attack second hand. The coffee was ready and he poured himself a cup then reached for the phone and dialed his apartment in Orlando.

Lisa answered on the first ring. "Hello."

"Good morning sunshine. How are you? You sound wide awake."

"I've been awake since about 3:30. I went to sleep fine last night but I woke up around midnight for some reason. I didn't sleep well after that so I just got up and showered."

Joe said, "I'm getting a pretty vivid picture in my mind. Now I'm wide awake. I wish I was there so we could take a shower together."

"Mmm, that sounds like good, clean fun." Joe chuckled at her little joke. She paused then said, "I'm visiting a couple of schools today; University of Central Florida and Valencia Community College. So far I like UCF better. They were real nice to me on the phone and very helpful. I got a ton of information about the school and their degree programs."

"That sounds great." He paused for a moment to gather his thoughts. He didn't want to change the subject but he had to get serious or he'd never tell her about the stun gun incident. "I need to tell you about something that happened last night."

"I knew that little Captain would get her claws into you," Lisa joked.

"Lisa, this is serious. That would be serious, too, but this is really serious. I wanted to tell you myself. I got hit with a stun gun last night while I was doing surveillance." Lisa gasped. "It knocked me out for about five minutes and I'm really sore this morning."

"Are you alright now? You're not in the hospital or anything, are you?"

"No, I'm fine, just a bit sore. My muscles feel like I've been working out for hours."

"There's no permanent damage, right?"

"Nope. No permanent damage." He smiled because he knew what was coming next.

"Good, cause I'm going to kill you when I see you. Then I'm going to kick your ass and kill you again." She paused then in a serious voice said, "You have to be crazy to continue on this mission. Can't you do something less dangerous?"

"We have to be getting close if they're doing some of these crazy tactics. I hope we can wrap this up soon." Joe waited for her response. All he heard was her breathing through the receiver. "Lisa, I love you. I won't let anything bad happen again. I'll be much more careful. There is one more thing. They got my wallet with my driver's license, military ID and credit cards. It might be a good idea for you to stay at your apartment while I'm gone. The manager hasn't moved you out yet, has he?"

"No, but he was planning on doing that next week. I can let him know that there might be a delay. Can we afford it?"

"For you, I can afford anything. You just make sure that you stay away from my apartment for a bit. When we catch these guys, we'll get moved back in and everything will be back to normal."

On the other end of the line, Lisa was smiling a nervous smile. Nothing was ever normal with Joe. She loved this guy but she was afraid that he'd get hurt or even killed and she couldn't stand that. Especially with having just gone through her father's funeral. "Joe McKinney, you be damned careful, do you hear me? I can't stand to lose another man in my life."

Joe choked on his response. "You know I will. I'll be home soon."

They talked for a few more minutes about what was happening in Orlando and about Pat, Diane and the kids. Lisa mentioned that Brian Purcer and his band, the Hot Licks were going to be in town for a concert the next week. She hoped that he could be home for the show. Pat already promised backstage passes for her and Joe if he could be there. Brian and Pat were best friends before Brian made it to the big time with several hit songs. He was on the fast track to stardom but he still remembered his friends.

Before they hung up, Lisa got very serious with tears starting to flow from her eyes. She said, "Joe, I love you. You have to remember I'll always love you. Please come home safe to me. I mean it. I couldn't bear to lose you."

Joe again choked up as he answered, "I love you, too, Lisa Goddard. I promise you I'll be home just as soon as I can. I'll call again soon." They both hung up, reluctant to end the call.

As soon as Joe hung up, the phone rang again. He picked it up and said, "Miss me already?"

Captain Brown said, "Why yes I do but I understand that you're already taken. Besides, I have bad news. Dean Gray's neighbor, Gerald Jamison was found shot to death behind a bar by the base. It's a pretty seedy part of town but we think it may be related to the robbery last night. He wasn't killed where he was found. It was a dump job."

Joe shook his head. "I'll be right in."

Chapter 33

The highway was thick with tractor trailers hauling everything from livestock to furniture, to steel rods and department store wares. They were all in a big hurry and had no patience for anyone driving under 75 miles per hour. Wanda Gray slept through most of Ohio. The Ohio Turnpike had been a maze of orange barrels and lane changes, warnings to slow down or be on the lookout for the poor road workers who were risking their lives to make a buck and make ground transportation better sometime in the future. That future never seemed to arrive as the turnpike was always under repair or in the midst of a widening project. She closed her eyes so that she wouldn't have to see the tight lanes between the Jersey barriers that temporarily established partial lanes and made for close-quarter driving. The only thing older and more run down than the Ohio Turnpike was the Pennsylvania Turnpike and its ancient toll booths. The turnpike was narrow with only two lanes that wound through foothills north of Pittsburgh. She'd been asleep for several hours and only woke when her husband, Arthur Gray, pulled off the turnpike to pay the overpriced toll. Mr. and Mrs. Gray exited the Pennsylvania Turnpike at Route 18 and headed south towards the town of Morado. So far, they weren't real impressed with Pennsylvania. Every bridge they'd passed over appeared to be crumbling and in disrepair to the point that rusted rebar was visible and the crumbling concrete was in small piles at the edge of the road. The roads also appeared to be in need of resurfacing with large cracks and potholes forming everywhere they looked. Some of the potholes were filled with water from an afternoon storm though the sun was now out and shining brightly. It didn't help the feeling of dread that hung in the air because of the shabby condition of the roadways.

The buildings along Route 18 were a mixture of new retail stores and old, rust belt era small factories. The contrast of old and new was dramatic and added to the feeling of despair. The little that Arthur Gray saw made him feel there wasn't any hope for the future of the people living around Morado. There were probably many good jobs but the prospects for the future didn't look positive. There was much work to be done to get this area turned around and prosperous again. The Beaver River flowed along with them to their left. Two sets of railroad tracks were on either side of the road and another set of tracks snaked along the far back of the river, an indication that there had once been factories and other commerce in the area. Art Gray thought to himself *No wonder kids are fleeing this area to the military. There's nothing for them here.* Then he thought how ironic it was because his son was in the military. His son's wife went to a military town looking for work. He figured that there was little difference in joining the military or working for the military under contract. These were tough times for kids, not like when he was growing up and there were jobs everywhere.

He looked at his wife who was rubbing the sleep from her eyes. He was just about to wake her when she was stirred by the bumpy turnpike exit ramp. "How was your nap?"

She yawned, "Fine." She paused and looked around. "Where are we?"

"We're about ten minutes from the Lippus' house as best I can figure."

"Ten Minutes? Why didn't you wake me? I have to straighten up some." She reached for her purse by her feet on the floor of the Lincoln LS. She pulled the visor down on the passenger side and flipped up the mirror cover. The illuminated mirror showed her reflection to which she exclaimed, "Oh my gawd. I look terrible. You should have woken me. I can't be ready in ten minutes. We've been riding in this car for hours."

"Okay. We'll stop at a restaurant and get a quick bite and you can freshen up. Deal?"

She smiled at her husband and said, "Deal. Where are we going to find a decent restaurant around this place?"

"Don't worry. I'm sure that there's a shopping district close by. Beaver Falls looks like it may have more to offer than Morado."

They drove through the heart of Beaver Falls. There were no restaurant chains except those that offered the usual burgers and fries. Art knew that Wanda wouldn't stand for that. He pulled into the parking lot of a convenient store and pulled out the internet map of the town. He looked to see if there was a street heading out of town and near a limited access highway. Highway 60 was to the west of town so he thought that there may be more choices in that direction. Then he noticed across the street on 8th Avenue a sign that read 'The Evergreen Café.'

"Hey Babe, let's try that little café. It looks nice." Wanda agreed and they stopped. It was a nicely run diner. The food was good and the restrooms clean. They were in and out in thirty-five minutes. As Art started the car, he asked, "Are you ready? It's only about five minutes to their house. I hope they don't mind the surprise."

"Well, it didn't look like we'd ever meet them unless we came out here so let's do it."

It was just after 1:00 pm when Art turned the Lincoln onto the main street going north through Beaver Falls. When he got to 18th street, he turned right and went the four blocks to 4th Avenue and turned left. The homes here were turn of the century two story buildings. Most had been re-sided with aluminum or vinyl siding. A few still had asphalt shingles that were torn and tattered. Just a few blocks east, Art and Wanda could see the

Beaver River. When they got to the address on the internet map they turned into the driveway. It was a two story house with white vinyl siding that looked as if it needed to be washed. The driveway had two cars. The one in front of their Lincoln was a late model Chevy Malibu. The car in front of the Malibu was an older Buick Regal. The Regal's hood was opened just a bit and the front end was jacked up. There were a number of car parts scattered around the front of the car. They looked as though they'd been there for a while. Oil appeared to have been spilled on the concrete drive and not cleaned up. Beyond the Regal, an old garage stood. The garage was leaning to the right and appeared that it could collapse at any moment. The garage door was either opened or missing all together. The garage was crammed full of lawn equipment, car parts, wood, tools, and junk. The front lawn was mainly weeds with a few spots of real grass.

Art turned to Wanda and said, "We can turn around and leave. No one will ever know that we were here."

Just as he finished speaking, a man came out of the house and walked slowly towards the Lincoln. He was short, about 5'6, and weighed about 280 pounds. His arms were thick and looked as if they were muscular at one point in his youth. He wore blue jeans and a black and gold jersey with the Pittsburgh Steelers logo on the front. He had dark hair that was thick on the sides but very thin on top. He looked to be about fifty-five years old. As he approached, Art pressed the button to lower his window.

In a gruff, smokers voice, the man asked, "Can I help yuns with something?"

"Yes, is this the Lippus residence?"

"Yes it is. I'm Dan Lippus."

Art opened his door and got out. He reached out his hand to Dan Lippus and said, "I'm Art Gray." He leaned over a bit and said, "This is my wife, Wanda. We're Dean's parents."

Dan Lippus looked at Art with a blank expression, like he'd just heard Chinese for the first time. He turned his head slightly to the side, still squinting, trying to shield his eyes from the sun. He said, "What was that name again?"

"Art and Wanda Gray. We're Dean's folks. Dean is your son-in-law."

Now the look on Dan's face was turning to anger. "If this is some kind of joke, it ain't funny."

Now it was Art's turn to look totally confused. He kept his eyes on Dan Lippus as his mind raced to think of what to say. This was very awkward. Then he said, "Maybe we have the wrong Lippus family. Do you have a daughter named Julie?"

"What kind of game yuns playing here? My daughter Julie died years ago. She's been dead since 1979. She died of leukemia. What's going on here? Yuns pulling some kind of scam or something? 'cause I'll punch your lights out right here and now."

"No. No I assure you we're not. Our son Dean married a young lady a few weeks ago and her name is Julie Lippus. She says she's from Beaver Falls. Is there another Lippus family in town? Maybe we've made a mistake." Art was clearly shaken. Wanda was still sitting in the car listening to the entire conversation. She was scared to get out for fear that Dan Lippus might assault them. Who could blame him? They had just opened a very deep wound in this man's heart. She took a deep breath and got out of the passenger side and came around the car. Dan was about three steps from her husband and appeared ready to hit him.

She said, "Mr. Lippus, this is my fault. I thought that it would be a good idea to come here and get to know our son's wife's parents. I had no idea about your daughter. There must be some mistake about her . . . our son's wife's identity. Can we talk for a few minutes? Maybe we can figure out what's happened here."

This seemed to calm Dan down a bit. He thought for a moment and then said, "Sure. Yuns should come inside and get out of the heat. Where yuns from?" They turned and walked towards the house as Wanda spoke.

"We're from Des Moines, Iowa. We left yesterday afternoon and stayed overnight in Indiana. Our son, Dean is in the Navy. He's stationed at Norfolk. He called us a few weeks ago and said that he met the most wonderful woman. Before we knew it he was married. It happened really fast." Everyone was quiet as they entered the Lippus' home. The interior of the house was well lighted with the drapes pulled back. The carpet was older and a bit worn but clean. Everything in the house was spotless in sharp contrast to the exterior of the house. As they stepped into the living room, a short plump woman came from the kitchen into the dining room. She asked, Dan, "Who are our visitors?"

"Honey, you should come in and sit first. I'll introduce them once you're seated." She had a puzzled look but sat on a worn chair in the living room.

"Honey, this is Art and Wanda Gray." He turned to Art and Wanda and said, "This is Lucille. We've been married for 32 years." He turned back to his wife and continued, "Lucy, the Grays have a son in the Navy down in Virginia. Their son married a young lady who claims to be Julie Lippus from Beaver Falls." Lucille's face turned to shock then turned red. She faced her husband with tears forming in her eyes. She pulled a tissue from a box on an end table next to where she sat and took a moment to compose herself. Lucille was short like her husband and about 190 pounds. She had short salt and pepper hair that framed a round face. Her chin appeared to be too small for the rest of her facial features and her neck was thick starting at her jaw down to her shoulder blades. She wore a house dress with a small floral print and an apron with the Pillsbury Doughboy across the front of her chest.

She spoke. "I guess that's why we've been getting all the junk mail with Julie's name." She turned to her husband, looking for confirmation. "About five months ago we started receiving charge card applications in the mail for Julie. It started out of the blue. We hadn't had anything like it ever before. We just figured that a mistake was made and she ended up on mailing lists. They sell those things all the time." Lucille took a deep breath and looked at Dan.

Dan picked up where Lucille left off. "We got one recently that looked different. It looked like a charge card bill instead of an application so we opened it. That's exactly what it was. There was about twenty-eight hundred dollars worth of charges on it. We were shocked to say the least. That's why I was getting mad when yuns started talking about Julie out there. I figured yuns were in on it."

Wanda spoke softly with compassion, "I assure you that we knew nothing about Julie or the charge card. Have you contacted the police or the FBI?"

Dan said, "No. We just contacted the company that issued the card and told them that there must be a mistake. It had to be identity theft. We never had to pay a dime but we spent a lot of time on the phone and sending letters to the credit card company getting it straightened out." Dan Lippus paused then said, "They used Julie's social security number and everything. These folks got some gall, using a dead girl's identity like that."

Art asked Dan and Lucille, "Can you tell us where the charges were made? What state?"

"Yes. The charges were in several different states but mainly in Georgia, North Carolina and Virginia. We didn't look at all the charges but most were for woman's clothing stores and gas."

Art and Wanda exchanged a glance. They knew their son was already out to sea. Art was thinking that they should cancel his business trip and head down to Norfolk to Dean's apartment. He didn't have a key but he figured he could work with the apartment manager. Maybe they could catch the woman that was taking advantage of their son.

Wanda was apparently thinking the same thing as she looked at her husband. She turned to Dan and Lucille Lippus and said, "Is there anything else that you can tell us that's happened involving Julie's name or identity?"

"No. Just the mail and charge card thing. It's really had us upset but we didn't know where to turn for help." Dan paused then said, "What do you plan to do? I mean, this is yuns' son who's being taken for a ride. He may not even know who he's married to."

Art and Wanda exchanged a glance. Art said, "We'll figure it out. In the mean time, here's my card. It has our home phone and my cell phone. If you can't get through, just leave a message and I'll call you back." He took a deep breath then continued, "We are both very sorry. We really had no idea. We really had good intentions. I hope you'll forgive us."

Dan turned to his wife who was now sitting quietly with her hands in her lap. He turned back to the Gray's and said, "We'll be alright. Julie's been dead a long time. It hurts to think about her and the suffering that she went through but we're at peace with her passing. But yuns need to find out who this imposter is and get her off the street. I wish we could help but we don't have the means."

Wanda's face brightened a bit. She said, "There is one way that you can help. If you don't mind, do you still have a copy of Julie's bogus bill?"

"Yes, I believe we do."

"Could we get a copy of that bill? We'll pay to have it copied and return the original to you."

Dan thought then said, "I guess that'd be alright. Just copy it and mail it to us. Can I ask what yuns plan to do with it?"

"We're going to follow the trail that's in these bills."

* * *

The mountains rose on either side of the road. A number of clearings in the trees allowed some pretty good views of the valleys below. The sun beat down in the early afternoon but this made for some good driving conditions. Art was driving along at seventy-five miles per hour even though the limit in this stretch of interstate was sixty due to some sharp curves atop Town Hill. Heading south on Interstate 70 just north of Berkeley Springs, West Virginia, Art and Wanda started to put their plan together. First they wanted to look over all the charges in Julie Lippus' name and see if there was some pattern that they could decipher. Then they were going to the Naval Base at Norfolk and report this woman. They wanted to put a stop to her theft before she got her hooks too deep into their son. He'd done well for himself and the last thing he needed was some twisted bitch ripping him off for everything that he'd worked so hard to acquire. It was only money and they were certain that Dean was going to make plenty, but if he got ripped off bad, this would be a major setback.

As Wanda looked over the map of the Eastern United States, she noticed two things that were obvious. The first was that all the charges were along the Interstate 95 corridor between Richmond, Virginia and Saint Mary, Georgia. Wanda noticed a pattern. Most of the charges near the bases were at department stores. The charges along the interstate were for gas. Another thing she noticed was that the charges near each base occurred over a period of a few days then stopped. There would be a couple of days where the charges were for gas then the department store charges started again near another base. Wanda knew that her stepson didn't travel between bases. He was too busy with his investments and other hobbies to travel much. This woman was using Julie Lippus' name for several months before she even met Dean. If she was traveling between military bases as it appeared by the pattern of charges, then she could be pulling this scam on other unsuspecting soldiers and sailors. Wanda's eyes grew wide at the potential scale of theft that could be happening. She wondered if this woman was doing this alone or if she had an accomplice.

Art looked over at his wife. "You've got that look. What's up?"

"Well, if I'm reading this right, Dean's got himself in a really bad situation. This woman is taking him for a serious ride and it looks like he might not be the only one. These charges go up and down the east coast and are centered around military bases. I think she's finding and marrying young military guys. No offense, dear, but Dean got suckered. How long has he been out to sea?"

"About a week. Maybe she hasn't had time to clean him out yet. First stop is his apartment. I should probably call his command now. Is there a rest area ahead?"

"I'll look." Wanda looked over the map and found the next rest area about 15 miles ahead. She said, "How low can a person be to take advantage of a soldier or a sailor who is risking his life to protect our country? Anybody caught taking advantage of a soldier should be charged with treason or something serious." Wanda shook her head. She wasn't a big fan of the military machine but she did support the troops. Her Father was killed in Vietnam in the mid 1960s. She never knew him. After her Father was buried, her Mother moved to Iowa to be near her older sister, Wanda's Aunt. She wanted nothing to do with the military and never remarried. She wanted to make sure that Wanda didn't marry a soldier. Her heartache ended her life. After Wanda turned 21 and moved out on her own, her mother committed suicide.

Wanda was devastated and never married herself until she met Art Gray. He was like a father figure to her but was much more important to her than that. He had been recovering from losing his wife and so they shared a common bond of grief. That bond grew to love and they were married after several years of being together in various stages of a loving, growing relationship. "Any idea how long before we get to Norfolk?"

Art thought for a few seconds. "Let's see; we're just north of Berkeley Springs. We have to take I-70 to I-270 to I-95 to I-64. . . my guess is five hours, maybe six. If we stop twice for food and bio-breaks it might take six and a half. It's 4:30 now. It'll be about 10:30 to 11:00 when we get to Norfolk. Remember, too, that neither of us have been to Dean's apartment. It might take some time to find the complex, then to find his apartment. I have some pretty decent directions but Norfolk's a big city. We have to get a room for tonight. Maybe we should stop in Williamsburg."

Wanda listened to her husband. She let him ramble when he thought he knew best. She already had the plan worked out in her head so it didn't much matter what he said anyway. They would call the base from the upcoming rest area. They were going to stay in Norfolk. They would find

Dean's apartment in the morning, then call the local police. If there was an FBI office, they'd call them, too. She figured since this woman was crossing state lines, it was beyond the jurisdiction of most local law enforcement departments. They wouldn't have the resources to track a crook to all the locations that this woman traveled. She moved too quickly for anyone to catch her. This was one smart cookie or she was working with someone who had the brains. This woman had to have charm and a way with words. She probably had a body to beat the band. So they were looking for a smart, charming, sexy woman with balls. *Well, we'll see who's got balls.*

Wanda reclined her seat and told her husband, "Wake me up with a bit more warning this time please. Ten minutes isn't enough time to get myself together after sleeping in a car."

Art looked over at her and said in his best Morgan Freeman, "Yes Miss Daisy."

She hated when he said that, but smiled despite herself.

Chapter 34

The aroma of steaks on the grill filled the air as Brian and Ginny approached the front door of Pat and Diane McKinney's house in Dunnellon, Florida. Brian was on a break from the Hot Licks tour. The band had toured most of Florida and southern Georgia and was on a break before heading into the Carolinas and Virginia. So far the tour was a major success. He and the band were flying high on the rush of fame and early fortune. Ginny, Brian's fiancé, was a bit overwhelmed. She knew that Brian's success was imminent but she had no idea that he was going to be a gold record artist and a highly sought after bachelor. She was amazed at the number of young girls out there who would throw themselves at Brian with such abandon. She was quickly coming to terms with the realization that she would constantly have to be on her guard against such an onslaught of temptation to her man.

Brian was taking it all in stride. He'd been warned by his band's manager that there would be times when he would be so exhausted from touring or studio work that he'd let his guard down. Love in this business was fleeting. There were few truly successful rock and roll love stories and most of those were contrived for publicity purposes. Brian was new to this gig. He was also new to being in love. The combination of the band's success and his success in his relationship with Ginny made him feel invincible. He was glad that the band had a break. It didn't matter that the break was only for three days then they had to board a plane for South Carolina. As long as the record company would let Ginny come along for free, he was happy. It was the summer and Ginny was on break from school. There were no hassles from the rest of the band. In fact, Rick Wessler, the band's drummer told Brian that Ginny was the best thing that ever happened to him. He said that since Ginny had come into Brian's life, he was a new man with more energy on stage and a calm disposition. Brian wasn't sure if it was Ginny, the Band's success or the fact that he was getting paid for doing what he loved most that changed his mood. Maybe it was a combination of everything right that was happening in his life. He didn't know but he was happy and healthy and he wanted it to stay this way forever.

They reached the front door of the McKinney residence. Before ringing the doorbell, Brian thought back to the first time he stood in front of this door. He hadn't met Diane yet. But Pat had written to him with their new address and told him to stop by and meet his family. When Brian had taken him up on the offer Pat wasn't home. Diane had answered the door and looked out at a skinny, young freak with long, frizzy hair and a face that hadn't seen a razor in days. Brian must have looked like a deranged drug addict to her. But he assured her that Pat, who was his best friend, had invited him to the house to meet his family. When she'd let Brian in, she was clearly distraught because she didn't know where Pat had gone. She only knew that Pat wasn't himself and appeared to be under tremendous pressure. Brian and Diane talked for a couple hours. During that time, Brian had inadvertently told Diane many things about her husband that she didn't know; things that Pat hadn't told her about his past. One of those things was that Pat had a couple of legal businesses that were worth a fair amount of money. He didn't tell her that Pat had been involved in the marijuana trade and had made a small fortune. He felt that Pat should be the one to come clean on that.

Pat finally did tell Diane everything. Well almost everything; but not before Brian and Pat had a come-to-the-mountain meeting. They cleared the air as much as possible but Brian still had a feeling that Pat was hiding something. If what he thought was true he believed that Pat should take that information with him to the grave. He believed to this day that Pat had killed to avenge his sister-in-law's murder and his Brother Mike's suicide.

"Are you going to stare a hole through the door or should I ring the doorbell?" Ginny was looking at Brian as he snapped out of his trance. "What were you thinking about? You had such a serious look on your face."

"Just remembering the first time I was here. It was the first time I met Diane." Before Brian could say another word, Pat opened the door and smiled broadly at Brian Purcer and Ginny Parks.

"Are you two coming in?"

Brian smiled back at Pat and held out his hand while still keeping an arm around Ginny's shoulder. "Pat, my man, how are you doing?"

"Great. You look well and Ginny you look beautiful." Ginny blushed. "Come on in. We're out back so just keep on going through the kitchen and back to the patio. Grab a beer or let me know what you want and I'll fix it. The steaks are on the grill. We're planning to eat in about twenty minutes." Pat led them through the family room and the kitchen out to the patio where the grill was smoking. The aroma from the steaks was strong and inviting. When they reached the patio they recognized Lisa Goddard, Joe's fiancée, sitting in a lawn chair next to Detective Johnny Poleirmo and his wife Rachael and Emma McKinney. Brian grabbed a beer from the cooler and Ginny asked for a whiskey and Seven Up. Pat whipped it up in a flash. Sean and Anna, Pat and Diane's children, were playing with their new puppy. They were taking turns throwing a rubber ball to the pooch and chasing him when he wouldn't bring it right back to them. They laughed as they chased the puppy all around the yard.

Ginny went right over to Lisa and started a conversation. They talked about Brian's tour and life on the road. They talked about Lisa's dad's passing and then about her and Joe's engagement. They shared their recent highs and lows. They had quite a lot in common with their love lives, school, and common friends. Brian also talked about his recent success but this wasn't easy for him. Until he became a rising rock star, he was a humble, quiet man. He still was nearly an introvert in social situations and didn't like talking about himself. He knew he was successful but liked to attribute it to luck rather than any talent he possessed. Everyone at the party knew different. Brian was the reason for the band's success even if he didn't acknowledge it.

Ginny asked Lisa if Joe would be coming to the party. "I'm afraid not. He's in North Carolina or Virginia. I'm not sure which one at the moment. He's supposed to call any time now."

"What's he doing up there?" Ginny asked.

"He's been recalled to the Marines. He's working on an investigation. There's some woman ripping off soldiers and sailors for their life savings and he's on a team that's trying to catch her."

Ginny frowned. "They recalled him to be a cop? I hope he's not being sent to the Middle East. There's no real ground war but who knows. They should just send an assassination team over there and take that nut case out."

Ginny noticed that Lisa looked uncomfortable talking about this so she changed the subject. "Brian is going to be playing up in Norfolk in a week or so. I forget the date but maybe you could fly up there, meet Joe and the both of you come to the concert. It'd be on us. I know Brian would love it."

Lisa's face brightened. She thought it was a great idea. "I'd love to and I know Joe would, too. When I talk with him I'll ask him. I'm sure it'll be fine. Just let us know the dates."

Ginny yelled over to Brian who was talking with Pat and Diane. "Brian. Can we have some guests at the Norfolk show? I want to have Lisa and Joe come to the show. Pat and Diane should come, too. It'd be a great time, don't you think?"

Brian smiled. "Yea. We can do that. We'll set it up and let you know the details."

Pat and Brian clinked the long necks on their beer bottles, sealing the deal.

The phone rang and Diane went in the kitchen to answer it. She came back out, smiled, and handed the phone to Lisa. "It's Joe."

Lisa immediately stood and walked towards the house with the phone. "Hi, Honey. I miss you."

"I miss you, too. How's your mom holding up?"

"She's doing pretty well. She's been going out with some friends and staying busy. I talked to her yesterday and I was surprised how upbeat she was. I think she's really starting to get on with her life without Dad."

"That's great. That has to be a load off your mind."

"Yes, but I've got a few other things on my mind. One is school. I've got to pick one and get registered." She paused. "The other thing is you. I hate it without you here. When are you coming home?"

Joe answered flatly, "I'm not sure. I wish I had a good answer for you, Babe. All I know is that I'll be home as soon as I can. This is getting real messy. I can't give you any details." Joe didn't want to go on but he figured he'd better be the one to tell her. "One of my investigators was shot and killed last night. Another guy got hit with a stun gun and knocked out like me."

Lisa gasped. Diane and Ginny had been talking not far from her and they both heard her. They turned and saw the look of horror on her face and moved closer to her.

Joe continued, "We must be getting close. They wouldn't be taking these desperate measures if we weren't."

"Oh my God, Joe. You've got to be careful. If you die on me, I swear I'll kill you." That brought weak smiles to both their faces. Lisa's voice took on a very serious tone as Diane and Ginny stood on either side of her. "Joe, please be safe. You do what you need to do but please make sure you come home to me. I couldn't stand to lose you."

"I will, Lisa. I will." There was a silence for a moment then Joe said, "Lisa, can I speak to Pat, please?"

"Sure. Hey, before I turn you over to your brother, Ginny and Brian are here. Brian's band is playing in Norfolk next week and he's invited us to go to the show and hang out back stage. If I make it up there can we go? You'd get a needed break and we'd have a chance to spend some time together."

Joe was smiling at the prospect of spending a night with Lisa. He really needed a break from the case and a concert might just be the ticket. "That'd be wonderful. Get the details and let me know. Have Brian get the arrangements together. It's a date."

"We're going on a real, live date. I can't wait." Lisa paused again. "You be careful, Joe McKinney."

Lisa walked the phone over to Pat and handed it to him as tears welled in her eyes. "It's Joe." She walked into the house followed by Diane and Ginny. As Ginny consoled Lisa, Diane started to prepare the sides for their dinner. From previous experience, they all knew that Joe could take care of himself. He was very competitive, focused and determined. When he set a goal, he always worked hard at achieving it. Lisa was worried though, especially with the death of her father; a man she thought was invincible.

Now she had a fiancé she thought he was invincible. She didn't want to be proven wrong twice.

Outside on the phone, Pat and Joe discussed details of the case. When Joe got to the part about one of his partners being shot, Pat winced. He knew that the case was getting more dangerous by the day. It seemed that they were getting closer to the perpetrators and that always spelled danger. Any time you cornered an animal, they became more dangerous.

"Do you have names for these bastards yet?"

"No. We've seen their faces though. Private Steers saw them both pretty clearly and I saw the guy that zapped me. If I'd had a picture of this guy beforehand I could've nailed him. There has to be a third perp though. Private Skiff was shot from the side as he approached the man and woman. Steers said he saw a dark colored van and smoke from the gun coming from that direction. By the way, if you ever have an opportunity to get stun gunned, pass it up. It hurts like a son-of-a-bitch."

"I'll try to remember that. So what's next?"

"We've got the local police looking for the van but there are lots of vans that fit the description. We're also trying to run down the BMW that they were loading up with Dean Gray's stuff. That's a one-in-a-million shot, too. How many black Beamers do you think are in the greater Norfolk area?"

Pat replied, "You're right about that. It's going to be tough. Johnny Poleirmo is here. Should I ask him if he's got any ideas?"

"It can't hurt."

Pat put his hand over the receiver and shouted, "Hey Johnny, come on over for a second. Joe's on the phone. He'd like to know if you have any ideas."

Johnny Poleirmo was a Sheriffs Detective. He worked in Vice but had been in Homicide before that. He was a smart cop with 10 years experience outsmarting murderers and dope smugglers. He helped bust two major drug figures in Orange and Lake Counties. It had put a major, though temporary dent in the drug trade around Orlando and earned him a commendation from the County Commissions of both counties. During the process, he determined that his partner and his captain were on the take from one of the dealers. His partner was killed by an unknown assailant. His captain was busted and is awaiting trial.

Today, Johnny was relaxing at Pat and Diane's but he was always willing to help a friend. He considered Pat and Joe to be two of his closest friends in the world. He took the receiver from Pat and said, "Hey, Joe. I hear this investigation is turning into a free-for-all. Tell me what's happened so far. I'll ask questions when I need more information."

For the next twenty-five minutes, Joe told Johnny the details of the case especially the details surrounding the murders. Johnny sat in a lawn chair listening and asking probing questions. Finally he told Joe that there were definitely at least three people involved but that they weren't working together. Joe found that hard to believe.

Johnny said, "From what you just told me, the woman was totally shocked when the shooting started. That tells me she didn't expect it to happen. Plus, Steers was hit with a stun gun. If they were working together, the guy would have shot him in the head. He'd be a corpse by now. Instead he got zapped. And what about you? He could have lured you into the parking lot and set you up to blow your brains out. Does that sound like a guy who's working closely with a killer? Hardly."

"Maybe the man and woman just don't have the stomach for murder but their partner doesn't have a problem with it. Maybe he gets off shooting people."

Johnny paused for a second before answering. "If these characters were working together, they'd plan the killing better. All the murders except the one in North Dakota were in public places. Unless they're trying to get caught, they wouldn't commit the murders in such a public place, not on purpose anyway." Johnny thought for a moment. "They're getting careless now."

There was a period of silence on the line.

Johnny said, "You mentioned a vehicle that's been at the scenes."

"Yea. The dark van's been spotted twice now; once at the house in Grand Forks and now at an apartment in Norfolk."

"Well Joe, here's what I think. Your killer is the person or persons in the van. Your alleged sister-brother team, they're crooks, not murderers. Using a stun gun doesn't equate to murder, but shooting someone in the back definitely is cold blooded. That's electric chair material in my state."

"We started out looking for a couple of thieves and now we're dodging bullets. I still can't believe that these folks may not be working together. But what you say makes sense." Joe took a deep breath. "So do you have any recommendations on what we should do next?"

"I'd continue the bar surveillance but I would try doing it from a distance. Don't try to engage the girl or apprehend the guy. You've seen them and have either pictures or artist's drawings. Use them to find the thieves. Then when you find the thieves, look around and you'll find the murderer or murderers. I can't imagine what the connection is between the two but there's some reason why the person in the van is following your thieves. One other thing; when you find the thieves, catch the murderers first. They're the more dangerous of the two."

On the other end of the phone, Joe took another deep breath. He wanted to catch the crooks. That was his assignment. He also couldn't do that if he was dead. This bastard or bastards had killed a fellow Marine. He felt duty bound to avenge that death. Joe had survived battlefield conditions where the bullets were flying everywhere. It was as likely to be killed by a stray friendly fire shot than enemy fire. This poor, young kid was murdered on American soil. He didn't even have a chance to defend his own country. That hurt Joe more than anything else. He was protecting the bad with the good. He was afraid that no matter what he did, this would always be the case. The righteous would have to live along side the bottom feeders. But it was still the best country in the world.

"You there, Joe?" Johnny asked.

"Yea. I was thinking. I have to talk with the Captain about our next move. We're too close to let this get away. Thanks for the insight, Johnny. If you'd like to visit us up here we could sure use you."

Johnny said, "I don't think the boss would like that." He glanced at Rachael to make sure she didn't hear his last comment. "You want to talk with Pat again?"

"Yes please. Later Johnny."

Pat and Joe chatted again for a few minutes then Joe asked to speak again with Lisa.

"Baby, if you were trying to steal everything I owned, how would you do it?"

"It'd be easy right now. You're gone. I know you're going to be gone for at least a while longer. A few friends and I could empty your apartment in no time flat."

"Could you and one friend do it?"

"Sure. It would take a little longer but if I knew you were going to be gone for several days, it would be easy to clean you out. Why do you ask?"

"I'm trying to figure out how these two are getting away with this. They always seem to be a step ahead. We're getting closer but they could pull up stakes, head for another city and we'd have to start over again. We can't figure out how a woman can convince a young guy to get married, clean him out, move to a new location and do it over again, all in a matter of two or three weeks."

"Maybe they're overlapping. You know, meeting one guy, hooking him then going to another city and meeting another guy. Then going back to the first city and continuing with that relationship. There are always excuses to be gone for a week or so at a time. Business trips, visits to family, job hunting. You name it."

Joe thought about this for a minute. She could be right. Maybe this woman has two or three guys on a string at a time. Each base is less than a day's drive from one to the other. She could be setting up marriages all along the east coast. How could she keep her stories straight? *She told me her name was Becky Lippert. I wonder where she got that name? Some poor, dead child most likely.*

They finally said their good byes to more tears from Lisa. She said that she was looking forward to the concert and would get him the details as soon as possible. Lisa went back to the bar-b-que and Joe went back to the investigation. They were both aching for each other but that pain would have to wait to be soothed. There was work to be done. Joe had the investigation. Lisa had to find a college and get enrolled. Life would go on for them even with the emptiness in their hearts.

* * *

Becky Lippert was wide awake and showered. She booked another day in her suite. She was dressed and ready to head down to the restaurant for lunch when a knock came on her door. It was Ace Glover. He was dressed in light shorts, a light green golf shirt and sandals with no socks. He looked handsome with a magnetic smile. He hadn't looked this good earlier that morning near the soda machines.

"Good morning, Becky."

"Hi," she said quietly and smiled back. "How did you know this was my room?"

"We saw you come back to the room last night, or this morning I guess it was. Anyway, Mom thought that maybe you'd like to join us for lunch. We just got up and got ready ourselves. There's a nice place just up the road."

"I don't know. I usually eat alone."

"No way. As pretty as you are, I can't believe that you do anything alone."

Becky smiled and gave Ace a shy look. "Well it's true. I'm a little shy around people. But I'll tell you what; I'll go with you and your mom. After that I have to get on the road." The lie came out just like water from a glass.

"Great. Are you ready 'cause we're ready anytime you are."

"Sure. Let me get my purse and lock up."

They left the Hotel and headed for a mid priced chain restaurant. Becky was starting to feel comfortable with Ace. She wasn't sure about him the night before but he had a smooth manner about him that put her at ease. He was like a little brother. She had no idea how true her instincts were.

Chapter 35

The office was a small room off the main hallway at the headquarters building of the Norfolk Naval Base on the west end of the city. The walls were painted white but had a yellowish tint from cigarette smoke. Smoking had just recently been banned in the building but the walls bore the ugly sheen from years of tar-filled smoke in the air. The office was typically used to conduct welcome aboard meetings. The room had a single wood desk and three wooden chairs with leather seats and back pads. All the furniture looked like it was ready for the surplus yard. The walls had pictures of the President of the United States, the Norfolk Naval Station Commander, and Admiral Hyman G. Rickover, father of the Nuclear Navy. There were also several photographs of warships; the aircraft carrier USS Nimitz, the battleship USS Iowa, and the Los Angeles class submarine USS Dallas. There was also a painting of the frigate, Old Ironsides, the first USS Constitution. Above the door was a clock not unlike the ones used at most high schools across the country. It made a slow, methodical tic-tic-tic as it counted off the seconds. The sound seemed to echo in the room. There was a single window high in the wall of the room that faced out to the front of the headquarter building. The room was lighted by four banks of fluorescent lights. The lighting was like that of a doctor's office. Two banks of lights would have sufficed. The room had an institutional odor, like it had just been cleaned and fumigated. The floor was highly polished so that you could almost see your reflection. It was also slick and Wanda Gray slipped and nearly fell when she entered the office.

Arthur and Wanda Gray sat in the chairs across from Captain Nancy Brown, Sergeant Joe McKinney, and Private Jeff Steers at the Norfolk Naval Station Headquarters. Private Steers was still sore from the attack at Dean Gray's apartment. He had two very dark purple bruises where the slugs from the 9MM hit his Kevlar vest. He also had a pair of burn marks from a stun gun. Joe got as many details as possible from him about the man, the woman and the van.

After going to their son's apartment and finding it marked off as a crime scene Art and Wanda went to the command office of Dean Gray's ship. They claimed that their son's new bride was a fraud and that their son's wife had tricked him into marrying her. She was now on a spending spree up and down the Atlantic Coast. They had the credit card receipts to prove it.

The Officer–in–Charge looked at the information that Art and Wanda presented. It was evident that the Gray's were upset and, if their story was true, Julie Gray was indeed a fraud. The call was made to Naval Criminal Investigative Service. Major Hartnett immediately contacted Captain Brown.

Nancy slowly looked through the receipts for a pattern when Wanda Gray piped up. "If you're looking for a pattern, I've already done that. Here's a map that shows every receipt logged at the location, date and time of purchase. I even color-coded the dates so that you can easily see where she was on each day." As Nancy looked the map over, it was very clear that Julie Lippus Gray was moving up and down the coast settling near military bases but only staying in one place for a few days, then moving on to the next location. She would then travel back to the previous town and stay for several more days.

"This is very good work, Mrs. Gray. Did you take any notes while you made this map?"

"Call me Wanda, please. Yes I did. I kept a log of dates and stores." She dug around in her purse and pulled out a notebook which she handed over to Nancy. Every receipt was meticulously recorded in clear penmanship. It was laid out like a spreadsheet with more details than were recorded on the map. The spreadsheet was divided by location where the expenditures took place. Two things were very clear. First, Julie Lippus didn't let the grass grow under her feet. She was never in one place more than three days. Second, Wanda Gray was one organized, determined woman.

"So, Wanda, how did you come across these receipts?"

"Art and I visited some folks who were supposed to be Julie Lippus' parents. But when we started talking, it was immediately clear that Dean's wife was not their child. The real Julie Lippus has been dead for years. She died of cancer. This woman, whoever she is, stole her identity. Mr. and Mrs. Lippus started getting these credit card bills in the mail and they knew someone was using their deceased daughter's name. They didn't have the financial means to do anything more than write the credit card company and let them know that it wasn't their daughter. At least they aren't stuck with the bills."

"We had some evidence that indicates identity theft but this is a clincher. Does your son know anything about this yet?"

"No. We don't want to get him worked up while he's at sea. He just left about a week ago. We're heading over to his apartment after we're through here."

"Dean's apartment was cleaned out of anything of value. He's lucky in a way. Past victims of these people were cleaned out completely, down to the bare walls."

Art asked, "Did you find a safe in the apartment?"

"Yes we did. It wasn't really a safe. It was more of a strong box."

"No. I mean a safe with an electronic keypad for the combination."

"Well, no. Why?"

"Dean had a safe, not too large but about eighteen inches square. He kept important papers and account numbers and passwords in it. If that safe is missing, whoever has it might be able to get into Dean's investment accounts. He's pretty much a wizard at stock trading. He actually has about a quarter of a million dollars in investments. If the safe is still at his apartment, then the majority of his money is safe. He kept the strong box for ready cash and some stock certificates but the bulk of his wealth or access to it is in the safe. We should look for that sucker. He told me where it would be if anything happened to him."

"Did he seem worried about his new bride? I mean did he ever tell you that he didn't trust her? Is that why he told you about the safe?"

"No. He never said anything about not trusting Julie." He hesitated as if he didn't know what else to call her since they now knew that Julie Lippus wasn't her real name. "He was really happy about her. He said she was the best thing that ever happened to him. We weren't at all happy about it. It was all much too fast. We never met her. We only talked to her on the phone a couple times. She seemed like a real nice girl, almost too nice. But he's an adult and he usually has a pretty good head on his shoulders."

Nancy gave Art a thoughtful look then asked, "Did he have much experience with woman before now?"

"Not really. He did date some but he was more interested in making money. He was fascinated by it. Girls didn't come into the picture much until this one came along. She really swept him off his feet. He was on cloud nine, as they say."

Wanda chimed in, "I thought that he might be gay when I first married Art. He was so disinterested in girls and into money that I was worried. When he called and said he'd met a really wonderful woman we were thrilled. Then it moved so fast, we didn't quite know what to do. I guess we should have said or done something. But what could we do? Like Art said, he's an adult."

"There probably wasn't anything that you could have done. At least he's alive. We have three military men dead and the father and mother of another. He could have been one of them."

Wanda and Art Gray held each other's hands just a bit tighter. Then Art said, "Is that all, Captain? We'd like to get to Dean's apartment and see if we can find the safe."

"Yes but we'll go with you. It's a crime scene and I have to be there to escort you through the apartment."

They all stood and headed for the office door. It was a short drive to the apartment but it would seem much longer in the heat of the Virginia day.

* * *

Patrolman Larvel Williams was called to the lobby of the Holiday Inn Select on a disturbing the peace call. It appears that a gentleman took exception to his bill. He had four hours of pornographic films on his bill and he became belligerent when the clerk actually expected him to pay for the three movies. He swore that he never ordered the films even though the room's keypad history showed all three titles being ordered and the movies being watched in their entirety. He began cursing the young female clerk and calling her a slut, claiming that she'd been the one to order them and watch them in the office of the hotel. She told the gentleman that it wasn't possible and that if he called her a slut one more time she would call the police. He did. Then she did and Officer Williams was the closest car to the hotel, so he responded. He entered the lobby and found the man and the hotel clerk still trading verbal jabs though it apparently was toned done from before. It was a matter of minutes before the officer had everyone calmed down, with the customer apologizing to the clerk, the clerk accepting his apology and him admitting that he did order the films. He paid his bill then remembered that he'd forgotten his shaving kit in the room. Officer Williams offered to escort the man back to his room mainly because he didn't want the man to have a change of heart and trash the room after he'd paid his bill. The entry into the room went as planned. He retrieved his shaving kit, got into his car and pulled away.

That's when Williams noticed a maroon colored van in the hotel parking lot. He walked around the van once, then again. It was Chevy van, about ten years old with worn tires, a broken side view mirror, and some minor rust. There was a rectangular area on both the driver and passenger side doors where the paint wasn't faded as bad as the rest of the van. There apparently had been a magnetic sign on the doors for some company but the signs were removed. It looked as though it had one time been a van used by a construction crew for a communications or contract electric company. He was trying to remember the information from the morning briefing about a dark colored van, possibly maroon, that was involved in a murder about ten minutes from the hotel. He looked up and down the walkway and at the rooms in the immediate vicinity of the van to see if there was any indication which room the van owners occupied. He wrote down the license plate numbers and headed for his car. He called in the license plate number and a description of the van and waited for dispatch to reply. Then he decided that he should check with the front desk and try to get the name and room number of the owner. It wasn't strictly legal, but he thought that maybe the clerk wouldn't know that and would hand over the information. After all, she might be grateful for resolving the issue with the previous customer.

When the dispatcher came back on the line and said the van fit the description of the van reported in the murder he requested backup and immediately asked that dispatch call the hotel clerk and request the information for him. He didn't want to leave sight of the van for even a few minutes. He got back into his patrol car and waited for backup to arrive. As he watched the van, a door to one of the rooms opened and a young man with blond hair came out and walked towards the van. He was about 18 and slender. Behind him, a woman who appeared to be fifty or older followed. They both moved towards the van. As they did, Officer Williams tensed and moved his right hand to unsnap the restraint of his holstered gun. He had his left hand on the door latch to his patrol car as he watched the two move ever closer to the van. He was about to open the door to his patrol car when the two walked past the van and headed to a parked car across the lot from the van. The car was a late model red Ford Mustang with temporary plates. Williams relaxed a bit, snapped the gun restraint strap, and continued his surveillance of the hotel. The young man and woman pulled away and headed for the exit of the hotel lot.

Another door opened and a young woman exited. She was slim, well built and had short black hair. She walked with a sexy gait. She had Larvel Williams' full attention. She turned and looked directly at Williams and he felt like looking away. She had on a loose fitting halter blouse that hung low in the front and she obviously wasn't wearing anything underneath. She walked right up to his patrol car and looked in at him. He rolled down his window and asked, "Can I help you, ma'am?"

The young woman smiled, leaned over exposing most of her chest and said with a strong southern accent, "I sure hope so. You see that van? Two black men have been in that van all night playing rap music so loud that I couldn't sleep. It was rattling the room windows it was so loud." Officer Williams had a difficult time keeping his eyes on the woman's face. "If you see them, those men, I mean, can you please arrest them for disturbing the peace or something? I don't know where they went. They might even be asleep in there for all I know. But that sure is rude, don't you think?"

Larvel, himself a black officer with little tolerance for annoying people regardless of race, smiled back at the woman and said, "Yes, ma'am, I do. Can you describe these two?"

"Well, they were both about 6 feet tall and muscular. One had a beard and the other had a mustache. The bearded one had his hair in those braids like a Jamaican. The other guy was bald."

That narrows it down to about 100,000 black men in the greater Norfolk area. "Will you be staying another night here?"

"Yes, unless these two are out here. I'm not putting up with this for another night."

"If they start the noise again tonight please call the police. I'll advise my sergeant of your complaint and the night shift will take care of these characters. Miss, can I get your name, please so I can log it on the report?"

"Rebecca Lippert." She gave her real name to the officer. She figured it was too dangerous to give him her most recent name, Julie Gray. The police and the military would be watching for a blond woman with that name. Since she was neither at the moment, she was pretty confident that she'd be safe.

"Miss Lippert, is there anything else I can do for you?"

"Thank you, Officer," she looked at his name tag and followed with "Williams. You've been most helpful." She turned and walked away passed the van to a black BWM. As she pulled away, Larvel Williams went back to his surveillance of the van and hotel as he heard sirens approach the hotel parking lot. His back-up had finally arrived. After a briefing by Patrolman Williams about the two black men and their descriptions, the officers cautiously approached the van and looked in the driver and passenger side windows. The van appeared to be empty. One of the back-up patrolman produced a 'Slim Jim' from the trunk of his patrol car and they unlocked the van. The smell of cordite from a fired weapon was evident but it wasn't within the last couple of hours. It could have been from the previous night but there was no way to tell with any certainty. There were a number of shell casings in the back of the van. Williams called dispatch again and asked for a crime scene investigation team. He was told that a team would be dispatched. The ETA was about twenty-five minutes. Williams thought that it wouldn't matter because the occupants of this van were long gone. Dispatch came back with a room number and name for the van occupants; Abbie and Ace Glover, room 129.

Officer Williams looked at the rooms in front of him. There it was, room 129; the same room that the woman and young man exited not 10 minutes earlier. He smacked himself on the head and told the dispatcher to put out an all points bulletin to every patrol car within a 10 mile radius of his position. They were to look for a teenaged, blond kid and a woman, approximate age fifty. They are driving a red Ford Mustang with temporary tags. He gave additional information about their dress and a few other physical characteristics. Then he added, "Also be on the lookout for a young woman, short black hair, approximate age twenty, wearing a dark halter blouse," *very sexy halter blouse*, he didn't add, "and bright red lipstick, driving a black, late model BMW. She may be an accessory to murder. These three are to be considered armed and dangerous." *And I have to be the most gullible cop in Norfolk.*

* * *

Art and Wanda Gray entered their son's apartment with Nancy and Joe. They were surprised to see how empty the place looked. They looked in the spare bedroom for his prized electric guitar and amp. They were both gone. Art went to the closet in the spare bedroom and looked on the top shelf to the far left. He saw the fake wall that his son had constructed to make the appearance of a ventilation duct. He reached for the fake wall and moved it to the right. As he did a safe came into view. At first he was relieved. He reached for the safe and lifted it from the shelf. This took considerable effort as the safe weighed about seventy pounds. As he did, the door of the safe swung open. Wanda and Nancy yelled 'Watch out" in unison. The door hit Art hard on the right side of his forehead. He yelled in pain and dropped the safe which came crashing down on his left foot. He yelled out again and fell backwards on his back. He immediately put one hand on his foot and the other on his forehead. Wanda and Nancy both ran to him, one on each side. They moved the safe away from his foot. Wanda asked if he was alright. At first he said no. Then he said yes, he was okay all the while sucking air through his teeth and rubbing his injuries. He was definitely embarrassed for his clumsy move.

Wanda said, "Take your hand away from your forehead and let me see." There was a small cut and some swelling that was growing by the second. They all forgot about the safe for the time being. Nancy went to the kitchen to get some ice. Luckily the freezer was still on and there were plenty of ice cubes in the tray.

As Wanda tended to her husbands minor scrapes, Nancy turned the safe upright and looked inside. It was empty. If there was any important information in the safe, it was gone. Nancy was sure that it was in the wrong hands.

"There's nothing here," she announced to Wanda and Art. "Do you know what companies he dealt with? And did he trust you with his account numbers? If we want to stop this woman from making off with his money we have to act fast."

Art pulled Wanda's hand away from his head. "I have the list in my wallet with the brokerage house and his bank where he did most of his trading. I think we can get to them in time. I know his broker, too. I think that if someone would try to clean out his accounts they'd question it. They know he's in the Navy and often deployed. If someone tried to make trades, they might not suspect anything as long as the trades were done on-line, you know, over the internet. But if someone tried to cash out and request a check, they'd probably question the transactions and at least try to contact Dean. They might even contact me if Dean wasn't available."

"Let's hope you're right, Mr. Gray." Nancy looked back in the safe then looked around the rest of the empty apartment. Her mind flashed to Private Skiff. This case was costing a lot of good young men their lives. It was one thing to steal everything a man had. It was quite another to rob him of the rest of his life. They had to catch these bastards and fast.

* * *

Becky had pulled the dark wig off as soon as she left the hotel parking lot. She drove for nearly an hour and got another hotel room. She skipped lunch with Abbie and Ace. She really wanted nothing to do with them. She'd enjoyed a couple of days on her own, shopping and relaxing. She even drove to Virginia Beach for a day in the sun.

But it was time to confront Bobby.   She headed directly for the apartment that she and Bobby shared. She had time to think and she wanted to give Bobby a piece of her mind. She was scared. She knew that he must have known about the murders before they happened and she wanted no part of it. She was ready to split the money and go their separate ways. She was actually beginning to feel sorry for the young men that she had seduced. She never before cared about the people that she and Bobby ripped off but now her conscience was starting to bother her. All she ever wanted to do was have a little fun and make a little money. No one was supposed to get hurt. She wanted it back the way it was originally; take the money and run. Never see any of their faces again. Now there were a number of her victims whose faces she would forever see in her mind. This had to stop.

She pulled into the parking lot at the apartment and bounded up the steps. She walked right in to the living room. Bobby was sleeping on the couch with a computer in front of him. The computer was on but the screen saver was activated. She sat on the couch next to Bobby and moved the mouse. The web site for a stock broker was on the screen but a message said that the third attempt had been unsuccessful and therefore the user would be locked out for 24 hours. Stock broker's statements and note pads with Dean Gray's handwriting were scattered all around the computer and on the floor. Becky briefly examined them and saw that there was a small fortune in the accounts. It was obvious that Bobby was trying to gain access to the accounts but had been unsuccessful opening at least one of the accounts. Becky shook her head, got up and headed to the kitchen for a beer. As she opened the refrigerator, Bobby stirred and opened his eyes slightly.

"Becky, is that you?"

"No, it's the frickin' boogey man. Who the hell else would it be?"

Bobby woke quickly hearing her nasty tone. He didn't like it. His temper was rising along with his body and mind. "Why are you taking that shitty tone with me? Where the hell have you been anyway?"

"Look Bobby, I had to get away so I could think. This is getting way out of hand." She moved back to the dining area and took a seat on a chair that needed to have its legs re-glued. She set her beer down and prepared for the inevitable fight. She continued, "You knew about the killings, didn't you. You knew there was some nut case following us killing these guys. Who is it? And why?"

Bobby's face was turning red now. He walked slowly to the table and took a seat next to Becky, trying to keep his temper in check. "I don't know what you're talking about. I'm just as surprised as you about it. I have no idea who these folks are."

"There! You liar! If you don't know then how do you know there are two of them? Who are they?" Becky was getting red in the face, too.

She'd had enough lies and she didn't want to go to prison, especially for something that she didn't do. She was going to get it out of Bobby one way or another.

Bobby was flustered. He'd screwed up. He actually didn't know Ace Glover. He knew that Abbie had a son but he didn't know that her son was with her. So in a sense, he didn't know that there were two people involved but he was pretty sure that Abbie wasn't doing the shooting alone.

Becky threw another question at Bobby, one which he wasn't expecting. He never had any idea that Becky was paying attention to the money and where it was going. "What happened to that $10,000 that's missing from the insurance money?"

Bobby paused, then looked away. He was caught and he had no plausible explanation. He wasn't fast enough and Becky was all over him.

"Where is it, Bobby? Do you have some slut following us? Are you getting a little on the side? Child support? Alimony? What?"

Now his embarrassment was fueling his temper again and he turned towards Becky. "Shut up, Becky," he growled in a low tone between clenched teeth.

"Why, what are you going to do? Have your girlfriend kill me, too?"

"I said shut up! You're talking crazy, now just shut up!"

"Where is it?" Becky continued to needle. "That was my money, too, you bastard. I want my half."

"I'll give you your half." Bobby stood and grabbed Becky by the arms and threw her into the living room towards the couch. She landed on the floor and scrambled to get up but Bobby was on her before she could get to her feet. Still lying on the floor, her blouse had shifted and her left breast was hanging out. Bobby grabbed her by the left arm and turned her to face him. He grabbed the front of her halter and yanked hard, ripping the blouse from her and tossing it aside. He quickly reached down and with a quick pull, broke the snap on her jeans. Before she knew what was happening, he was up and grabbed the jeans by the legs and pulled upward. The effect was that Becky was nearly standing on her head. With another quick jerk, Bobby pulled the jeans from her body. Becky yelped in pain as the carpet burned her shoulder where it rubbed like fine grit sandpaper. Within just a few seconds, she was naked down to her thong panties. But Bobby wasn't finished. Almost as soon as her legs hit the floor again, he was on top of her, turning her onto her stomach, pinning her arms behind her back.

"You want your half? Here it comes." Holding her wrists together hard with one hand, he grabbed her thong with the other and ripped the skimpy undergarment from her body. The friction of the seams of the panties burned her crotch and legs. She yelped in pain again. She thought about screaming for help but she was afraid of what Bobby might do before help arrived.

Bobby straddled her torso and sat on the small of her back. He raised his arms and removed his shirt. The computer screen was back to the dark screen saver and she could see his face reflected there. She could see the evil smile on his face and she braced for a rough half hour of nearly sadistic sex. Bobby stood and placed his right foot on her back between her shoulder blades and said, "Don't move a muscle if you know what's good for you." As he said this, he unzipped his pants and started to pull them down.

Just then, the apartment doorbell rang. Bobby stopped. He knelt down next to Becky and whispered, "Don't make a sound." The doorbell rang again. Bobby waited. Becky's breath was coming in short, deep spasms. She wanted to scream out for help but she didn't know who was on the other side of the door. Bobby waited another 30 seconds, then a loud pounding on the door followed by a woman's voice, "Open up, Bobby. I know you're in there."

Becky's jaw dropped upon hearing a woman call him by name. She was angry but was in no position to do or say anything. Bobby whispered, "You pick up your clothes and get in the bedroom. If you make a sound, you'll be one sorry little bitch. Is that clear?"

Becky nodded. Bobby let her get up and she quietly gathered her clothes that were now rags. She headed for the bedroom as she thought of a dozen ways that she'd get back at Bobby for this. Tears had streamed from her eyes but she showed no other signs of crying.

Bobby yelled to the door, "Just a minute," as he zipped his pants and pulled his shirt back on. He quickly gathered up Dean Gray's account papers and stuffed them under the couch. He closed the laptop computer, rubbed his hands through his hair and headed to the apartment door. Before he looked through the peep hole he knew who was knocking at his door.

Becky slowly dressed in a different set of clothes. The ones she had on were now rags after Bobby's attack. She stopped to look in the dresser mirror at the rug burn on her shoulder. Her crotch burned where Bobby had ripped her panties off. She hated Bobby even more now than when she first arrived at the apartment. She moved her face closer to the mirror and looked at the lines that were evident around her eyes. *I'm too young to look like this. I'll end up looking like an old maid, like that Abbie from the hotel.* Just then, she heard a muffled, but familiar voice from the living room. Then she heard a man's voice that was also familiar. *It can't be. How did they follow me here?* It was Abbie and Ace Glover.

It sounded like Abbie was raising her voice to Bobby. But why would she do that? She doesn't even know him. Becky was confused by the brewing confrontation in the next room. Then she heard something that enraged her. Abbie was demanding money. Actually, she was demanding more money, meaning that Bobby had already given her some; the missing $10,000. She finished dressing and stormed out of the room.

"What is going on here?" She demanded.

They all stopped arguing and looked at Becky, surprised by her sharp demand. Abbie's gruff demeanor softened. She looked lovingly at Becky. She took a step towards Becky, looking her over from head to toe. She noticed the burn on her shoulder and turned to Bobby, her face screwed up in an angry stare. "What have you done to my little girl?"

Becky looked at Abbie in stunned amazement. "What did you say?"

Abbie turned to her with a smile and opened her arms. "You are my little girl and Ace is your little brother."

Chapter 36

"Look Honey, I can't control my boss. He tells me what I need to do to keep my job and that's what I do." Jim Hollis was exasperated. His wife was demanding that he come home early and take her out to dinner. It was Friday night after all. That's what couples did on Friday night. They went out to eat at a decent restaurant and then went to a movie or went shopping. At least that's what Jim Hollis' wife expected. He looked around his cubicle at the stacks of files in his inbox then looked at the calendar with red marks where deadlines were etched. His anxiety level grew with each passing minute. He had to make quota and he wasn't making any progress with his wife constantly calling.

What Jim knew was that he had to work late. His case files were stacking up and he was getting further behind. His boss had called the department together earlier in the week and told them that he was setting a new, higher quota for processing claims. Each adjuster had to meet the minimums or face getting terminated. The latest merger to take advantage of the synergies of the combined companies only meant that the employees left after downsizing were going to have to work harder and longer. The board of directors had promised the shareholders that the savings from the merger would be substantial. Earnings per share were going to double and there would be bonuses for each employee in February of each year. He'd heard all this before. The last merger was supposed to produce tremendous results. And it had for the top ten executives of the company. They all enjoyed six figure bonuses. Except the CEO who received a generous seven figure bonus and a comparable rise in base salary. The rest of the employees were told that they had to work harder just to keep their miserable jobs. He was working longer hours for the same money. The company was reaching into his and his co-workers pockets to balance the books. They preached family values but in truth, the only family the big wigs valued was their own.

He heard his wife tersely say, "You aren't even listening to me."

"Honey, yes I am. I'm just swamped here and I'm trying to finish up so I can get home. Honestly, dear, if I can get back to work, I can be home by 7:45. Please be patient." As his wife answered, he looked down at the file on his desk. Dean Gray. United States Navy. Killed in Action. Accident in the engineroom of the USS Nimitz. *I don't recall any accident on the news. Maybe it was a minor incident.* "Honey, I have to go now. I'll see you in a couple of hours. We'll go to that restaurant across from the mall that you like." That seemed to calm her some, but it took another 5 minutes to get her to finally hang up and allow Jim to concentrate on his work. As he looked over the Dean Gray file, something on the form looked familiar. He couldn't place it but he sensed that something was wrong with the claim. He looked over each page of the form from top to bottom but still couldn't find anything technically wrong. He leaned back in his chair and looked up at the ceiling with its four foot by two foot tiles and fluorescent light fixtures. He rubbed his eyes. He was mentally exhausted. Physically, he knew he was in for another night of little sleep as his mind would run through the files as if he were still sitting at his desk. And his wife wouldn't let up on him for working the overtime hours for free. He was being eaten alive by alimony payments from his former wives and he wasn't getting any closer to a secure retirement. *It's no wonder people commit fraud to get a big payoff. It was easier than going through this hell every day.*

He picked up the phone and dialed the number for Dean Gray's wife, a Mrs. Julie Gray. She answered on the fifth ring.

"Mrs. Gray, please?"

In a solemn voice, Becky Lippert answered, "This is Julie Gray."

"Mrs. Gray, this is Jim Hollis from NatFed Life Insurance Company. First I want to say that I'm sorry for your loss."

"Thank you, Jim." She recognized his voice from when he called her about her 'husband' Edward Sharp. She was ready for him to ask the same boring questions. Yada yada yada. Just get it over with.

There was some shouting going on in the background as Jim tried to concentrate on his standard questions. He heard Julie Gray cover the phone and shout, "Would you people shut up? It's the insurance company." The shouting went silent.

"Sorry Jim, go on please."

"Mrs. Gray, I have a few questions before we mail your claim check. First, did your husband have any other policies in force at the time of his death?"

"No."

"Can you please verify your address?"

Becky provided the address of her and Dean's apartment which was now a crime scene. By the time the check was mailed, the crime scene would be cold, Dean would still be at sea and she and Bobby would be able to claim their money. But now there might have to be a four way split and Becky was not happy about that possibility. The questions went on from there and five minutes later he was finished. He said, "That's about it. Do you have any questions?"

Without a moment's hesitation and in a voice that was a little too matter-of-fact for Jim Hollis' liking, Julie Gray said, "How soon will I get my check?"

Jim was taken aback by the cold delivery of the question. Any remorse that this woman felt was gone. It was a statement more than a question. Then Jim remembered another claim. *This woman sounds exactly like . . . what was her name? Lisa . . . LouAnn . . .* He remembered. *Laurie Sharp! Her husband was Edward Sharp, Private Edward Sharp.* He'd been reprimanded for processing the claim because Private Sharp had been alive at the time of the claim. He was later murdered outside of his apartment. The claim had been processed but the money wasn't paid the second time. They hadn't recovered the payout from the false claim yet. The trail that started out in Jacksonville, North Carolina went cold when Mrs. Sharp disappeared but not before she'd cashed a check for $100,000.

"Mrs. Gray, the check should be in the mail within a week to ten days."

"Okay." The line went dead.

Jim's mind raced. He pulled up the claim for Edward Sharp and compared it to the Dean Gray form. The names on the form were different but the signatures had very similar characteristics. He looked at the dates and the way the numbers were formed and he concluded that the same person had written both forms. He wasn't an expert but it didn't take an expert to see the similarities. He was convinced. Should he call his supervisor and tell him he suspected that he was processing a fraudulent claim? He faced the fact that he had no choice. He'd already been reprimanded for his failure to do so before. One more missed opportunity to find fraud and he'd be on the unemployment line. As much as that eventuality was appealing, given his current work load and the poor hours, he didn't want to face the prospect of having to start over in a new job. He also had to remind himself of the alimony payments. He made up his mind. Maybe this time he'd get a promotion for discovering a cheat and saving the company big bucks. Maybe he'd get a cut. Maybe he'd just keep his miserable job. But that beat getting fired. He picked up his phone and dialed his supervisor.

He answered on the first ring. "Harper."

"Mr. Harper, I need to report a potential fraudulent claim."

Dan Harper ran a hand down the front of his face. Why do these things always happen on a Friday late in the afternoon? Now he'd have to call his wife and explain that he'd be late again. He looked around his office at the white walls with motivational posters. He fixed on the one that said Attitude. It bore a beautiful picture of a soaring eagle with a brilliant blue sky in the background. He pictured himself with a shotgun on the cliff of a nearby mountain ready to blow the eagle out of the sky. *I'll give you attitude.* "Okay, Jim, I'll be right over." He hung up the phone with Jim Hollis. He despised Jim. He hated talking to him because there was so much strain on his shirt's buttons that he was afraid that one of them would burst off and hit him in the eye. He always dressed like a slob. His pants were always too short and his shirts were never pressed. His shirt-tails were on the verge of pulling completely out of his pants and the sweat rings were evident no matter the time of day. He hated talking to Jim Hollis only slightly less than talking to his wife and explaining that he'd be late but that was a call that he had to make. He picked up the phone and dialed his home number then prepared for a severe tongue-lashing. He wasn't disappointed.

* * *

"This is huge. This could be the break we've been looking for." Nancy Brown and Joe were looking over the information they'd received from NatFed Life Insurance Company. They now had an opportunity to set up surveillance at Dean Gray's apartment. They also had a commitment of cooperation from the insurance company's fraud prevention unit. The unit consisted of five agents with military intelligence backgrounds, which didn't impress Joe McKinney in the least. He told Nancy that he was personally going to review their files and interview each to make sure they understood the ground rules. The first ground rule was that they were support and were to take directions from Nancy and Joe. They were not to do anything on their own. The last thing they needed was some cowboy going off trying to be a hero for the insurance company.

Joe said, "Let's get the plan together and walk through it. We have time to plan it out and set up several contingencies. We can't let them get away again. I want to get Pat back up here. He's kind of an expert on plans and contingencies."

"I thought he was a Navy nuke."

"Yea, but he learned the hard way that you have to cover your ass and all your bases. He knows plans; what works and what doesn't. We can use his perspective, trust me on this."

"Okay, Joe. Call him and we'll put him back to work."

It was 7:00 on a Friday night. Joe half expected to leave Pat a voice mail message when he dialed and was surprised when Pat answered the phone on the third ring.

"Hey, Pat, what are you doing home? I thought you two would be having a night out on the town.

"Well we would be except Anna decided to catch a cold last night. She's not feeling well at all. She kept us up pretty much the whole night."

"Too bad. Is Anna getting any better?"

"A little but then Sean will probably catch it next."

Joe heard in the background as six year old Sean yelled, "I'm not catching a cold."

"The little expert has spoken." Pat asked Joe, "So what do we owe the pleasure? I'm sure you didn't call to hear the medical news."

"We have some real strong leads on the suspects. They tried to file another false claim with NatFed. This time the adjuster recognized the woman's voice. He compared the claims from the two files where she was the beneficiary and sure enough, the handwriting on the claims matches."

"Wow, little brother. Sounds like you may have a shot at catching her with her hand in the cookie jar."

"Pretty corny, Pat, but it may work out that way. We'd like for you to come up to Norfolk and oversee our plan. The claim check will go out in about 10 working days. When they come to pick it up, we'll be waiting to snag them. We need an expert to make sure we're not screwing something up. That's where you come in. We'll have the plan put together by the time you get here. You can sit down and pick it apart, step by step. Then we can rebuild it again." Joe stopped and waited for Pat's reply.

"I don't know, Joe. Anna's pretty down with this cold. Diane's tied up taking care of her and the house. It'd be tough to get away right now."

Joe heard Diane in the background. "What would be pretty tough?"

"Joe, can you hang on for a second?" Pat talked to Diane for about two minutes. Joe couldn't hear a thing since Pat had the receiver covered. Then he came back on. "Hey Joe, I can make it but I have to wait a few days to see how Anna is feeling. In the mean time, you guys can work on the plan and critique it yourselves. Just be hard on yourselves. Try to look at it from someone else's perspective. Then fax it to me or scan it and e-mail it."

"Sounds like a plan, man."

"Speaking of corny . . ."

"Look who's talking, brother."

* * *

Joe, Nancy and Jeff Steers worked on the plan for hours. They received Dean Gray's apartment complex blueprints that showed all the building positions and the parking lot including the entrances and utility accesses. The complex was bounded on three sides by a brick fence that was about 7 feet high. A grown man in good physical condition could leap the fence but it would be tough. There were some gated entrances for foot traffic to an adjacent shopping center. The complex had a single road access that turned into a large circle road. Parking was segregated; one parking area for each set of three units, each two stories high. The complex was bounded by two smaller apartment complexes, a shopping center and an older neighborhood off West Little Creek Road south of the Navy base. They needed to rent an apartment with a clear view to Dean Gray's mailbox. They needed unmarked cars to help block the single escape route by car from the complex. They needed at least a dozen personnel besides the folks driving the blocking vehicles. As they were going over the high level needs of the plan, Petty Officer Wilson Brush entered the office. The three looked up and stared at the young man. They couldn't believe that he was here all the way from Georgia.

Nancy spoke first. "Petty Officer Brush, what are you doing here? You're supposed to be at King's Bay, keeping an eye out for Tanya."

"She's not down there, Ma'am. We all know that. I came up here to offer my services to help find her and catch her. I can't let any other men get used by her. I heard that she's killed some of her late husbands." He raised his fingers in quotes. "I can't let that happen again. I couldn't live with myself if she did it again and I didn't try to stop her."

"Aren't you supposed to be on duty down there?"

"No, Ma'am. I requested leave. I have 2 weeks off. I am ready to help in any way I can. Please let me do this."

He was begging to be part of the team but Joe didn't want just anyone to drop in and offer themselves unless they brought some skills to the table. "Petty Officer Brush, what can you do to help us? What skills do you have that will aid in this investigation?"

"Well sir, I spent 2 years in Criminal Justice in college before joining the service. I'm also a good investigator. I worked part time for the police department while in school. They said they liked my work. I was able to find a couple of guys who they thought were on the run. They were living a few blocks from the police station and the detectives didn't even know it."

"Do you have a few references so we can check out your story?" Joe was being difficult on purpose to see if he could rattle Wilson but the young sailor was unflappable.

"Yes, sir, I do." He provided four different names of detectives and police captains from the Columbus, Ohio Police Department. Joe was finally impressed.

"Okay, Petty Officer Brush, you can start by reviewing this plan. You met my brother Pat. He's going to review the plan when he gets here in a few days. It has to be flawless by then. Let me give you the details. We think that Julie Lippus, or Tanya as you know her, is going to try to pick up a benefit check for her husband, Dean Gray. He was supposedly killed in action. In reality, he is alive and well on the USS Nimitz in the Atlantic Ocean. He is not yet aware that this is going on and we want to keep it that way for at least the next couple of weeks. The check is supposed to be delivered to the post office box at their apartment here in Norfolk. We want to allow her and any accomplices to get to the mail box unmolested. Once there, we'll apprehend them. There is a twist. The shooter, whoever it is, usually isn't physically with them. It appears that they're in a separate vehicle or positioned in such a way that they can provide cover for Julie and her accomplice. So, Petty Officer Brush, let's do some analyzing." Joe turned to look at the blueprint on the table then stopped. "One last thing; stop calling me 'sir'. My parents were married."

Nancy frowned at Joe at the officer joke. She just shook her head and looked down at the blueprints along with Wilson, Joe, and Jeff. She said,

"Remember, Sergeant McKinney, you are still active duty." She gave Joe a sideways smile.

"Yes, Ma'am. Whatever you say, Ma'am."

Chapter 37

Becky sat on the couch in Bobby's apartment. She was stunned from everything she had been through in the last five minutes. She'd had her clothes ripped from her body and was on the verge of being raped by her boyfriend. She learned that a young man she'd met just days before was her brother. She'd met her real mother for the first time in her life. Her head was spinning.

She looked at Bobby, Ace and Abbie as they continued to argue over each other's role in what Abbie called their new plan. It was all Abbie's plan from what she could gather. Becky looked closer at Abbie. Something about her looked familiar. Seeing her and Bobby argue gave her a feeling of déjà vu. Then it hit her. She was the woman that Bobby was talking with in the parking lot at Tommy's bar at St. Marys, Georgia and the same woman she saw at Dee's Pub here in Norfolk. Abbie had to be following her and Bobby everywhere they went. These were not just chance encounters. As the arguing continued, Becky tried to piece together any logical reason why her own mother would follow her and her boyfriend around the country and never step up and tell her who she really was.

She obviously knew Bobby. From bits and pieces of the argument Becky could tell that they knew each other well and for a long time. She heard Abbie say, 'When we were in Jacksonville, you never knew how to make the most out of a score. You're whole plan was take their stuff and hock it. Now that I taught you how, you want to cut me out.' Becky was listening, but she wasn't sure she was hearing this right. Was her mother Bobby's old girlfriend? Did she work this scam before with Bobby? Is this where Bobby learned how to work this game? Becky was becoming more angry but even more bewildered. She was thinking back on when she met Bobby. She was minding her own business on a beach in the Florida Keys when Bobby approached her. He seemed to know that she was a hustler but why did he pick her? Maybe someone told him. No, it couldn't be. She was a loner, a one woman show back then. Only when she and Bobby teamed up did she confide in anyone else and the person was him. He was the only one, besides her former victims and their recent victims who knew what she was doing for a living.

She wished that those days were still here. It was much easier back then. She ran the show and took the profit. There was no one to tell her what to do or to take her hard earned dollars and keep them from her. Sure Bobby's 'Killed in Action' scam brought in more money but she wasn't sharing in any of the spoils. Bobby was keeping that to himself. If she didn't use her husbands' credit cards she wouldn't get a dime. That was another thing that was pissing her off. Then there was the missing $10,000. She just heard Abbie complain that all she got from Bobby was a lousy $10,000. *That was my money, too. Why did he give it to this woman? This woman . . . who is my mother? How do I even know that's true? And Ace is my brother. Is that really true? I don't even know who my father is.* The questions were coming too fast for her mind to process and the noise from the argument wasn't helping. She wanted to scream and that's just what she did.

"Ahhhhh! All of you shut up! Just shut up!"

The arguing stopped immediately and all three turned and looked at Becky who had tears streaming down her bright red face. Her eyes were darting from Bobby, to Abbie, to Ace then back to Bobby. She was angry and confused. She needed answers and she hardly knew the questions. But she was not going to let the arguing go on until she had control over her emotions.

Bobby took a step towards her to try to comfort her, but Becky held up both hands and yelled "Stop! Just stay away! I don't want any of you near me! Just listen!"

The three of them looked at each other, not knowing what to do or say, so they each stood still and looked back at Becky, waiting for her directions. Becky took three deep breaths then in a calm voice said, "All of you sit down and let me think for a second."

They did.

Becky continued and without blinking looked Abbie directly in the eyes and asked, "How long have you been following us? Wait, that's not the right question to ask first. Are you really my mother? My real, biological mother?"

Abbie shook her head affirming that yes, she was Becky's mother. "Yes baby. I'm your real momma, flesh and blood."

"Who's my father?"

Abbie's hesitation was a bit too long for Becky's liking.

She asked in a more stern voice putting emphasis on each word, "Who is my father? Do you even know?"

"Yes baby. I know but you don't know him and there's no real good reason to tell you his name. You see, he's been gone for so long, before you were even born."

Becky seemed to take the answer in stride. She just shook her head, wiped the tears from her eyes and sniffed snot loudly. Ace ran to the bathroom, brought out a box of tissues, and handed one to Becky. She took it without a word and blew her nose. She then asked Abbie and Bobby how long they'd know each other. Bobby started to answer that they'd just met and Becky cut him off. "Liar! I know you gave her money; at least $10,000. Tell me the truth or I swear I'll cut off your balls!"

Bobby saw the look in her eyes and knew that she wasn't playing. She was pissed off and stressed more than he'd ever seen her before. He wanted to tell her another lie but he wasn't certain he cold trust Abbie to back him up. He started to answer again but Abbie chimed in, "We've known each other for at least ten years. Bobby was in trouble and was being tossed out of the Navy when we met at a bar here in Norfolk. I helped him through his rough times. We teamed up and did a few business deals together."

Becky thought about the time frame. She was in Norfolk ten years ago. It was one of the first times she'd ever pulled a scam. She was only about fifteen years old and running away from a foster home. She learned how to please men and so she was working hard at making her own way. She was making good money because she looked at least eighteen. She was beautiful and knew all the right moves. Young sailors and soldiers fresh out of boot camp appreciated her talents and she soon was able to get her own apartment. That didn't last long though because she needed to be mobile. When guys found out that she was taking more than her pay for her services, they came looking for her. She knew when it was time to move and she never encountered any of the men that she cleaned out. Many of them were too embarrassed to tell their friends or supervisors that they'd been taken by a hooker. Soon she found that hooking wasn't as lucrative as pretending to marry the poor suckers just before they left for sea or a deployment overseas. She would gain their trust through their crotch then clean them out when they left. It was a sweet, lucrative game. Ten years ago she was in Norfolk but then left to go to South Carolina near the submarine base. She spent a year in Summerville, Ladson, North Charleston, and Goose Creek. When she finished her work there, she decided to treat herself to a Florida vacation. No Mickey Mouse for her. She went straight south as far as she could go and ended up in Key West. That's where Bobby approached her and their joint business venture began.

Could it be possible that Abbie and Ace followed her all those years, watching her? How could they have done that without her noticing? Surely they'd have run into each other more than just the bar in Georgia and the one here in Norfolk. How could she not have seen them in North Dakota? Why would they follow her there anyway? Why did Bobby take us up there? The trio was waiting for her next question. It was a question that made Bobby and Abbie uncomfortable.

"So are you two lovers?"

"No." Bobby's answer was immediate and to the point. He wanted to make sure he answered before Abbie had a chance to say anything. But the look on Abbie's face told a different story. She was offended and hurt by his answer. The look on Ace's face was equally out of place. He looked angry that Bobby would disown his mother like that. He knew that they'd had a long relationship that included a lot of sex. He knew because he could hear them going at it through many motel room and trailer walls. At the time he couldn't believe what his mother was doing but over the years he learned to ignore it. Then he was angry when Bobby abandoned them to hook up with Becky. He didn't realize at the time that it was part of Abbie's plan. Now he knew.

Becky knew that Bobby was lying again. She had to know the whole relationship here. If Abbie was her mother and Ace was her brother, who was her father. Was Ace's father also hers or were they just half brother and sister? Abbie said she knew who her father was but that it shouldn't matter to her because he'd been gone for so long. But Abbie had also been gone for just as long. Neither had ever been in her life. They left her alone to be shuffled from one foster home to another. She hated them both for that. They'd forced her into a life of deceit just to survive. It was the only life she knew. But she'd survived on her own until Bobby came into her life, supposedly with a better deal. Now she had to wonder whose deal it really was.

She asked Abbie how long she'd been following her. Abbie replied that it had been too long to remember. She'd been following Becky from state to state since before she was a teenager in foster care. She learned of her whereabouts before she met Bobby. That's what brought her to Norfolk in the first place.

"Why?"

"Why what?" Abbie didn't understand the question.

"Why did you try to find me after all those years? Why didn't you keep me when I was a baby?" As she spoke, Becky's voice became louder, her movements more animated. She was losing control over her emotions again and she was headed for a meltdown. "Why did you let me get passed around like a rag doll, like worn, hand-me-down clothes? I was in homes where I was beaten every day, where the boys raped me and threatened to kill me if I talked! I was pregnant at 13 and forced to abort my own baby because my foster parents would lose money and get in trouble if the case workers found out!" Becky was screaming at Abbie as the tears flowed down her face and dripped on her tank top. She stood and started to pace the living room floor like a trapped animal. She paced for nearly a minute shaking with anger and pent up feelings of hate for her life and the people who put her here. She stopped pacing right in front of Abbie and looked her right in the eyes. "Do you really expect me to love you after all you've put me through?"

In a timid voice, Abbie answered, "No." She paused then continued. "There is nothing that I can tell you that will change anything about yours or my past. You see, I got pregnant when I was raped by . . . . Well, it doesn't matter. The fact remains that when you were born, I hated you. Not you, but what you represented. I was only 15. I was all alone. I couldn't keep you. As bad as it was, you were better off with all your foster families then you'd have been with me. I'd hoped that the adoption agency would place you with a loving family. I had no idea that you'd be put in foster homes." She fell silent again. She was near tears but that was never an option for Abbie. She'd never shed a tear since she was a child. "When I found you, I hoped that we could meet and make a new start."

Becky sarcastically shook her head and said "Right. Just walk in and everything's rosy. Over twenty-five years of pain just goes away. Now all you can talk about is how you're going to whore me out and start your son on the same career path. You're a piece of work."

"Baby, its all I know. It's what I've done all my life; that and stealing. We could make some real money. You've got the skills, baby. Ace is a natural, too. All he needs is some coaching. Between you two we could all be rich. Bobby has some skills with paperwork. I know how to spot good prospects. You know all the right moves. Look, don't answer me right now. Think about it and we can talk tomorrow. I know this has been a shock."

That was an understatement. Becky was exhausted, mentally and physically. She was bruised and burned from her earlier scuffle with Bobby. She still had thoughts racing through her head about the events of the day and questions about her past. Maybe Abbie was right about one thing; she needed time to think. Maybe she could decide what she wanted to do in the morning. Right now she needed a shower and sleep.

"I am going to get cleaned up and go to bed." She looked at Bobby and said with feeling, "Alone." When I get up in the morning, we're all going to talk about this idea. Before we do, Abbie, you and I are going to talk about us. I have questions and I want answers."

"That's fine, baby girl."

"And stop calling me baby girl. I stopped being that a long time ago, if I ever was your baby girl." Becky turned and walked to the bedroom, grabbed her nightgown, and headed to the bathroom to take a shower. When she finished showering, she could hear the three of them arguing about how to carry out their plans. They hadn't listened to a single word she'd said. It was only a matter of time now and Becky would have to make her escape. She hated her mother more now that she knew her than she ever did as a figment of her imagination. Now she had flesh and blood to attach to her hatred. She didn't fall asleep right away as her mind continued to race. She didn't know how long she laid there wide awake but when she finally did sleep, she dreamt about four men taking turns having sex with her. It was straight missionary position sex, nothing fancy or kinky. She didn't really fight but she didn't want to be there. Every time she tried to get up, one of the men pushed her back down and penetrated her again. When she awoke, she was alone in her dark bedroom. She had no idea what time it was but it was before dawn. Becky cried herself back to sleep. When she awoke again, the smell of coffee, bacon, and eggs were evident. She wasn't the least bit hungry.

* * *

"What do you think? Are we ready for a dry run?" Nancy Brown put the question to the team. Joe, Jeff, and now Wilson Brush ran through the plan again in their minds to try and find a hole in the plan. From what they could see, there were none. Then they talked through all the possibilities that they could imagine. Joe was hoping that Pat would be there by now. The apartment layout blueprints were in front of them showing the positions of the teams that would allow Julie Gray and her accomplice entry to the complex but cut off their escape. They had 'X's and 'O's in places denoting possible locations for any vehicles that might be used for the shooter. If they were fired upon, there wouldn't be any surprises. They had an apartment rented that had a clear view from across the parking lot to the Gray's apartment. They also commandeered Gerald Jamison's apartment. A large blood stain was found on the floor in his bedroom. The crime lab determined that his blood was inside the van found at the Holiday Inn Suites. They also found a pen that had his blood on the tip. He wouldn't need his apartment any longer. In Gerald's apartment the team set up listening devices and cameras through the walls. If anyone entered Dean Gray's place, they'd know about it instantly and a recording would be made of every noise from inside. They could clearly hear conversations that we mere whispers. The cameras were so small that they barely looked like specs of dust on the walls but the picture clarity was amazing.

"I really wish Pat were here. He'd spot a dozen holes in this plan without batting an eye." Joe turned away from the group and started to pace, wondering what was keeping Pat. He should have been there by now. He'd said he would be in by this time today and he was usually early. Joe, in typical, serious fashion, went for the phone on his desk. As he put the receiver to his ear, the office door opened and Pat strolled in. He looked around the room at the serious faces.

"Hey, you guys look serious. You need to loosen up or we're never going to catch these characters."

Joe replaced the receiver and walked over to Pat. "You can be such a jackass. What took you so long?"

"I had to do the dishes before I left. The family is finally getting over their colds but it's been a long week." Pat turned to the group and said hello to each in turn, starting with Nancy Brown. He got to Wilson Brush and said, "So, you joining the team here?"

"Yes sir, I mean, Pat. I really need to catch this lady before she hurts more people."

Pat looked Wilson Brush in the eyes and said as serious as he could, "You just make sure it isn't you that she hurts. You can't afford to let her talk you out of doing what you need to do, when you need to do it. A hesitation, a look the wrong way could get you killed. Do you understand?"

"Yes sir." He paused then said, "Before the ship left port Hatch told me to tell you pretty much the same thing. He said, 'You tell Pat and Joe McKinney to mind their training and watch their backs. I don't want to come home to any funerals.' You and Hatch must be friends."

"You could say that. He saved my life and taught me every thing I know about weapons and shooting and staying alive. He was on the 'Bama when I got there and he was there when I left. He just transferred to the Nevada recently."

"He said that this is his last tour. Said he's getting too old for it. He also told me to tell you that he expects a free concert from that other buddy of yours. How in the heck do you know Brian Purcer? He's a rock star."

"It was from a former life. I knew him when he was a mailroom kid loading newspapers for a living. It wasn't all that long ago either. But that's another story." He looked around the room at the team and said, "Let's get a look at this plan."

For the next hour the team tore the plan apart and rebuilt it. Like Joe said, Pat ripped gigantic holes in the plan that the others hadn't thought about. Nancy Brown was impressed. Pat did it in a way that made the others feel good. He built up their confidence that they could cover most any contingency. What started out as a road block and an assault turned out to be a method to peacefully take the subjects into custody without any hassle, if all went right. Pat assured them that it would not go exactly according to plan. They would encounter unexpected obstacles and the subjects would act differently than prescribed by the plan, regardless of how many different scenarios they went through. The big unknown was the shooter. They knew from the previous shootings that Dean's wife and her boyfriend didn't do the shooting. That left at least one unknown assailant from an unknown location. It would be hard to predict the whereabouts and movements of the shooter. One thing they knew was that there had been a dark colored van used at one scene, the one in North Dakota and a van had been found that had GRS or gun shot residue on the passenger side window. Now the van was out of the picture.

There was one good thing about this plan. They had plenty of time to change it if necessary. They'd take a break tonight and look at it again in the morning with fresh eyes. Sometimes that's what it took to see the flaws that you couldn't see in the heat of discussion. After three hours of going over the plan, Pat finally said, "Let's call it a night. You guys have been at it all day and I've been driving all day. We'll hit it right after breakfast. Tonight, get a good night's sleep and don't think about this. Read a good book or listen to some good music. Fresh eyes and clear heads will help us catch these bastards."

Chapter 38

"I'm sorry Mrs. Gray but we were held up in the claims process for a day. We had our computers down and couldn't process any checks at all yesterday. I am looking at your claim right now. It is through the review and has been approved for payout. It should be printed tomorrow and should be in the mail by Friday."

"I've been waiting for this check for a long time," Becky protested. "How long will it take to get from Richmond to Norfolk, can you tell me that?" Becky was good at acting out frustration and playing the part of the grieving widow when she wanted. Normally she just acted indifferent but she needed this check soon so that she, Bobby and their new partners could move on to bigger and better things.

"Ma'am, you can expect to receive it either Saturday during normal delivery or no later than Monday. I wish I could speed it along. I know that you need the money for moving and all, but it really is the best we can do."

Becky sighed loudly into the receiver and said, "Well, I guess if that's the best our government can do for the widows of our fallen men, then I'll just have to wait." She sighed again and hung up.

"Not bad Mr. Hollis. You did well."

"Thanks. She sounds so convincing. The last time I talked to her she sounded like a teenager who'd just won free tickets to a concert. What a difference." Jim Hollis was feeling pretty good. His boss told him that he might get a bonus for saving NatFed a substantial amount of money if the woman was caught and prosecuted. He could use the money, too. His wife and ex-wives were eating him alive. A fat bonus check would be just the ticket to get him ahead of the game, if only for a few weeks.

"Let's get those tapes rewound so we can review them and see if we can pick up any more info." Nancy was barking orders left and right and her team was jumping. They had just a few more days until they had a real shot of getting this woman and her accomplices off the street. If all went well, by Saturday this little tramp would be behind bars awaiting arraignment.

"Mr. Hollis, we need to use your computer for a few minutes. We're going to download the Gray files onto a disc, so can you guide us to the correct files?"

"Sure," Jim Hollis replied. He was real cooperative, especially in front of his boss and several executives who wanted to watch every move that the investigative team made. There was a load of money at stake. If they could stop this woman, they could use the publicity to show what a great steward

NatFed was of its client's money. They were playing every angle. They sure couldn't use Jim Hollis in a commercial but they could get an actor to play the ever diligent agent.

The files were printed out at the nearest printer. As they came off, Nancy and Joe looked at the forms and compared the writing on the .pdf files. There was little doubt that the same person filled out the forms. They must have used the same pen, too. An expert in handwriting analysis would have to confirm it, but Nancy and Joe were confident. If they found the writer of one form, then they found the writer for the others. "What else do we need while we're here?" Joe asked.

"Nothing. We have to make sure the check is marked and of no real value. If they get away, we don't want them to actually cash this check. It has to be written in a way that will ensure they don't get away with another big payday." Nancy looked at Jim Hollis' boss. "How will you make the check out so that they can't cash it? Besides us, what's to stop them if they get away from us?"

"The check has the words VOID printed all over it but you can't see the words until you get it under a black light. Most banks have a series of black lights at teller stations so that they can see these types of markings on bills or checks. When a teller sees those words, they're trained to call in security. Nobody wants to get caught accepting bad checks or counterfeit money. It's bad for your future banking career."

"Okay. I guess that'll work. Hopefully we won't need to worry about that. How big is the envelope?"

Jim Hollis looked puzzled. "What do you mean by that?"

"I mean, what size envelope will be used? Standard #10, a full sized 9" X 11", or some specialty envelope? Is it big enough for a passive tracking device?" Joe was hoping that they could use a little technology to better track this woman and her boyfriend and whoever else might be involved. Some kind of tracking device might give them the edge.

"We do have some larger envelopes but they aren't typically used to deliver claim checks. That might be a give away. Remember, this woman has already received at least one of our checks. If she gets something in any other type of envelope she might be smart enough to suspect something's up. She might get spooked and run."

Joe was rubbing his square chin, feeling the stubble that was in danger of becoming a beard if he didn't shave soon. Being an active duty Marine, he could be reprimanded for being out of uniform. He was staring off in the distance, deep in thought when he remembered a microscopic device that friends of his said could be used to track anything. The device was like a black dot the size of one of those circles that you fill in when taking standardized tests. Joe always hated those things. He had to work at studying. School work was always harder for him than it was for Pat. But, with help from Pat and his other brother, Mike, he managed to make it through high school with decent grades. He shook his head. His mind was wandering as the fatigue and lack of sleep wore on his mind and body. Joe spoke to Nancy, "Do we have any connections with the satellite folks. If we could get them to agree to let us use one of their miniature tracking devices it would make this a whole lot less nerve wracking. We could remain out of site and track the check without putting anyone in harms way. We could pick the best time and place for the apprehension if we knew their movements. What do you think?"

Joe's idea sounded good, at least on paper. Nancy said that she'd speak to a friend of hers that was in the SatCom unit at the Pentagon. It was worth a shot. They could only say yes or no.

"Alright, when is the check hitting their mailbox?"

Jeff Steers said, "We spoke to the Post Master. He has his regular guy on that route briefed that there will be a special delivery on Saturday morning. He doesn't know any details. He was only told that he is to deliver the mail as he normally would but that he shouldn't stop for lunch anywhere in the vicinity of the Colony Arms Apartments. He was also told not to speak of the conversation to anyone. He's a pro but he's nearing retirement. He won't do anything to jeopardize that."

"Alright. We have one more chance to go over the plan and the contingencies. Be at the office at 0700 hours tomorrow. We'll have a complete walkdown. We'll also go over to the apartments in groups of two and three. Wear civilian clothes that will look natural at an apartment complex. We have to be inconspicuous. We also have to be thorough. We can't afford to miss anything so if you have anything on your mind between now and tomorrow before we finish, you bring it up. There are no stupid questions except the one left unasked. Are we clear on that?"

They all answered in unison, "Yes ma'am."

* * *

Pat and Joe sat in a booth at a pub in Chesapeake. It was a typical bar that held about 150 people max. Joe and Pat were at a table to the right of the bar that was in the center of the main room. A back room to the left of the bar had a pool table, dart board, half a dozen arcade games, and a foosball table. It was only about 10:00 in the evening so the crowd was still a little thin, about fifty people, mostly in their early twenties. Pat and Joe felt like they were parents spying on their kids. But there were only one or two that looked like they were in the military. They wanted to go to a bar away from the base. It made Pat nervous being near all those sailors and their Navy talk. He disliked the Navy when he was in and he disliked the Navy now. The only good thing about the Navy for Pat was that he got the training he needed and he met his good friend William 'Hatch' Hatcher from Moniac, Georgia.

Hatch was a bit of a paramilitary freak. He was in the Navy on a Trident Submarine but he trained during the off crew with a g.oup that could very easily be on a number of government watch lists for anti-government activity. He swore that he was with the group solely for the exercise and weapons contacts. Pat almost believed him. William Hatcher owned a section of land off the southern edge of the Okefenokee National Wildlife Refuge, or "the swamp" as Hatch called it. He inherited the land from his parents when they were brutally murdered. His younger sister was also killed in the attack. The murders were never officially solved but rumor was that Hatch had tracked down the murderers, two redneck brothers from a rural part of Georgia near Folkston. The brothers had bled to death after being bound, gagged, shot in the genitals. Pat was wondering if Hatch was out to sea or if he was home at the swamp. He was rubbing the scar on his chin when Joe smacked his hand away from his face. "Cut that out, man. You're going to rub another hole in your face."

"Sorry." Pat rubbed his wrist where Joe had slapped him. *Punk.* "I was thinking about Hatch. I wonder what weirdo military crusade he's on now? Wilson said he was still on the ship but they're due back in port pretty soon."

Joe said, "We could sure use him and his skills right now. If there's a shooter out there, Hatch can spot them a mile away. The dude's got a sixth sense or something." Joe looked at Pat and said, "Why don't we see if he'd like to join us in this little venture, if he's in port that is."

"That's exactly what I was thinking. I'll call his place before we leave here tonight. Wilson said he learned a lot from Hatch, both Navy stuff and how to protect yourself. He said Hatch has a regular following on the ship. Guys are spending time with him learning about weapons and tracking and I'm sure a few things that the Navy doesn't want to know about. What a character." Pat shook his head thinking about Hatch's ability to appear then disappear in a flash. "He was there when we needed him, that's for sure."

"Let's have another beer then you can try and call him. Maybe they made port already. Hatch swore he was retiring from the canoe club last time we talked with him. Every patrol is his last. Do you know why he keeps going back? He could quit anytime, right?"

Pat thought about that. He wasn't sure what Hatch's commitment to the Navy was but he had to sign on for at least an additional two years beyond his original enlistment if he decided to stay in. He couldn't remember Hatch's potential discharge date. "I guess we'll know when we talk with him."

They flagged down a waitress and ordered another round. Joe said, "I've got to call Lisa while you try Hatch. She's looking forward to the concert next week. That's a week from Saturday Night you know. We have to wrap this apprehension up early or we'll miss Brian's concert."

"Yea, I know. What a bummer that would be. Diane is looking forward to it. She hasn't had a chance to get out in a long time. It was

290 P. J. Grondin

really nice of Mom to offer to watch the kids. She'd be real reluctant to leave them with anyone else."

"It'll work out fine. We grab these folks, get them locked up, and we're good to go to the show. Sound like a plan?"

"Sounds too easy."

"Yea, it does. Nothing ever goes that smooth."

Their beers came and they each took a long pull on their long necks. They both put their bottles on the table when Pat stared past Joe. He turned pale. The look on his face was as if he saw a ghost. Joe noticed and was about to turn around and look when Pat said "Don't move a muscle. You won't believe who just walked in."

Pat quietly told Joe that standing across the bar from them was Julie Lippus. She was facing away from them and apparently hadn't seen them. She was talking with a tall, skinny, pale faced guy with straight black hair. Without a word they both turned away from the couple.

Pat said, "Okay, what do we do now? We can't risk trying to take them down here and now."

"You got that right. I have to get out of sight. He's seen me close up. If he sees me, they're gonna run. We can't afford that. You need to keep your head down, too. We look enough alike that they might spot you and think that you're me. Then they'll see me and freak out."

Pat lowered his eyes to his beer so that the couple didn't have a good look at his face. They were both silent for a few minutes, then Pat said, "Let's head for the other side of the bar one at a time. I'll go first. We just have to make sure that we look away from them and don't show our faces. Once we get to the other side of the bar we should be able to watch them from a distance. Maybe we should just get out of here and call Nancy. She may want to try a pickup here."

Joe shook his head. "There's too many things left to chance if we try a takedown now. We have a plan, let's stick to it." They both looked casually around the bar. Julie Lippus and her friend had moved to the back of the bar and found some open seats near the pool tables. "Now's our chance, let's move."

Pat and Joe headed for the opposite side of the bar from Julie and her companion. They left their nearly full beers and headed for the door. Joe was shaking his head. "That was too close. Should we try to wait them out and follow them to wherever they're staying? If we could find out where they're staying we'd have more options than trying the take down at the apartment."

Pat thought for a second then said, "Maybe we'll have enough time to get some help with that. Let's make the calls. I'll see if my cell phone has coverage from the car. If not we can call from the drug store across the lot. I think we have time. I don't think they saw us."

* * *

"Did you see those two guys sitting at the table behind the bar? One of them was the guy I stunned at Dee's Pub."

Becky looked alarmed as they moved back into the game room of the bar. Her back was to the table where Bobby saw the two guys who looked almost like twins. The one he had stunned was bigger and he had his back to them so maybe Bobby and Becky were safe. He'd never seen the other guy so maybe he didn't know Bobby's face. He chose Chesapeake and this bar to get away from the base. He figured that they wouldn't be followed or spotted this far away from Dean Gray's apartment. Worse, Abbie and Ace were going to show up any minute and they didn't have a way to warn them off. Even if they tried, Abbie would be suspicious that he and Becky were trying to make a run for it and get away with all the money for themselves. This was to be their first planning session and a toast to their new partnership. It was a partnership that Becky and Bobby agreed to reluctantly. They had little choice because Abbie threatened to set them up and send Bobby to prison for a long time.

Becky remained outwardly calm but the butterflies were doing a number on her insides. She didn't want to go to prison. She had no desire to be some big woman's bitch. As small as she was, that was likely. She could hold her own in most situations. She'd learned how to protect herself during all those years in foster care but she knew she'd be no match for a hardened, big-mama lesbian in an enclosed cell. She looked at Bobby as he thought of their options. Bobby looked anxious. He grabbed her arm, a little too hard and moved her to an open table against one wall of the game room. A barmaid with Asian features approached the table and Bobby said, "Can you leave us alone?"

The barmaid turned and walked away but not before turning back and saying, "Fuck you very much, asshole." Becky watched her and noticed that she said something to the bartender, who in turn called a big, burly guy over and looked in their direction. Becky knew the conversation went something like 'Keep an eye on that asshole in the black shirt and pants. He's trouble.' Becky knew that whatever the conversation, Bobby was already bringing unneeded attention to the two of them. Whatever they were going to do, they needed to do it fast.

"Bobby, let's get out of here. We can swing by the apartment and grab the money. We'll leave before Ace and Abbie get here and get out of town. We don't need the check from Dean; we have enough money to last a long time. Now's our chance to . . ."

Bobby cut her off.

"Can you shut up? I can't think while you're rambling on." The terse rebuke left Becky stunned. She was on the verge of getting up and walking out but she kept her seat and tried to keep her emotions under control. Someone had to maintain control in this situation and it wasn't likely to be Bobby. The last thing they needed right now was for Bobby to make a spectacle of himself but that was probably going to happen if they stayed in the bar much longer. A couple of the guys around the pool table heard Bobby snap at Becky and one was staring directly at him. If Becky didn't get him out of there, she could see it in this guy's eyes that a fight was imminent. Bobby could never back down from a fight, especially when it came to Becky.

She could never figure Bobby out. He would help set her up with guys to extort money from them, knowing that she had to screw their brains out. He would get so jealous that he would end up calling her a whore and abusing her for his own pleasure. Then he would lose his mind in a fit of anger if another man would approach her. Becky figured he was going insane and that was another reason she had to get away.

Becky stood. "I have to use the bathroom."

"We don't have time. We have to get out of here."

The guy who was staring at Bobby walked over and said, "The lady wants to use the little girl's room, buddy. Why don't you just relax?"

The guy was half a head taller than Bobby but that didn't bother him. He looked at the guy who had a pool cue in his hands and said, "Why don't you just play your game and mind your own fucking business? My girl and I are having a private conversation."

"It sounded pretty public to me." As the two exchanged words, the crowd started to quiet down to listen to the exchange. Becky knew that they had to get out of there now so she stepped in between the two and looked up at Bobby. "Sweetie, we don't have time for this. Remember, we have more important things to do right now."

Bobby didn't even look at Becky. He continued to stare at the guy with the pool cue. He said to Becky, "Yea. Okay." Becky grabbed him by the arm and tried to turn him towards the door.

By this time, the big guy that had been talking with the bartender came into the room. He was a much larger than both Bobby and the pool player. "Is there a problem here?"

Becky immediately said, "No. We were just leaving, right Bobby?"

Bobby didn't even look away from his adversary. Becky was pulling him away now. He was moving towards the outer room but slowly. He continued to stare, then turned and started walking towards the main entrance to the bar. The crowd in the game room started to cheer and fling names in Bobby's direction but the bouncer yelled, "Knock it off. Let that loser get out of here. We don't want any trouble tonight."

Just inside the front door of the bar, Becky jerked on Bobby's arm. "Get your head out of your ass. The two guys are gone. That means they might be waiting for us outside. Why do you do this shit all the freaking time?'

Bobby's head was still in the bar trying to pick a fight. Finally he looked down at Becky and said, "Let's get out of here. You have a plan?"

"Yes. We head to the apartment, grab the cash and head for anywhere but here. We leave Abbie and Ace behind. I don't want anything to do with them. I don't care if she is my blood mother or that he's my half brother. They can both go to hell. Let's go."

They walked out of the bar into the dimly lit parking lot towards their car. Before Bobby could unlock the door, Abbie and Ace pulled up next to them. Becky's look of exasperation was shielded by the darkness of the parking lot but Bobby started to get worked up again. Abbie rolled down the driver's side window and barked at Bobby in an accusatory tone, "Where are you two going?"

Bobby barked back, "We're getting out of here. The guys who've been watching us were in there. We have to get out of here and now. Where in the fuck have you two been anyway? I thought we were supposed to meet here half an hour ago."

Ace was tired of the way Bobby talked to his mom. He got out of the passenger side of the car and marched right up to Bobby. He got right in his face. "Don't ever talk to Mom that way again." He raised his index finger and pointed it right in Bobby's face and said, "If you do, I'm gonna kill you. Understand?"

Bobby looked back at Ace. They were nearly the same height and build, but Ace was younger by ten years. Bobby had a lot of experience fighting dirty so this didn't appear to be much of a threat, as long as Ace wasn't holding a gun, that is. He was more afraid of Abbie. He figured that Abbie was doing the shooting so he knew he could handle Ace.

Abbie yelled, "Ace, get back in the car. We don't have time for this and we're drawing too much attention."

"You, too, Bobby." Becky was at her limit. If Bobby didn't stop now, she was going to walk away from them all. There was too much at stake for this macho display of testosterone. "We just got out of the bar and you're making a scene in the parking lot. We have to get out of here before someone sees us."

It took a minute or so, but the two men backed away from each other.

Abbie asked, "Where are we going to meet now?"

Becky said, "I don't know. First we have to get out of here. Hell, the police are probably getting ready to surround us here in the parking lot right now." Becky Thought for a minute. How could she send Abbie and Ace on a wild goose chase and give her and Bobby a chance to get away? She said, "Look, we have to split up to throw these guys off our tails. It'll be harder for them to track us if we head in different directions. You and Ace head to Smithfield. Get a room at the Econolodge. Bobby and I will meet you there in an hour. We'll go by the apartment and get some clothes, enough for a few days. We have to let things settle down here." Becky gave Abbie directions to Smithfield. She could tell Abbie didn't trust her and she had good reason. "Look, we'll be there. We can't afford to not be there."

Bobby had calmed down some and said, "Look Abbie, if you want this to work, do what Becky says. We'll be there."

Abbie didn't say a word. She rolled up the car window and drove away.

Bobby asked, "So which way are we headed?"

"We're heading west, but on the north side of the river. Get in. I'm driving from now on."

* * *

Pat's cell phone didn't have service so they drove Pat's rental car to a parking spot by the pay phones that still had a clear view of the front door of the bar. Pat dialed Nancy's private line. The answering machine picked up and went through Nancy's very business-like greeting, then beeped. Pat left a message that he'd try to call again and that he and Joe needed assistance for some surveillance. He kept the phone to his ear as long as he could in case she was there to pick up if she recognized his voice, but the machine cut off and the dial tone sounded. He hung up the receiver.

Joe was on a phone next to Pat. He was talking to Lisa in low tones. He sounded like a high school sophomore after his first date. *What a lucky bastard.* Pat turned away to give his brother some privacy and to get a better view of the front door of the bar. Several people were coming and going. About five minutes later, Joe hung up and turned to Pat with a wide grin. "She's coming up tomorrow. I can't wait to see her."

"I can tell." Pat watched as the front door to the bar opened again and Julie Lippus Gray and her friend exited and headed towards the parking lot. They stopped at a black BMW. As they started to get into the car a Mustang pulled up. A window in the car rolled down and a woman's voice could be heard over the traffic from the nearby road. Pat and Joe couldn't hear the conversation but it appeared to be getting heated. A passenger got out of the car. It was a young man with short blond hair. He was walking aggressively towards the pale skinny guy but paleface wasn't backing down. They were face to face now but no punches were thrown. Julie was shouting for them to stop. The woman in the car yelled something as well. After about a minute of the two doing little more than staring each other down, the young man got back in the car and after another minute the car sped off.

Pat and Joe watched as Julie got into the driver's side of the Beamer and Bobby got in the passenger side. They sat for a minute longer then headed off in the opposite direction. Pat and Joe jumped in the rental and tried to follow Julie's car. They got caught at several lights and lost track of the Beamer. They thought that they picked it up again about half a mile north on Wilson Road, but when they pulled up near the car that they were now following, they noticed that a young guy in a business suit was driving and he had no passengers. They'd lost Julie Lippus in traffic. Pat slammed his hand on the steering wheel. Joe pounded the dash. They looked at each other. All they could do was shake their heads at the lost opportunity.

* * *

"Why are we turning around?" Ace seemed bewildered. His mom had circled the block and was heading back into Norfolk.

"Oh my naïve young man, you know so little of women and of the world. Becky and Bobby have no intention of meeting us at Smithfield. They're going back to their apartment, getting the money, and heading for anywhere but here."

Ace looked at his mother, his faced scrunched into a look that screamed I don't understand. He didn't understand why Becky hadn't welcomed her mother into her life. Why would she want to continue to live without a family? And why would she stay with that loser, Bobby? He was an abusive bastard. He treated her like a doormat and she didn't deserve that. She'd be better off with family. She could teach him lots of things about what women like. He wanted to learn. He knew he could run Becky's scam on female soldiers and sailors. It was in their blood. If Becky could do it he could do it, too.

"Listen, son. You need to steer clear of Bobby. You may be his height and weight and stronger than him, but he fights dirty. He always has and he always will. If you have to confront him in a serious way, you use this." Abbie picked up the Glock 9mm that was on the car seat between them. "And if you have to pick this up against Bobby, you pull the trigger. He's a devious bastard. He treated me as bad as he's treating your sister and he won't cut you any slack. One day soon we'll get rid of him and it'll be down to a three way split. We're gonna be rich, son, don't you worry."

Ace looked down at the gun that his mother had laid back on the car seat. He smiled as he thought about pointing the gun directly between Bobby's eyes. He enjoyed the look on Bobby's face that only he could see. It was so vivid in his mind that he could almost smell his fear. He enjoyed pulling the trigger and watching as Bobby's brains and skull fragments sprayed all over the room behind him. He replayed that part in slow motion in his mind several times. It was almost like when he shot Kevin Reardon.

Chapter 39

They hadn't spoken a word since they got on Interstate 64 heading west. They took the bypass north of Richmond and were nearing the Interchange with Interstate 81 when Bobby asked where they were headed. Becky still was in no mood to talk but she said, "Tennessee."

"If we're headed to Tennessee, why are we headed north? Tennessee is southwest of here. We should have taken 95 to 40. We'd be lots closer to Tennessee by now." Bobby looked at Becky and waited for a response. She just kept watching the road and driving. She was in no mood for another of Bobby's *I know everything* speeches. She was in charge now and she was going to stay in charge. When they got to the apartment back in Norfolk, he tried to call the shots. She just kept moving, packing what she needed and making sure he got all the money together. When they got into the car, she made sure she had the leather computer bag that held the money. When he tried to get into the driver's seat, she simply said, *I'm driving.* He tried to argue but to no avail. He reluctantly moved to the passenger seat. As Becky left their apartment, she doubled back several times to make sure they were not being followed. She didn't really know what she was looking for but there were no cars or other vehicles on their tail. Bobby didn't look as if he were interested in helping to look for a tail. He just pouted all the way across Virginia. When they pulled onto the entry ramp for Interstate 81 heading south, Becky finally spoke. "I took this route because it's pretty much all open road. If we were being followed it would be pretty easy to spot someone. I've been speeding up and slowing down and watching to see if any other cars did the same thing. We have to stop for gas pretty soon and we need to get some sleep."

Bobby yawned as if on cue. "You're right. Let's find a place to stop."

They pulled off the interstate at Lexington and found a room at the Colonial Inn. They paid cash and slept until just before noon. Then they showered, dressed, got a sandwich to go from the restaurant by the hotel and filled up with gas. There were no cars following so they headed back out onto Interstate 81 again. Becky still had not told Bobby their ultimate destination so he just sat back and let her play her power game. He knew that he still had ultimate control over her and the money. She always came back to him, even after major blowups like the other night when she raced out of their apartment complex with their car. He had her and he would always have her.

They drove for hours until they were on the western edge of Knoxville, Tennessee. Becky got off the interstate at exit 380 and pulled into the parking lot of a Holiday Inn near the West Town Mall. It was in the heart of a sprawling shopping area. Becky turned to Bobby and said, "For the next week we are going to relax. We're going to do nothing but eat, shop, sleep, and swim at the hotel pool. We have a big paycheck waiting for us back in Norfolk but we're in no hurry to get it. We may decide to not get it at all, depending on what happens after our little vacation. We may decide it isn't worth the risk to go back. You know Abbie and Ace are going to be staking the place out. If they're doing it then someone else could do it, too. Somebody knows too much, Bobby. I'm scared and I'm not going to prison. Is that clear?"

Bobby let her vent. He agreed with most everything she said. Maybe it was time to cool it for a while. They had plenty of money. They were safe and far away from where everyone expected them to be. They could relax. If they wanted, they could take on new identities and never go back. But the money would only last so long and they couldn't live out of hotel rooms for long either. The money would be gone in a flash. But they had time to think things through and decide their next move. There were two pay checks waiting for them, one in Norfolk, Virginia and one in Saint Mary, Georgia by the sub base. If things got tight, it wasn't a real long trip to Georgia. Nobody was expecting them to go there. Maybe that was their best move. He'd talk with Becky when she was more relaxed. *A little shopping will do her wonders. Maybe I can get her a sexy night gown. She always looks so hot when she dresses like that.*

"I won't let you go to prison. You know I love you." He said it but even as he did, he knew it wasn't true. He loved what she could do for him and he was jealous when she did it for others. "Well, let's get that room. What do you say we start out with some hot sex?"

"You're going to have to wait on that, lover boy. I started my period yesterday and I'm not in the mood. We'll see in a couple of days."

Bobby cursed his luck. He would still buy that sexy night gown. It would give him something to look forward to.

* * *

Ace loved two things more than anything else. One was guns. He loved to shoot guns and he loved to learn about different guns. He was impressed with different statistics on the strengths and weaknesses of guns. He read reports on gun manufacturers and their quality control and which guns were least likely to jam in a given situation. He was particularly interested in handguns and the types of ammunition used for handguns. He read reports on which bullets produced the most damage to the human body and which were least likely to be available to the average citizen. He was also aware of the laws surrounding the possession of certain types of ammunition and the penalties associated with possession.

Ace's other love was for electronics. It was beyond computers, radios, or disc players. Ace loved miniature monitoring devices. He loved Radio Frequency Identification Devices or RFIDs. The greatest thing about RFIDs was that they could be so small they could be hidden in just about anything. A person could have one in their pocket and not even know it. For a person with Ace's skills it was child's play to plant an RFID on a car. Bobby and Becky had no idea that they were being followed. Ace simply monitored the hand-held computer with the GPS software to keep tabs on the BMW. When Bobby and Becky stopped for the night at the Colonial Inn, Ace and Abbie stopped at the motel a few miles down the road. It was too easy.

Now they were in Knoxville, Tennessee. Abbie was familiar with Knoxville. She spent a year there near the campus, making a living on her back at the expense of wealthy parents of some Tennessee Volunteer male students. Knoxville had been good to her until she headed to Norfolk. She was curious why Becky would come here but that question could wait. They were here and she felt good that her Becky was safe. After all, that's what family did; made sure each other was safe. She was sorry that she couldn't have provided that for her sooner, but she was here now and she would do everything she could to make sure she fulfilled that responsibility.

* * *

The Surveillance and Apprehension Team had been in position starting early that Thursday morning waiting for the postman to deliver the $100,000 check to Dean Gray's apartment. They expected that Julie Lippus and her companion would be there within minutes to open the mailbox and grab the check. They waited for hours and nothing happened. They waited well into the night and they were starting to get concerned that the check would sit and not be retrieved. At 9:55 PM, or 2155 hours, a young woman pulled into one of the open parking spots and walked towards the apartment building. She was blond, slender with a good build and was a close fit with Julie Lippus' description. Nancy asked the team in the apartment if they had a good view of her face. The team replied back that they did not. The lighting in the vestibule area of the apartment building wasn't as good as it should have been. One of the lights that normally illuminated the area had blown as the lights clicked on for the evening.

Over the radio, Nancy Brown heard a report from the team inside the apartment across from Dean Gray's apartment. "Captain, this woman is not, I repeat not retrieving her mail. She walked past the mailboxes without even looking at them. And she is heading to apartment one-Charlie, say again one-Charlie. Subject is not Julie Lippus, Ma'am."

A collective sigh was let out by the team. It was a sigh of disappointment versus a sigh of relief. The team had hoped to have this wrapped up by now but that was not to be. Nancy was ready to turn the operation off and leave a skeleton crew in the apartment for surveillance.

"Okay, ladies and gentleman.   We're moving on to minimum coverage. The first team scheduled to take the watch, take your posts. Check in with me via phone every 2 hours regardless of the time. I want to know if a fly moves around this apartment tonight.   Squelch to acknowledge."

Six clicks sounded over the radio indicating that all stations acknowledged the change in plans. Nancy turned to Joe and Pat with a disappointed look, shaking her head. "Where did we go wrong this time?"

Pat offered, "I don't think we did anything wrong. It's possible that they saw Joe and me at the bar the other night and got spooked. If we'd have known that, we would have tried harder to follow them but we didn't."

Joe was also thinking hard about what could have gone wrong. "I don't know. Maybe they just aren't in a hurry to grab this check. They still might have a lot of cash from their last job and they aren't in as much of a hurry as they appeared to be. Do we still have a team in Georgia?"

"Yes," Nancy replied. "But they're not seeing anybody approach the mailbox down there. Not like we expect to since that check isn't due to be delivered until next week. Maybe we're going about this all wrong. Should we regroup and take a different approach?"

Pat considered this for a moment. He rubbed his scar as he thought. Finally he said, "I don't think there's anything wrong with our plan. I think we should just sit tight for now. Maybe we'll catch a break. For now, let's make sure the team gets a good night rest. I won't be able to sleep much. I'll be tossing this around in my head all night."

Joe and Nancy both agreed that neither of them would sleep much either. Nancy's radio crackled to life. Captain, you have a call at the office that you should take. I cannot give you details over this line, Ma'am."

"Roger, out." Nancy looked at Joe and Pat again. "I wonder what this is about."

"Only one way to find out." Pat pointed towards the road. "Let's get back to the office."

The call was from the North American Bank Card Company. They'd been requested to have a special watch for suspicious charge activity on Dean Gray's credit cards. They had several hits during the day from several stores in Knoxville, Tennessee. Of particular interest was a Target store. The clerk was contacted and described a young woman with blond hair and a male companion, pale skin and jet black hair. The credit card company's investigator recorded his phone interview with the clerk.   The clerk remembered the couple because she was so nice and her boyfriend was a rude bastard. She wondered why such a nice lady would be hooked up with such a freak. The investigator played the interview for Nancy, Joe, and Pat.

Investigator: What did the pale man say to the woman?

Clerk: He said, *Becky, why are you using a credit card. We should pay cash.* He seemed real nervous that she was using a credit card.

Investigator: Are you sure he said 'Becky'?

Clerk: Yes, absolutely.

Investigator: Did he say anything else?

Clerk: He did but he turned his head so I couldn't hear him. He was getting pretty red in the face, like he was mad or something.

Investigator: How did you know the card was being monitored?

Clerk: It came up on my screen. When the warning came up that this card should be reported without confiscation, I almost blew it. I've never seen that warning before. I almost said that their card had been turned down, but then I read the whole message. It said to process the card then report it to my manager once the transaction was completed. I did exactly what the message said.

Investigator: Miss Tanzy, you did just fine. We'll call you if we have any more questions.

"That's it. The woman we know as Julie Lippus and Tanya Brush and others has a name; maybe a real name this time. Becky. Short for Rebecca?" Nancy looked at Joe.

"Probably. Remember at Dee's Pub, the woman I talked to said her name was Becky Lippert. Maybe that's her real name. We should try to run that down."

Nancy continued. "The investigator also said that they have the store video. He was transmitting it to our video communications boys at the Norfolk Naval Station. From there they're going to convert it to an .mpg file and e-mail it to my Laptop computer. We should have it in about three hours. Isn't technology grand?"

Pat said, "Wow. A few years ago, this would have taken days. What will they think of next, tracking cars and people on a mini computer?"

Joe looked at his brother as if he'd just fallen from outer space. "What planet are you on? We have that stuff now. I'm surprised that it's going to take that long."

When they received the film clips from the store security cameras, both Joe and Pat were certain that the woman was Julie Lippus, and Tanya Brush and Laurie Sharp and Becky Lippert, and maybe others. Wilson Brush was near tears when he viewed the video but bucked up after a few seconds. All he wanted was a chance to talk with her and find out why she'd screwed him over, but first he wanted to make sure she was captured and put behind bars where he was sure she belonged.

"Okay, now that we know where they are what are we going to do about it? Are we heading to Tennessee?" Wilson Brush's question made the collective wheels in the room grind away. Nobody had the answer right away. It was a good question. Do you uproot the entire team and head for Knoxville? Do you break down the team even further and send a small group to Tennessee and leave the rest behind? Or do you keep the team in Norfolk and wait it out until news drives you to a new place?

Pat seemed ready to offer his opinion then held back. Nancy saw him waiver and walked over to him, rolling her hands as if to say, let's have it. Pat finally spoke up. "These two seem to be pretty mobile. Whenever we think we have a handle on where they are, by the time we catch up with them, they've moved on. If we look at the map that Dean Gray's step mom provided, you'll see that they travel to a location, stay only long enough to take care of business then move on or move back to a previous location. In my opinion, I think we stay put in Norfolk and let them come to us. We know that they have a big check sitting in a mailbox at Dean Gray's apartment. We also know that they will have another big check sitting at Wilson's mailbox in St. Mary, Georgia. If we keep chasing them, the team will be spread so thin it'll be a miracle if we catch them." Heads nodded agreement all around the room. "We have a plan in place, let's stick to it."

Joe looked at Nancy and said, "What about getting some FBI support for surveillance at Wilson's apartment? Would they go for it?"

"We can ask. I'll make the call."

Nancy looked around the room at Joe, Wilson, Jeff Steers, and a number of others on the surveillance team. All heads were nodding approval. "Alright. We have what appears to be a consensus. We stay in Norfolk and let them come to us. We maintain minimum coverage until we have confirmation that they're coming this way and then we beef up the coverage and execute the apprehension plan. This is going to take lots of patience, folks. We'll keep the credit card monitoring going. That way if they leave Tennessee and head somewhere, we'll know it."

Joe and Pat walked out of the briefing room together. "I have to call Diane. I think her and Lisa are going to ride up together tomorrow. That will give us a few days to do some tourist type stuff before the concert Saturday. I just hope that the takedown doesn't interfere with Brian's concert. That would totally suck."

"Yes it would," Joe replied. "Lisa and I have some catching up to do. Man, I miss her."

"Where are you staying while she's here?"

"I don't know for sure. Brian's band is staying over night at the Courtyard. Lisa and I will probably stay there, too. It's pretty convenient to the arena. Plus we don't plan to get out much." Joe smiled.

"Oh man. I don't want to hear any details, alright?"

"Okay. Look I'm heading back to the room. I'm calling Lisa to get the last minute details on their trip up then I'm hitting the hay. Do you want to meet for breakfast before we go on duty tomorrow?"

"Sure. Let's meet at the Cracker Barrel then we can head over to the complex and relieve the night shift guys."

"Sounds like a plan, brother. See you then."

Pat headed back to his hotel room and called Diane. They talked for over an hour about their kids, the case, the concert, her and Lisa's trip up,

Pat's mom and how much they missed each other. Before they hung up Diane said, "I'll see you tomorrow. I miss you so save your strength."

"You know I will, Babe. I love you. Say good night to the kids for me."

They disconnected. There was a knock at Pat's door. It was William Hatcher.

"So, you just going to stand there with your jaw on the floor or can I come in?"

"As long as you leave that Navy smell outside, come on in."

For the next hour, William Hatcher and Pat caught up on about five months of history. Hatch hit on one subject that Pat didn't really want to discuss but it had apparently been on Hatch's mind.

"You know, Pat, I've never told anyone but you about my family and those two bastards that killed them. You're the only one who knows. At one time, I thought about turning myself in but what good would it do? My family's gone. Those guys took them from me. I'm not throwing my life away because the police and the courts couldn't do what needed to be done."

Pat didn't know where Hatch was going with this information. But he figured he'd get to the punch-line sooner or later. "Hatch, I've already had that one-on-one with God. What I did had to be done. There's no turning back the pages. I'm resigned to the possibility that I may end up in hell over this but hey, I'll be shaking hands with all my friends." He tried to smile but Hatch's gaze was steady.

Finally Hatch said, "I was there the night you pulled the trigger. I was trying to get myself into position to do it. By the time I put the van in gear, I saw the muzzle flash and knew that you'd already started taking care of business. I knew I had to work fast to get ahead of you."

Hatch had done exactly that. A plan the McKinney brothers had put in place to get revenge on their former friends took off and the McKinney's didn't even raise a finger. Not after Pat took the first step that is. But that was all in the past now. The door was closed on that chapter in Joe and Pat's life. If it ever came to light, hell would be the least of his worries.

"So, how are you going to help us now, Mr. Hatcher?"

"Well I'll tell you what. I like Tennessee. So with your permission, I'll head over to Knoxville and do a little snoopin' around. If I find anything I'll call you and let you know what's up. Will that work for you?"

Pat didn't give it a moment's thought. "That will work just fine."

The two shook hands and did a half-assed man-hug. It was awkward and they both chuckled about it.

After Hatch left, Pat went to the night stand drawer and picked up the Gideon's Bible. He opened the Good Book to the New Testament, Luke, Chapter 11, verses 9 and 10. He read, *And I tell you ask and you will receive; seek and you shall find; knock and the door will be opened unto you. For everyone who asks, receives; and the one who seeks, finds; and the one who knocks, the door will be opened.* Pat wished his faith were strong enough to believe. It was written in the Bible, so it must be true. But it also says, *Thou shall not kill.* So which line wins; the commandment or the verse? Pat knew he had a lot more praying to do. He planned to do a lot of asking, seeking and knocking. He didn't like his chances but the Bible says, "With God, all things are possible."

Pat stood and went to the mini-bar. He needed a beer.

* * *

Becky Lippert held the cell phone and cleared her throat as she dialed the office of NatFed Life Insurance Company. She was now Tanya Brush, grieving widow of the late submariner Wilson Brush. She was trying her best to sound distraught. After all, the insurance company was taking their time processing her claim and she needed that money desperately. How could they in good conscience keep that money from her?

"Nat Fed Life Insurance Company. How may I direct your call?"

At least you talk with a real person when you call. In a whimpering voice with a southern accent Becky said, "Yes, I'd like to speak with Mr. James Hollis, please."

"Your name please?"

"Mrs. Tanya Brush."

"One moment and I'll connect you, Mrs. Brush."

After what seemed like five minutes but what was actually two, a voice came on, "Hello Mrs. Brush. This is Jim Hollis. What can I do for you?"

"Mr. Hollis, last time we spoke you said that you were processing my check. I still haven't received it." She stopped to blow her nose as if she were crying. "Is there some problem? I'm getting desperate here."

"Mrs. Brush, let me pull up your file." There were several minutes of silence on the line while Jim Hollis was supposedly looking for the file. In reality, the agents in Mr. Hollis' cubicle were franticly trying to trace the call. Meanwhile Becky was trying to keep her sad demeanor for when he got back on the phone. She noticed Bobby shifting in his seat. He looked at her as if to say, '*What's taking so long?*' Finally Jim Hollis came back on the line and said, "Mrs. Brush, there was a mix up with your paperwork. It was supposed to go to processing yesterday but the file ended up back in the claims department by mistake. We're very sorry for the delay. I promise you the check will be in the mail by tomorrow at noon. You should receive it at your apartment in Georgia by Monday's delivery, Tuesday at the latest."

He paused to see if she would be satisfied with his answer. She had to contain herself, thinking that they'd have two big paydays within four days. Again putting on her whimpering voice and trying not to giggle with delight at the same time, Becky said, "If that's the best you can do for me sir, I guess I'll just have to wait."

"I'm sorry ma'am but that is the best we can do and I apologize again if this has caused you any problems. It was an honest mistake."

I'll bet it was, you crooks. Isn't it ironic? Me calling you guys crooks. I guess we're even now, or will be Monday. "Thanks for at least not giving me the runaround. Good-bye Mr. Hollis."

"Good . . ."

Before he could finish the phone clicked in his ear. He said to the two agents who were recording the phone call, "It's funny but Tanya Brush didn't have a southern accent last time I talked with her. She's a good actress but she's apparently forgotten her part."

* * *

Becky thought that she'd put on an Oscar-winning performance. She was smiling from ear to ear when Bobby got her attention by grabbing her arm. "What did he say?"

"Well, Bobby, you and I are going to get another big payday on Monday. All we have to do is take a little drive down to St. Mary. Then we can start a long vacation. First we have to pick up the money at the apartment then head south. Once we cash that check we should get a new car. I'd really like a newer Cadillac CTS." She looked Bobby in the eyes. "I think we're going to be very happy together."

Bobby looked back at her with sinister eyes with a touch of perversion. "Yes we are."

Chapter 40

The drive to Knoxville was relaxing for Hatch. He loved to see the mountains, especially the Blue Ridge as you approached them, with their dark outline below the sky. It was always neat to see the shadows of the clouds move up the mountainside then disappear as if flying off the mountaintop. Then another set of shadows of a different shape move in behind the one that had just disappeared. The air was cleaner up here and the noise level lower. The winding highway kept drivers on their toes especially as you drove through the western section of Virginia. It was fun to look at nature in all its beauty but the task of driving along Interstate 81 was always a challenge even in the best conditions. You couldn't afford to get too distracted by the beauty. But Hatch was used to the pressure of working on a nuclear powered ballistic missile submarine. As a Radar Technician, he was responsible for keeping track of the equipment that pinpointed a submarine's position. That was necessary in order to determine the exact launch point of the missiles carrying nuclear warheads. He knew that his job was a crucial link in maintaining the balance of power between Russia and the United States. If one country determined that they had a clear advantage and the wrong mad-man was in charge in either country, the world could be thrown into a nuclear exchange that could end in total destruction. As he looked around at the beauty of his country, he was certain that there were places all over the globe with similar beauty. He hoped and prayed that he would never see the day when that beauty was destroyed by an impulsive act of a man with too much power.

He thought about the madness that occurred on an individual level. He had experienced that madness in his own family. Two drunken fools had gone to his parent's cabin on the Okefenokee Swamp and killed them for no apparent reason except that they were insane, bored and looking for a good time. Their idea of a good time was to murder his parents. That wasn't enough for them. They also murdered and raped his little sister. She was only 14 years old. All this happened while he was out at sea, unknowing and unable to help them. When Navy officials learned of the tragedy, they evacuated Hatch from the submarine in the middle of the Atlantic Ocean and flew him home. Until he set foot in the offices of the Trident Fleet at Kings Bay, he had no idea why he was taken from the sub. He thought that he was being arrested for running guns, which was a hobby of his since he was a teenager. Only when he was seated in an interview room did he learn that is family had been slaughtered. He learned the gruesome details from the county sheriff. He said they had suspects but that the evidence that they had wasn't good enough for an arrest. Hatch didn't shed a tear or show any outward emotion. He held it in, like a nuclear warhead that hadn't been detonated. The power was contained but the destructive potential was only an ignition switch away. All that was needed was a trigger at the right moment and the unleashing of destructive power would take place.

And it did. Hatch determined on his own the real perpetrators of the crime against his family but he didn't have the skills necessary to make them pay for their crimes without putting himself in jeopardy. So he trained himself how to perform covert surveillance. He learned about weapons of all types; from hand guns to rifles to automatic weapons. He found out where he could buy these weapons and make money selling them in the process. He was careful not to sell guns to street thugs, though. He didn't want to empower the very type of characters that he was hunting. He learned how to kill and he learned how to maim. He practiced different aspects of warfare every day. Then he learned the laws surrounding acts of violence. He determined why his family's killers were still walking free while he was restricted to living within the bounds of the law. And he figured out that he couldn't wait for law enforcement and the judicial system to take action for him. In the Old Testament the lesson was an eye for an eye. In the New Testament the lesson was turn the other cheek. In Hatch's mind, he knew he would never be able to live by that edict. He knew he couldn't live with himself if he didn't avenge the death of his family. He figured if there was a hell then he would be knocking on hells door when he died. He knew what the Bible said but he also knew he couldn't look his family's killers in the eyes unless they were the lifeless eyes of dead men.

His training paid off. He made good on his post mortem promise to his parents and his kid sister that he would not let their deaths go unpunished. The side bonus of his actions was that he now had a new set of skills that very few people possessed. He was keenly aware of everything that went on around him. He processed everything and he knew when danger was imminent. He knew when to fight and when to go undercover. He knew who was most dangerous and who was not an immediate threat. And he knew how to kill. That's why Pat McKinney and Hatch were friends. Hatch was Pat's mentor when he needed skills. He was Pat's supplier when he needed hardware for a particular job. And Hatch was the man that took care of business when necessary.

That's why Hatch was on the road to Knoxville. Pat had a feeling that the surveillance team was playing by the rules to a fault. Nancy Brown was a good leader and his brother Joe was smart, strong, and dedicated to the cause. But the team had boundaries. They had to stay within those boundaries or they'd pay a high price as if they were criminals themselves. Pat knew the rules. He knew that the rules were there to make sure good people didn't go bad trying to uphold the law. The problem was that the rules were too cut and dried. He knew that the law was allowing Julie Lippus Gray, Tanya Brush, Laurie Sharp, Rebecca Lippert and whoever else this woman called herself, and her accomplices, to get away with murder. He knew that Hatch would obey the rules until they got in the way of justice. Then his instincts would take over and he would get the job done. Pat hoped that it wouldn't come to that but Hatch didn't care one way or another. His fellow servicemen were getting hurt while they were most vulnerable; while they were deployed overseas in a foreign country or at sea defending America's freedoms. He would not allow this woman and anyone associated with her continue to get away with their crimes.

Hatch used caution while the traffic from Interstate 40 merged with the southbound traffic from Interstate 81. He was getting close to his destination. Just a half hour more and he could start his search for Julie Lippus and her pale-faced accomplice. His adrenaline was ramping up, his heart pounding just a little faster. The pleasant drive was nearing an end. It was time to take care of business.

* * *

Becky and Bobby enjoyed their stay in Knoxville. The few days of shopping and lounging by the pool helped Becky relax and gain some perspective on how quickly they were spending their money. At the rate they spent, it would be about six months and they'd have to make another score with the insurance company or they'd have to collect on both the checks that were out there. Becky made a call to NatFed to see if her check had been mailed for the death of her poor husband Wilson. After all, she needed that money to buy groceries and pay rent and other bills. But for now, the trip back to Norfolk would be a leisurely one. She convinced Bobby that they needed to take their time getting back to Norfolk and that they needed to leave a few decoys around the southeast.

So they drove through Pigeon Forge and some of the worst traffic that they'd ever seen. They continued through Gatlinburg and into the Great Smokey Mountains. Once through the mountains, they stopped in Cherokee at Harrah's Casino and dropped over $1000. They would have lost more but Becky hauled Bobby out before he started playing any table games. From Cherokee, they hopped on the Blue Ridge Parkway and drove the speed limit until they reached Asheville, North Carolina. They took Interstate 26 to Interstate 95 then headed south towards Kings Bay. At 10:30 at night, they got a room at State Route 17 and I-95 in South Carolina.

When Becky and Bobby checked out of the room, they stopped along the interstate for gas. Becky purposely left one of Dean Gray's credit cards at the pump. When Bobby saw her drop the card he said, "What are you doing?"

As she sat in the passenger seat, she said, "That's our insurance card. You see, someone is going to find that card and whether they use it or not, word will get back to whoever is following us that the card was found down here. And like good little policemen, they'll all head down here to see what we're up to in South Carolina. Then we can go get our paycheck in Norfolk."

Bobby thought for a moment then smiled at the ingenuity of her plan. He reached his hand behind her neck and pulled her to him for a kiss but she pulled back and removed his hand. "Not now, Bobby. We have to keep our heads on straight. Remember what I told you in Knoxville. I am not going to prison. We can't afford to make public scenes."

"You can't even kiss me here in the car? That's not a scene." Bobby gave her a mean stare. He said, "Is this how it's gonna be from now on? Cause if it is, I don't like it."

"Look, Bobby, you're the one who was so damn serious about concentrating on the plan and making sure we did everything right. Now I'm serious and all you want to do is screw around. You can't have it both ways, now let's get rolling before somebody sees the card and wants to give it back to us."

Becky was hoping that the plan would work and very soon after they were back on the interstate, it did. Two teenaged boys were heading into the convenience store to buy rolling papers after skipping the last two periods of school when one of them came across the credit card in the parking lot. He thought he'd won the lottery. He and his buddy headed south towards Savannah and stopped to get gas. They filled up then used the card to do a little shopping for clothes. They were nervous as they paid for the seven pair of designer blue jeans and half a dozen tee-shirts. They moved on to the next store and repeated their shopping spree. Finally they found a guy who was willing to buy them a couple of cases of beer if they charged one for him. By the time they finished their shopping spree, they had a trunk full of clothes and enough beer for a big party. All in all, they spent over $1300.00, all courtesy of Dean Gray who was still out at sea. He had no idea that he was being abused and his credit would be turned to crap before he could return from his deployment.

The credit card company's investigators watched the charges pile up. They tracked the movement of the cardholder as they went from store to store, then to a second gas station. Something wasn't right though. All week the card had been used to buy clothes, some male and some female. The charges that went on Thursday were all male. Of all the charges that took place in Knoxville, none were for cases of beer. The only alcohol that was purchased was with dinner at nice restaurants. It was clear that the spending habits had changed. But what caused them to change? The last charge made before most stores closed was for a carton of cigarettes, a bottle of whiskey, and some Seven-Up. It sounded like an underage drinking party was in the making. They called the surveillance team in Norfolk to report the card use.

Nancy was shaking her head. She wanted to send the team from Kings Bay to try and track down Julie and her boyfriend but she didn't want to leave the area around Wilson Brush's apartment unattended. Just her luck the couple would head down there and pick up the check as it was being delivered and disappear again. They couldn't afford to let that happen. She wanted to get Joe and Pat's opinion to make sure that her judgment was sound.

"Hey guys, what do you make of all this?" Joe was shaking his head. He agreed with the credit card investigations team that something had changed. They whole nature of the charges was different and it didn't make sense. Why would they change from a big city like Knoxville to Beaufort, South Carolina? "Should we send someone down there to check it out?"

"I don't know. This doesn't make sense at all. Do we know any law enforcement in the area?"

Pat's question drew looks from both Joe and Nancy as if he had three heads. "Do they have any law enforcement down there? If they do, it's probably just a couple of county sheriffs. I wouldn't count on any support." Joe turned away and looked back at the faxed report from the credit card company.

"But what could it hurt?" Nancy asked.

"It can't hurt. Let's just call and see what happens." Pat reached for the receiver to call information then set it back down. "What's the name of that city and county?"

Joe said, "I think its Podunk."

"Which one, the city or the county?"

Nancy and Joe answered in unison, "Both." They looked at each other and laughed. They'd all been at this too long.

* * *

Hatch found out all he could in the Knoxville area. He determined that they had stayed in Knoxville for several nights, gone shopping quite a bit and basically relaxed as if they were on vacation. He got a description of the car, which wasn't much help. There were at least one hundred thousand black BMWs on the road. He did get a license plate number but it was different than the one they had when they were in Virginia so they must be stealing plates and swapping them out. He also figured out that they liked to drive around a lot. They had to have put well over 500 miles on the car even after they got to Knoxville. They took a trip to Nashville and enjoyed a concert and drove to the Fontana Dam and back. Hatch learned pretty much all he wanted to know about Becky and Bobby then he found out something he didn't know.

"They didn't know it but they was being followed."

The innocent comment from the hotel clerk stopped Hatch in his tracks as he was about to exit the hotel lobby. He walked back up to the desk. The clerk was in her late forties. She had jet black hair cut short. It was fluffed out a bit like an old Linda Ronstadt style. She had slight streaks of gray mixed in. She wore too much blush on her cheeks and dark red lipstick. Hatch said, "Come again?"

"They was being followed by a middle aged woman and a young man. It may have been her kid but they was following Mr. and Mrs. Gray, I'm sure of that. It's like they didn't want to let them out of their sight but they didn't want to be seen neither. Ya know what I mean?"

Hatch smiled at the strong southern accent of the clerk. He put a little extra twang in his own Georgia accent when he asked, "Do you know where the woman and her man were stayin'?"

"Nope. I know they wasn't stayin' here. They shoulda stayed here though, cause they was here most of the night. They parked their car over thar just outta sight of the Gray's room. I'd of called the police but they didn't do nothin' but watch. So I figured leave 'em alone long as nuthin' was happenin'. You're not a cop are ya?"

"No, ma'am . . . " Hatch looked are her name tag. It read Lorna Jean. ". . . Lorna Jean. That's a pretty name. Did either one of them happen to mention where they was headed?'

"I overheard the Gray's sayin' that they needed to get on the road 'cause their vacation was almost over and money was runnin' out fast. That was Mrs. Gray talkin'. She was more relaxed than her husband. He looked like he fell outta one a them punk bands, all pale faced and black haired and all. She was a real pretty thang. Don't know what she sees in ole Dean, I mean Mr. Gray."

"Lorna Jean, you've been a real help. If you think of anything else you give me a call at this number. Don't hesitate 'cause this is important. I can't tell you why but trust me, it is."

She gave Hatch a look like it would be their little secret. She smiled and actually blushed a bit, then stuffed his card in the smock's front pocket. "Sweetheart, you can come visit me anytime. And if I remember anything else, I'll be sure to give you a call."

Hatch left before Lorna Jean could ask him out on a date. He had a feeling that Becky and Bobby were headed back to Norfolk but it was only a feeling. The only thing he had to base that feeling on was that Lorna Jean heard Becky say that they were burning through the money. They'd need to recharge their stash of cash soon. That meant picking up a check and the only one that was available to them now was the check at Dean Gray's apartment in Norfolk.

As Hatch left the parking lot, he called Pat from his cell phone to get an update on any card activity. "Hey Pat."

"Hatch, what's the latest?'

Hatch told Pat everything he knew and everything that he suspected. Pat listened and wrote down a few notes. What Hatch said made perfect sense. Then he told Hatch about the credit card activity in Gatlinburg and Cherokee. The latest activity was at a gas station in Beaufort, South Carolina within the last forty-five minutes. He told Hatch about the change in spending habits. Immediately Hatch said that it was a decoy and that the team should shrug that off. "Get some county sheriff to look into that and call you with what they find. Ten to one it's a couple of kids who found the card. If the store has surveillance tapes you can wrap that one up quick."

"That's what we thought, too." Pat and Hatch both paused to think then Pat said, "Where do you think they are right now?"

"You must have been reading my mind. I think they're on their way to Norfolk. It's Thursday and they want to get that check and cash it before the banks close. If I were you I'd make sure your team was in place by later this evening. My guess is that they're going to go after it first thing in the morning, maybe before daylight."

Pat gave this more thought. He expected that they'd wait until Saturday, thinking that the team would stand down or lighten up on the watch teams over the weekend. But with the recent activity on the charge card as a decoy, Pat thought that maybe Hatch was right.

"Hey Pat, I'm going to head back towards Norfolk and try to get a hotel room tonight, maybe around Richmond. I'm going to try to get about five hours in the sack then head to the apartment. Where do you want me to find you and how should I approach?"

They made the arrangements. Hatch would plan to be there around 3:00 in the morning. He'd meet up with Pat and Joe at the perimeter of the apartment complex. If Hatch was right, it was going to start getting busy real soon.

The sooner the better, Pat thought as he hung up the phone. He spoke briefly with Nancy about his conversation with Hatch. He motioned for Joe and Wilson Brush to join them. They discussed all the details of the plan and the information that came in most recently. They all agreed that they needed to be ready to move by early morning. Then he called out into the hotel suite's outer room to the rest of the team, "Hey gang, listen up." As the last man entered the office he began, "I just spoke with Hatch. He believes that the suspects are coming to Norfolk tonight. Captain Brown and I agree with that assessment." He looked at Nancy for her to take over the brief.

She looked around at the team then said, "The apprehension plan is still a go. Does anyone need to go over any details?" No one responded. "Good. If Hatch is right, and I think he is, we've got a real busy morning ahead of us. Everyone except the on-sight team, go home and get some sleep. We meet back here at 2 am. That'll give everyone about 10 hours if you count a half hour commute to your homes. You have to be sharp. Get some rest. These folks have already killed at least five people for no good reason. You don't want to become their next victim."

Chapter 41

Diane McKinney yawned. She was tired from the eleven hours on the road from Dunnellon, Florida to Norfolk. Now that she and Lisa Goddard were nearing their destination, fatigue was setting in. Lisa asked if she wanted her to take over but Diane said no, that she would be fine for the last ten miles of the trip. Traffic was not as bad as they had expected as they approached I-64 where it intersected I-264. They would take the I-264 into the heart of Norfolk before exiting near the hotel where both Pat and Joe were staying. The drive had been pleasant and the women enjoyed each other's company during the drive. They shared many stories about the men in their lives. Diane confessed that she was concerned about their marriage and the prospects for its survival after she learned about some of Pat's past mistakes. But it was obvious to her that he was a different man from his youth. She chocked it up to youthful indiscretion.

"Pat and I are concerned about Sean as he gets older. He seems to have the personality trait that lends itself to excess. We can already see it. He's also got a terrible temper and a stubbornness that I don't really understand. Pat has a stubborn streak but nothing like Sean. He gets on something and won't let it go."

Lisa confided that she saw that same trait in Joe. "When we work out, he gets into a mode of concentration that's almost dangerous. He's oblivious to his surroundings. We met in the weight room at the apartment. He was lifting alone when I got there. His face was so red and contorted that I thought he was having a heart attack. I interrupted his routine because I was worried. When he looked at me, it was with such hatred, I thought he was going to kill me. But he said that's just the way he concentrates. He wasn't mad at me, he was mad at those guys that they knew in Orlando. Anyway, he sure is stubborn and he still scares me when he works out like that."

Another few miles and they'd be at the hotel. Diane yawned again. Lisa asked again, "Are you sure you don't want to pull over for just a minute or so and stretch?"

"I'm okay, really. Just keep talking to me and I'll be fine. It isn't too much further if Pat's directions are right."

After another five minutes, they pulled into the parking lot of the Courtyard by Marriott. Pat and Joe each had a room at the hotel. Brian Purcer and the Hot Licks were also supposed to stay here the night before and the night of the concert. Ginny Parks was with Brian, too. Since Brian and Pat McKinney were best friends, Ginny was introduced to Diane and

Lisa at a barbeque at Pat and Diane's house. The three became close friends, though they rarely spent time together because of Brian's concert schedule and Ginny's school schedule. But it was summer and Ginny was able to go on tour with Brian. He was thrilled and the band was okay with it so far. The good news was the tour would be over by late September and Ginny would be back in school at University of Central Florida. Lisa and Diane were anxious to meet up with Ginny and shop.

Diane parked the car in the lot and the ladies went to the front desk. "We'd like to ring the rooms of Pat and Joe McKinney, please."

"Yes ma'am. Right away." The desk clerk was a male in his mid thirties by Diane's best guess. He had dark hair that was perfect. It looked like a piece but she couldn't tell. His perfect red vest was pressed to perfection and his hands were manicured. He could have been a model for a Courtyard commercial. After about half a minute, the clerk said, "There is no answer at Mr. Patrick McKinney's room. I'll try Mr. Joseph McKinney's room now." He punched in the numbers and went through the same routine. He came back with the same answer; nobody in either room. Diane sighed. Lisa looked disappointed.

Lisa said, "I'll call his office and see if they've left yet. Joe did say that they would meet us here about now."

She pulled out her cell phone and hit the #3 speed dial for Joe's cell phone number. He answered on the first ring.

"McKinney."

"Goddard."

"Lisa! Baby it is so good to hear your voice. Where are you calling from?"

"The Courtyard. You and your brother are supposed to be here, remember?"

"Oh Shit. Is it that late? We'll be there as soon as we can. In the mean time can you get into our rooms?"

"We haven't tried yet. Did you leave instructions for the desk clerk to give us keys?"

"Yes. Just ask the clerk, I think the guy on duty now is Bryce. He knows that you're going to be asking for a key." Lisa glanced at Mr. Perfect Courtyard Clerk's nametag. It read 'Arlen'. She guessed that they needed to speak with a different clerk to get the keys and directions.

"Okay Dear. We have to find Bryce and get the keys. If we have any problems we'll call you right back. How soon will you and Pat be here?"

"That's a tough question, Sweetness. We're finishing up now but finishing up sometimes takes longer than the meetings. We're only about twenty minutes away so it shouldn't be long. You two get into the rooms, I'm sure you're both tired. Relax, help yourselves to the bar or room service and we'll get there as soon as we can."

"We thought maybe we would get a bite to eat. We're both pretty hungry. If you're going to be awhile, maybe we'll head to the hotel restaurant then go to the rooms." Lisa finished talking with Joe and they disconnected.

They first hunted down Bryce who was happy to assist them with room keycards and directions. He also recommended that they see the concierge about tickets to the Brian Purcer concert Saturday night. The tickets were going fast. Diane impressed Bryce with the news that they didn't need tickets because they already had backstage passes. Bryce gave her a sly smile and a wink as if to say, 'What did you have to do to get that?' Diane blushed just from the look on Bryce's face.

Lisa piped in and said, "Her husband and Brian are best friends. She's too nice for anything like that, but I'm not too proud." She winked at Bryce and his face colored a deep shade of red.

He picked up a few papers and fanned himself saying "Oh my."

Diane and Lisa left Bryce still fanning himself and headed to the restaurant. They had a light dinner in the elegant dining room then went up to their rooms.

* * *

Nearly two hours later Pat McKinney walked into his apartment to see a sleeping Diane on the bed, fully clothed except shoes. She was snoring and didn't budge when he closed the room door behind him. He let her sleep for a bit while he washed his face in the sink then collapsed in the chair near the bed. He watched his wife sleep for about ten minutes, then cleared his throat just loud enough to wake her. She opened her eyes, saw Pat sitting there and smiled. "Who's the intruder?"

"Just the boogey man. Want to boogey?"

He got up and lay down next to her. They kissed lightly but with passion. They kissed longer and harder. Within minutes they were naked and expressing their undying love for each other with a touch of lust thrown in for good measure.

* * *

Joe walked into his room and looked around for Lisa. He didn't see her on the bed or in the kitchenette. He said into the room, "Hello. Is anyone home?"

Lisa stuck one long leg covered with a white fishnet stocking out from the bathroom doorway and moved it around seductively. Then she moved out a little more so that all Joe could see was the lower part of a very sexy teddy. "Sergeant McKinney, is that you?"

Joe's knees were getting weak as he watched Lisa slowly expose more of the sexy outfit that she wore; a red very shear teddy with a heart-shaped bra, red thong panties, and a red garter belt holding up the white fishnets. She moved slowly towards him and ordered, "Sergeant, keep your hands where I can see them and don't move a muscle."

Joe did as he was told with one exception. There was one muscle that he couldn't keep from moving. Lisa couldn't help but notice. Her lips turned up in a wicked smile.

* * *

Lisa and Diane weren't happy when they heard the news, separately, that their men had to get up at 2:30 in the morning and head out for a possible apprehension at an apartment complex across town. Diane was especially ticked off since her husband was basically doing this for free. He wasn't in the military, he had no orders. He was just along to help out. This was like a hobby to him but it was a dangerous one. People had already been killed and Diane had no desire to be a widow at her young age. She didn't want her kids to grow up without a father either.

"So tell me again why you're doing this? You feel an obligation to your brother and your country?"

"That's right."

"That's a load of bullshit!" Diane's swearing got Pat's attention. Diane rarely used anything stronger than 'darn it'. On occasion she would say 'damn' but that was usually as strong as it got. So when she said 'bullshit' Pat was listening. "You want to be some kind of hero. It's been on your mind since you helped with the bust in Florida. You've had this fantasy of being some big-shot detective."

"That's not true." As he said it he knew it was on the borderline of being true. He knew that she could see through it, too. "Well, maybe it's not completely false. It does feel good to do something right, for the good of my old military buddies. You know, some of these kids are very naïve. They're fresh out of high school. For some of them it's the first time they've ever been away from home."

"Not a man of the world like Mr. Tough-guy, Pat McKinney, you mean?" Diane was digging into his ribs with her finger.

"Boy, you are a mean woman." He smiled at her trying to ease some of the tension. "Look, I'm committed to doing this so let's try to be civil. I promise I'll come home safe and sound."

"You should be careful of the promises you make. If you don't come home to me, I swear I'll kill you. Do you understand me?" Diane was kidding, but not really.

Next door, Joe was having a similar conversation with Lisa. Diane understood the commitment that Pat used to have to the Navy. She lived through his deployments on the submarine. She understood that a military wife had a lot of responsibility on her shoulders. Lisa didn't know Joe when he was active duty in the Marine Corps. She only knew the Marines through the stories that Joe told her and they were usually sanitized for her benefit. She never lived through an overseas deployment. She never feared that he wouldn't come home when she heard of attacks in Afghanistan where Marines were killed. She never felt the empty heart when he was gone for three months or more at a stretch. Military life was as foreign to her as being an astronaut. She never had the experience so she couldn't comprehend the emotions. Until now.

Joe had been active duty for just a short time. She expected that they'd be able to spend the entire evening together and make love all night, then sleep in late and get breakfast in bed and make love again. But Joe was explaining the reality of their first night together in many weeks. He had to leave her in the middle of the night for what; the possibility of getting shot and killed? She was angry and scared and sad and lonely all at once. She didn't want Joe to go but she knew he had no choice. All she could do was hold him close and let him get some much needed sleep. There would be more nights in bed with mornings that would turn into afternoons in bed, holding each other. She had to believe that there would be or she'd start to cry. She didn't want to do that in front of Joe. She wanted him to know that she was strong, physically and emotionally. She wanted him to know that she was behind him so he wouldn't be thinking of her while he needed to be thinking of the dangerous business that he would face later that morning.

"Here's the bet, Sergeant McKinney. You make it home safe to me and I'll make love to you all night Sunday and into Monday. Then I'll fix you breakfast in bed and if you can keep up, lunch, too."

Joe cocked his eyebrow at her. "That's some bet. I don't think you can hang, Miss Goddard."

Her smile turned wicked and she rubbed one hand over his bare chest while the other rubbed the back of his neck. "Oh, I can hang alright. As a matter of fact, you're gonna beg me to stop."

Joe laughed out loud. "I don't see that happening. Not in your lifetime." Joe stopped at his poor choice of words. He went on to cover his tracks. "I'll up the stakes. When this is over and I win, I'll take you on that vacation to Fort Myers. And we'll go spend the entire week in the Keys. Deal?"

"It's a deal but I'm telling you, you're going to be too worn out to enjoy that vacation. You'll sleep the entire time."

"We'll see. Right now, my dear, I have got to get some sleep." Joe reached over and turned out the bedside light then turned back to face Lisa. "I want you to know how much I love you." He kissed her soft and deep. When he pulled back she followed him and wouldn't release. They held that kiss for several minutes before falling asleep in each other's embrace.

Chapter 42

Bobby finished pumping regular unleaded gas into the tank of their Beamer. He hung the pump back in its holder and walked into the convenience store to pay the bill. Becky was at the fast food sub shop next door getting sandwiches and drinks. Bobby went to the cooler and grabbed a six pack of tall boy Busch Beer and headed to the counter. As he reached for his wallet, he remembered that he didn't have any cash on him because the cash was in the trunk of the car. He didn't want to open the trunk to get the cash out for fear that someone would notice the nearly $200,000 cash in the vinyl tote so he decided to pay for the gas and beer with a credit card. He pulled out the first card that he touched and handed it to the cashier. When the cashier came back and said that the card was denied, a look of fear momentarily crossed his face. He mistakenly used one of Dean Gray's credit cards. Apparently there had been a stop placed on them in the last twenty-four hours. He nonchalantly took the card back and handed her a second card. This one went through with no problem. He gathered his beer and met Becky back at the car.

"What's wrong?" Becky asked. She could see his face twisted with concern.

He looked over at her and said, "Nothing. Don't worry about it."

Becky knew when there was something to worry about. When Bobby said don't worry, it was time to worry. "What happened in there?"

"Nothing." He paused. "I used Gray's credit card by mistake and it was denied. They must have tracked the card that we left in South Carolina. I guess they figured it was being used by someone other than Gray. When we get this last check we're using cash until we get new identities in place. I can't believe I fucked up like that."

Becky wanted to say that she could but she figured he'd slap her so she let it slide. Once again she was thinking that this was too dangerous. Bobby was making too many mistakes and with Abbie and Ace trying to get control, there was no telling how crazy things were going to get. She just hoped that they lost Abbie and Ace forever. She didn't need a mother or a brother. She lived her whole life so far without them. She sure didn't need either now. As they pulled into traffic and headed north towards Norfolk she started to wonder what it would be like to have a man who treated her right. She knew how to keep a man happy. Maybe she could go straight and fall in love with a man who had money and could take care of her. So far her life was full of misfit foster families who treated her badly. She didn't deserve it though she did learn how to fight back. She learned how to get even and get ahead when needed. She may have been abused but it wasn't without consequence to the abusers in her life.

"When we get to Norfolk we have to be ready to get in and out fast. We need to grab that check and get back on the road." Bobby was already giving orders and they were at least three hours from Norfolk. She looked at him in the dark car, his face silhouetted by the lights from cars passing in the opposite direction. His physical features, like his personality, had contrasts that were extreme. His nearly black eyes and black hair framed his pale face. His dark personality was in vivid contrast to the loving person he could become when he had to turn on the charm. That's how he won her over when they first met in Key West. She was taken by his charming manner. His confidence was evident in everything he said and did. Any woman would have fallen for him, especially a young woman. Even though Becky had become a street-wise, worldly woman at a young age, totally out of necessity, she fell for Bobby when he approached her on that beach. He already knew much about her past. He'd done his homework. Plus he learned from Abbie. She was the link from Bobby to Becky, unbeknownst to her. After they got to know each other, he made her a deal. They'd be partners and lovers. They'd take advantage of both of their skills and make themselves rich. It sounded so simple back then.

At first he was a kind, gentle lover. He would talk sweet to her and the passion was strong. Then when they started their plan in motion, he became more aggressive. It seemed the more she worked at winning over the soldiers and sailors that they targeted, the more Bobby became jealous and his love making became punishment. He acted as if she was doing something wrong by doing the very things that they'd agreed she would do. Most recently he was becoming abusive. He was bruising her far too often and she was growing fearful that he might hurt her badly. As she gazed out the passenger side window, lightning began to light up the sky. A few more miles down the road, the rains started and the lightning strikes were getting closer accompanied by thunder. Finally, they were driving through a full fledged thunder storm with the thunder claps occurring immediately after the bright streaks of light. Bobby slowed the car as water started to accumulate on the road. This only put the exclamation point on Becky's mood. She was in a deep, dark place in her mind. She closed her eyes and wished the rain would stop. She wished her life were different. She wished she knew how to pray but it had never been a part of her life. *People who pray swear it works. I wonder if it would work for me?*

Bobby spoke and broke into her thoughts, "I think we need to stop until this rain lets up. Check the map and see what's up ahead."

Becky came out of her trance and picked up the map. She turned on the map light and started to search for the area of North Carolina where they were driving. She found Highway 17 north of Jacksonville, North Carolina. "What was the last city that we passed?"

"New Bern."

"There's Vanceboro but I doubt there's much there. Are we just stopping until the storm passes? We still have to eat these sandwiches."

"See those lights? Can you tell what it is?"

Becky looked through the rain soaked windshield. It was difficult to see anything through the rain and sloshing of the wipers but she finally saw that there was a parking lot for a rural church on the right. *This must be some sort of sign from God.* "It's a church parking lot. It's empty. I think we should stop."

Bobby agreed and they pulled over under the light. They ate their sandwiches and relaxed, both staying silent as the storm raged on. Finally, the rain and thunder began to weaken. Becky looked at the church, thinking about her lack of knowledge of prayer, religion, and God. She thought about all the churches that she'd passed over her lifetime and how crowded they seemed to be on Sundays. But they always seemed to be empty throughout the week. Only on a rare occasion did she see anyone in a church in the middle of the week. *They must all be out sinning during the week like me. That's why they're so busy on Sundays. It must be a good business to be a preacher.*

"Are you ready?"

Bobby's question broke into her thoughts. "Why don't we sleep here for tonight? I mean, would it hurt anything?"

"Do you want to do it right here by the church? What if someone sees us here and calls the cops?"

Becky looked at Bobby with a look of disgust. "I wasn't talking about doing it here. I meant sleep. You've got a sick, one-track mind. How sick can you be to suggest that we do it in a church parking lot?"

Bobby put on an angry look, reached for the ignition, started the car and headed back out on the highway. He pulled out and headed north on highway 17 again. He was mad and he picked up speed fast. He never looked back at Becky and she could tell he was getting angrier by the mile. She looked at the open space between the seats at the 9 mm Glock that he kept loaded with the safeties off. She was afraid that he might just go off the deep end and use the gun on her. She looked out the window again and wished that she were anywhere else but there in that car.

The bright multi-colored lights startled them both. A Sheriff's car had pulled up close behind them and was signaling for Bobby to either pull over or get out of the way. He hadn't sounded his siren yet but Bobby was shaken. He wasn't sure what to do. With the wet conditions trying to make a run for it was senseless. He looked at Becky as if to say, 'what should I do?'

"Bobby, first get it together. Then pull over at the first place you see that isn't dangerous." She covered the gun with a bag from the sub shop. Bobby saw a spot near an intersection where the shoulder widened, so he pulled over. They sat for several minutes while the sheriff was apparently gathering information on the car and its potential occupants. Bobby looked down where Becky had covered the gun and reached down to see how it was arranged in case he had to quickly grab it and use it on the sheriff.

Becky said, "Don't even think about it." She looked back and the door to the sheriff's car was opening. A tall, well built man, about six feet 4 inches tall and muscular stepped out of the car and put his sheriff's hat on. Becky couldn't see his face because he was backlit by the spotlight from his cruiser. He slowly approached the car with a flashlight in his hand then he paused and looked at the back of the car. As he came up to the driver's side window, he made a rolling motion with his hand instructing Bobby to roll his window down. Bobby was clearly nervous. Becky was scared that he'd reach for his gun and they'd have a whole new set of problems.

Bobby asked, "Is there a problem, sheriff?"

As the sheriff was about to answer he received a call on his walkie-talkie. He responded. Bobby and Becky couldn't understand the lingo that he was using and wondered how law enforcement people could even communicate with the static and jargon that was used over the radios. When he finished talking to the dispatcher he turned to Bobby.

By this time, Becky had loosened the top buttons on her blouse and leaned over close to Bobby. The sheriff shined his flashlight towards Becky. She asked in a sexy voice, "Is there a problem sheriff?"

He couldn't help but see lots of cleavage. Her breasts were nearly popping out of her bra and he stammered on his words. "Uh, yes ma'am, there is. Your taillight on the passenger side is out. I was going to give you a ticket but I have to scoot. There's been an accident up the road. I'm writing a quick note letting you know that I've advised you of the problem. This should be sufficient to keep you from getting a ticket at least for the next day or until Monday anyway. You should have that taken care of as soon as possible. Drive careful, now." He shined his light back on Becky's chest one more time before he left, then headed back to his cruiser and took off for the accident scene.

Bobby turned to Becky and angrily said, "You didn't have to act like a slut. I had it under control."

"Bobby, you thought about pulling the gun and shooting him. Nothing about you is under control right now. You're freaking me out. Everything's a crisis. I can't live like this anymore." She'd let it out. There was no taking it back. "First, you set me up to be some high priced whore then you get jealous when I do exactly what you say. I can't please you anymore."

"That's not true. You make me very happy."

"Yea, when you're screwing my brains out. When that's not happening all you do is sit around and scheme and sulk. This used to be fun but now that there's serious money involved, it just isn't fun anymore. You're not fun anymore."

Becky's sadness poured out. Tears filled her eyes. Bobby looked over at her and his eyes strayed to her open blouse. She reached down and buttoned the two buttons that she'd undone earlier. "See. All you think about is sex and money. We never do anything to relax."

"What do you mean? We just spent a week shopping."

"If I wouldn't have insisted that we get away from that psycho, Abbie and her nutcase kid, we would never have done that." She paused and the silence filled the car. The rain started to fall again but just a sprinkle. "Bobby, let's go. It's almost 9:30. Let's get a room and some shut eye. We can get up about 2:00 am and head into Norfolk. I want to get the money and get out of here. Maybe we can take a break from this and pick it up later when the heats off and you're not so obsessed with making a score every couple of weeks. We're putting too much pressure on ourselves. If this is what being rich does to you, I don't want to be rich."

Bobby pulled his black hair behind his ears and started the engine. After a few miles of silence Bobby said, "Maybe we should slow down the pace a bit. Have you ever been to Texas?"

"No but I'm not sure I want to go there. They execute people there."

"Good Point."

* * *

"What the hell is taking them so long? That sheriff's been gone for almost ten minutes."

"Relax son. They'll get moving soon. Besides, we know exactly where they're going. It doesn't matter if they stay there all night but I'll bet they're headed directly for the apartment as soon as they get going again. They have enough gas, that's for sure."

Abbie was trying to keep her son's impatience from getting the best of him. He's young, he'll learn in time. "So, what's the first thing you want to buy once we get our share of that money?"

"A dirt bike. I've always wanted a good dirt bike. I rode one once and it was fun. It took a few times to get the hang of it but once you learn how to handle it, it's fun. And I want an electric guitar and a big amp. I know how to play a few cords but I know I could be a star."

"I know you can, too son. You can get both if you want. We'll get a place by a lake, secluded from neighbors. That way you can play as loud and long as you want." Abbie stopped talking as her mood went dark. She had a bad feeling about the money pickup. She knew that Bobby would try something deceptive to keep from sharing it. She knew it wasn't Becky that decided to fool them and drive to Tennessee. They were blood and family doesn't work that way. Sure she was bitter about being given away at birth but she had explained all that to her. She was better off then. But now that Abbie is back on her feet, she could help her. It's that Bobby that's making all these bad decisions. He's a bad influence on her. He's not family. He never will be family and that might be a problem for their partnership in the future. She and her two kids would be united at last. The outside influences would have to go. That meant Bobby.

Ace said, "There Momma, they're on the move."

Abbie saw the brake lights then the reverse lights flick on momentarily and the car moved out onto Highway 17 again. Then the car pulled into a flea bag motel near Vanceboro. Ace and Abbie watched as Bobby went in and paid for a room.

Abbie turned to her son and said, "Get comfortable. We're going to be here awhile. I'll bet they get up early and head into Norfolk before anyone's up. It's only about two and a half hours to the apartment. My guess is they'll shoot for four o'clock in the morning. Nobody should be up except the very early risers and there are very few of those. That seems like a good time for picking up a hundred grand."

Abbie smiled at her son. "Get some sleep my dear boy. It's payday."

Chapter 43

FBI agents Ralph Lewis and John Sears were on the night watch for an apartment in St. Marys, Georgia. They'd been on this watch for over a week now working 12 hour shifts for no apparent reason. The apartment was outside the Kings Bay Submarine Base and they were told that they should watch for a blond woman and a tall, skinny, pale-faced guy with jet black hair cut just above his shoulders. They had a more detailed description but if they could see those features they didn't need anything further. They were told that it was unlikely that they would need to worry but that they should be on their toes anyway. They were in an apartment that was across the parking lot from the Wilson Brush apartment. Brush was supposed to be at sea but he was in fact in Norfolk with the apprehension team. Why he wasn't down here at his apartment was a mystery to the agents but they didn't question their orders. They were getting time and a half after eight hours so it didn't matter to them what the guy from the apartment was doing.

The agents had to admit that the set up in the surveillance apartment was pretty slick. There were several cameras throughout the complex all of which were pointing towards Wilson Brush's apartment. The cameras were equipped with night vision technology so that the agents could see sharp images of the complex even at night, though the night view had an eerie green tint. But the detail in the pictures was outstanding. The monitors were all flat panel, high resolution screens. Each monitor could be individually recorded. Inside Wilson Brush's apartment two cameras were set up to monitor anything that occurred in the apartment, which for days was absolutely nothing. Ralph and John were both bored and tired. The only interesting thing that happened all week was a young woman walking towards the complex pool lost her bathing suit top. They managed to get it on disc and when they were bored they played back the clip. They tired of that so they erased it to make sure that they wouldn't get in trouble for unauthorized surveillance, not to mention getting the department sued for who knows what.

It was just after dark. John and Ralph were in the middle of a pizza dinner when John noticed a young couple walking along the apartment complex walkway that led to Brush's apartment. They had never seen this couple before which was odd because they were starting to get to know the tenants, not by name, but more by nick-names that they'd unofficially assigned to them. There was poof lady with the poofy hair in building 7. Her hair looked the same when she left in the morning and when she came home in late afternoon. She must have poofed it up during the day. Then there was the young real estate sales couple from building 6. They carpooled to work together in the car with the real estate signs on the driver and passenger doors. They looked like book ends in their matching blue blazers. They were a cute couple, according to John. But the husband would sometimes come home at lunchtime with a different female real estate agent. She also wore the company blazer but it wasn't Mrs. Real Estate agent it was some Miss Easy Real Estate agent. When they left the apartment after 'lunch' they'd look around quite a bit, looking guilty as carnal sin. They were probably showing each other the importance of location, location, location. Then there was the honky rapper. He was a pale skinned, blond haired white kid with several earrings and lip rings in his face. He always wore a hat cocked to one side and walked with such a herky-jerky movement that Ralph and John thought he'd broken a hip or had a bum knee. When he got into his car the rap music was so loud and distorted that it shook every window in the complex. They heard dispatch call the nearest car to investigate the loud music in the complex on more than one occasion. Finally there was Petty Officer squared away. This cat dressed so sharp in his Navy uniform that he looked like a commercial for the Navy recruiter. They watched him walk to his car with sharp turns as if he were in a drill team in a parade on the fourth of July. He was apparently stationed at Kings Bay and was on the off crew. He was home a lot.

Now here were two new players. It wouldn't have caught the detective's attention except that the couple kept looking over their shoulders like they were afraid of something or making sure no one was watching them. *Too bad for you two because big brother is watching you.*

Ralph said, "I wonder what these two are up to." They watched for a minute or so more. "Do they fit the profile of our perps?"

John looked over the description of the two that they were supposed to watch and said, "They're not off by much if you consider that the hair color is not exactly right. The guy has hair nearly to his shoulders but it looks lighter than what the bulletin says. He looks pretty pale from here. The chick looks kinda blond but it's hard to see colors when the screen is night vision green." They continued to watch as the couple stopped to look around. It didn't look like they were going anywhere in particular and the way they looked around it appeared as though they were casing the Brush apartment building.

"Should we call Captain Brown?" Ralph wasn't convinced that these two were Tanya Brush and her accomplice. They couldn't get close enough with the zoom on the camera to get a good facial shot.

"Not yet. Maybe we can get a better shot with one of the other cameras." John played with the joy stick and maneuvered the lens of one of the cameras so that it had a better angle on the couple, but as soon as he moved in close, the slightest movement by the couple caused their image to move off the screen. John couldn't get a happy medium where there was enough detail on the screen to make an ID or a close enough shot with a stable picture. "Well, if we want to see their faces, we're going to have to go out there and confront them and I know we won't get clearance for that. Especially if we're not sure it's them."

They sat quiet for a moment thinking of their options. They knew from the reports that the two suspects could be dangerous. They also knew that they weren't supposed to be here. There was no bait for them here. The check from NatFed was only going to be delivered if the apprehension failed in Norfolk. If that happened they wouldn't have to worry about being alone at their lookout. The place would be swarming with agents crawling all over each other to make the collar. Many of the agents in this region were ex-military. They'd love to be the one to take these two down.

John said, "You know what else we should be looking for? There's a possibility that one more person, possibly two are involved. The latest report said to be on guard for a middle aged woman and a teenaged kid. She's got blond hair with gray streaks. He's got short blond hair and is about 6'2" or so, slender build, kind of a pretty boy look."

Ralph looked at the flat screen, still trying to adjust it and asked, "So where are these other characters supposed to be?"

"Report says that the older woman and the kid follow this Tanya woman around and show up wherever they go. It says that the older woman or the kid may be the shooter. That means we can't just lock in on those two." Ralph looked away from the monitor for a moment, trying to analyze the situation. They'd gone from nearly a week of absolutely nothing happening to a possible apprehension. They weren't supposed to see any action. They were just there for surveillance.

John said, "How about if you keep trying to get a fix on those two. I'll scan around the lot with one of the other cameras."

Ralph continued to hone in on the couple near the apartment but he still couldn't get in close enough. John maneuvered a second camera out towards the parking lot, scanning cars, vans, mini-vans, and a number of SUVs as he moved away from the couple who were still standing on the sidewalk near the Brush apartment building. As the night vision camera panned across the lot, a car entered the parking lot and backed into a space about 150 feet from the young couple. John directed the camera at the car but the lens took several seconds to readjust to the headlights that were still on. After a moment, the car engine cut out and the lights went dark. A few, long seconds went by again as the night vision camera readjusted to the changing light conditions. John zoomed the camera in on a man and a woman in the car. Something wasn't right. The man and woman in the car were both young. There was a young blond kid but he wasn't a handsome kid like the reports said. He had a broad face with a hint of a beard. The woman in the driver's seat was more a girl than a woman. She had a very slender face and dark hair. They were looking over at the couple on the sidewalk as if they knew them. John saw something he didn't like at all. The passenger lifted his hands above the dashboard and cocked what appeared to be a 9mm pistol. He smiled and looked over at the girl. She shook her head as if to say, *put that thing down before you hurt yourself.* He put the gun down on the seat between them. He raised his hand in the direction of the couple on the sidewalk. When he did, the couple exchanged words and moved towards the Brush apartment.

Ralph and John looked up from their monitors at the same time. John asked, "What do we do now? Should we call the locals for backup or try to take them ourselves or just let it happen because these folks aren't our suspects?"

Ralph was the more experienced detective so John felt that he should have all the right answers. Sometimes there weren't any right answers. Sometimes you just had to make judgment calls. He decided that the right call was two-fold. He told John, "I'll call Captain Brown and tell her the situation. You call the local police and get back-up. Once we make the calls, we'll either get direction or we'll take our own actions.

John nodded and grabbed the note pad with the local emergency numbers by the monitor. He punched in the number for the St. Mary Police Department. While he was waiting for the dispatcher, Ralph was dialing Captain Brown's home phone. She picked up on the first ring.

"Brown."

"Captain, this is Detective Ralph Lewis. John Sears and I are working surveillance at the Brush apartment in St. Marys, Georgia and we have a situation."

"What's going on?"

"Ma'am, there's four people casing the Brush apartment or at least in the vicinity of the apartment. They could be our suspects but they don't exactly fit the descriptions."

Nancy said, "Can you describe them to me?"

"Yes, ma'am." Ralph described the four suspects. They had not moved yet but they were getting more animated as the minutes past. As he was finishing up his description of the four, the driver's side door opened and the young woman exited the car. She was walking towards the couple standing on the sidewalk. "Captain, I have to go. There's activity and I have to get back to it."

"Detective, can you put your phone on speaker and can you and your partner talk through what is happening as you monitor the situation? If that's too distracting then don't bother. I could listen in and provide recommendations if appropriate."

"Yes, ma'am. We can do that."

A moment later, Nancy heard a click then a hollow sound as agents Lewis and Sears maneuvered the monitors and called the local police for backup. They never spoke directly to Nancy but continued to watch as the young woman from the car stopped and talked for a moment with the couple. The three of them looked around suspiciously then slowly made their way towards the Brush building. At first they walked tentatively then headed up the stairs of the building with purpose. John adjusted his camera to zoom in on Wilson Brush's apartment door where the three were congregated. The man had pulled out some kind of tool like a knife and was working the door lock. He worked at it for several seconds and appeared to be getting frustrated. The women were starting to get nervous and were looking around to see if anyone was watching.

In the surveillance apartment, John and Ralph listened as the microphones in the Brush apartment picked up the noise from the front door. From the sound of the noise he was making trying to unlock the door the man was not using a key. They could here him swearing as he tried to jimmy the lock.

Ralph commented, "With him making all that racket, we didn't have to call the locals. The neighbors will cover that for us."

Finally, the door lock pulled back and the three entered the apartment. John switched from the parking lot camera to one of the cameras inside the apartment. As the three entered, it was clear that these kids were teenagers, maybe twenty at the most. They entered the empty living room and their expressions changed from anticipation to dismay. The apartment had been cleaned out. The walls were painted apartment complex antique white and were void of any wall treatments. The kitchen was clean. The only thing out of place was a can of paint sitting on an old newspaper on the counter. These kids were expecting something totally different. The man went quickly from the living room to the bedroom hallway and looked in both bedrooms. He went into one bedroom and opened the closet. It was bare. He ran into the other bedroom, opened the closet; empty as the first. He yelled to the women, "Check the kitchen cupboards." When they just stood there with blank expressions, he ran to the kitchen himself. Every cupboard was empty. He stopped in the kitchen, leaned on the counter and looked around. He heard a sound like a tiny motor. He looked around the kitchen trying to place the sound. *What an odd noise. I can barely hear it. Where's it coming from?* He continued to try and pinpoint the source then it stopped. He moved towards the sink and the noise came back then stopped. He looked at the pantry door then moved back to the counter as he watched. There it was again. Then it stopped again. He walked directly to the pantry door and opened it. He looked into the empty pantry, puzzled. He looked at each shelf, but there was nothing. He heard the noise again, a bit louder and very close to his ear. He looked at the back of the pantry door and all he saw was a plastic shelf mounted on the inside of the door. It was the kind used for boxes of plastic bags or bottles of cleaning supplies. It was solid, not like the plastic coated wire shelves. The young man looked inside and saw a small mechanical device with a tiny antenna. It was attached to the shelf. He inspected the front of the pantry door and there it was; a tiny pin hole through the door where a camera lens looked back at him. At that moment he heard the sirens off in the distance.

"Oh shit, we've been set up! Let's get out of here!"

The three headed for the door and met their fourth partner as he was bounding up the stairs to warn them. "Come on! The cops are coming!" he yelled as the sirens grew louder. They turned and started to head back down the stairs and stopped in their tracks as they stared at two 9 mm Glocks pointed back at them. The chunky man from the car held his gun at his side and didn't move a muscle.

Ralph Lewis said in a deep, commanding voice, "You with the gun, real slowly set that gun down! Don't twitch a muscle because I'll shot you and splatter your brains on your friends. The rest of you keep your hands where we can see them; that means real high in the air."

The four complied as the first of seven police cruisers pulled up with guns drawn. They quickly understood that the situation was well in hand. They took the four into custody and headed to St. Marys police headquarter building. The ranking officer spoke with Ralph and John. He assured them that they'd be able to question the suspects when they were able to get down to the station.

The agents went back to the surveillance apartment and cued the disc to the point when the three entered the apartment. They watched as the three looked around at the empty rooms and closets. Ralph said, "Okay, here it comes." They watched and laughed as the man looked directly into the camera in the pantry before he realized what it was. Then John played with him a little, moving the camera from side to side. At this point he left the camera alone because they had to get across the parking lot to greet them as they came down the stairs. On the screen, the man's eye was nearly taking up the entire screen. Then they heard the very loud "Oh shit, we've been set up! Let's get out of here!" The agents were laughing so hard that they both had tears in their eyes. It was so loud and raucous that the people in the next door apartment pounded on the wall for them to shut up.

When they calmed down, they heard a voice. "You guys having fun?" It was Captain Brown. They forgot that they were still on speaker phone.

Ralph said, "Well, yes ma'am we are." He wiped the moisture from his eyes as he started to fill Nancy in on the details of the bust. "We'll be heading to the local police station to question these kids. That's all they are, really. They look like high school kids. We inspected the gun. It wasn't even loaded. We could've shot the kid dead and he wasn't even a real threat."

"We all know you can't take that chance. You have to protect yourself and your partner. It sounds like you did a good job. Now the question is; why were these kids there in the first place?"

"I hope we can find that out in about twenty minutes, Captain."

"Call when you have anything."

"Yes, ma'am."

* * *

When Joe and Pat got the call to report to the office at 10:30 at night, they were both bummed and dead tired. Both had just fallen asleep and were in the heavy haze of sexual gratification when the hotel phone rang and woke them. Diane and Lisa were both angry, but they were more worried than angry. They hadn't been able to spend any real time with their men and now they were being drug off to who knows where.

Pat kissed Diane and told her to go back to sleep. He wasn't sure how long he'd be but it shouldn't be too long. Joe was more realistic with Lisa. He said he had no idea when he'd be back but that he would call her cell phone when he knew. He also told her to not worry and go back to sleep. When they both left their men at their hotel room doors, Lisa went over to Diane's room and they talked for almost an hour. It was near midnight before Lisa made it back to her and Joe's room. She fell asleep but it was an uneasy sleep. She dreamt as she drifted off.

Diane didn't even try to sleep. She knew she wouldn't be able to sleep right away so she took out a novel and read. After she read several chapters, she started to drift off to a deep sleep. It didn't last too long. She was jolted from her sleep by a vivid dream. Pat had been shot in the chest and was bleeding. The blood was pumping out of his chest in a solid stream and his face was as white as a ghost, like he had white makeup powder all over. He was talking normally as if nothing unusual had happened. Diane was screaming at him, "You've been shot, you're bleeding to death. I told you to be careful." She was sobbing in her dream but Pat was smiling at her, saying, 'It's okay. It's only a flesh wound.' When she finally woke, her face was soaked with tears and she had a horrible feeling of dread. She couldn't sleep another wink. Then a knock came at the door. She was frightened to open it. She walked to the door and peered out the peep hole and saw Lisa standing there in a hotel robe.

When she let her in, Lisa said, "Are you alright? I heard you crying in my room. I wasn't sleeping much anyway, but it sounded like you were sobbing." Without a word, Diane held out her arms and they embraced. She began to cry again, this time it was no dream. Lisa cried right along with her.

* * *

"It turns out the kids were paid to burglarize the apartment. Once they finally realized how serious it was they all sang like the Vienna Boys Choir." Nancy was telling Pat, Joe and Wilson about the events at Wilson's apartment. Wilson sat stone faced hearing that his personal space was again the target of ill intent. "Anyway, the youngest girl, sixteen years old and the driver found out all the charges that could be leveled and she described in detail how they came to be at the complex. A woman approached her older brother about making some money and a little bonus. He agreed to listen. She paid him twenty bucks to break in to the apartment. She said that there was a safe with over $3,000 bucks in the master bedroom closet. She even gave him the combination and directions on opening the safe. She said the door was easy to open that the lock and latch weren't long enough to keep anyone out. All he had to do was to use a knife to pry open the door slightly then bang the door with his shoulder and it would pop right open."

"That's pretty good incentive but why would this woman want the apartment burglarized in the first place? Why would the kids believe her?"

"She told them that her husband was screwing around on her and she wanted to pay him back." Nancy shrugged her shoulders. "What can I tell you? They're teenagers. What do they know?" Nancy smiled as if she had a secret.

"Okay, Captain. What else do you know?"

"Well, this woman said that if they pulled it off, she'd give the guys a blowjob. Apparently they were hesitant until she put that on the table as a bonus. The guys jumped at it. The girls were pissed. So for the girls, she said they could do anything that they wanted to her son or they could have him do anything that they wanted him to do. That calmed them down some but the girls really weren't that interested, or so they said."

"Did they give a good description of these two?" Joe asked.

"Yes and they sound exactly like our suspects."

Pat looked at Nancy who was still smiling like Cheshire Cat. "Do they have a name?"

"That's the best news of all. The woman is Abigail Glover. The young man is her son, Ace Glover. One last bit of information. She told them to do this job this evening, not before and not after. Sounds like part of a plan."

"If they're headed back here to get that check, we've got to get some shut eye. It's already 11:00 pm and we have to be back here by 2:00 am if we're to be in place on time. Maybe we should skip the sleep and head over to the apartment. We can take turns getting some shut eye at the stakeout." Nancy's idea was looking more like reality than just a thought. If they went back to the apartment, they'd never get back to sleep and get up in time to get in place for the stake out.

"I'm game," Joe said. "I think we're better off doing that rather than trying to get a half assed nap at the hotel." Joe knew that if he went back now he'd never get any sleep. The first thing he'd have to do is explain to Lisa what was happening and why they were called in. Then more time would be spent undressing, quick shower, a bite to eat, redressing. He figured he'd never make it. "Let's spend a few minutes going back over the game plan then head over to the apartments. Are all the others on their way in?"

"Yes. Right before you got here I figured that this was how it was going down so I called everyone and said to be in by 11:30. As soon as they get here we'll start. You might as well get the coffee started. It's going to be a long night. I sure hope this is it. We can't afford another slip up. Major Hartnett said that if we don't make the collar this time, the FBI is going to move in and take over. This is our last shot."

Pat and Joe looked at each other then back at Nancy. Wilson Brush headed for the coffee machine and made a fresh pot. As they started to drink, the other members of the team arrived. Within a few minutes the entire team was assembled. They went over the plan one last time. It wasn't so much a plan as it was a strategy to contain anyone who went to the mailbox outside Dean Gray's apartment. They wanted to take these characters without incident. They had to move fast so that the suspects knew they had no chance to escape and therefore would offer no resistance.

The setup of the apartment didn't lend itself well to the plan. There was too much open area between the apartment building entrance and the parking lot and there were very few trees or other means of cover for the team. So they had to hope that they could move in fast and quiet. One advantage they had was the apartment parking lot lighting was pretty poor. They were also wearing bullet resistant Kevlar vests. But that was no advantage when a gun was pointed at your head.

Chapter 44

The grounds around the parking lot were wet from the rain that had fallen within the last hour. Lighting still flashed in the sky to the northeast but the storm was finished dumping on the eastern half of Virginia, at least for now. The local FM station said that there was a chance for a few trailing showers but nothing like the downpour that had resulted as the storm front moved through the area. The storm cooled the air some but the lingering humidity promised to be oppressive once the sun rose and heated the earth and all the moisture that the storm left behind.

The team was in place by 2:30 am. At 4:05 am the team was still waiting for the suspects to show. There were twelve team members in all. Pat was paired with Wilson Brush in a car to the left of the apartment entrance. Nancy and Joe were in the command van. The van was about fifty feet from the building but directly in front of the apartment entryway with a full view of the mailboxes and the top section of Dean Gray's basement apartment door. Another car was to the left of the building and a team was in the parking lot behind the apartment building. They were to watch for anyone trying to escape through the window at the back of the common area of the apartment building. One other car was parked near the exit to monitor for cars trying to flee the complex. Nancy had everyone keep radio silence unless immediate action was required. That would only be broken if the suspects were fleeing or life was endangered. So far, it was a boring two hours. Everyone was awake and bored but anxious. The rain drops on the windshields of the three cars made it difficult to see, especially when they were trying to keep low and out of sight. But they dared not get out and wipe their car or van windshields and windows for fear of being spotted.

From inside Dean Gray's apartment Jeff Steers and his partner took turns watching through the peep hole while the other watched the monitor that showed an image of the entry to the apartment. The camera was directed at the space right in front of the mailboxes for the apartment building. It encompassed a view that would pick up anyone coming into the common area in front of the boxes. So far, only two people came into view. A young man with a military hair cut coming home at 0300 hours, apparently drunk, stopped and checked his mail. He pulled a few envelopes from his box, belched loud, and went upstairs to his top floor apartment. At 0345 a woman who appeared to be in her mid thirties had come out of one of the apartments near the mailboxes. She was dressed in the kind of smock worn by grocery store clerks. Jeff figured she was on the early morning shift at Food Lion. The colors matched the stores scheme. She'd waited under the sheltered portion of the building for several minutes hoping the rain would slow. When neither happened, she'd run into the parking lot and was out of view of the camera. Since Jeff and his partner didn't receive a 'go' signal they figured she was of no interest to the team. From inside the apartment, that was all the action for the early morning so far.

Out in the parking lot there were several more 'contacts' logged. Over the past two and a half hours the team spotted seven different vehicles. There were four cars, one mini van and two SUVs. The minivan belonged to the grocery store clerk. She got in, started it up and headed out, apparently to work. One of the cars was the drunken military man. The other three cars and the SUVs were of various combinations of people looking pretty normal in their coming and going. Most of them hurried out of their vehicles and to the shelter of their apartment building overhangs. Then they'd shake off the rain and head inside without looking around or drawing any undue attention. All looked normal around the parking lot and none of these folks apparently spotted any of the surveillance team.

As Nancy sat in a van with darkened windows, she thought that maybe the rain would help keep the team concealed. Everyone was in a hurry to get in or out of their apartment so they didn't have time to look around the lot to see the cars and van that were not normally there. She knew that having this many team members in such a concentrated area might draw undue attention from people who cared about their little neighborhood. So she was happy for the rain for now. She was also thankful for the early morning hour of the stakeout. Once the sun started to rise, they would have to go to plan 'B' which had members of the team driving off and back again. That was always harder to pull off since there were more people coming and going, moving around the complex. People noticed things out of place. Unfamiliar people sitting around in cars were definitely out of place. Nancy hoped that this would be over before dawn.

Across the parking lot in a rented, gold Dodge Sebring, Abbie and Ace sat watching the apartment entrance. They'd been there since 1:30am. Abbie was wide awake. She'd been thinking about how much money $100,000 was and that she'd never seen so much cash before when they were at Bobby and Becky's apartment. She was also thinking that dividing it by three was much better than dividing it by four. After Bobby left her high and dry several years ago, she never trusted him. She'd introduced him to her daughter . . . in a way. She helped him get up the courage to approach Becky down in Key West on that beach she watched from a distance. With Abbie's coaching and encouragement he walked right up to her and charmed her like a pro. That's when the trouble between them began. Until that day she was his lover. Once he started talking with Becky, he was through with Abbie. Becky was young, beautiful, and confident. She was already pulling scams on men much older than herself. Bobby was charming in his own way but he had rough edges and a short temper. There was a lot of maintenance involved with having a relationship with Bobby.

When Bobby first met Becky, his temper seemed to disappear. It looked as if he'd licked his problem. Even when he was with Abbie, he was smiling to himself and calm. He would talk about Becky and how wonderful and beautiful she was. It bothered Abbie that her daughter had that affect on him. But his temper was just on hold. It was just buried deep inside of him and it was building pressure, looking for a release. Bobby found that release in rough sex. At first Abbie thought it was exciting, that their relationship was getting rekindled. Then it became painful, physically and emotionally when she finally realized that it wasn't a strengthening of their relationship but a punishment for her growing older and not being as beautiful as her daughter. Finally, when Bobby wanted to break it off totally with Abbie and stay with Becky, it became violent. It was as if Bobby was trying to screw her to death, and maybe he was. Finally he just tried to run away with Becky. That's when she thought it might be a good idea to get Bobby and Becky to learn the identity of Becky's real father. She thought that Bobby might take out his anger on the man that had ruined hers and Becky's lives. But that didn't work out. They weren't in North Dakota long enough for the plan to work. One day she hoped to find that bastard again and finish their business once and for all. But for now a $100,000 payday was more important.

Ace stirred and looked over at his mom. "What time is it?"

"It's a little after four. How are you feeling?"

"I'm fine, just real tired. Anything happening yet?"

She smiled. "Not yet. I'll wake you up as soon as I see them pull in. I expect that it'll be pretty soon. We got ahead of them when they stopped to eat. Speaking of that, what would you like for breakfast? Once we get done here, I'm treating you and your sister to Cracker Barrel or Bob Evans. No more greasy spoons, I promise."

"I always liked Cracker Barrel." Ace smiled as the thought of a large plate of pancakes, sausage, bacon, and a couple of eggs over easy crossed his mind. He could almost smell the dining room of his favorite breakfast restaurant. He turned in his seat and stretched. When he did, his wrist hit one of the 9mm pistols sitting on the console between them and it fell to the floor of the car on a passenger side.

Abbie jumped then scolded Ace, "Be careful. The safeties are off on both of them. You trying to get us killed before breakfast?"

"Sorry Mom." He reached down and put the gun back on the console. He was wide awake now after the rush of adrenaline. "That was some storm. I had a hard time sleeping. The lightning . . ." He stopped in mid sentence as he noticed a black BMW enter the parking lot. Instead of pulling straight up to Dean Gray's apartment building the car circled the parking lot, moving slowly.

"There they are. Keep your head down." As the Beamer passed Abbie and Ace, they crouched low below the dashboard. They nearly stopped breathing when the car passed within ten feet of the parked Sebring. Finally, Abbie peeked above the dash and saw that Bobby was headed towards the Gray apartment entrance. Bobby found an open spot at the end of the building close to the exit road. He put the car in park but left it running. From the Sebring, the BMW was nearly out of sight but they still had a clear line of sight to the mailboxes in the apartment building. Abbie figured when Bobby and Becky pulled the check out of the mailbox, they'd start the car and block them into the parking spot. From there it would be easy to convince Bobby that he needed to renew their partnership or pay the consequences. Even if it went that far, they didn't need Bobby to cash the check anyway.

"Get ready, son. There's a small fortune waiting for us in that mailbox."

Nancy clicked the radio twice to signal that something was happening. She and Joe each checked their guns to make sure that safeties were on but that the straps holding them in the holsters was unsnapped. When they left the van for the apprehension, guns had to be drawn and aimed. There was no time to fool with a sticky snap. They didn't want the noise of a snap to alert the suspects and ruin a quiet and quick collar.

Pat and Wilson looked to their right as the BMW parked. They saw the reverse light flash momentarily as the driver put the car into park then the brake lights went off. The car exhaust continued to billow fumes into the air telling Pat that they had no intention to stick around once they went to the mailbox. Pat could see through the rain spotted window and the darkness in the parking lot that there were two people in the car. He saw the driver, a male with long dark hair, move in his seat and look around the lot. Pat and Wilson were crouched in their car seats, staying as low as possible. The BMW was only about 25 feet from where Pat and Wilson were parked but at such an angle that neither person in the BMW could get a good look at their dark colored sedan. Even so, Pat and Wilson were very still and barely breathing. They'd already checked their guns at the first radio click. They were ready to go whenever they heard Nancy say the word 'Green'.

Inside the apartment, Jeff Steers and his partner waited quietly. They also had their guns ready and in hand. They had to be extra careful during the actual take down. They were coming in from behind the suspects and could possibly get caught in dangerous crossfire. Jeff was well aware of the dangers. His friend Lenny Skiff was killed in what should have been a routine arrest. He wasn't going to let that happen again. He kept thinking about the van in the parking lot when Lenny was killed. The killers had ditched the van at a hotel not far from this apartment complex. *What are they driving now and is it out there in the parking lot?* Jeff was still uneasy about the possibility that someone was out there waiting to ambush the team. He shivered and a chill went up his spine. His partner watched the monitor. Jeff looked over at him with a look that asked the question, *'Anything yet?'* He shook his head and Jeff resumed looking through the peep hole on the door.

* * *

Bobby and Becky sat with the engine running, lights out, and radio off. They each looked around the parking lot for any signs of trouble. So far in their tour of the lot, they didn't see anything. They were nervous and anxious. Becky thought they should just walk right up to the mailbox, grab the mail and scoot. Bobby wanted to be more cautious and since Bobby was driving, he won the argument.

"Okay, we'll leave the car running and go get the check together. Do you have the key?"

Without a word, Becky held up the key.

"Alright, when we leave the car, we walk normally together so we don't attract attention."

Becky shook her head and rolled her eyes. "Bobby, look around. There's nobody out here. How are we going to attract attention? Sitting here with the engine running and no lights on will attract attention. Let's get going. The longer we sit here the more nervous I'm getting. Somebody might call the police and then we're sunk."

Bobby thought about that for a second. What Becky said made sense but he was nervous. He wanted to make sure everything was perfect before they made their move. But there was no time like the present. "Okay, are you ready?"

"I've been ready." She was tired of waiting and opened her car door. Bobby paused for a split second then followed suit. They got out of the car and headed for the apartment mailboxes just under the overhang of the building common area. They paused at the mailbox as Becky put her key in and opened the box. The box was nearly jammed full of mail, mostly advertisements and assorted junk mail. She reached in to pull out the stack of mail. She put magazines and advertisements back into the box as she inspected the stack for the one envelope with the big check.

She found it; addressed to Mrs. Dean Gray from NatFed Life Insurance Company. She handed the remaining stack of mail to Bobby and ripped the envelop open. She peered at the check for $100,000. She stared for a moment before she tucked the check back into the envelope and turned to smile at Bobby. Her smile turned to a frown as she noticed the reflection of light in the glass front case of a fire extinguisher. The light was coming from the parking lot and it appeared to be a car dome light.

Bobby saw the expression on her face and his heart sank. He reached for the gun that was tucked in his belt at the small of his back.

Nancy put the radio to her mouth and said, "Green." Almost immediately six car doors opened and the team began their approach. They each were about sixty feet from the entryway to the apartment building and they moved together as they closed the distance. As they approached, they staggered so that they weren't in a straight line across. If the suspects ran, they wanted to be able to cut them off if they broke through the first line. Their hope was that they wouldn't need to take any aggressive action. They hoped that the suspects would see the helplessness in fighting and go peacefully. Pat looked around the parking lot as he and Wilson approached from the left. He didn't see anything on his side but he did notice a light come on at the back of the lot. He signaled to one of the team members approaching on the right and motioned towards the light. He wanted to make sure that if a threat came from behind, they were covered. They planned for this but in the intensity of the moment, you couldn't remember every detail. Pat turned back to the approach and continued along with the remainder of the team. They were within about twenty feet now and would round the corner of the entry. The suspects would be in full view any second now.

* * *

Abbie saw the car doors open in unison. She knew that Bobby and Becky were trapped. There was no escape without help. Ace saw the team starting to move in, too. He straightened up and tensed.

"Mom, look!"

"Let's go! We have to get her out of there." With that Abbie grabbed her gun and was out of the car. She didn't shut the door. She just started running towards the apartment building, gun at her side. Ace sat there, stunned and unable to move. He watched his mother approach the advancing team. She was about one hundred feet from the team when he saw her raise her gun as she continued to run at the apartment.

* * *

Bobby raised his gun and fired at the first person he saw. The shot went high over Nancy's right shoulder. On hearing the report, the team stopped, crouched and prepared to return fire. Nancy and Joe were the only ones with a clear shot at Bobby. But that ended when Bobby grabbed Becky around the throat with his left arm and used her for a shield. Becky was horrified but couldn't get away from Bobby's grasp. He continued to fire two more rounds, the second grazing Joes left arm. He felt the sting and immediately knew he'd been hit. He also knew it wasn't serious. He took aim at Bobby's head and steadied to fire. Before he did, one of the team members from the right side took aim and fired several rounds at Bobby and Becky. The first shot hit Bobby's arm that was around Becky's neck and passed through, catching Becky in the lower neck. The bullet severed her carotid artery. Blood spurted from her neck, spraying the mailboxes and the entryway. Her now dead weight was too much for Bobby to hold while trying to fire on the approaching team. When Becky's body slid from his grip he rose up, aimed and started to squeeze the trigger. That was his last thought. Joe squeezed off two rounds that hit the center of his face and exploded out the back of his head. Bobby was dead instantly. The team rushed in and tried to stop the profuse bleeding from Becky's neck to no avail. Her bleeding was coming in shorter and shorter spurts. It was only a matter of time.

Abbie saw Becky get shot as she approached. She was about sixty feet away when she screamed and started to open fire on the apprehension team. As Pat turned to see her running, he caught a slug in the chest and was knocked backwards onto his back. The team member Pat had alerted to the possibility of a rear assault fired back at Abbie and caught her in the chest. She went down immediately. Joe had been trying to stop Becky's bleeding and looked up just in time to see Pat fall on his back. In horror he ran to his brother's side. He saw the hole in his shirt in the center of his chest. Pat looked pale. Joe thought he was dead. After a few seconds kneeling there, Pat coughed and started to breathe. He opened his eyes and looked up at Joe. He gave Joe a weak smile as he struggled for each breath and said, "Those . . . Kevlar vests . . . were a pretty good . . . idea." Joe smiled back and nodded his head. "But it feels like . . . someone took a . . . baseball bat to my chest." He coughed.

"Are you just going to lay there or can I help you up?"

Joe offered his hand and Pat grabbed it. Pat started to move forward then groaned and said, "Maybe I'll just stay here for a few minutes."

"Suit yourself but it's gonna hurt worse if you don't get up and move. Trust me."

"Okay you pushy bastard." He grabbed Joe's hand again and struggled to his feet. He noticed the blood on Joe's shirt sleeve and asked, "Are you alright?"

"Yeah; just a flesh wound. It took a little meat and it burned a little but I'm fine."

Wilson Brush walked over to where his former wife lay, grotesquely spread out on the concrete floor of the apartment entry. Her blood was everywhere. He leaned over her body. Her eyes were still open and she turned her head towards Wilson. Her lips moved. He thought she said 'I love you' but he couldn't be sure. Her skin was extremely pale as she quickly approached death. As he crouched looking at her he asked a dozen questions to her in his mind. *Why did you have to let me love you? You had me hooked from the moment I laid eyes on you. I would have given you all of the money you needed. You didn't have to do this.* The tears started to flow and he broke into a deep sob sucking in air loudly as he did. One of the team tried to console him but he shrugged them off. He'd needed this moment for a long time.

Joe helped Pat over to the entry where the bodies of Becky and Bobby lay. He shook his head. Then he glanced at Abbie's body lying about 50 feet away in the parking lot. "All this . . . and for what? That's at least eight people dead. Those are the one's we know about."

"People have been killed for a lot less. Think of the number of convenience store clerks that have been killed over twenty or forty bucks. All they were trying to do was bring home enough money to feed their families." Joe wanted to get away from the scene and head for his hotel room. He wanted to hug Lisa and tell her how much he loved her. This was totally depressing.

Nancy came over to check on them. She was checking on all the members of her team. Everyone was alive. That was first and foremost on her mind. "We had a few injuries but for the most part, everyone's okay. Jeff Steers took a bullet to the upper left part of his vest. It bruised his collar bone terribly. He's going to be transported to the hospital. How about you, Pat? Do you need to go?"

Pat's answer was short and firm. "No! I'm fine!" He took a couple of deep breaths and said again, "I'm fine, really."

Local police had arrived on the scene and a couple of ambulances. The coroner was going to be summoned to the scene before any bodies were removed.

Pat had a look of confusion on his face when Nancy and Joe looked at him. Nancy asked, "What is it, Pat?"

"That's Abbie Glover, right? Where's Ace? Wasn't he with her?"

Both Joe and Nancy got a concerned look on their faces. Nancy said, "Gather the team members and the local police. Let's get a search party together. We really need to secure this scene before any of the neighbors trample on the evidence. She came from that direction, right?" Nancy pointed towards an empty space across the parking lot. "Let's do a search of the area. Maybe we'll track him down. Chances are he's still here. It's only been about five minutes since we moved in."

Pat thought, *five minutes. It feels like hours.* But it had been just those few minutes. A drizzle of rain started again and the local police got tarps from their cruiser trunks to cover the bodies as the team started to fan out and search the apartment complex. After twenty minutes they gathered back on the empty space where they figured Abbie had come from. Apparently Ace was there but he was gone now.

* * *

At 5:10am, Ace walked back out of Bobby and Becky's apartment with a duffle bag in his hand. He knew that Bobby wouldn't need the money any longer and nobody would stop him from taking the remainder of the cash. No sense leaving it behind for the cops. He drove the Sebring west on I-64 until he was west of Richmond. Then he got on US Route 250 and paralleled the interstate to near the Virginia border. He was exhausted by noon so he pulled off the interstate and got a room in McDowell, Virginia. He slept for the rest of the day into Saturday morning. When he awoke, he knew what he had to do. He kept driving west until he found a Wal-Mart store. There he bought a road atlas and plotted a course for the northern plains. Then he thought about his mother. He sat in the Sebring in the parking lot of the Wal-Mart and cried for ten minutes. Then he scolded himself for shedding a tear. His mother was all he had. He didn't know his father. She'd never let on who he was even if she knew. But he knew a few things that had gone wrong in his mother's life and he reckoned to even the score. He put the Sebring in drive and continued northwest.

* * *

The paperwork wasn't real clean for the bust since all the perpetrators were dead. But all in all, Major Hartnett was pleased. *It's fine that they're dead. They shouldn't have screwed with our boys.* He commended Nancy on a job well done. Nancy was not as pleased as the Major seemed to be. She wanted to bring Bobby and Becky in alive and make them suffer the way they made their victims suffer. But they weren't going to let that happen. At least Bobby Garrett wasn't. She looked at his service record and saw where he got his skills; a Navy Yeoman. What better position to learn how to manipulate the system.

They finally learned the identity of the young woman who could turn a man's head because of her beauty and his heart because of her charm and sexuality. Rebecca Jean Lippert had been disowned at birth; called a bastard by her own flesh and blood. According to the adoption records that Nancy had obtained, her adoptive parents, Robert and Sheila Lippert, were killed in an accident in the mountains of Colorado when Becky was a toddler. She was placed in foster care and lost in the system, passed from one foster home to another. When she was eleven years old she was removed from a foster home amidst allegations of sexual and physical abuse. By the time she turned fifteen, she'd run away from her foster homes nine times.

The last entry in the file by Family Services stated Rebecca Lippert had disappeared. She was considered a runaway. No other trace of her was found in their official records. As far as they were concerned, Rebecca Jean Lippert no longer existed. No one questioned where she went and apparently no one cared.

Nancy and her team would never know the details of Becky Lippert's life. They'd never know about how she learned how to take care of herself the hard way. She'd learned what men like. Through her rough life, she'd managed to keep her body in shape and protect herself from abusive men. She'd learned how to treat men and gave them what they liked. And she learned how to avoid danger.

Once away from the Foster Care system and until she met Bobby Garrett, she was satisfied with her life. She was taking advantage of people but she felt justified because of the way people had taken advantage of her. When Bobby came into her life, he wooed her with promises of money, fine clothes, and fancy cars. He'd said that with his skills and her talents, they were an unstoppable team.

At first, Bobby's promises seemed to be on track. Then his temper and controlling personality started to surface. The relationship started to unravel long before their tragic end when Bobby's hunger grew for physically abusive sex. Becky knew she had to get away from him before he really hurt her. She'd already been through that as a young teen in the many foster homes to which she'd been shuffled. She knew she had to get away from Bobby or she would end up seriously hurt.

In the end, her life was snuffed out as tragically as it began. Though she never intended for anyone to get hurt, she impacted the lives of many others. Some of those sucked into this horrible mess were innocent people. Their lives were destroyed for reasons that they would never know or begin to understand.

Chapter 45

Pat, Joe, and Jeff Steers all decided to go to the hospital. Actually, Nancy insisted. In unison they'd said "Yes Ma'am." It was a good thing that they did. After each was examined it was determined that Jeff had a chipped collar bone and a fragment of the bone had to be removed. The doctor said he risked painful infection if he left the fragment in place. Joe was given a prescription for antibiotics and an antibiotic cream for his flesh wound. Finally, Pat was given a chest x-ray. The bullet had bruised his sternum so badly that the doctor said he would think he was having a heart attack the next morning. He warned Pat of the other signs of a heart attack and told him that if he didn't have other signs besides a sore chest to ignore the pain. He gave him a prescription for Vicodin and said to be careful moving around for a few days. If the bruise was deep it could actually cause reduced lung function therefore shortness of breath and some of the symptoms that mimic a heart attack.

"Great. Diane's gonna kill me anyway. I should take several of those Vicodin because I don't want to feel it when Diane beats my ass."

"I have no clue what Lisa's gonna say. I hope she's in a good mood."

"After she sees that bandage, don't count on it. You'll be lucky if she doesn't sock you right on the bandage."

Jeff Steers walked out of one of the emergency room cells. His arm was in a sling and he looked like he was walking on air. He had a smile that looked painted on his face. "Who's driving back to the office?"

"Well it sure as hell isn't you, pal." They all laughed, except Jeff's was delayed by about two seconds as it took awhile for the joke to clear the fog in his head.

Pat asked, "Did either of you guys see Wilson after the shooting stopped this morning?"

Joe and Jeff both shook their heads. Jeff looked at Joe then realized that he should shake his head no as well.

"I hope someone talks with him. He was still in love with that crazy chick, Becky. I think he really wanted to save her and help her see what she could make of herself. He talked with me for quite a while about her and how smart and beautiful she was. It tore him apart to realize that she was evil."

Joe looked quizzically at Pat. "You have to be careful of your harsh judgments of people, Pat. Just think back a few years and look in the mirror. It's easy to take a wrong turn and once you do it's really hard to get back on track. We had a good family and a good life, remember? Then look what happened. From what I understand, Becky spent most of her life in foster homes. How tough is that?"

Pat did a little soul searching and thought about how right his younger brother was. They were on the wrong track for several years and it cost them a brother and sister-in-law. Who knows what kind of emotional pain it put their parents through? "I wish I could argue with you but you're right. We were on a fast track to nowhere. It took tragedy to get us to wake up."

They both looked at Jeff Steers who was leaning against the wall nearly falling over. Joe said, "Speaking of coma, we'd better get him out of here or he's gonna end up on the floor."

It was 7:30 in the morning. They were in and out of the emergency room quickly. The staff wasn't real busy that morning so they got right in and were treated and released. The morning was sunny. It looked to be a real scorcher later. The showers from earlier would only help to raise the humidity to intolerable levels. They got Jeff outside and into the rental car then headed back to the office with Joe driving. He was the only one that wasn't on serious pain medication. Once they dropped Jeff off with Nancy, they headed back to the hotel room to see their women. It was a reunion that they both anticipated with mixed emotions. Pat was anxious to see Diane but he knew he was in trouble. But it was time to face the music. They hopped back in the car and headed for the hotel. Joe reminded Pat that they had to get some sleep today because Brian Purcer's concert was that evening.

"Oh shit, I forgot about that. You don't have to worry about me getting rest. These Vicodin are knocking me out already. Just make sure I go into the right room."

In the car, Joe started talking about the turn of events that brought them to this day. He was rambling on about how if they hadn't screwed up their own lives so young that he would never have gone in the Marines. If he'd never have gone in the Marines he'd never have met Major Griggs and Major Griggs would have never recalled him to service. Of course if that never happened he'd never have called Pat to help out. And . . . he looked over at Pat just in time to hear him snore. He was out cold.

So much for my confession.

When Joe parked the car at the hotel twenty minutes later, he had to shake Pat to wake him. He also had to help him into the hotel lobby and the elevator. The few people that saw the two must have thought that Pat had been on an all night drunk. Joe did nothing to dissuade that belief. He just smiled as the elevator door went closed and he punched in the number for their floor. A few minutes later he was at Pat and Diane's door knocking. Diane answered and saw Pat barely awake being held up by his younger brother. Her expression was at first fear, then when Joe smiled her expression changed.

"What happened?"

"It's a real long story, Diane. Can it wait until later today? Or if you like we can drop Pat on the bed and you can come over and hear me explain it to Lisa. I might need some protection."

Diane put her hands on her hips and said, "Sorry Joe. You're on your own there. Lisa's been worried sick about you. You are one lucky bastard, do you know that?"

"Uh, yes I do. I hope my luck doesn't run out."

"Just get over there, would you?"

Joe headed to his and Lisa's room, knocked on the door and waited. He didn't have to wait long. Lisa opened the door, took one look at him and leaped into his arms. He winced at the pain burning in his left arm but he held on tight. They kissed in the hall then they slowly made their way back into the hotel room. Lisa was in a robe and nothing else. As they held and kissed each other her robe loosened but she didn't care. Within seconds the robe was on the floor and she was undressing Joe until she felt the bandage on his arm.

"You're hurt! What happened?" She stared at the bandage. It had just a slight spot of blood showing through the bandage.

"It's nothing really. A bullet grazed me this morning. The good news is it's just a flesh wound and will be healed in no time." He looked at her face and he saw the fear. She was afraid that she was in love with a guy who lived a very dangerous life. He had to dispel her fears and fast. "I'm going to ask for a discharge from the Marine Reserves. I had to take this assignment because I'm in the reserves and I was ordered to do it. But I did my part and we finished the job we were asked to do. Now its time for someone else to step up. I only have a little time left anyway."

Lisa looked into Joe's eyes. "You'd do that for me?"

"I am doing that for us. I can't leave you like this again."

"But you love the Corps."

"But I love you more."

"Her face brightened and she smiled as she met his lips. They made their way to the bed where they made love for a good part of the morning that remained. They fell asleep just before 10:00.

* * *

At just after 2:00 pm, Pat awoke from his drug induced slumber. He started to role over but someone hit his chest with a hammer, or at least that's what it felt like. Then he remembered the morning's events.

"Hey sleepy head. How are you feeling?"

"Uh, great. What time is it? How long have I been out?"

"Oh, about six hours. Do you remember getting here?"

"Uh, not really. The last thing I remember was being at the hospital." Oops.

"So, smart guy, why were you at the hospital?"

"Well, Joe got shot in the arm so he had to get stitched up or something. And Jeff Steers got shot in the collar bone so they had to look at him. I think I drove them." He saw Diane's look and decided he'd better come clean. "And there was one other thing. I got a bruise on my chest somehow."

"Somehow? You were shot, Pat! Shot in the chest! Right where your heart is supposed to be. Of course it probably wouldn't have hurt you 'cause you obviously don't have a heart!"

"Honey, I had a vest on. I'm okay. It's just a bruise."

"You're alright now. Wait until I'm through with you. You'll wish you'd taken that bullet."

Pat hung his head. He took a big gamble joining this team for no good reason except to support Joe. He had no commitment but he chose to do it.

"Pat, you have to choose. You have a family. I had a nightmare last night after you left. I dreamed that you were shot . . . in the chest . . . and died." Tears formed in her eyes. I can't lose you, I won't lose you. If you have to do this stuff, okay, but understand that there may come a time when I can't take it anymore. I'm just not that strong." Pat slowly got out of bed and moved to his wife. They embraced gently.

"I'd hold you tighter but I'm afraid I'd pass out from the pain." They stayed that way for a while then Pat said, "I'll never leave you. I'll always be there for you and the kids. There are some things that I feel I have to do to make up for some of the bad things that I did in my earlier years. I know you shouldn't have to atone for my sins but I do. Will you help me get through this? There will come a time when I feel like I'm even again, but I'm not there yet."

"You'd better get there in a hurry because we may not be around when you get there."

His vision of Diane faded as she said again, "You'd better get there in a hurry because we may not be around when you get there." Then he woke up. The dream was over and Diane was sitting on the chair watching him.

"Finally ready to wake up?"

"Yea, what time is it?"

"It's nearly 3:30pm. I just got a call from Brian. He and Ginny arrived at the hotel and checked in at about 3:00. They'd like for us to go to dinner with them before he has to get to Scope Arena. He wants Joe and Lisa to go too. He said he'd treat and he won't take no for an answer."

"Well I guess I better get up and shower." Pat moved and pain shot through his chest. "Ouch, does that hurt."

"That is some bruise. How did you get that?" She gave him a menacing look like she already knew the story.

"I'll tell you later, maybe on the way home while we're in a moving car. That way you can't hit me."

Diane just stared for a few seconds. Then a smile curled at the corners of her lips. "I don't know what it is. I just can't stay mad at you."

"Because you love me," Pat said as he slowly moved off the bed and headed to the bathroom for a shower. When he took off his shirt and looked in the mirror, the bruise was deep purple, almost black in the center. Close call. He touched the bruise then felt around its perimeter. It was sore at least an inch all around it. He looked closer and the bruise was in the shape of a heart. *There's a message in this somewhere.*

As he showered he wondered if the conversation that he thought was a dream really was a dream or if it was real. Had Diane said those things? He didn't have the courage to ask. He knew he had to make some changes though. If his subconscious mind was that hard on himself, there were things he needed to come to terms with or he'd lose his family. He couldn't live with that. He finished his shower and dressed for dinner with his best friend from after high school and newest rock star from the southeast, Brian Purcer.

* * *

Dinner was fantastic. The six got along well and enjoyed good food and good drinks. Brian held back on the drinks because he had to perform but they had a wonderful dinner. Brian gave them their backstage passes for the show and told them to come anytime before, during, or after the show. The band would be staying overnight at the Marriott so they could get a late breakfast before the band left for Philadelphia in the morning.

"There's one more thing I wanted to tell you guys. Ginny and I are getting married." Ginny blushed and smiled brightly. She was so much in love with Brian. Pat had never seen him happier. He was on top of the world. His band, Brian Purcer and the Hot Licks had a number one single, *I Know You Better Than You Think*, a number one album, *The Hot Spot*, and he was in love with a good woman. Pat thought that he'd never see the day. Pat, Diane, Joe and Lisa raised their glasses in a toast to the happy couple. The ladies gave hugs all around, the men shook hands, and they left to get ready for the concert.

* * *

That night, the Hot Licks put on one of the greatest concerts that Pat and Joe had ever seen, and they'd seen plenty. Brian's guitar was smoking and the crowd was into it from the opening cord to the grand finale. The two and a half hour show left the crowd exhausted. Pat couldn't believe the intensity of the music and the lyrics. Brian truly was a superstar.

Backstage after the show, Brian handed out beers and drinks for everyone. He got everyone's attention and said, "I have a toast. To my band, the Hot Licks who make the greatest music in the world." Everyone started to yell 'cheers' but Brian went on. "I'm not done yet. To my friends, Pat and Diane McKinney, Joe McKinney and Lisa Goddard-soon-to-be-McKinney, who have stood by me when I wanted to give up. They kept me going.   Finally, to Ginny Parks-soon-to-be-Purcer, who has made me the happiest man in the world.   I love all of you."

"Cheers!"   Applause broke out in the dressing room.   It was a magical night for everyone.

After an hour of hanging out with the band, Pat, Diane, Joe, and Lisa hugged Brain and Ginny again.   They left with promises to stay in touch and attend Brian's concerts whenever they could.   Before they walked out the door, Brian said to Pat quietly, "Thanks for hooking me up with your financial guy.   It's working out exceedingly well."

"It's the very least I could do, Brian.   After some of the things I've done in my life, I need all the brownie points I can get."

Brian's face took on a serious look.   "Pat, all that stuff is in the past. Let it go, man."   Pat shook his hand and started to pull away.   Brian grabbed his hand tighter.   "I'm serious.   Wipe the slate clean.   You've made amends. Good God, man.   Just be happy.   If you ever doubt that you've done the right thing, just look at your wife.   You're the second luckiest man on earth, next to me of course."   Brian's smile widened.   It was definitely contagious.

"You're right.   I am.   Thanks Brian.   He paused for a moment looking Brian in the eyes.   "Good luck with the rest of the tour.   After seeing you guys tonight, it's a slam dunk."   They hugged a man hug then Pat turned and ran to catch up with Diane, Joe and Lisa.   He waved to Brian over his shoulder as he ran, feeling one step closer to breaking even.

Chapter 46

The drive took nearly three full days. The scenery along the back roads and highways was beautiful and diverse. The landscape changed along the way from green mountains in the east to rolling hills and flatlands in northern Ohio and Indiana to wide open fields in Iowa, then to the forests and lakes of Minnesota, finally giving way to the flat, rolling land of Eastern North Dakota. Now Ace Glover saw wheat fields for as far as the eyes could see. The distance between cities in the east was mere miles. In the Northern plains the cities were much further apart and much smaller. The population density in this agriculturally based part of the country was a fraction of states like Ohio and Virginia. But that was good for Ace. He didn't want to be around people. He preferred to be alone, at least for the time being. He was on his way to an important interview. The interviewee was an officer in the Air Force and on the way up in the military hierarchy. When Ace asked him for the interview, he initially declined saying that he was nearing the end of his tenure at Grand Forks and was getting ready to move to Washington, D.C. He didn't have time at the moment. He suggested that Ace wait and talk with the new commander but Ace countered that the new man wouldn't have his experience and insight. Ace promised that the interview would take less than thirty minutes. It would really improve his grade to have an interview with an Air Force Colonel, especially one in his position. Finally, the colonel agreed and the interview was set for late in the day out at the old Minuteman III missile silo that the Air Force hoped to turn into a Cold War Museum.

Ace drove down the treeless road to the site. He feared that the wide open terrain might be too visible. As he drove on for several miles he realized that there was nobody around. The area was deserted. Only hearty souls ventured out here during the heat of the summer. It was late afternoon, nearly 5:30pm. The sun was still high in the sky in this northern region of the country. The heat was oppressive. The humidity was low and Ace was glad he'd thought to bring a liter of water along. He already downed about a third of the water on his way to the site.

As he approached the site, he was surprised by the isolation. He expected to see several large buildings with a large parking area and other support facilities such as a building to house the missiles in case they needed to be removed from their silos. There was nothing but a small building that looked so small he doubted that three people could stay there comfortably. There was a small picnic table under a pavilion style shelter. That's where he and the colonel would meet. It was within site of the road

but that didn't matter. By all appearances, nobody came down this road.
And they want to preserve this for a museum. Hmm. Good Luck.
Ace took a seat at the picnic table and waited for the colonel. He set
his water on the table and a note pad with several pages of notes already
scribbled out as if he were really gathering information on a report. He set
a couple of pens next to the pad, stood and looked around the area. There
was barren land as far as he could see. There was no sign of human life.
The only thing that kept this area from looking like the surface of the moon
was the white sage covering the untilled earth.   In the distance Ace could
see the edges of wheat fields, geographically laid out surrounding the
missile site. He looked at the underside of the roof overhanging the picnic
bench. Wasps had built their nests in the corners of the wood beams and
spider webs covered much of the space between cross beams. Some were
new, but most had been there for a long time as evidenced by the dried
vegetation blown in by the prairie wind, clinging to the web's sticky fibers.

There was no security fence keeping anyone off the site but the
building had a padlock and chain on the only door to the small building.
That didn't deter vandals and their cans of spray paint from desecrating the
place with graffiti. He tried to read some of the words but most had been
overwritten by more recent trash.   The artists in North Dakota weren't
nearly as talented as those he'd seen back east. But the kids in the slums in
Virginia had lots of practice. *Too bad they couldn't put that talent to good
use. Why do people have to screw up other's lives to benefit themselves?*
Then he thought, *that's why I'm here; to settle a score.*

As he sat waiting and thinking, he thought about his mom. She had
meant everything to him. She taught him how to survive and how to be
cautious of people who tried to take advantage of him. She schooled him
on how to be charming and nice to women and not take advantage of them
like almost every other man that she knew. She was determined that Ace
would turn out different. She taught him that bad men needed to be taught a
lesson, like that bastard Bobby Garrett. He needed his ass kicked. If he'd
survived, Ace was planning to do it. But he'd read in the paper before he
got out of Virginia that Bobby had been killed, along with his sister and his
mother.

He wished that he had a chance to get to know his sister better. He
knew just from their brief encounter that he would have liked her. She was
a lot like him. She was beautiful and full of life. She knew how to be nice
to people. He smiled to himself remembering the only real conversation he
had with her at the hotel in Norfolk, that early morning when she left
Bobby. He thought she was leaving that prick for good but it didn't work
out that way. *Too bad, because it would have changed the whole outcome
of the last few days. I can't dwell on that.*

He thought about his mother again. He missed her. They'd been
together constantly through nearly his whole adolescent life. She got him

away from that horrible foster home and told him that she was his real mother, that she came back to take care of him. She apologized for giving him up at birth and wanted to make it up to him. She did her best and as far as Ace was concerned, all was forgiven. He didn't have it as bad as his sister in foster care. But he was a male and he managed to stay out of the other kids way when trouble seemed imminent. He was only assigned to two different families in his foster care years. The first family was working fine until the parents got divorced. The kids were taken away and sent to different families. Ace ended up with a very caring, but very religious family. Up to that point, he knew nothing about God or churches and he had little interest in religion at eleven years old. He liked girls and that kept his attention pretty much full time. Then when he turned twelve, his mother found him and he left his foster family for good. He left in the night and they never found out where he'd gone. He read the papers about his own disappearance and was pleased to know that they gave up after a few months.

But his life had taken an ugly turn now. He had to take the lessons he learned from his foster care years and his mother's instructions and survive on his own. It would be much easier with over $150,000 cash but that didn't guarantee success. He had to be cautious and make sure the money didn't leave his sight. He had to guard it with his life. That money was his ticket to finishing a job he planned out on his way to North Dakota over the last three days.

He looked up as the official car approached and parked next to the rented Dodge Sebring. Ace tore off the sticker that identified the rental car company. The clerk had questioned his being twenty-five when he rented the car but his fake driver's license from Virginia bore out his claim. He would buy a new car when he was finished with his 'report'.

The tall man exiting the car was distinguished looking. His expression didn't give away any emotion or mood. His long slender face was business-like. He was in his light weight summer uniform hat, pants and shirt, a light blue with applets and the eagle insignia of an Air Force Colonel. Ace stood and greeted him with a smile and a hand shake.

"Hi, Colonel. I'm Ace Williams. Thanks for meeting with me. I know this is a bit out of the way for you and you're a busy man."

Milton Chester's face didn't change a bit. He didn't smile or let on that he was happy, angry, annoyed, or any other emotional state. He just said, "My pleasure, son. I have to be back in town by 7:00 pm so what did you have in mind?"

"Well, sir, I'm doing some research on life in the military, particularly on the life of officers. Part of it has to do with life around weapons of mass destruction. I've thought about entering the Air Force Academy and wanted to know what life was like for an Air Force Academy graduate."

The colonel's jaw tightened slightly. "You could have come to my office for this kind of interview. We didn't have to meet at a remote missile site for this." He looked Ace directly in the eyes and saw something more than a curious youth looking for answers on the Air Force Academy. "My assistant, Major Hull, said you wanted to know about missile programs and how we keep control of the still active missiles. What are you up to son?" Ace stared at Colonel Chester. *That was the second time you called me 'son'. I'm not your son, you son of a bitch but you are my sister's father. My mom had the paperwork to prove it.* It was time to get this game on the table.

Ace's face took on a tense, matter of fact look. "You're right. I'm not here to talk about the Air Force. I want to know how you can have a daughter and let her life be destroyed while you enjoy the good life." Ace's face grew red with anger as he went on, explaining his real business here. "I want to know how four Air Force cadets can get away with destroying a woman's life; how they can go on living their lives like nothing happened while the woman they raped was forced to live like trailer trash nearly her whole life."

Milton Chester's face finally showed emotion as he realized the potential danger that he was in. He was standing near the picnic table with a kid who had knowledge of something that took place almost thirty years ago. How did he know? Who was he? Why did he care? "Listen son . . ."

"Stop calling me 'son'! I'm not your son! But you did have a daughter, or did you even know that?!"

The colonel started to turn away but Ace wasn't nearly finished. "Sit down and don't move!"

The colonel hesitated then continued. He wasn't about to let this kid order him around. "I'm leaving now," he said calmly.

Ace pulled the 9mm silenced Glock from the waistband at the small of his back and shouted, "Sit down now!" His face was bright red with rage.

The colonel stopped, staring at the gun pointed at his face then did as he was ordered, slowly sitting down at the picnic table. He kept his eyes on Ace's finger which was dangerously close to putting enough pressure on the trigger to blow his brains all over the pavilion. "Okay, son . . ." He put his hands up and quickly said, "I'm sorry. I didn't mean to say that. What do you want from me? I don't even know who you are."

"Like I said, you had a daughter that you probably don't even know about. Look in that notebook on the picnic table. There's a paternity test that proves it." The colonel looked at him without moving as if he didn't understand what Ace said. "Look! It's in the folder!"

Colonel Chester turned the folder around and flipped through several pages until he found the official looking form from Penrose-St. Francis Medical Center, Colorado Springs, CO. It listed a baby girl, named Rebecca Jean, Mother - Abigail Jean Glover, Father – Milton Hamilton Chester. His jaw dropped slightly. Then his heart sank to the bottom of his stomach as he remembered the party before graduation at the apartment near the academy in Colorado Springs. This kid wasn't even born yet. Why did he care? He looked up at Ace who was still holding the gun level with his head. The opening in the silencer looked large as he stared back at the deadly weapon.

"Look Ace, that was almost thirty years ago. I was a kid. You're a young man. Surely you can understand that we were just trying to have a little fun. I didn't know anything about this girl until you just showed me this form. If I'd have known I'd have done the right thing by her. How are you involved with this?"

"That girl was my sister." Tears were starting to form in his eyes as he talked about Becky. "I say 'was' because she was killed the other day by some more pricks like you. They shot her down like a dog. And remember the girl that you and your buddies had such a great time raping?" Colonel Chester winced when Ace said 'raping'. "She's dead, too, shot by the same bastards. But it all started with you and your buddies at that party. You used her like a party favor then threw her out in the street. I heard all about it. That woman was my mom, Abigail Glover."

When Ace said the name the second time, he remembered seeing a young woman at the Wal-Mart store in Grand Forks. She looked like the girl from the party many years ago. It had spooked him at the time. Then he realized it couldn't be the same woman. She was too young. Then he remembered seeing an older woman who looked like the young woman's mother. *That must have been the woman that he's talking about. Could it be true? Could that young woman have been my daughter?* He stared off into the distance for a moment then realized that he was in extreme danger. He had to take action or he was a dead man.

He turned back to Ace and said, "I'm so very sorry. Your mom and your sister are gone. I can't bring them back. What can I do to make it up to you?"

"I'll tell you exactly what you can do. Do you see that folder and the pen? You take that folder and find the last page with writing on it. Then you take that pen and write down the names and addresses of the guys that helped you rape my mother. Just add it to the list of names." Colonel Chester paused. "Do it now!"

"I can't do ... "

Before he finished, Ace squeezed the trigger and a silenced bullet ripped through Colonel Chester's left bicep. He shouted, "Mother Fucker," and grabbed his arm. The pain shot through his arm to his shoulder and down to his hand. The wound felt like a bad bee sting followed by a flame. "What the fuck?"

"You pick up that pen and you write down the names of the men who helped you rape my mom!"

He hesitated again. This time Ace shot the colonel in the left hand.

The shot blew off his pinky finger and part of the next digit. The colonel yelped in pain again. He looked at Ace as if he were a madman, which in fact he was.

"I am not going to tell you again! You write those names and addresses or you will bleed to death right here and now!"

The colonel said in a strained but calm voice, "You have no plans to let me live. I will not give you these names. These men do not deserve to die for something that they did almost thirty years ago. Kill me if you like but we're done here." He pushed the notebook back towards Ace and leaned back on the seat, the pain etched on his face.

"I knew you'd do this. That's why I already got the names. I just wanted to see if you would do the right thing and name them." Ace reached into his shirt pocket, pulled out a small flip folder and tossed it on the table. The names, addresses, and phone numbers were written on the pad. Colonel Milton Chester looked up at Ace in horror. He started to jump up and run but Ace shot him in the leg. The colonel fell to the ground, facing Ace as he walked around the table. He leveled the Glock at the colonel's chest, and as the colonel looked back in sheer terror, he pulled the trigger three more times. Colonel Milton Chester, Commander of Grand Forks Air Force Base, was dead.

Ace turned back to the table, put down the gun, and picked up his notepad and pen. He looked at the names already crossed off his list, the dried, rust colored lines of blood soaked through the paper. Sergeant Kevin Reardon, Private Edward Sharp, and Bobby Garrett. He bent over the Colonel's body and stuck the pen's tip into the oozing chest wound. In the colonel's own blood, he crossed his name off the list and tossed the pen aside. Nine names remained on Ace's list.

Colonel Richard Aims
General Adam Wesley
Colonel Carl Dempsey
Private David Wallace
Petty Officer Wilson Brush
Petty Officer Dean Gray
Captain Nancy Brown
Sergeant Joe McKinney
Patrick McKinney

The End